Praise for Patrick Taylor

"*Pray for Us Sinners* is written with heartfelt urgenc... than demonize the place and the population. A deeply felt thriller and a very valuable one." —*The Globe and Mail* (Canada)

"Flawlessly researched and . . . nails the chips-and-guns-with-everything atmosphere of violence in mid-1970s Ulster." —*Quill & Quire* on *Pray for Us Sinners*

"Taylor masterfully charts the small victories and defeats of Irish village life." —*Irish America* magazine

"Taylor . . . captivates and entertains from the first word." —*Publishers Weekly*

BY PATRICK TAYLOR

Only Wounded
Pray for Us Sinners
Now and in the Hour of Our Death

An Irish Country Doctor
An Irish Country Village
An Irish Country Christmas
An Irish Country Girl
An Irish Country Courtship
A Dublin Student Doctor
An Irish Country Wedding
Fingal O'Reilly, Irish Doctor
An Irish Doctor in Peace and at War

The Wily O'Reilly: Irish Country Stories

"Home Is the Sailor" (e-original)

NOW AND IN THE HOUR OF OUR DEATH

PATRICK TAYLOR

A TOM DOHERTY ASSOCIATES BOOK NEW YORK

NOW AND IN THE HOUR OF OUR DEATH

Copyright © 2005 by Ballybucklebo Stories Corp.

A Forge Book
Published by Tom Doherty Associates, LLC
175 Fifth Avenue
New York, NY 10010

www.tor-forge.com

Forge® is a registered trademark of Tom Doherty Associates, LLC.

The Library of Congress has cataloged the hardcover edition as follows:

Taylor, Patrick, 1941–
   Now and in the hour of our death / Patrick Taylor.—1st ed.
     p. cm.
   ISBN 978-0-7653-3519-7 (hardcover)
   ISBN 978-1-4668-2143-9 (e-book)
1. Undercover operations—Fiction. 2. Political violence—Fiction. 3. Northern Ireland—Fiction.
4. Vancouver (B.C.)—Fiction. I. Title.
   PR9199.3.T36 N69 2014
   813'.54—dc23

                              2014014686

ISBN 978-0-7653-3522-7 (trade paperback)

Forge books may be purchased for educational, business, or promotional use. For information on bulk purchases, please contact the Macmillan Corporate and Premium Sales Department at 1-800-221-7945, extension 5442, or write to specialmarkets@macmillan.com.

First published in Canada by Insomniac Press

First Edition: July 2014
First Trade Paperback Edition: May 2015

Printed in the United States of America

0 9 8 7 6 5 4 3 2 1

To Dorothy

Ave Maria, gratia plena, Dominus tecum.
Benedicta tu in mulieribus, et benedictus fructus ventris tui, Jesus.
Sancta Maria, Mater Dei, ora pro nobis peccatoribus, nunc, et in hora
    mortis nostrae.

Hail Mary, full of grace, the Lord is with thee.
Blessèd art thou among women and blessèd is the fruit of thy womb,
    Jesus.
Holy Mary, Mother of God, pray for us sinners, now and in the hour
    of our death.

BOOK ONE

PRELUDE

CHAPTER 1

A small handgun, six hollow-point, .25 calibre cartridges, a plastic bag, and an open jar of Vaseline lay on top of the chipped enamel toilet tank. Erin O'Byrne disassembled the revolver, slipped its components and the bullets inside the bag, and tied a short length of white string round the neck. She shuddered as she scooped Vaseline from the jar and lubricated the package.

Someone hammered on the door.

Erin almost dropped the bag.

"Get a move on." She heard the tension in her brother's voice.

"Christ, Cal, you near scared me to death."

"You're going to be late."

"Take your hurry in your hand." She put one foot on the toilet seat and reached under her skirt. The plastic was cold against her. She spread herself with her left hand and worked at the slippery bag, feeling it slide into her. The stiff gun barrel could have been Eamon—she felt the familiar tingle—but the bag was cold and, God knew, Eamon was always so hot. Used to be—until the Brit bastards lifted him.

"Move it, Erin."

She lowered her skirt, washed her hands, and opened the door.

"What the hell are you getting yourself worked up for? I'm the one that's taking the risks. I'm the one going into the Kesh."

Sited on a disused aerodrome outside Lisburn, 'the Kesh' had been called Long Kesh in 1974 when the Security Forces sent Davy McCutcheon down. They hadn't thrown the book at him. They'd chucked the whole bloody Linen Hall Library. Fifteen years for arms possession. Arms possession. Christ, he'd been the best bloody Provo bomb maker in Belfast. They'd given him another twenty-five for what they'd called the murder of the British soldier Davy'd shot while trying to escape from a farmhouse in Ravernet—not ten miles from where he lay in his cell.

Murder, my Aunt Fanny Jane, Davy thought. In his mind and in the opinion of the Provisional IRA, the Provos, the Brit squaddie had got his in a legitimate military operation. The Brits had been tipped off that the Provos were planning to mount an attack from the farmhouse. Soldiers had launched a raid and trapped Davy there. Davy hadn't even known at the time that he'd killed a soldier.

While the man Davy'd thought he could trust—a man who called himself Mike Roberts—had been downstairs, greeting the attackers under his real name, Lieutenant Marcus Richardson, the bastard who'd given the fucking Brits the tip-off, one member of the British attack group had rushed up to the bedroom where Davy was hidden. He'd let go a blind burst of automatic fire through the locked door. Heard the thump of a falling body. That was all. Davy'd been too busy trying, and failing, to blow up a bridge over the Ravernet River and, with it, the then British prime minister, Harold Wilson.

Today, Maggie Thatcher was prime minister, the Beatles were history, Bob Geldof was all the rage, the Troubles were into their fourteenth year—and Davy was nine years older.

Bloody good thing the Brits hadn't tried to nail him for Richardson's death, too. Someone *had* shot the young man, but Davy had to give the authorities their due. Their forensic experts had shown the bullet that killed him could not have been fired by Davy's weapon. They'd concluded Richardson must have stopped a random shot when the soldier Davy *had* killed loosed off a burst as he fell.

That had been nine years ago. Nine fucking years, and it wasn't even half of his sentence. The twenty-five years they'd given him for murder were to be served in full without any chance for parole. He could earn remission time for the arms-possession charge, but by his reckoning the twenty-first century would have arrived before he was on the outside—unless the Brits declared an amnesty or the Provos won the bloody war. He was going to be in the Kesh for a long time.

When he'd first arrived, the prison was a collection of Nissen huts surrounded by barbed wire cages. The Brits had replaced the corrugated iron structures with eight pairs of single-storey concrete cell blocks, each pair joined by a central corridor—the H blocks. Each block housed 160 prisoners and was surrounded by its own thirty-foot, barbed-wire-topped fence.

The entire complex lay behind a twenty-foot-high, antiscale perimeter wall. The perimeter wall was anywhere from half to one mile from the H blocks. There'd be no "great escape" by tunnel.

The British changed the name from Long Kesh to the Maze. The Republicans still called the place the Kesh or the Lazy K, as if it were an American ranch. They were good at that kind of sarcastic naming. A huge housing development on the outskirts of Belfast might be called Turf Lodge by the city planners. To its Republican inhabitants, it was known as the Ponderosa after the Cartwrights' spread in the TV series *Bonanza*.

Davy had lived—if you could call it living—in cell 16, D wing, H-block 7, through the weeks of the "blanket men," Provisional IRA inmates who, demanding the right to be treated as political prisoners, not criminals, had refused to wear prison uniforms. They spent their days naked, draped only in blankets. Davy, although sympathetic, had ignored the suggestions from the Provos' internal command that he should "go on the blanket."

Even in here there was a strict hierarchy that had nothing to do with the Brits. Each cell block had its own commander, who in turn reported to an overall Provo officer commanding the Kesh. Inmates were meant to "obey all orders and regulations issued . . . by the Army authorities and . . . commanding officers." That was part of the *Óglaigh na hÉirann* declaration he had made when he had joined the IRA as a boy.

He'd believed back then. God, he'd believed. Wouldn't any sixteen-year-old whose father had fought against the British in the Black and Tan war in the '20s, whose father ate, drank, and slept Irish independence—the Cause? But now? One of Davy's bombs, one he had planted himself with an army patrol as its target, had accidentally killed a farmer and his family, and Davy had been forced to watch as a little girl was roasted alive in the furnace that had been their car. After that, his faith in the Provos and their goal of Irish freedom was shattered.

Jesus, he thought, if I was a priest, the rest of the true believers would consider me an apostate. He didn't give a shite what anyone thought.

Davy had told the self-important little git who thought he ran cell-block H to go fuck himself, and when the blanket men upped the ante with the Dirty Protest, Davy had not been one of the 341 Republican inmates who had stayed in their cells for three years, unwashed, unshaven, with their uneaten food and excreta daubed on the walls. The place was bad enough without having to live with the stink of your own shite.

By then, even the Provo Officer Commanding the Kesh had got the message. Davy McCutcheon wanted nothing to do with any of his 850 fellow prisoners, was putting in his time and that was that. When the hunger strikes started in 1981, no one had bothered to suggest to Davy that he, like Bobby Sands and eight other prisoners, should starve himself to death.

He lay on his cast-iron cot as the screws made their morning rounds, clattering their billy clubs on the doors of the cells. He stared at the walls. Christ, he knew every crack in the cement, reckoned he could call the spiders that infested the walls by name.

He watched as his cell mate rose. Eamon Maguire from County Tyrone was twenty-nine, another lifer caught after a shootout when two Royal Ulster Constabulary men had been killed. Eamon had been in for three years. The day Maguire'd arrived, Davy had recognized the man for what he was. Tough as an old boot, deeply committed to the Cause, but once in a while he let his friendly side show. In their first year together, Eamon had broken through Davy's reticence, called the older man Father Davy, and asked Davy's advice but didn't always take it. Eamon had paid no heed when Davy had tried to warn him off getting mixed up in the circle of that really hard shite, Brendan McGuinness.

McGuinness. Davy shook his head. As Officer Commanding the 1st Battalion, Belfast Brigade, Provisional Irish Republican Army, McGuinness had been the man behind the raid that had cost Davy his freedom. He was a man Davy avoided. Detested. Served the hoor right that he'd been lifted at the same time as Davy. The pair of them had unfinished business—a lot of unfinished business—and it was a bloody good thing that McGuinness was in C wing, not in a cell near Davy.

McGuinness was a bitter man, a vengeful man who reveled in the violence of the Troubles. When they had been working together on the outside, Davy had seen through McGuinness's protestations of love for Ireland. He was in the Provos because that gave legitimacy to his love of killing and maiming. And he had treated Davy like a has-been old idiot, someone who was expendable, had even told Davy on one of the rare occasions that they had come face-to-face in here that it served him right that he'd been captured. That he was a liability to the Provos anyway. It had taken three men to pull Davy off McGuinness. Bastard.

Davy threw back the blanket and swung his legs over the side of the cot. He rubbed his left thigh. The ache was always with him. His thighbone had snapped when Davy had jumped from that farmhouse window. Three hundred yards from the Ravernet Bridge, and one hundred yards from the motorbike that would have got him away. If his fucking leg hadn't given way, he'd be in Canada now with Fiona.

No use crying over spilt milk, he told himself, and recognized the lie for what it was. Not a day went by that he didn't think of her and what might have been.

"Time you were up, Father Davy." Eamon, carrot-red haired with two front teeth missing, grinned and flicked a towel in Davy's direction. "It's not likely the screws'll be bringing you breakfast in bed."

"Away off and chase yourself, son." It was good to have Eamon for a friend, the only friend Davy had in the whole bloody place—in the whole bloody world. His best mate from the old days, Jimmy Ferguson, lived in Canada. He did write, but it wasn't the same as the pair of them sitting together over a pint, having a bit of *craic*, the banter so ingrained in the Irish character, Jimmy spouting the lines of his hero, William Butler Yeats:

> *Romantic Ireland's dead and gone,*
> *It's with O'Leary in the grave.*

Aye, or with Davy McCutcheon in the fucking Kesh.

Eamon said something.

"What?"

"I'll shave first. Erin's coming today. I want to get my breakfast early."

"Fair enough."

Davy half paid attention as Eamon brushed his teeth, filled the cracked enamel basin, lathered his face, and shaved with a safety razor. Cutthroats were not permitted. He heard the water run out and Eamon refilling the basin.

"There you are. Room service."

"Piss off," Davy said, but limped to the basin. He had to stoop to look in the mirror. Whoever had hung it had not made any allowance for a man who stood six feet tall. He shaved carefully, peering at the face that looked back at him, blotched in the places where the silvering had peeled from the back of the glass. He saw a pair of deep blue eyes, crow's-feet at the corners, and it wasn't constant smiling that had put those lines there. His moustache, trimmed over firm lips, showed not a trace of its original black. All silver now like his thinning thatch. He still carried a scar over his left eyebrow, a reminder of the head-butt from a drunken youth in a Republican drinking club.

Eamon said, "Hand me that wee glass."

Davy lifted a water-filled tumbler from a shelf between the basin and the mirror and gave it to Eamon.

"Ta." He removed a dental plate from the water, gave it a quick rinse, popped it into his mouth, and grinned at Davy. "That's better. Got to look my best for Erin." As he left the cell, Davy heard Eamon say in a stage whisper, "She's bringing me a wee present."

Erin felt the string of her "wee present" rub against the inside of her thigh. Maybe she'd left the cord too long, but how else was she to get the package out? Eamon had told her that other women smuggled things—a miniature camera, messages stuffed in the top halves of ballpoint pens—and for all she knew others might be in the gunrunning business, but, Jesus, Mary, and Jo, why had she let Eamon talk her into this?

She squeezed the steering wheel until her knuckles whitened. The drive from Tyrone to the Kesh seemed to be taking forever. At least she was off the narrow winding roads of County Tyrone and on the M1 Motorway. She just wanted to get to the prison, get this over with, and get home.

She knew that she would be body searched. What would the female prison officer think when she saw that Erin was not wearing panties? She felt the blush start. The embarrassment would be desperate. Then Erin smiled. Typical Catholic girl. Here's me taking the biggest risk of my life, and what I'm really worried about is that my mammy always told me that nice girls would never go out without their undies on.

When it worked out the way Eamon said it would, she'd soon be wearing a lot less than just no knickers. And there'd be something inside her a lot nicer than her wee bag and its cold contents.

Eamon wriggled in his chair in the visiting area. Erin was late. Christ, if the screws had found what she was bringing, it would fuck up two years of planning. And that didn't bear thinking about. He'd been in on it almost from the start because of his expertise with firearms. The Provo Officer Commanding in the Kesh, Bic McFarlane, had approached Eamon last year. Without preamble, he'd asked, "Could you fix one of those wee .25 pistols if it was busted?"

"Aye, certainly."

"Fix that." McFarlane threw the components of a small revolver onto the table in Eamon's cell.

"That's a fucking . . ."

"I know what it is. Fix it."

It had only taken a minute to reassemble the weapon.

"Keep your mouth shut about it."

Eamon bristled. "Of course I fucking well will. What do you take me for?"

"A sound man, or I'd not be here."

"What's up?"

"One day a bunch of us are getting out, and you'll be coming with us, but only a few of the lads know. So not a fucking word. Not to nobody. Right?"

"Fair enough." Out? Dead on. Eamon hugged the thought.

"Me or Bobby Storey'll be in touch." McFarlane put the revolver into his pocket.

Eamon, who was in no doubt about the need for security—he couldn't even tell Davy—had been willing to wait, as he waited now, and wished to God Erin would get a move on.

The Provos weren't the only security-conscious lot in this place, but Eamon knew that security's only as good as those who try to make it work, and for two years the Provo inmates had been working at undermining the prison warders. He had gradually learned the intricacies of the planning. He thought back as he waited.

The first step had been to ensure that one H block, H-7, was rid of any Loyalist prisoners. The Provo leadership had deliberately provoked fights with the Protestant bastards. Not one was in H-7 now. Good riddance to bad rubbish.

Then Bic McFarlane and his mates had put pressure on the Northern Ireland Office to let the prisoners work, maybe get back some of the remission time that they'd lost during the blanket protest. For a year, many of the men of H-7 had worked as orderlies. This gave them access to each of the block's eleven electronic gates. The screws had got used to them being there, and close to the guards. That was bloody important. If it were going to work, twenty-six guards would have to be captured before they could raise the alarm. Total surprise would be everything. Surprise, and five other small handguns all brought in the same way that Erin was bringing hers.

Eamon stood up and peered at the window in the entrance door. There she was. About bloody time.

The screw let her in. She sat opposite Eamon.

"What kept you?"

"Body search. The ould bitch noticed a piece of string hanging out of me."

"She didn't . . . ?"

"Not at all. I told her I was on my monthlies."

"Good lass. I'll get it from you in a wee minute." He turned to where another inmate sat several tables away, ignoring the woman opposite, staring at Eamon, who nodded.

The man turned to his visitor, smashed his fist on the tabletop, leapt to his feet, and yelled, "You fucking slut, you've been screwing Sean Molloy."

"Have not."

"I'll fuckin' well kill you. I'll kill you dead." The man rose to his feet, spittle flecking his lips.

Two warders rushed to restrain him.

"Now," Eamon hissed. "Now."

Erin passed him the package under the table. It slid through his fingers, clunked on the floor and slithered into plain view. He froze like a rabbit in a car's headlights. Erin slipped off her chair, scooped up the package and thrust it at him. Eamon dropped it down the front of his shirt and tried to control his breathing.

"Jesus, you done good, love." He had to raise his voice to be heard over the yelling of the decoy.

"Aye," she said, and ran her tongue over her upper lip. "And I hope you'll do good for me soon."

What was it about women? Eamon wondered. Was it fear that made Erin horny? "Soon, love."

"Now would be good," she said with a grin. "I'm not wearing no knickers."

He laughed and felt the package slip down under his shirt, the gun hard against his belly. It wasn't as hard as the bulge in his pants.

"I've to go now," he said. "But it won't be long. You just bide."

"I will."

"Right. And, Erin?"

"What?"

"Don't be wearing any panties that day either." He smiled and blew her a kiss, rose, and walked over to the nearest screw.

"'Scuse me, sir. Permission to go to the lavatory?"

"Go on."

Eamon headed for the toilet. His smile faded. To get back to his cell, he'd have to pass a body search. He knew there was only one way to do that. Pushing the Vaseline-lubricated package into his own rectum was going to be a real pain in the arse.

CHAPTER 2

Fiona Kavanagh looked out over Burrard Inlet. White sails and multihued spinnakers studded English Bay, the yachts' hulls tiny among the lines of moored cargo ships. Beyond Point Atkinson, Bowen Island tumbled down to Cowan Point and was etched against a sky as colourful as a Fair Isle sweater. Across the Strait of Georgia, the sun behind the mountains of Vancouver Island slipped into the Pacific Ocean and dyed clouds pink and mauve and scarlet.

The air was redolent of salt and drying seaweed, the sand of Kits Beach warm between her bare toes. Fiona let the evening's peace wash over her. Kits Beach was her "Lake Isle of Innisfree," where "peace comes dropping slow," and for her reflected everything about the tranquility of her new country. Vancouver was a far cry from tiny, self-absorbed, war-torn Northern Ireland, where the Troubles, the civil war, had ground on remorselessly since 1969.

She shook her head.

She'd sworn to put Belfast and the senseless slaughter behind her when she'd left that city in 1975 to come to Canada. The shootings, bombings, riots, and maimings were things to be forgotten.

She made it a point to turn off the sound of the newsreader's voice when the images of armoured cars on the streets, yelling youths hurling Molotov cocktails, and police and troops in body armour appeared on the television screen. Canadians always seemed to ask as soon as they found out where she had come from, "What is really going on in Northern Ireland? Is it ever going to end?" She would deflect the question by saying, "It's just the next chapter in a row that's been going on for eight hundred years. I'm from there and *I* don't understand it." That was a damn sight easier than trying to explain the convolutions of Irish politics, and allowed her to move the conversation away from a subject she preferred not to discuss.

A line of darkness crept up the North Shore Mountains. The west wind strengthened. Fiona bent, slipped on her shoes, and headed for her apartment in the big old house on Whyte Avenue.

Canada had been a new start for her—a new country and a new life. And, she thought, she'd succeeded fairly well in trying to become a Canadian, but, even after eight years, she couldn't completely escape from her heritage.

And why should she?

Ireland, Northern Ireland, was where she'd been born, raised, educated, where she had family and friends. Northern Ireland had formed her, made her what she was today.

Before the Troubles it had been a grand wee spot. A place to be remembered with affection, even if, after eight years, the memories were fading.

Most of the memories. Not all.

She'd fallen in love there in Belfast, not once but several times, and she half-remembered with affection those men. All save one. He still lived somewhere deep in her—but he was there and she was here.

Since coming to Canada, she'd had a number of short romances—but the right man? Perhaps Tim Andersen. She'd been seeing him for eight months, and he was meant to phone tonight. There might be a message waiting for her on the machine. She walked faster.

She nearly bumped into one of the great driftwood logs at the edge of the beach. "Watch where you're going, stupid." She'd better stop talking to herself. Back home, folks used to say that to do so was the first sign of madness.

Home? Dammit all, Vancouver *was* her home now. She had a good job, vice principal of Lord Carnarvon Elementary School, friends, new and interesting things to do. There was Gastown to visit, Stanley Park. The Gulf Islands were a short ferry ride away. Theatre, and her particular joy, the opera. And she could go where she pleased without being body searched, having always at the back of her mind the nagging worry that at any moment the day could be ripped apart by an explosion.

She crossed Arbutus Street onto Whyte Avenue, fumbling in her pocket for the front-door key. At home, McCusker would be waiting for supper.

She smiled as she thought of the overweight tortoiseshell cat. In her Belfast life, she'd had a ginger McCusker. He'd been kicked to death by a British soldier. Poor McCusker. Why, she wondered, had she given the same name to the stray kitten that'd appeared on her doorstep four years ago? Sentimentality? Had she needed something from her past to hold on to as a frightened child clutches a teddy bear? She opened the front door of the building.

She heard McCusker yowling, hurried down the hall, opened her door, and a spherical tortoiseshell hurled himself at Fiona's shins, the cat's howls changing to a basso rumbling.

Fiona bent and scratched the animal's head.

"Did you miss me?"

"Aaarghow."

"No, you didn't. You're missing your grub. Come on." Fiona walked into the kitchen, took out a bag of Tender Vittles, and poured the pellets into a bowl. McCusker attacked the food as if he hadn't eaten for weeks.

"Time you went on a diet." Fiona glanced down. "Maybe it's time I went on one myself."

She left the kitchen and entered the small living room, parquet-floored and two-thirds covered with two Persian rugs. They'd cost her a fortune, but apart from McCusker, who had she to spend her money on?

Through the tall bow windows, over the houses opposite, she could see the neon glare of the downtown towers and, beyond them, the lights of the Grouse Mountain ski run. They'd be getting it ready for the ski season.

She switched on a floor lamp and drew the curtains. It wasn't cold enough to light the false-log fire that sat flush in the wall flanked by two floor-to-ceiling bookcases where she kept her records segregated as classical or pop in the lower racks. She glanced at her books—old friends from Ireland and new Canadian acquaintances.

She looked over to a telephone and answering machine. No flashing red light. So Tim hadn't called and—no, she'd not call him.

She shrugged, selected *Carmen*, and slipped it onto the turntable. Modern science, she thought, is a wonderful thing, as she turned off the speakers in the room and turned on those in the bathroom. She'd done the wiring herself after she'd read about the option in an interior-decorating magazine.

The overture was finishing as Fiona switched on the bathroom light, threw a capful of Vitabath into the bathtub, and turned on the taps. At the sound, McCusker stuck his head round the door.

"Too hot, McCusker." The silly cat loved to drink from a running tap. Steam filled the room. Fiona slipped off her shoes. She inspected herself in a full-length mirror. She rubbed a patch clear.

Deep-set, dark almond eyes, slightly slanted and set between little fans of laugh lines peered back at her. She turned to see herself in profile. Nose straight, not too big; lips—she pouted—full but not too full. Chin firm. Forehead smooth—well, two shallow creases, but not bad for a woman of forty-three. A few more silver streaks in the raven-black hair that was cut to frame her face. Tim had asked her not to dye the silver. Said he liked it. To tell the truth, she'd been pleased. Why should she try to pretend to be younger than she was?

She stripped off her clothes. The room was warm and steamy, just like Kiri Te Kanawa's Carmen, who was beginning to seduce Plácido Domingo's Don José. "*Près les ramparts de Seville . . .*" She hummed along and examined her naked body in the mirror. "Not the girl you were ten years ago—but you'll do."

The telephone in the living room rang. "Go . . . away," but then it might be Tim. She hauled open the bathroom door and raced for the phone.

"Hello?"

"G'dye."

It was Tim. She'd know that Aussie accent anywhere.

"You all right? You sound a bit out of breath."

"I'd to run to get the phone."

"And I thought talking to me made you that way."

"If you could see me now, you'd be that way yourself."

"Why?"

"I'm naked."

"Yeah. Right."

The room was cold. She felt the goose bumps starting. "And you'd better tell me what you want. I'm going to freeze."

"You really starkers?"

"I told you. I'm freezing."

"I could nip over. Warm you up."

"Not tonight you won't. I've an early staff meeting tomorrow."

"Bugger. I'm working on Friday night. How about Saturday?"

"Love to."

"Seven?"

"OK." She heard the sound of a kiss and replied in kind.

"Remember that old song 'put on your high-heeled sneakers'? Get a bit swank, and I'll take you to Bridges."

"Fine."

"Now go and get warm." She heard him chuckle.

The phone went dead. She hung up, shivered, and scuttled back to the bathroom, into the tub and under the bubbles. Plácido sang, "*Parles à moi de ma mere . . .*" The water was warm and soothed her. God, but she was getting sleepy. Early to bed tonight.

. . .

Fiona rolled on her side, pulling the duvet under her chin. McCusker was curled in a ball at her feet. Sleep came softly, floating in on the pastel red and maroon clouds of tonight's sunset.

In her dream, she was wrapping herself in the sky's softness when lightning screamed over a black cloud that rose from a shattered building. One eye-searing flash, one single roar punctuated by the screaming of police sirens made Fiona thrash. She saw people running, silently openmouthed, faces grimed and bloodstained. There was shattered glass all over the street.

She flexed her sleeping legs and tried to run from the bed as she had tried to run on that day when she'd been shopping on Ann Street, not two hundred yards away from the blast. Above the street she saw the angel of death hovering, his tattered robe woven from the smoke of the burning building.

Her mouth opened, saliva dripping on her pillow. A low keening struggled from her lips. Her fists clenched and unclenched as she struggled awake, panting, the sweat clammy on her face.

She hadn't had that nightmare for more than a year. Why had it come tonight? She switched on her bedside light, her breathing slowing as she recognized where she was.

But why, safe in her own bedroom, could she still smell the smoke of the blast and hear the moaning of those left alive, see herself, hurrying away?

Fully awake she knew that her dream had been of the bombing of Belfast's Abercorn restaurant in 1972. The IRA explosives had killed two young women, ripped the right arm and both legs off Rosaleen McNern and wounded 130 others. And she hadn't stopped or tried to help. She'd hurried away to the house on Conway Street where she'd lived with Davy McCutcheon for four years.

She could remember letting herself in, tumbling into Davy's arms, sobbing on his chest. Big Davy, strong Davy, gentle Davy—Davy McCutcheon, the man she loved—Davy, who made bombs for the Provisional IRA.

"What's wrong, love?" She heard the concern, felt his hand stroking her hair.

"Everything."

He waited. Whenever she was upset—which wasn't often—he would be patient, listen, find the right words, hold her.

"Another bomb." She felt him stiffen. Why, she asked herself, why do I, a committed pacifist, stay with Davy when I know what he does? Why don't I just leave him, this house, and the whole of Northern bloody Ireland? Because—she felt his hand rubbing her back, insistently, comfortingly— because . . . She turned her face up to him. "Davy, Davy, I love you."

"It's all right."

But it wasn't.

"It's all right. Here." He gave her a handkerchief.

She dried her eyes but began to tremble.

"I'll get you a cup of tea."

Oh, Christ. Tea. The Belfast answer to every crisis from accidentally breaking an egg to just missing being blown apart. "I don't want a cup of bloody tea." She heard the pitch of her voice rise until she was almost screaming. "I want out of this." Before she could stop them the words came tumbling out. "I don't think I can go on living with you."

He flinched as if she had struck him. "Don't say that."

"Not unless you leave the Provos." She saw him flinch again. "Look, I've asked at Canada House. I can get a job as a teacher in Canada. We could go together. Start over." She saw his face harden.

"You didn't tell me."

"Why should I? I was just asking. Just . . ." She moved away from him.

"Fiona, I've never lied to you. You've always known what I do."

"Yes, but in the beginning you and the rest fought to protect the Catholics from the Protestant mobs when they started rioting, coming here to the Falls Road, burning houses. I didn't like it then, but I could understand. I've tried to close my mind to what you do. Just like a wife whose husband beats her. Pretend it's not really happening. But now . . . ? God knows how many people were killed today, maimed, shattered. I could have been one of them. I was on Ann Street."

"Oh, Christ . . ."

". . . and it could have been one of *your* devices."

"It wasn't."

"But it *could* have been."

"It wasn't."

"Get out, Davy. Get out and take me with you."

"I can't."

"Why can't you?"

"You know why."

"Because you believe? Because you gave your word?"

"That's right. I *believe* in Irish freedom. My da believed in Irish freedom. He died for it. I owe him and . . ." He put his hands on her shoulders. "And I owe it to myself. I promised."

"Jesus, Mary, and Joseph . . . You promised. You're just being stubborn." She made a fist and struck his chest. And she knew that one of the reasons that she loved him so was because his seeming stubbornness was merely the reflection of an integrity so deep that it was in his bones.

"What are we going to do? Davy, I do love you but I've had enough."

He pulled her to him.

She could smell the old smoke of his Woodbine cigarettes. She didn't like his smoking, but she put up with it. It was as much a part of Davy as his devotion to Celtic Football Club, his friend Jimmy Ferguson, Davy's love for Jimmy's daughter Siobhan, for all children, his acceptance of Fiona's decision that there'd be no children for the pair of them until the lunacy of the civil war was over, his unshakeable belief that if his bloody Provos could just make one more effort that they would win, that Ireland would be one country again, and that he and she could go back to living a normal life. She knew he was a dreamer, but she loved his simple dreams. "Davy. Davy . . ." And her resolve faded. She kissed him.

He took her through to the parlour, and she followed obediently. She let him stroke her, kiss her, caress her until her need for him grew and, fumbling at each other, urgency rising, they made love on the old chesterfield that she knew, but Davy thought that she didn't, stood over the secret place under the floorboards where he hid his equipment.

They went into the kitchen when it was over. Davy made a cup of tea. He always did that—after—and in the mornings for her before she rushed off to work, and he—she'd not think about that now.

Davy carried over her cup, and as he did he broke wind. They laughed together. They were on what her father used to call "farting terms," and Daddy had said no couple was really in love until they'd reached that state of comfort one with the other. And she saw that while she and Davy enjoyed sex—more than just enjoyed it—she loved him most for the little things.

The comfort of him. So what if she was better educated? Had established herself as an independent woman? Broken away from her slum roots? No matter what the crisis, Davy was her rock. Her "bridge over troubled waters." She could no more leave him than cut off her right arm.

McCusker, her ginger tom, jumped up on her lap—

Her Canadian tortoiseshell, McCusker, butted at her, weaving over her crumpled duvet, demanding attention. Fiona stroked the animal.

Poor Davy, she thought, brushing the cat away as she got out of bed and went through to the bathroom. God, but I still miss you.

She'd stayed with him for two more years, but when a bomb he had made killed the father of two little girls in one of her classes, she'd snapped, given him an ultimatum, "The Provos or me." And when he'd made his decision, she'd moved out.

Davy came after her weeks later, said he'd changed his mind, just one more mission and he would go to Canada with her. Those weeks without him had been the loneliest of her life. His promise about Canada had seemed to her then like having a doctor coming to her bedside and telling her that the diagnosis of cancer was wrong, that she'd live. She'd waited—but the mission had gone wrong. The court had given Davy forty years.

She could picture him the day she'd gone to the Kesh and told him she was leaving Ireland. His big hands twined and untwined on the tabletop, his face crumpled, and his eyes glistened with the tears that she knew he was holding back until she had gone.

She turned on the tap and filled a glass of water.

Inside her, the old pain whimpered. Oh, Davy.

She reached into the medicine cupboard for the Tylenol, found two, swallowed them, and put both hands to her temples.

Always when she had the nightmare, a migraine would start, the pain crushing like a woodworker's vice.

CHAPTER 3

Davy McCutcheon clamped a piece of wood in a vice, picked up his plane, sighted along the board's short length, and began to work. Shavings curled and fell on the floor of the prison's carpentry shop. He and seven other prisoners working in the shop had earned the privilege of learning carpentry. He was aware of them around him but kept his gaze fixed on his work. Forward, keep the pressure steady, let the plane bite, move along the wood's surface, lift and start again. Forward, keep the pressure steady . . .

Davy liked the shop. In here the prison stink—disinfectant, boiled cabbage, half-washed men, clogged drains, backed-up toilets—was masked by the smell of freshly sawn wood and hot glue. The rhythm of his work pleased him, made him feel for the moment like his own man, in nobody's debt. But today he was beholden. There was that promise made to Eamon.

He glanced to the workbench and confirmed that the plastic protector was firmly in place on the blade of a chisel. A peek down the room. The screw had his back turned. The woodworking instructor, a civilian, old Mr. Donovan—Pa to the screws and prisoners alike—was deep in conversation with another apprentice. Pa was so ancient that they said he'd helped Noah measure up his cubits and spans of gopher wood.

Davy did not smile at the old joke. Why the hell had he let Eamon talk him into this? Eamon and his, "Look, Davy, it's only a wee favour." Wee my Aunt Fanny Jane. He would lose his privileges and his remission time if they caught him. He wanted to learn this trade, and he didn't want to lose one day. He was going to be a different Davy when he did get out.

He put down the plane and picked up a set-square, but he used the back of his hand to nudge the chisel off the bench top onto a pile of shavings. Another quick glance round. No one had seen, or if one of the other inmates had, he was keeping that to himself. Davy kicked the chisel under the shavings.

He let out a long breath. He hadn't realized that he'd been holding it. Right. Back to work.

He ran the set-square along the length of the plank. Not quite smooth yet. He noticed as he picked up the plane that his hands trembled. He told himself to take a breather, leaned against the bench, and let his thoughts turn to the distant day when he would be free and to what life had been like before they stuck him in here.

Yes, he'd been a dyed-in-the-wool Republican. Yes, he'd made explosives for the "Cause," but there'd been more to life than that. He could see himself back in Belfast, in the stands watching a game of soccer.

"Oh, for fuck's sake, pass the bloody ball." These words were roared by Jimmy Ferguson, who stood next to Davy, one of the hundreds in the terraces, out in the open air, in the drizzle, leaning on iron pipes set in the ground like upturned, flat-topped U's.

"Jesus, Davy, that winger should be traded, so he should."

"Give him a chance, Jim. It's his first season with Celtic."

"It should be his bloody last. Christ, would you look at that?"

The Glentoran forward who had intercepted the misdirected pass was dribbling the ball down the right wing, coming nearer to the Celtic goal. He sent it soaring across the goal mouth to be fired by the centre forward straight into the back of the net.

The Glentoran supporters cheered.

The goalkeeper pointed at his full back in the gesture beloved by all goalies, as if to say, "That wasn't my fault."

"Do you know," said Jimmy, "I'm getting frozen. Do you fancy leaving early and going for a jar?"

"Fair enough. As long as I'm home by six. Fiona'll be expecting me."

They walked from the grounds and took a bus to their usual pub. Three snotty-nosed kids stood outside, each clutching a bag of potato crisps and a glass of orange Crush. Davy stopped and spoke to the biggest. "Would you lot not be better in the bus shelter out of the rain?"

Children were not allowed into public houses, so their fathers would be inside having a pint while the wee ones had to be content to shiver outside. It troubled Davy. He'd seen enough cold, underfed kids on the streets of the Catholic Falls district, aye and on Sandy Row, the Loyalist stronghold. He was fighting for the wee ones as much as for Irish freedom. Social justice was meant to be part of the Provos' agenda.

"My da would kill me if I didn't wait for him like he told me." The lad dragged his sleeve across his nose and sniffed.

Davy stuck his hand in his pocket and pulled out small change. "Here."

He gave it to the boy. "Away you and your mates to that wee café and get some hot chocolate inside you."

The child hesitated.

"Who's your da?"

"Willy McCoubrey."

"I know him. I'll have a word in his ear. Tell him where you've gone. You run away on now."

"Thanks, mister." The boy ran off, yelling at his friends to "come and get some hot chokky."

Jimmy shook his head. "You're daft about kids, aren't you? You're just a big softie."

"Not at all."

"Pull the other leg, Davy. Do you think my wee girl, Siobhan, calls you Uncle Davy because you're an ould targe?"

"Well . . ." Davy didn't want to talk about kids. Fiona had made it very clear she didn't want any. Not while the Troubles ground on and on. Maybe, because she knew that what he was trying to do was supposed to bring the civil war to a close, maybe that was why she still stayed with him. Jesus, but it had been a near thing the day the Abercorn was blown up. He'd thought she was going to walk out.

"Are we going in for a jar or aren't we?" Jimmy held the swing door of the pub open.

Davy picked up the plane. It would be great if wee Jim could hold the doors of this fucking place open as easily.

"How're you getting on, Davy?"

Davy swung round. "Jesus, Pa, you near scared me to death creeping up like that."

"Have you a guilty conscience?"

Bloody right he had.

"Here, let's have a look." Pa slid his callused hand along the freshly planed surface. "I don't need a set-square. There's still a bit of a bump." He took the plane, squinted, adjusted his stance—his left foot was less than an inch from where the chisel was hidden—and made two swift strokes. "Try your square now, son."

The metal arm of the tool slid along the surface as if it were gliding on ice.

Davy forced himself to smile. "You're a quare dab hand at that, so y'are."

Pa grinned. "You're no' so bad yourself. Is it next year you're goin' for journeyman?"

"Aye."

Pa clapped Davy on the shoulder. "You'll've earned it, but you'd two left hands when you came to me first. Couldn't tell a fretsaw from a mallet. You hadnae a clue."

Of course he bloody well hadn't, Davy thought. All his life, man and boy, in the old IRA and then the Provos, but he'd been a bloody good bomb maker. And that was all he was. No trade. No future. But he had had the Cause. He'd have died for it. And now? Shit. Davy almost spat, but he remembered that Pa was nearby. Well, anyway, he was going to see Eamon right. But for personal reasons, not for the Cause.

"Pay attention, Davy. You get your journeyman's certificate, and you'll have a good trade when . . ." Pa stopped. No one mentioned that in here. Men could have nervous breakdowns counting the days until they'd get out. Some had. Pa coughed. "I'll be off now. That lad over there"—he nodded to one of the other prisoners—"thinks a dog's hind leg is a straight edge."

"Thanks, Pa." Davy tried not to stare at the floor as the old man walked away. At least Pa was blocking the view of where Davy was working. He dropped to the floor, grabbed the chisel, lifted the leg of his trousers, tucked the handle under his sock, and secured the blade beneath an elastic band that he'd slipped over his ankle before coming here. He could feel the pressure underneath his sock.

He rose and saw the little hairs on his forearm rise and make goose flesh. He pulled his sleeves down and made a show of returning to his work. Damn you, Eamon Maguire, you and your "Could I have a wee word, Father Davy?" Eamon wanted a favour and that favour was now cold against Davy's calf.

Davy shook his head. Eamon and his friends were planning to break out of the Kesh. Bloody madness. They'd not have a snowball's chance. The screws, never mind the prisoners, couldn't go from one block to another without a daily password. There were double air-lock gates, guards everywhere—and their fucking Alsatian dogs. One push of a button in their communications room and the Brits could shut this whole place down tighter than a duck's arsehole. The outside walls were punctuated by guard towers full of soldiers with rifles and machine guns. Mad, the whole bloody lot of them, and yet Eamon had said that they were bound and determined to go—and that Davy could go with them.

He wrapped a piece of sandpaper round a block of wood and started to put the finishing touches to the now-smooth edge of the plank.

That had made him think. God knew he'd tortured himself in his first years here, dreaming of escape, of finding Fiona. Fiona, with the laughing, sloe-black eyes. Fiona, who'd promised to come back to him when he'd left the Provos but had visited him only once after they'd stuck him in here to tell him that it was no good. She was going to go to Canada, without him. Canada was a hell of a big country. He had no idea where she was. Break out? What was the point?

The sandpaper rasped, made wood dust. Davy sneezed and wiped his nose with the back of his hand.

What if Eamon's lot did get out? Where would they go? Ireland was a very wee place. They'd never get out of the country. They'd be lifted in no time flat, and then God knows how much longer they'd get. Davy'd time enough to serve. Even if they caught him with the chisel he was trying to steal, he'd lose his remission time and his woodworking privileges, and probably have more years added.

Davy started sanding again.

He knew it was stupid of him to have agreed to get the bloody tool. Eamon had asked as a friend. Even then Davy had tried to refuse, but when Eamon had begged Davy for help, not for the Cause but because Eamon was desperate to see his girl, Erin, the poor bugger had been nearly in tears. How could Davy have refused? He'd seen the pleading in the eyes of a man who wouldn't ask the devil for a glass of water. They'd grown close over three years in the same cell. Davy told himself he was an ould softie. He should have had more sense. And yet here he stood, the steel of the chisel cold against his calf. All he had to do now was get it back to his cell.

He put the sanding block down and picked up another blade from the bench, slashed it across the palm of his left hand and let a roar out of him like a banshee. "Fuck it. Jesus. Aaaaw."

Pa and one of the screws rushed over. "What's up, Davy?" Pa asked.

"I'm bleeding like a stuck pig." He thrust his hand under the guard's nose.

"Jesus. I can't stand the sight of blood."

Davy saw the man's face turn ashen. "Do something. Make a tourniquet."

"What?"

"Get a bit of rope or . . . Here, gimme your tie."

The guard fumbled with the knot.

"Hurry up, for God's sake." Davy's hand throbbed and burned. Blood dripped onto the pile of shavings where the chisel had been hidden. Pa hovered in the background making sympathetic noises.

"Here y'are." The guard turned his face away.

Davy grabbed the tie in his right hand, draped it over his left wrist, and tried one-handedly to make a knot. "Look, could you maybe tie that?"

The guard fumbled but managed to make a loop and tighten it. The flow of blood was reduced to a trickle, warm on Davy's fingers.

"Ah, Jesus, you've blood all over my tunic." The guard took a deep breath. "Come on to hell out of this. We'll need to get you to the infirmary." And to Davy's delight, the guard tugged him toward the back door of the workshop, not the front where the security equipment stood. And in the infirmary? It would be his hand they'd be looking at. Not his ankle.

"Be more careful the next time, McCutcheon." The prison doctor, a young man Davy reckoned was still wet behind the ears, was obviously unhappy with having had his day interrupted. He finished bandaging Davy's left hand. "See the nurse in a week and get the stitches out." He spoke to the guard. "Take him back to his cell."

"Yes, sir. Come on, you."

Davy rose. "Do I not get any painkillers?"

"What?" The doctor stopped in the doorway.

"It's throbbing like hell, so it is."

"The local anaesthetic should still be working."

"It never worked in the first place." Each of the six stitches had bitten his hand as it went in and came out. "And you're telling me to be careful?" Davy shook his head. "You were in too much of a bloody rush."

"Don't speak to me like that or . . ." The doctor reddened.

"Or what? You'll have me locked up?" Davy's smile was sardonic. He could hear the guard sniggering.

"I don't have to stand for this." The physician stormed out.

The guard said, "You're a better man than I am, Gunga Din. I'd not have taken a wheen of stitches if I could feel them."

"I've had worse." Like a shattered leg after the bomb explosion and no medical help but Jimmy Ferguson.

"I near took the rickets, so I did, just watching." The guard was solicitous. "Here"—he fumbled in his pocket—"here's a clatter of Aspirin." He gave the small box to Davy.

"Thanks, Mr. Carson." Davy stuffed the box into his own pocket. "Should we not maybe be getting me back now?"

"Fair enough. Come on."

Davy followed the guard along corridors where an inmate was cleaning. His mop spread a grey film of sudsy water on the grey concrete floor. A screw leaned against the wall, leafing through a copy of a kiddies' comic. He barely bothered to look up as Davy and Mr. Carson passed. They went through the electric gate from the infirmary and out onto the walkway to H-block 7.

Davy saw the perimeter wall with its manned watchtowers, where soldiers scanning the compound leaned on their machine guns. Davy could see no farther. Whatever world lay outside was hidden by the wall and by the cold rain that mizzled down on the sterile acres of the Long Kesh prison.

Mr. Carson had to give the day's password to the guard at the gate in the razor wire to be allowed to enter H-block 7. Walls, wire, gates, guards. Just like Davy had told Eamon. And Eamon was going to bust out of this? He must think he's Harry fucking Houdini.

"There y'are, Davy. Number sixteen. Home sweet home." Mr. Carson halted outside the doorway. "I'd better be getting back to the shop. Take care of that hand now."

"Thanks, Mr. Carson." Davy saw Eamon leap off his bunk.

"Jesus, Davy, what happened?" He stared at Davy's left hand. The bandage was the size of a boxing glove. Blood had seeped through, dried, and turned rusty.

"Cut myself."

Eamon backed inside to allow Davy to enter.

"Is it bad?"

"I'll live." But the cut pounded. "Would you get me some water?"

"Right."

While Eamon ran the taps, Davy fished out his Aspirin and fumbled with the box lid. "Could you open this? I'm all thumbs."

Eamon opened the box and took out the bottle of tablets. "How many? Two?"

"Aye." Davy popped the pills into his mouth, accepted the water, drank, and swallowed. He could sense Eamon's impatience. Davy lowered his voice. "I got what you're looking for. It's in my sock. I'll give it to you after lights-out."

"You did?" Eamon clapped his hands. "Fucking A-one."

"Aye, and if you're thinking of digging your way out with that wee thing, by the time your sentence is up, you'll still be fiddling away."

CHAPTER 4

The principal fiddled with an overhead projector, throwing yet another set of incomprehensible figures on the olive-drab wall of the teachers' common room. The chintz curtains were drawn. A single ray of sunlight sidled in through a tear in the material, and Fiona had to move her chair sideways to avoid the glare.

She fidgeted in her hard-seated chair and doodled in her notepad. Surely someone *must* have told the man that no visual aid should contain more than five facts, yet there he stood, pointing to the eleventh row of figures on this one slide, his back to his audience, mumbling at the makeshift screen. He turned to face the group of teachers and said, ". . . and I think that in a, quote unquote"—he extended the first two fingers of each hand like a pair of skinny rabbit's ears and flexed them rapidly—"student-centred learning environment, we must strive to build the children's self-esteem."

The remains of last night's migraine gnawed behind her eyeballs. She struggled to stifle a yawn. Glancing round the faces of her colleagues, she could tell that she wasn't the only one having difficulty staying awake. Fiona watched as her friend Rebecca (Becky) Johnston, who sat on the other side of the table, raised her eyes to the heavens, stared directly in Fiona's direction, and crossed her eyes.

A younger man sitting near the head of the table stroked his beard and asked the principal, "But why must we always concentrate on self-esteem at the expense of the three Rs? In the intermediate grades, two and two make four, have always made four, and will always make four . . . no matter how much that may bruise some little dear's ego."

Other voices were raised, one teacher talking over another.

Lord above, not that argument again? In the primary grades, kindergarten to three, the school's mission was to develop the kids' self-esteem and teach them how to learn. After grade three, in intermediate, the learning of facts began.

Fiona closed her eyes. Every week they struggled with this, never reaching any kind of conclusion. She thought about the ancient clerics who would argue about how many angels could dance on the head of a pin. The old boys had only been rank beginners when it came to the hair-splitting that went on at these meetings. Her colleagues didn't make the Mourne Mountains out of molehills. They went up and down both sides of a Mount Everest built from a single grain of sand.

She pushed her chair back from the table, eased her numb backside, and decided not to contribute to the futile discussion. It was far removed from the cut and thrust of the debates she'd grown up with in her years at Stranmillis Teachers' College back in the '60s.

The bearded teacher was pointing at the slide. That man could talk the hind leg off a donkey. She knew he'd hold the floor for what would seem like forever.

Funny how much he looked like George Thompson. She'd not thought of George for years, but she could see him clearly: beard, granny glasses, briar pipe. He used to stab at people with the stem of the thing to emphasize points he was making.

She could smell his tobacco, Murray's Erinmore Flake, hear his high-pitched voice.

"Look, Fiona's a Catholic, like the rest of you, and I'm a Protestant, but why should that matter in 1961?"

There had been a hum of agreement from the twenty other student teachers gathered in George's rooms in the college's halls of residence.

"Because, George," she said, "we're living in Northern Ireland. It's *always* mattered. Some Protestants have more than one vote. Catholics get shoved to the bottom of waiting lists for subsidized housing, get kept out of the good jobs. Taigs, Fenians as they call us, get beaten up . . . just because they're Catholic."

"Bloody right." A boy with ferocious acne stood up. "And do you think we're going to change that?" he demanded. "Not all Protestants think like you, George."

She glanced at him, saw a tiny smile as he said, "You're right, but once we qualify and get into the classrooms, we can work with the kids. Teach them about tolerance."

Paddy, that was the name of the one with the acne, Paddy snorted. "Jesus, George, maybe you will, but the rest of us? We'll only get jobs in Catholic schools. Worst bloody thing they ever did in this country was to keep the schools segregated."

Fiona butted in. "But we can change that, too."

"How?" Paddy shook his head.

"The same way Martin Luther King's doing in America."

"Rather you nor me, Fiona." Paddy muttered. "A lot of them American civil rights workers have had their heads smashed in. The whites have their Ku Klux Klan. Look what they did in Montgomery, Alabama, when the Yanks tried to integrate a school."

Another voice chimed in. "And here the Prods—sorry, George, but it's true—they have the Orange Order."

"And we," she said, rising and folding her arms across her chest, "we have NICRA, the Northern Ireland Civil Rights Association. One man, one vote. No more discrimination."

She heard the murmur of assent, smiled at the approval of the crowd, until Paddy growled, "Aye, and we have the IRA. They'll chase the Brits out, and *then* we'll get one man, one vote."

George was standing at her shoulder.

"No," he yelled, stabbing with his pipe stem. "Not by violence. You can't make people love you by shooting them. By throwing bombs at them."

"I agree," she said. "We need to use nonviolent methods, civil disobedience. We *need* one man, one vote."

"Fiona's right." George put his arm round her shoulders.

She snuggled against him and wished that the rest would go home so she could be alone with him, talk more freely, and then they'd take each other to bed. It was a good thing the British government had made the pill available on prescription this year. There were some advantages to having Northern Ireland as a part of the United Kingdom. Bugger what the priests thought. Fiona Kavanagh wasn't going to get herself in the family way. Not until she was good and ready. She had a career to make, and changes to make to her Ireland.

Those two resolutions had already cost her. None of her family would speak to her since she'd taken up with a Protestant. They'd thought she was daft when she told them that she was going to be a teacher. Women were housewives or secretaries, and she'd no right to try to rise above her station. She shuddered to think what they'd say if they knew she was here tonight working for civil rights. And work on she would, even if tonight—she glanced over at George—it meant that bed would have to wait. She knew that the arguments would rage on interminably.

Just like this staff meeting.

The flicker of slides being changed caught her eye. The principal had changed the subject. "Moving to the final item on today's agenda . . ."

Thank God for that.

". . . the budget."

Fiona began to pay attention. This would be interesting. She knew that there was going to be intense competition for funds between Becky Johnston, who mostly taught the primary grades, and Whiskers over there, who worked only in intermediate.

If it came to the crunch, Fiona would use her position as vice principal to wade in on Becky's side. Not that she thought she'd have to. Back in Northern Ireland, Fiona occasionally had enjoyed putting a few shillings on the horse races. In this one, she'd put the lot on Becky. The woman would fight with the mathematician for her students as fiercely as Fiona and George had fought in their last few months before their inevitable split.

He'd been a good lad, George, for most of the four years they'd been together, but she couldn't be sure if they had simply grown apart or whether their political views had diverged too far. He'd continued to believe in NICRA's insistence on staying within the bounds of constitutional methods. She'd been swayed by a young woman named Bernadette Devlin and the other leaders of a splinter group, which in 1968 became the People's Democracy, who went in for confrontational protest marches. Perhaps the cross-sectarian divide between her and George had been too wide to span. She'd missed him for a while, but she'd been young and had taken comfort from the old saying that men were like corporation buses—if you waited for a while, another one would come along.

Fiona kept a careful eye on her friend Becky as she argued her corner successfully. They'd have a good chat about that on their way home today, and next week they were going to the opera together. That would be something to look forward to, like dinner with Tim tomorrow night. She was expecting him to pick her up at seven in the evening.

CHAPTER 5

"Are we expecting anybody, Cal?" Erin O'Byrne stood back from the black cast-iron range when she heard knocking on the farmhouse door.

"Sammy's meant to be coming over, but . . . ?"

Erin watched Cal cross the tiled kitchen floor. It was probably only Sammy McCandless—but it wouldn't be the first time the Security Forces had paid an unexpected visit. It was no secret about her and Eamon Maguire, and since he was a convicted Provo she'd have been surprised if the O'Byrne family and the O'Byrne farm weren't kept under surveillance.

Cal opened only the upper half of the door. "'Bout ye, Sam. Come on in. Jesus, it's really bucketing down."

Erin relaxed as Cal struggled with the lower door half.

"Bloody thing's warped."

She heard Sam say, "Take your time. I'll not melt."

"Would you move, you stupid thing?" Cal tugged at the door. "Never been right since Da died."

And you've still not got round to fixing it, big brother, she thought. One day I'll do it myself.

The door screeched open. Sammy came in, shaking himself like a spaniel after a water retrieve. He pulled a cloth cap off a mop of badly cut, straw-coloured hair and slapped the duncher against his thigh. "Morning, Erin."

"Get them muddy boots off you, Sammy," she said, crossing the kitchen. "Don't you be dragging all that clabber in here."

Sammy left his Wellington boots beside the door. She heard the cackling of a hen trying to come in, Cal yelling, "Get away on out," and grunting as he pulled the door shut.

"Gimme your cap and coat." She held out one hand.

"Just a wee minute." Sammy bent, pulled a pair of bicycle clips from the ankles of his moleskin trousers, stood, untied a length of baler twine that served as a belt, and shrugged out of his Dexter raincoat. "Here y'are." He handed her the sopping coat and cap. He rubbed his hands. "I'm foundered. It would cut you in two out there."

"Fancy a cup of tea?"

"I do so."

"Sit down at the table." Erin hung the clothes on a coat stand in the corner of the kitchen. "Would you make Sam some tea, Cal? The kettle's nearly boiled."

"Not at all. That's woman's work." Cal's tone was bantering. "You don't buy a dog and bark yourself, do you, Sammy?"

Sammy had enough sense to keep his mouth shut.

"I'll kill you, Cal O'Byrne, but I'll see to it." Erin went back to the range. She smiled at her brother. He was allowed to take liberties.

He'd done it for as long as she could remember. He'd teased her even more since she'd been up at Queen's University in Belfast and discovered that women didn't have to spend their time barefoot in the kitchen or dropping babies like a brood mare. Like poor old Ma, dead of a haemorrhage after number six, Fiach, the youngest. He was off playing in a hurling match today.

The other three were scattered, two sisters in America and a brother, Turloch, in Australia. She'd half-thought of going off to Australia herself. Maybe finish her degree there. It was warm in Brisbane, so Turloch said, and nobody was shooting at anybody.

But then there was the Cause—and the farm.

She'd grown up here, knew every hedgerow, every ditch, and the fairy tree in the back ten acres that no one would plough within fifty yards of for fear that the little people might sour the cow's milk or have the lambs stillborn. Superstitious rubbish—and yet—Da had told her about the leprechauns. He'd believed in them, just as he'd believed in Irish freedom. And, like Da, she'd never budge in *her* belief that one day Ireland would be reunited.

And until that day, she'd stay here on the farm that Cal as the eldest son had inherited after Da died of cancer two years ago. Sometimes she felt it was time that old custom went. Why shouldn't a daughter inherit? Bridget, one of the two sisters in America, would have been first in line then.

But better one child got the whole thing than under the old Irish *Brehon* law that divided the property equally between all the sons. In about three generations the descendants were lucky to have a couple of acres each. Only sufficient for one crop—potatoes. And in 1845, the crop had failed. No one needed to remind her of the Potato Famine, or any of the other horrors inflicted on the Irish people by their English overlords.

Da had made sure that all of his children had learned their history, or at least his version of their history. It was very black and white. The Irish were good. The British were invaders and must be driven out. According to Da, the O'Byrnes had been fighting the British since the eleventh century. It was a family tradition. He'd explained to her their family name came from the Irish *Ó'Broin* and that meant "raven."

"Here." Cal set a tray of cups and saucers on the counter beside the range.

"I'll just warm the pot," she said, lifting a heavy iron kettle. That thing had stood on the range for as long as she could remember. How many times had she set it to boil on the old turf-fired range in this kitchen? The old kettle, the range, and the kitchen were the heart of the O'Byrnes' farm. And for her the farm was home.

After Da passed, working the farm had been too much for Cal and wee Fiach, even with the help of Sammy McCandless as a labourer, so she'd left university, not without regrets, and come home to help them.

She emptied the teapot, spooned in tea leaves, and refilled it. "Just be a minute."

She'd become used to playing the part of the farmer's wife, cooking for them—Cal would burn the water if he tried to boil an egg—keeping the house clean. But she'd made sure that her three years studying agriculture hadn't been wasted.

Cal was only too happy to listen to her suggestions about how to increase crop yield. She could plough a furrow as straight as anyone and chuck sheaves of barley into the threshing machine at harvest time when it was all hands on deck to get the ripe crop in before the rain.

She'd be willing to go on doing her job here—until the Provos sent the British packing. And she and Cal and Sammy were working hard to that end.

She watched Sammy pick his nose. He always did that when he was nervous. And he had reason to be. He wasn't here just to talk about the weather. He had a job to do that would, with the help of Cal and her, bring the day closer when the Brits would be gone. Then she'd go back to university, not just to finish her degree but also to further her education and aim for a faculty position at the Hillsborough Agricultural Institute.

She felt the warm side of the teapot and asked, "Do you fancy some bread and butter with that?"

"Dead on," said Sammy, wiping his finger along the side of his pants.

"Right."

She cut thick slices from a loaf of wheaten bread. The butter was hard, so she put the butter dish on the range top. As she waited for the butter to soften, she looked at the familiar faces of the men seated at the big bog-oak dining table.

Cal, twenty-seven, two years her senior, had craggy, ruddy cheeks, badges given to all Tyrone farmers by the sun and the rain and the winds that swept down from the Sperrin Mountains. He had green eyes—not as green as her own—and an unruly red mop that hung over the nape of his neck. She'd collected the family colouring herself, but she kept her shoulder-length hair piled into a ponytail, russet and shining as a polished horse chestnut.

Sammy was no oil painting. He reminded her of a ferret. Little black eyes that were never still, set to the sides of a sharp nose. Protruding front teeth. He only shaved every two or three days, and his mousy stubble completed the illusion.

And where Cal was broad, Sammy was so skinny and had such narrow shoulders that she could imagine him slipping down a rabbit hole to chase terrified rabbits out under the guns of the hunters. Where Cal was easy-going, Sammy McCandless had a vicious streak. And with the work the three of them did as an Active Service Unit of the Tyrone Provisional IRA, that wasn't necessarily a bad thing.

The cell had had four members. Eamon was in the Kesh, but she'd not much longer to wait for him. He'd be out very soon. And a bloody good thing. The look on his face when she'd given him that wee gun last Thursday. That look had been worth the risk she'd taken.

She tested the butter's softness with the flat side of a knife. The knife was stiff, the butter soft, soft as she'd be when Eamon brought his hardness to her. She held her arms to her sides, feeling her nipples being thrust against the stuff of her blouse, forgetting Cal and Sammy and thinking only of Eamon.

His family farm bordered theirs. She'd thought when he'd started court-ing her four years ago that he'd only been after her so that he and Cal could set up a family partnership, with her as the gift to seal the bargain. It was the way the old kings of Ireland cemented alliances, but it had been *her* he wanted. And she'd wanted him. Wanted him from the first day he'd kissed her. Wanted him for the nearly three years he'd been inside. The waiting hadn't been easy. She'd nearly given up two years ago.

A harder piece of butter stuck to the bread, and the pressure from the knife tore the slice apart. Erin would eat that herself. She pushed it aside.

Just like she'd tried to push Eamon aside. She'd nerved herself two years ago to tell him that she loved him but that no woman should be expected to wait for twenty-five years. It was all very well for the women's libbers at the university to argue that men and women should be equal. Erin had no doubts on that score, but slogans like, "A woman needs a man like a fish needs a bicycle" had been coined by someone who was out of touch with reality—or a nun or a lesbian. Erin needed a man, and not just for what he could do in bed, although what Eamon did made her gasp and shudder, and claw at him like a wild cat. She squeezed her thighs together at the thought of it.

But to expect her to remain celibate for twenty-five years?

And she had had no intention of sneaking round behind Eamon's back. There were plenty of lads in the village, secure in the knowledge that Eamon wouldn't be around for a very long time, who'd be happy to accommodate her.

She looked over at the table where Cal and Sammy were in deep conversation. That Sammy would be up her leg like a ferret up a rabbit hole if she gave him the slightest encouragement. She smiled at the stupidity of the thought. That would be a cold day in August.

Cold as the day she'd driven to the Kesh to tell Eamon it was over. She'd got colder still when she'd had to pull the car over to the ditch, get out, and throw up, her stomach knotted by the thought of what she was going to do.

She'd still been shivering when she'd gone into the visiting hall.

He was all pleased to see her, and she felt like hell, knowing what she was going to tell him.

"Eamon, I need to talk to you."

"And I need to talk to you."

"Well . . ." She'd rehearsed what she was going to tell him. That she still loved him but couldn't wait forever. That it wasn't fair to him and wasn't fair to her. That they'd get over it. That she'd still go on fighting with the Provos. She couldn't find the words to begin.

Maybe she would say nothing about it today, write him what the Americans called a "Dear John" letter? No. That would be a sleekèd thing to do to anybody, never mind Eamon. He'd said that he wanted to say something? That would give her a short reprieve. "All right. You go first."

"Lean over. I've to whisper."

She'd frowned and bent her head toward him.

"In about a year, me and some of the other lads are getting out."

She sat back in her chair. Out?

"Did you hear what I said?"

"I did, too."

"Will you wait for me?"

"What do you think?" Thank Christ she'd let him go first. "I love you."

"Great." He leaned forward. "I may need a wee bit of help."

And she'd given him that help two days ago. She'd just have to wait a little longer, and Eamon would be out. Here in Tyrone there were plenty of places to hide a man that the Brits could never find. Jesus, Mary, and Joseph—she glanced over at the table—but it would be grand to have him sitting there again.

Cal grinned back at her. "Are you churning that butter?"

"Take your hurry in your hand, Cal. It's ready. Here." She carried the tray to the men. "Help yourselves." She joined them and half-listened as they talked about the weather, the things that needed to be done on the farm.

Quite the rustic scene, she thought. Any strangers asked to join them would be charmed, unaware that they were sitting with three of the most committed Provos in County Tyrone.

Perhaps Sammy wasn't, but he was a damn good armourer who manu-factured their explosives, procured their weapons, stole cars, and that was all that mattered. She and Cal were completely dedicated.

Had been from the day Da started telling them his stories of the Irish and the English. He wove tales of Ireland that went back to prehistory: of Finn McChuaill, and Princess Macha, Cu Chulainn and his Knights of the Red Branch, and Maeve and Deidre of the sorrows. He told the children of rebellions that always ended in the glorious defeat, Fiach McHugh in 1580, the United Irishmen in 1789, the Easter Rebellion in 1916. He'd sung them the songs, songs that kept the folk memories sharp, the bitterness honed like a bright pike blade. Da had told them over and over that one day—one day Ireland would be free. Not just the twenty-six counties of the Republic but the six here in the north that still paid homage to the English Crown, that twenty-six plus six made one. Thirty-two counties, but one Ireland.

She chewed her buttered wheaten bread.

Never mind Da telling them things. He'd shown them.

He'd been a volunteer with the IRA since 1922. She could remember the nights he'd not been home and Ma had sat by herself in the kitchen—waiting, sometimes crying quietly to herself, once helping him in through the door— the bottom half didn't stick then—stripping his bloodstained coat and shirt away, binding the bullet wound in his right arm. Burning the bloody clothes in the range. Telling the frightened children they must never—*never*—say a word about it to anyone.

Ma yelling at constables of the Royal Ulster Constabulary to get off the O'Byrne lands the night they'd come looking for Da.

Erin, five-year-old eyes wide, had clung to her mother's skirt as soon as the pounding on the door started, did as she was bid when Ma said quietly, "Erin, get you under the table."

Peering out, she saw Ma open the door, and outside there were three big, beefy, red-faced RUC men in their bottle-green uniforms, black harps for their cap badges, rifles in their hands.

"You've no right to come in . . ."

"Out of the fucking way, you Fenian bitch." A sergeant shoved Ma aside. Ma fell, then sat up, stared at Erin, and held one finger to her lips. There was a trickle of blood from the corner of her mouth.

Erin crept farther under the table. All she could see were green-trousered legs, black muddy boots. She heard the crashes as furniture was overturned, the clumping of boots rushing upstairs, thundering through the bedrooms overhead. Shards of broken crockery skittered across the kitchen floor.

"Come out of there, you wee hoor." The man's face was upside down as he peered under the table. "Get out. Don't have me come in to get you."

She scuttled across the floor and clutched at Ma, who held her tightly. Ma was dry-eyed. Scowling.

Boots clumped down the stairs. One of the men had nine-year-old Cal by the ear. The sight of his tears brought on Erin's own.

"Nobody upstairs, Sergeant, except this wee skitter." The constable shoved Cal across the room, sucked his hand, then spat on the floor. "The wee cunt bit me, so he did."

Another constable said, "You'll need to get that disinfected. Them Fenians' bites is poisonous, so they are." He laughed.

Cal hurled himself at the man.

"You leave my ma and my wee sister alone."

He got a backhander across his face. One eye started to close.

The sergeant walked across the room and stood over Ma and Erin. From where she sat, Erin thought that he looked like a giant.

"All right. Where the fuck is he?"

Ma let go of Erin and stood. "Where you won't find him."

Erin could see the fire in Ma's eyes.

"Constable. Grab that wee lad."

She watched the man who'd been bitten grab Cal, twist his arm up behind his back. Cal struggled and then began to whimper. "You're hurting me. Stop it."

"I'll not ask you a third time," the sergeant said. "Where the fuck is he?"

"Let my Cal go," Ma yelled.

Cal's cries grew louder.

"All right," Ma said. "He's across the border."

Cal gave a high-pitched yelp.

Ma tried to go to him, but the sergeant held her back.

"I told you. He's across the border. In Ballybofey."

The sergeant released Ma and turned to the constable. "Let him go."

Cal made no attempt to join them. He just stood there nursing his arm.

"We'll be going now, missus." The sergeant and the other two marched to the door. "We'll be back," the sergeant said. "Maybe you and your brood should get over the border, too, take the rest of the fucking Fenians with you. And stay there." He slammed the door.

After Ma had tended to Cal, she took out a bucket, filled it with soapy water, got down on her knees, and started to scrub the place where the constable had spat. Ma hadn't cried, just scrubbed and scrubbed. And, Erin resolved, the bloody Brits would never make her cry either.

And they hadn't. Not since that day. She glanced across to the crack between the floor tiles where, eighteen years ago, Ma had scrubbed her fingers red-raw.

After that night, it had been no wonder that Cal had joined Da in what the pair of them called "the family business." The other brother and sisters had taken a different tack. They'd got the hell out of Northern Ireland. Fiach hadn't been born back then. As soon as she'd been old enough, she'd asked Cal if women could join the Provos. He'd told her that girls weren't allowed to. They had to join the *Cumman na mBan*, the woman's auxiliary. The hell they had to.

She'd found that out when she was at the university. There *were* women who were full members of Active Service Units. They mostly came from the poorer districts of Belfast, Derry and towns like Coalisland in East Tyrone, where sectarian oppression had flourished for centuries, and they fought as tenaciously as the men. All of them were driven by one goal—the fight to free Northern Ireland. And why shouldn't she join? She wanted a free Ireland as much as, maybe more than, the next person.

She soon persuaded Cal to get her in, and anyway, County Tyrone wasn't like Belfast with its formal structure of brigades and battalions. Down here there was a brigade, but the Provos were organized into independent cells. Only one member of any small group was known to a single man from another. If the Security Forces penetrated a cell, the chances of the Brit buggers finding out about another Active Service Unit were slim. Cal had sent word up through the chain of command. Erin had been in, and proud to be in for—she had to think—five years now.

She finished her tea.

The men were still going on about a broken fence in the back ten acres. She looked fondly at her brother, the big lig, as he held a teacup in a fist like a ham. He was one of the best, and she loved him dearly. Not the way she loved Eamon but for his humour, his ability to put off any job, like fixing the kitchen door, his way with the horses, and for always being her big brother.

"You're back, are you?" Cal grinned at his sister. "You were away off on a powerful daydream."

"Daydream? Listening to you two *craic* on would put anyone to sleep. I know that the fence needs fixing in the back ten acres."

"I'll do it on Monday, Erin," Sammy said. His tone was ingratiating. "We've to see to the horses today."

She could see his gaze resting on the front of her blouse. Let the wee bugger look. He'd never said a word, never tried to touch her, but she knew that Sammy McCandless wanted her. If it was Sammy's desire for her, not a commitment to Ireland, that kept him in the Active Service Unit, who cared?

Anyway he *was* in, and, as the Provos were fond of saying, "The only way out is feetfirst." They meant you either died in battle or, if you showed the least sign of disloyalty—and wanting out, except under very special circumstances, like an illness, was considered to be disloyal—they'd take care of you themselves. Permanently. Sammy was in whether he liked it or not, and as long as he did his job right—and fair play to Sammy, he was a damn good armourer—he'd nothing to worry about. And that was really why he was here this morning.

"So, when are you going to do the other thing, Sammy?"

Sammy hesitated and glanced at Cal.

"Tell her, Sam."

"I'll need your Land Rover and the horse trailer tonight. I was going to steal a car in Derry, but I nearly got lifted. Bloody great peeler come over and asked me what I was about."

"Damn," said Cal. "I'd rather you weren't using ours. You have to get across the border, and there's a checkpoint. We'll need to change the number plates."

"Stay here for your supper," Erin said, "and the three of us can see to that after."

"Fair enough."

"Usual suppliers in the Republic?" she asked.

"Aye. I'll pick up the shipment in Ballybofey, run it over at Clady, and take them up to the churchyard at Ballydornan. The ArmaLites and Semtex won't come to any harm in the grave, and if the Brits do happen to find them it'll throw them off the scent about this place."

Cal growled. "Don't get caught. Not in our 'Rover."

"I'll not get nicked." Sammy grinned.

Watching him grin, Erin thought that she'd been wrong about Sammy looking like a ferret. He was more like a weasel.

"See you don't," she said, "or you'll end up in the Kesh."

"If I do, I'll get to see your Eamon."

"Don't be too sure of that. He's . . ." She bit her lip and saw Cal sharply shake his head. They hadn't told Sammy about the impending jailbreak. Informers had been the curse of every Irish independence movement.

"He's what?" Sammy asked.

Erin gave him her most come-hitherish smile. "Nothing."

"Come on, Erin. Something's going on, and you won't tell me? Do you not trust me?"

Cal rose and looked down on Sammy. "Listen. You know the rules. The less folks know, the less they can tell."

"I'd never tell nothing."

"That's what we thought about that shite Christopher Black. Bloody super-grass, singing his head off like a fucking canary. Thirty-five of our lot lifted on his word."

Sammy stood and leaned, taking his weight on his hands that were splayed out on the tabletop. "Don't you make me out to be like Black. You think I'd turn informer?" There was spittle on his lips. "Fuck you."

Erin put her hand over Sammy's. "Not at all, Sam. It's just the way we do things. You know that. We will tell you when the time's ripe." She looked up at Cal. "Sit down, the both of you. You're like a pair of strange roosters in the one barnyard."

"Jesus, Sam," Cal said, "if we can't trust you, who can we trust?"

Sammy seemed to be satisfied. "I'm sorry I lost the rag there, Erin, but . . ."

"Never mind." She squeezed his hand. "We trust you, Sam, and we've to rely on you tonight."

Sammy forced a smile. "The night? Just you wait 'til you see. It'll be easy as playing marbles."

CHAPTER 6

From her window, the grass of the playing fields of Lord Carnarvon Elementary School shone dew-sparkle bright. The four baseball diamonds looked like pieces cut from the same brown pie. On the verges of the avenues surrounding the fields, the birch trees' September leaves had the dusty, dying look of pages in a book left too long on a library shelf.

Fiona leaned back in her chair and looked around her office. Bookshelves ran from floor to ceiling on two of the walls of the little room. Files of minutes of meetings, textbooks that were being used by her classes, books about pedagogy, chief among which was a battered copy of *Bloom's Taxonomy*, filled the available space.

Her desktop was cluttered with memoranda, current files, letters awaiting her signature, and next week's schedule. In her in-box, the pile of paperwork she must deal with before Tuesday crouched like a bad-tempered cat, daring her to reach out her hand and risk being clawed. At least the pile wasn't growling at her. Och, well, "Sufficient unto the day is the evil thereof." Tuesday was next week.

Three chairs stood in front of her desk. She had a parent-teacher interview scheduled this morning with the Papodopolous family. Young Dimitris was a holy terror, and his parents, both Greek immigrants, had not a word of English between them. The family should be here soon.

The high-pitched shouts of the Little League baseball teams playing a post-season recreational game outside sought no permission before intruding through the open window.

"Batter, batter, batter."

"Good eye. Good eye."

Fiona had learned enough about the game to understand that "good eye" meant one team was encouraging their batter not to swing, in the hope that the opposing pitcher would throw a fourth ball and give the batter a walk to first base.

To her ear, the words sounded very like the "g'dye" that was Tim's standard greeting. Australian for "good day." It was funny, she thought, how little things, like the ballplayers' cries, could bring him to mind. She often found herself thinking of him at incongruous times. His image had a habit of popping up like an unexpected scene in a Bergman movie. Totally unexpected, yet always welcome.

"Good eye. Good eye."

"G'dye." That's what Tim would say when he picked her up tonight to go to Bridges—which was where he'd taken her on the January day they'd first met. She let herself savour thoughts of seeing him tonight and of how they had met.

The weather then, she thought, looking at dust motes shimmering in a visiting sunbeam, hadn't been as pleasant as today's, and the last thing she had been expecting was to meet a new man, especially one like Tim Andersen.

She rose, walked to the window, and watched as a little lad took an almighty swing at the ball—and missed, lost his balance, and sat down heavily right in the middle of home plate.

"Go on," she said, knowing that he couldn't hear her, "pick yourself up and have another go."

It was advice she could have used herself not so very long ago.

She'd started seeing a writer last July. He was younger than she was, a bit bohemian with his beard and ponytail and complete disregard for the establishment. God, but he'd made her laugh. Some of his friends were weird by her standards, yet there was always an excitement in their company. He'd made her feel ten years younger, until, quite by chance, she had discovered that he was married. That had come to light in November. She'd told him to go to hell, never seen him again, decided to give men a rest for a while and to be satisfied with her own company and that of her immediate circle of friends.

Three months later, her anger and disappointment, her sense of betrayal, had faded sufficiently, and she could smile at herself for being so easily taken in.

One Saturday, feeling housebound, she'd decided to go to the Art Gallery. She'd walked from Kits to Granville Island, intending to take the water-bus across False Creek and walk down Burrard Street to West Georgia.

It had been a day when the January clouds had seemed to be welded to the tops of the North Shore Mountains. The sky had opened.

Despite the warmth of the morning sun today, just thinking of how suddenly soaked she had become made her shiver.

The nearest shelter had been Granville Market, and she was turning to scurry over there when, from nowhere, a voice said, "Excuse me. Excuse me, miss."

She'd turned and seen a tall man in foul-weather gear standing in the cockpit of a small moored yacht.

"Me?"

"Yes. Come aboard out of the rain." His Australian accent was noticeable.

She hesitated.

"I don't bite, and you're getting soaked."

She stepped to the side of the dock.

"Take my hand."

He helped her aboard.

"Down there." He guided her to a hatch.

She found herself in a small cabin. She sniffed. There was a faint smell of diesel fuel. The thrumming of rain on fibreglass drowned his next words.

"Pardon me?"

"I said, 'Park yourself on one of the seats. By the table.'"

"Thank you, Mr.?"

"Andersen. Tim Andersen." He threw back the hood of his oilskin jacket.

She saw the beginnings of pouches beneath grey eyes. Sandy eyebrows with uncut longer hairs. Wide forehead under a receding hairline. Bent nose—a result, she would later learn, of the Aussie-rules football he used to play in Melbourne. He wasn't going to beat Sean Connery for the title of World's Sexiest Looking, but looks weren't everything.

"Fiona Kavanagh."

"Welcome aboard. You from Ireland?"

"Years ago. I live here now." She knew her accent had given him the clue.

"I'm from Oz. Canada's a country of immigrants. Do you like it here?"

"I love it on the west coast."

"Me, too. Except when it rains like this. West coast? More like the bleeding *wet* coast."

She'd heard that one before but still laughed, and, as her head shook, she felt her hair wet against her face. She must look a sight. "You wouldn't have a towel on board, Mr. Andersen?"

"'Course. I'll get you one." He moved to a small doorway, entered, and returned carrying a towel. "And it's Tim to my friends."

She accepted the towel and dried her hair. "God," she said, "I must look like a drowned rat."

"You look pretty good to me," he said, taking back the damp towel.

She noticed his look of appraisal, and found that she didn't mind. Not one bit.

"Thank you . . . Tim."

"Aw, no need for thanks when a bloke tells the truth."

That made her smile.

She heard the rain hammering on the deck above her head.

"Tell you what," he said, "I was going to make a cup of tea. Would you like one?"

Why not? She nodded. "Great."

"Listen," he said, turning from where he was filling a kettle, "it's stopped raining."

All she could hear was the soft creaking of the boat tugging against her mooring lines. "I really should be running along. Thanks for rescuing me."

His face fell. "No tea?"

"Well . . ."

He glanced at his watch. "I've a better idea, Fiona." He hesitated. "It's all right if I call you Fiona, Miss Kavanagh?"

That was Old World courtesy, and she appreciated it. "Of course."

"Why don't you let me buy you lunch at Bridges? Unless you've something better to do?"

She hesitated. "You're not a writer, by any chance?"

"Me? Nah? You should see my scrawl. Anyway, I didn't ask you to a reading. I invited you to lunch." He smiled, and the look on his face was that of a small boy who had brought a stray puppy home and was asking his mother, "Can I keep him, Mum? Can I?" That look tipped the scales.

"No," she said.

His face fell.

"No. I mean I don't have anything better to do."

"Good on you, mate. Let's go."

Something better? She knew, now, that meeting Tim had been the best thing that had happened to her in years. She blessed the downpour that had brought them together. There'd be no rain today. Outside the window, there was not as much as a wisp of cloud to be seen in the sky.

She closed the pane, muffling the cries of the Little Leaguers.

Someone knocked on her door. Fiona went and opened it, expecting to greet the Greek family.

Becky Johnston, fiftyish, bespectacled, tall, her grey hair pulled back in a bun, stood in the hall. She carried herself with the formal rigidity of a sergeant major.

"Morning, Becky."

"Toiling in your vineyard, I see." Becky's parents came from the south of England and had brought their seventeen-year-old daughter with them when they'd immigrated to Vancouver. She'd never lost her plummy Oxbridge accent.

"Parent-teacher in a few minutes. The Papodopolouses."

"Dimitris been acting the maggot again?"

Fiona nodded. "The in-house counselor thinks he's hyperactive."

Becky snorted. "Rubbish. Psychological mumbo jumbo. He's just a busy little ten-year-old, that's all."

"Busy? If we could harness his energy, we could use him to power half the streetlights in Kits."

"You have my deep abiding sympathy." Becky had a grin on her face. "I'll leave you to it. I came in to work on next week's teaching plan." Becky looked out through the window. "It really is a lovely day, and I'll be finished soon. Would you care to go for coffee when you've finished?"

"Please." Past Becky's shoulder Fiona could see the Papodopolous family walking along the corridor. "I'm going to need one. Dimitris's parents haven't a word of English, and I'm never sure if the little devil translates exactly what I'm saying."

"I'll skedaddle. Do come along to the common room when you've finished."

"I will."

Becky left, and Fiona stood aside to let the parents of a black-haired, damson-eyed boy precede her into the office. "Good morning," she said.

She listened to Dimitris's rapid-fire Greek. "*Kalee mairah.*"

Fiona heard the liquid sounds of words that were meaningless to her, as would be hers to the parents, when the father said, "*Kalee maira, kay efharistoumai pou mas dethikatai stou yrafiosas.*"

Dimitris was obviously enjoying being in charge. "My father says, 'Good morning and thank you for seeing us.'" His English was barely accented.

"Please have a seat." Fiona pointed to the chairs in front of her desk and waited until the father, who was dressed in what was obviously his best suit, preceded Dimitris to the chair to Fiona's right. He sat, a heavyset, balding man, crossed his legs, and waited.

Dimitris came next. When seated, his legs did not reach the floor.

"*Efharistoumai,*" said the mother. She was wearing a flower-patterned dress. Fiona couldn't help noticing the woman's jewellery, two enormous finger rings and a golden crucifix that swung from a fine gold chain around her neck. Mother waited until her husband and son had been seated side by side before joining them. They were, Fiona thought, like "three dicky birds all in a row."

Dimitris immediately began to swing his legs back and forth.

Fiona sat. "Dimitris, please tell your parents I'd like to talk to them about you."

"*Thelee nas sas maleesi ya mena.*"

"*O Dimitris enai kalo ped, poli kalo pedi,*" the mother said.

"She says I am a *very* good boy." Dimitris translated, grinning. "*Poli kalo pedi.*"

"I know that," Fiona said, trying to smile, "but you can be disruptive in class." Would he tell his parents that?

"*Toe keseri oti emai kalo pedi . . .*"

Those were the words, "*kalo pedi,*" the mother and Dimitris had used for "good boy." He *was* embellishing what she was saying. She understood why the lad would try to cast himself in as favourable a light as possible, but could she trust him to convey some of the less flattering things that she must tell them? Fiona studied the parents' faces.

". . . *alla poles foress emai nohleticos stin taxi,*" Dimitris continued.

She saw the father frown. The mother shook her head, grimaced, and heaved a huge sigh. Something that had not pleased them had been transmitted. Perhaps Dimitris was doing his best to tell them what she was saying, and she could hardly blame the boy for trying to sugarcoat the pill.

This wasn't the first time Fiona had been forced to surmount the language barrier. She decided that she would use an old tactic that had worked before. She would not *tell* the parents anything. She would ask specific questions, and from the answers hope that she would be able to see if the message had got through. That, of course, assumed that Dimitris wasn't quick enough to garble the translation and still give her what she would think were the parents' responses. She didn't think a ten-year-old would be as clever as that—at least she hoped he wouldn't be. And watching their expressions and how they sat would help.

Dimitris kept swinging his legs so that now there was a rhythmic drumming of his shoes on the desk front.

The father growled and put one hand on the boy's leg.

"*Eni kalo pedi,*" the mother said emphatically, then spun round and clipped her son firmly round the ear. "*Dimitris! Katsai eseehos kai mein klotsas to trapezee.*"

The kicking stopped. Dimitris sniffled. "Mother says I should stop kicking."

She hauled him to her bosom and made soothing noises. He grinned at Fiona but kept up the sniffles for his mother's benefit, leaving Fiona in no doubt that, as she already knew, he was a bright lad and, being bright, could probably play his mother as an angler plays a fish. "All right," Fiona said, "let's all just take a minute and settle down."

Did that thump mean that the boy was beaten often? Not likely. As far as Fiona knew, Greek mothers were, if anything, overprotective. Certainly she had been quick to comfort the boy after the punishment had been given. It was more probable that she spoiled the boy at home.

"Now," she said, "shall we continue?"

The interview lasted for nearly an hour. By the time it was over, Fiona had been able to persuade herself that they had made some progress. She thought one of the little lad's difficulties was that he had not yet fully developed the ability to make the critical connection between cause and effect. That actions—his actions—would lead to consequences, and understanding the simple fact was the basis for understanding the concept of personal responsibility.

The parents had agreed that Dimitris would be allotted some specific tasks, like feeding the family dog—he'd seemed to be excited about that prospect—or helping his brother and two sisters with the washing up. Rewards and punishments had been defined. If he failed to wash his share of the dishes, his next meal would be served on the dirty plates. As a last resort, she had told the parents, if Dimitris was behaving badly, they should simply walk away from him and shut themselves in another room. That message had been passed by Dimitris with a look for Fiona that would have frozen water.

She had privately resolved that he would need more attention from her and the other teachers—lots of TLC—but that was some of what teaching was about, not just the three Rs so beloved by the mathematics teacher.

It had been agreed that they would meet again in one month to discuss Dimitris's progress, and—Fiona had breathed a quiet sigh of relief—the parents would bring an adult friend to translate.

As the family was leaving, the father said, "*Efharisto, Despeneice Kavanagh, ya tin prosohesou ston Dimitris. Adio.*"

"My father says, 'Thank you, Miss Kavanagh, for looking after me.' And"—he looked down at his neatly polished shoes—"I'll try to be good. I promise." He looked up at her. She could still see the imp that lurked behind those damson eyes, but she couldn't stop herself from reaching forward and tousling his hair.

He grinned at her—and took off racing down the corridor, his mother yelling after him, "*Dimitris. Dimitris, pearpata, mean trayhes . . .*," which Fiona presumed meant, "walk, don't run."

She shook her head, closed the door, and sat at her desk. Lord, she thought, the joys of parenthood. Once the cuddly baby stage was over, raising the little ones was a full-time job, and in her opinion did not receive the recognition it deserved.

She asked herself, did she regret never having had children of her own? It was a tough question, but nothing, nothing, would have persuaded her to bring a child into the lunacy that was Belfast back in the '70s. Perhaps if Davy—there he was again—perhaps if they could have come to Canada together, she would have enjoyed being the mother of their children, but it hadn't happened, and now? The media were talking about a woman's "biological clock," and, at forty-three, she knew that hers was ticking very fast.

Yes—she answered her own question—there was and always would be a tiny, nagging regret, but she knew that she, unlike Dimitris Papodopolous, did understand cause and effect. It had been her choice to be childless, and she now had to live with the consequences of that decision. And she did have a kind of a family—Dimitris and all of the other children in the school—and although the faces changed every few years, that family would never really age and move away. They'd always be there as long as she was a teacher. There was one other thing to consider (selfish as she knew the thought to be): Her school family went home at three o'clock and on weekends.

She picked up her pen and began to write her report of the interview.

"All done?" Becky sat, back straight, shoulders back on an elderly sofa in the teachers' common room. "How did it go?"

"It's over, thank goodness. I think I've given them something to work on."

"I'm absolutely sure you have." Becky stood. "I can't say I'm overly fond of meeting with parents, but as an old mentor of mine used to observe, 'In this life, there will always be a certain amount of shit to be shoveled. My advice to you, Miss Johnston, is to stop complaining, get yourself a long-handled spade . . . and start digging.'"

Fiona laughed at the incongruity of the coarse sentiments being expressed in accents that would have done a BBC newsreader proud.

Becky grabbed her coat from a clothes tree and said, "Come on. Coffee. You've earned it."

Fiona followed her friend out of the school to where Becky had her car parked.

"How about that coffee shop on Fourth?" Becky asked.

"That's fine by me. We could walk."

"I always say, if God had meant us to walk, He wouldn't have invented the internal combustion engine. Hop in." Becky pulled away from the kerb, drove the short distance from the school to Fourth Avenue, parked and climbed out.

Fiona asked for a table on the patio. "It's far too nice to be stuck inside any longer today."

She followed Becky as the waitress led them to a table for two in the corner of the wrought-iron-railinged enclosure. Becky ordered a latte, Fiona an espresso.

"Isn't that sari absolutely gorgeous?" Becky said, inclining her head toward the sidewalk.

Fiona saw a Sikh couple, the woman in a sari as iridescent as the tail feathers of a peacock's fan, walking beside a man wearing a bright orange turban. Behind them, a group of Chinese women was striding along talking loudly in what she assumed was either Cantonese or Mandarin.

Becky leaned forward and said quietly, "I wonder why the Chinese always have to yell at each other? It's a bit common, you know."

Fiona laughed. Becky had kept more than her accent. Occasionally, she let something slip that told Fiona that, in the eyes of the English expatriate, *Britannia* still ruled the waves.

"It's just their way. You get used to it. I think it's wonderful that so many people from all over the world live here in Vancouver and seem to be able to get along," Fiona said. "Not like where I come from." There was a tinge of sadness to her voice.

"Quite so," Becky said. "Live and let live."

The coffees arrived.

"I'm serious." Fiona sipped her espresso. "The family I saw this morning is from Cyprus. The father's half owner of a taverna. The other owner is a Turk . . . and all the waiters are Italian."

"Regular little League of Nations. I suppose the exception does sometimes prove the rule." Becky had a moustache of latte foam. "I'm not too fond of Cyprus. We, the British that is, lost a lot of boys there in the fifties. Peacekeepers. Trying to keep the Turks and the Greeks from each other's throats. Still, as you say, it is a rather promising sign that Johnny Turk and a Greek are going into business together over here."

"Johnny Turk?"

"That's what my grandfather called them. He fought the Turks in Gallipoli in the First World War. He did say they were damn fine fighting men. Damn fine. And it wasn't the Turks the British soldiers had to contend with in Cyprus. It was EOKA, the Greek Cypriot terrorists."

Fiona lowered her cup to its saucer. All this talk about war, about

Cyprus. EOKA. Sudden memories ran in her mind—like the nightmare—memories she would rather forget.

Becky ploughed on. "The Greeks wanted *enosis,* political union with the Greek mainland, and to chuck out the Turks. They still do, and that Archbishop Makarios?" Becky scowled. "The Greek Cypriot leader? Nasty piece of work."

"I know," Fiona said softly. Cyprus. Cyprus. She frowned. She hadn't talked about Connor to anyone in Canada, but—she looked at Becky's open face—they'd become close friends in the last few years. Why not tell her?

"My big brother, Connor, was killed there. In nineteen fifty-five, when I was fifteen," she blurted.

Becky sat upright. "Good Lord."

"He'd joined the British army. They sent him to Nicosia. He was shot dead when he was off-duty, Christmas shopping on a place called Ledra Street."

"Well, I'll be damned." Becky leaned toward Fiona. "I didn't know. I really am very sorry."

"It's all right. It was a long time ago." Fiona sipped her coffee. "It really shook me up then. I was hardly more than a child, and it seemed to me that Connor had been killed in the middle of someone else's fight."

"It never changes. British boys are still dying trying to keep ethnic and religious groups apart."

"In Cyprus?"

Becky looked deeply into Fiona's eyes, hesitated, then said, "And, forgive me for saying so, in Ulster."

And that was the truth. "I know," Fiona said, and thought of Davy and the soldier he'd killed. And the forty years Davy was serving in the Kesh. "There've been too many deaths there."

"I seem to remember that once upon a time you actually tried to do something about it."

"I beg your pardon?"

"You told me you'd been up to your neck in the Ulster civil rights movement. A regular . . . what's the American word . . . ? Peacenik. That's it. You said that you'd worked hard for them."

"Yes. I did." What was Becky driving at?

"It seems to me, at least from what you said, that you did your best over there."

"Well, I . . ."

"I'd even wager that your brother's death was what got you involved in the first place."

Fiona's eyes widened. Becky was right. It had been Connor's death that had made her try all those years ago—along with George Thompson and the rest of NICRA—to put an end to the useless sectarian violence.

"It's hardly your fault that your countrymen are still at it. Queen Elizabeth the First knew that it was a waste of time trying to civilize the Irish."

"Becky, it was your Good Queen Bess who was responsible for the Troubles."

"In God's name, how? She's been dead for three hundred years."

"She was the one who decided to ship thousands of Lowland Scots as colonists to Ulster. They were Protestants. They called it the Plantation. She gave them the land that Catholic natives had owned. The natives didn't like that. They still don't."

Becky fiddled with her coffee cup.

"Come on, Becky. Cheer up. It's hardly your fault. It all started so far in the past."

"And that's a foreign country," Becky said pensively.

"A what?"

"A chap called L. P. Hartley once said a marvelous thing, and I quote, 'The past is a foreign country; they do things differently there.' And d'you know what? He was absolutely right."

"A foreign country?" Fiona toyed with the line, then said, "I try not to think about it too much. Sometimes . . . sometimes I wish we could blot out our pasts. Clean them off like chalk from a blackboard."

"Ah," said Becky with a small grin, "we can't, however"—she hoisted her latte—"we *can* polish off our coffees, and, if you'd like, I'll run you home and you can take me for that walk." She patted her stomach. "I probably could use a bit of exercise."

Fiona could hear her friend breathing heavily as together they reached the top of the little hill in Vanier Park, a favourite spot for Vancouver kite fliers.

"I," said Becky, "need a breather." Then she plumped down on the grass.

Fiona sat beside her and watched the kites, multicoloured fabric birds that caught the breeze and dived and soared. "Aren't they graceful?"

"Pretty," said Becky. "You'd think they were all trying to break free and go tearing off on their own. Of course, you know if their strings snap they don't soar off into the wild blue yonder. They prang."

"They what?"

"Prang. My dad was in the Royal Air Force. Prang was RAF slang for crash." Becky turned her head to follow the aerobatics of two crescent-shaped creations that raced across the blue. "I wonder . . . remember you said you'd like to be able to blot out your past . . . ? I wonder if our pasts are like kite strings?"

"Whatever do you mean?"

"You said you'd like to be able to wipe out your past."

"Well, sometimes I would."

"I think everything that has happened to us is *our* string. We may think it's an encumbrance, but all that has gone, all we remember, even the things we try to forget, remind us of who and what we are and keep us on an even keel. As long as we don't dwell there too much."

Fiona considered what her friend had said and recognized that she, Fiona, *had* been dwelling too much on her past in the last few days. The bloody nightmare always did that to her. It was a good thing that it seemed to be coming less and less frequently. Perhaps, she grinned at the idea, perhaps it was like a teenager's acne. She'd grow out of it.

One of the kites swooped close to her, rose, stalled, and plunged to earth. She saw a little boy running to it, pulling a man by the hand. The lad lifted the broken thing, stared up at the man, and said, tearfully, "But you can fix it, can't you, Daddy?"

Poor wee fellow. The boy didn't know, as she did, that there were some things even a daddy couldn't fix. He'd learn as she had learned. Northern Ireland couldn't be fixed, at least for all her efforts she and her NICRA friends hadn't been able to fix it. And as they said there, "What can't be cured must be endured"—or left behind as she'd left Belfast to carry on with her life. And Tim was now part of that life. He was taking her to dinner tonight.

She stood. "You've said a mouthful, Becky, and I think you're right. In fact . . . I know you're right."

Becky struggled to her feet. "Doctor Becky usually is. Rather boring, don'tcha know?'

Fiona laughed at her friend's fake upper-class Victorian expression.

"Not one bit. Come on. Let's go home."

CHAPTER 7

Sammy McCandless just wanted to get this over with and get home. He slowed the Land Rover. Through the drizzle, its headlights lit a signpost. Clady was the last town on the County Tyrone side of the border with the Irish Republic. Underneath the pointing finger that read CLADY ½, nailed to the post, was a metal white-painted triangle surrounded by a red border. It wasn't one of the usual traffic signs where the picture in the triangle, say of cattle, warned the motorist that this was where cows might cross the road and be a hazard to traffic.

The picture was of a balaclava-hooded figure holding an ArmaLite rifle aloft. The slogan beneath proclaimed, SNIPER AT WORK. Not even the thickest British squaddie could fail to be aware of the effectiveness of a sniper, concealed in a clump of whin bushes or tucked in behind a dry-stone wall, firing from the Republic of Ireland side of the border. An ArmaLite's .223 round could pierce body armour.

He pulled the Rover to the verge, stopped, took a torch from the passenger seat, and got out. One last check in the horse box.

He dropped the tail ramp and climbed in. Plenty of straw on the floor. Enough horse apples. He shoved the yellow stalks aside and shone the torch's beam along the floorboards, each fitted to its neighbour by a tongue-and-groove joint. It would take a skilled eye to see how a section could be lifted and allow access to the hollow floor of the vehicle. It had seen a lot of use, this old horse trailer—and not just for gunrunning. Old man O'Byrne had made a bit of extra cash cross-border smuggling. It had been a way of life in all the border counties for as long as Sammy could remember. Tyrone in the North and Donegal in the Republic were neighbours. Before the partition of Ireland, both had been part of the old nine-county Province of Ulster, where today only six counties remained.

About forty miles south of here, in South Armagh, "Slab" Murphy's farm was half in Ballybinaby in County Louth in the Republic and half in Cornoogah in Armagh. He had oil storage tanks on both sides of the border and simply pumped oil from the side where the prices were lower to the side where the oil could be sold for more. He was supposed to be worth millions. An illegal traffic in grain and pigs always followed subsidies offered to farmers by the British or by the Republic of Ireland. There was big money in that, too.

Money? Sammy kicked at a pile of horse turds. He'd been short of doh-ray-me all his life. The wages old man O'Byrne and now Cal paid a farm labourer would hardly keep a wood louse in wood chips. No wonder Sammy'd got in with a bunch of lads who bought pigs in Ballybofey, trucked them north, claimed the eight-pounds-per-animal subsidy at the border, then herded the animals back across the fields at night to repeat the trans-border run the next day—and collect another bounty. Made him a good fifty pounds a week. With that amount of extra cash to spend, life hadn't been too bad—until the day, three years ago, when Erin smiled at him.

He sat down, let his leg dangle over the open back of the trailer, switched off the torch, pulled out a Park Drive—cheapest fags he could buy—lit up, and thought of her and her bloody smile.

He'd been mucking out the byre, shoveling cow clap into a wheelbarrow, when she'd come round the corner.

"Morning, Sammy." Her hair was down, and the light behind her shone through the strands like evening sunlight on a rippled lake. He could see the silhouette of her legs, long, slim legs, through the material of her skirt.

"Erin."

"Have you got a wee minute?"

For her? She could have the rest of his life and his share of eternity. How often had he watched her move about the farm, graceful, young, high-breasted? How many nights had he sat alone in his cottage flipping the pages of an old *Playboy*, zip of his pants undone, tissues on the sofa beside him, staring at the nude American girls and picturing Erin O'Byrne, naked, lips pouting, beckoning to him? Why could he never get her out of his mind? She'd not even glance at a fellah like him, and anyway there were plenty of girls in Strabane who'd let you take them to the pictures on a Saturday night, fumble with their bra straps in the dark, give you a bit of the other up against a wall in a dark back alley, but still . . .

A man could dream, although Sammy kept his dreams tucked in the bottom of the sock drawer of his mind as he used the dresser back home to hide his *Playboy*s and a dog-eared photograph of Erin smiling down from her horse.

"Aye, certainly," he'd said, putting the shovel into the barrow and walk-ing to the byre's open door.

"Great day," she said.

"Aye." He wished he was quicker with the repartee, but the best he could come up with was, "It'll bring the crops on a treat."

"Sam, I was wondering if you could do me a wee favour . . . ?" She tilted her head to one side, and her hair caressed her left cheek and fell to her right shoulder in a copper cascade.

"Aye, surely." She probably wanted her horse saddled.

"It's a bit . . . you know . . ." She looked down at the floor of the byre. "A bit tricky."

It wasn't like Erin to be hesitant about anything.

"Are you all right?"

She laughed in her throat and looked up. Her eyes, bright as emeralds, shone for him. "Aye. It's just a wee thing." She moved close to him and put her lips close to his ear. Her breath was gentle on him as she whispered, "I know you get stuff in from the Republic . . ."

He started. What he and the boys got up to was meant to be a secret.

She took his hand, and he felt the soft warmth.

"I need a parcel brought over the border . . . tonight."

Brought in? For her? He didn't hesitate. "What is it?" Lots of things, he knew, could be bought at a considerable discount over the border because of different taxes levied by the governments of the two countries. "A new skirt? Nylons?" He thought of her pulling the sheer stuff along her calf, her thigh.

"Guns." Her voice was matter-of-fact. She might have been asking him to smuggle a pound of butter and a couple of hams. "You'll do it for me, won't you?"

"What?"

"Guns."

"Jesus Christ." He'd suspected for years that Cal was an active Provo. That was none of Sammy's business. He'd no interest in politics, their fuckin' "Cause," but was Erin mixed up, too?

"No," she said calmly, "we don't need Jesus Christ. There's enough pic-tures of His Bleeding Heart around here. *We* need guns . . . and *I* need you to help."

He hoped to see pleading in her eyes. If it had been there, he could have refused her nothing, but her eyes were cold like the eyes of a newt.

"I'm not . . ." He let go of her hand.

"Yes, you are, Sam. For me." And then she'd smiled.

He'd be seeing that smile on his deathbed.

Sammy tossed the butt into the ditch. If he hadn't given in to it, he would never have made that first gunrunning trip, nor have been drawn deeper and deeper into the Provos, until two years ago he had made their declaration, accepted full membership.

She'd kissed him that night, told him she loved him, but he knew it was only a word, one that she might have used to a girlfriend. "Nancy, I love your new blouse." That's all he was to Erin O'Byrne. A friend's new blouse. All he'd ever be.

And look where joining the Provos had got him. Fighting for a cause that meant nothing to him. Risking jail or worse—much worse—and for what? A united Ireland? That meant nothing to him. He'd never been further than Ballybofey in his life, and the few Donegal lads he knew were no different from himself. Working men who liked a smoke and a pint. What difference did it make to anyone if the government of Northern Ireland was in Dublin or London? The buggers would still tax the bejesus out of them.

He'd only gone in to please Erin. He'd not known then their saying, "The only way out is feetfirst"—but by God he'd soon learned. And now there was that other matter—Christ, what a fuckup. Sammy shuddered.

He slammed the tailgate, stamped back to the Rover, climbed in, and drove off, sucking a peppermint. He wound down the window, let the night air blow in, turned a corner, and there, up ahead, two RUC constables and four soldiers were waiting for him at the old customs post, on the Tyrone side. Once past them and over the bridge with its walls built like small battlements, he'd be in Donegal—in the Republic.

One of the body-armoured constables stood in the middle of the road, torch aimed at the Rover. Sammy stopped and got out. He might as well. They'd want to search the trailer.

Ahead, the officer bent and shone his torch at the front of the vehicle. He'd be making a note of the plate number. Let him. The Provos had known that since 1974 the army had been using a computer programme called Vengeful. It took thirty seconds, once a security man had entered the numbers at a remote terminal, for the programme to find out anything he needed to know about the vehicle in question.

Good luck to the bugger out there. When he sent the plate information in, he'd find the Rover was registered to a big landowner in Sixmilecross. Sammy and Cal had seen to that after they'd had their supper. Plates were easy to forge, and no Provo in his right mind would go out on any mission in a vehicle that could be traced.

The big peeler, with the ponderous gait of his kind, moved up to Sammy.

"Evening, sir. Can I see your licence?"

"Aye, surely." Sammy produced the pink cardboard square.

"Thank you, Mr. Pollock." The constable wrote something on a clipboard. Sammy knew that every crossing would be logged. Time. Driver's name and address. It was a good thing that British driving licences did not carry photos and, like plates, were easy to forge. An Active Service Unit in Newtownstewart had a graphic artist as a member. He took care of the forgeries.

He returned the licence. "I'll hae to take a keek in the beck."

The way the man said "hae" for "have," "keek" for "look," "beck" for "back," and the sibilance of his s's marked him as a County Antrim man, not a local who might have recognized Sammy. So much the better.

Sammy accompanied the constable as he walked to the rear of the horse box.

"Open her up please, sir."

"It's empty."

"I'm sure it is, sir, but I still need to hae a look."

Sammy unlatched the tailgate. "Help yourself."

The police officer swung up inside and scraped the loose straw aside.

Sammy's palms started to sweat.

"Sorry about that, but you never can be sure." The policeman dismounted. "Bit late to be going down to the Republic."

"I've to pick up a horse in Stranolar." The town was near enough to Ballybofey, and you *never* told the peelers exactly where you were going. "I'll be back this way in a couple of hours."

"I'll still be here. I'll be here all fuckin' night."

"Rather you nor me."

The constable shrugged. "Goes wi' the job." He nodded at the tailgate. "Close her up, Mr."—he consulted his clip board—"Pollock, and away you go."

"Right," said Sammy and bent to his work.

"Sorry to have held you up. I'll give the *Garda Síochána* detachment on the other side a bell, let them know you're clean."

"I'd appreciate that."

"Night, sir."

"Night." Sammy snibbed the last latch.

Sammy passed a finger post that pointed back along the road he'd traveled. BEALACH FÉICH 6. He was glad to be leaving Ballybofey. It had taken longer than he'd anticipated to load the ArmaLite semiautomatic rifles and five hundred rounds of .223 ammunition. Sammy had recognized the guns as

Bushmaster XM-15 M4 A3s, an American civilian version of the U.S. Army's M16. Thirty kilos of Semtex, and separately wrapped consignments of RDX and PETN, the explosive components of Semtex, to be used in the manufacture of detonating cords, completed the load, all tucked in safely beneath the floor—and under the sharp hooves of a bad-tempered chestnut gelding.

He didn't anticipate trouble at the border. The *Gardai* and the RUC detachments would be tired by now. More careless. He'd told the peeler that he was meant to be collecting a horse, and what was in the back? A fucking great horse. All he had to do once he'd passed the checkpoints was get the horse into the paddock and the shipment into its hiding place in Ballydornan churchyard. Then home, a wee whiskey, and bed.

Sleep would be good. The only other thing he had to do before turning in was to make a phone call. From a coin box. A call that couldn't be traced.

He thought about the hint that Erin had let slip about something that might be going to happen at the Kesh. Would that be the key to let him out of the mess he was in?

There was a public phone about a mile away. He accelerated, reached the kiosk, stopped, and turned off the Rover's lights.

Coins in the slot. Double ring. A sleepy, "Hello?"

"It's Sunshine." Stupid fucking code words.

"Yes?" Interest in the voice now.

"I've something for you. Something big."

"Have you? Tell me."

"Not now. The light's on in this kiosk, and I'm stickin' out like a sore thumb."

"All right. Tomorrow. Ten A.M. Point Alpha."

"Right." Sammy hung up. His breath had steamed up the windows of the call box. He stepped outside, leaving the door ajar. The automatic light went off, and Sammy shrank into the darkness. The sooner he was out of here, the better. He didn't want Cal or Erin to be missing him, but if he didn't get the horse into the paddock soon, one of them might start to wonder what had held him up.

CHAPTER 8

"Damn. Just missed another one. I told you parking would be tight at Granville Island on a Saturday night." Tim hunched over the wheel.

"Look. There." Fiona pointed to a space near the grey silos of the Ocean Cement Company. "That car's backing out."

"Bloody good." Tim stopped, indicated left, waited for the other car to pull out, and slipped his BMW into the spot. "Hop out and I'll lock up."

She joined him for the short walk to Bridges restaurant. He took her hand, and the warmth of his pleased her.

"Have I told you you look smashing tonight?"

"Thank you, sir." She had been satisfied with the effect of her carefully chosen white silk blouse and bottle-green skirt. She'd left the top two buttons of the blouse undone to show just enough cleavage. Three open would have been tarty.

He glanced down and said, "Best gams in Vancouver."

Her dark pantyhose did set her legs off well, and the curves of her calves were accentuated by her black patent-leather pumps, the high-heeled sneakers Tim had asked for.

"You try walking in these heels."

"Nah. I'd rather look at you in them, and anyway we're here."

A hostess greeted them, showed them to a window table in the upstairs nonsmoking section, and left two menus. "Your waiter'll be with you in a moment, sir."

The place was packed.

Tim held Fiona's chair. He sat opposite.

"Fancy a drink?"

"Wine, please." Ten years ago, she might have had one glass of sherry, but Tim had taught her about wines and she particularly liked Chardonnay.

"Let's have a bottle." Tim leaned across and whispered, "I'm as dry as a dead dingo's donger."

Fiona adopted her best schoolmarm voice. "Tim Andersen. What a thing to say to a lady," but her words were masked by a wide grin. "I think it's true what they say about Aussies."

"And what might that be?"

"That God invented Australians so that Americans would at least *appear* to be cultured."

"Too right." Tim laughed and picked up his menu. "Now. Let's see what looks good in this."

She practically knew Bridges' menu by heart. As he read, she looked out of the picture window.

Not quite the same vista as from Kits Beach. The single span of Burrard Street Bridge blocked the view.

As usual, False Creek was busy. Water-buses dodged between incoming and outgoing sailboats, their wakes crossing and criss-crossing and sparkling in the evening sun. To her left, the slips of Burrard Civic Marina were crammed with commercial fishing boats, sharp-bowed, businesslike. Behind them, moored pleasure crafts' masts were an aluminum forest.

Fiona half-heard Tim discussing the wine with the sommelier.

A kingfisher, iridescent blue, its flight sudden and jerky, skimmed over the water, scolded the gulls, swooped over the fishing boats, and vanished among the pleasure crafts rocking in their berths to the wakes from the creek. Tim's boat, *Windshadow,* was among the yachts.

Tim loved that boat. The day he'd asked her to come in out of the rain and she'd admired his vessel, he'd said, "I love this little darling." He'd had the kind of look on his broad face that she imagined Romeo would have had under Juliet's balcony.

He was still reading the menu. She would take a bet with herself that he'd order calamari to start with, then red snapper. That's what he'd had when he'd brought her here for lunch back in January. It had been a different hostess eight months ago who had greeted Tim like an old friend. "Hello, Doctor Andersen. For two?" she'd said.

Fiona had been surprised that he hadn't made a fuss about being medically qualified when he'd introduced himself. She'd liked that. A lot.

She had followed him to a table, and they'd sat on soft-cushioned, cane-backed chairs. The cane, she remembered, had felt lumpy against her rain-dampened sweater.

"*Doctor* Tim?" she'd asked.

"'Fraid so, and to get the rest of the questions out of the way, chief of endocrinology at Saint Paul's Hospital up on Burrard Street, prof. at UBC, fifty-six years old, came to Canada in fifty-five, married a Canadian . . ."

"You're married?" She'd sat back in her chair. Hard. Not another one. She'd started to rise.

"Was. My ex and my two boys live in Ontario."

"Oh." She'd sat down.

He'd leaned across the table, smiled, and said, "Now, you know everything about me. Let's order, and then you can tell me all about Fiona Kavanagh."

She couldn't remember what she'd ordered, but he'd had—

"I'm going to have calamari . . ."

"And red snapper." She laughed.

"How did you know that?"

"It's what you had the first time we came here."

"And you had oysters and fish and chips."

So she had. Trust him to remember. The pair of them were like a couple of sixteen-year-olds getting dewy-eyed when they heard the tune that had been played at their first dance together. For old times' sake, then. "Oysters Rockefeller and Atlantic cod and french fries, please." To hell with diets, even though McCusker had been switched to a low-fat cat food.

"Fish and chips? You can take the girl out of Ireland, but . . ."

The waiter leaned past Fiona. He showed the wine's label to Tim, who nodded.

The waiter poured.

She sipped. It was a Chardonnay, crisp and fruity.

"Would you care to order, sir?"

Tim ordered.

"We're very busy tonight. It may be some time."

"No worries."

The waiter left.

"Cheers." Tim lifted his glass.

"*Sláinte mHaith.*" This was a damn sight better than parent-teacher interviews. The wine was cold on her tongue.

Tim pointed to the marina. "Fancy taking *Windy* out tomorrow? Forecast's good."

"Love to." He'd started taking her sailing in April, and she'd taken to it like a duck to water. "Where'll we go? Where the wind blows?"

"Bowen Island?"

Around them the hum of the conversations of the other diners was punctuated by the gulls outside that bickered like the women of the Falls hanging out their washing and calling insults to their neighbours across the backyard fences.

"Lovely. I'd enjoy . . ." Fiona was conscious of someone standing near her.

A harsh voice said in a thick Belfast accent, "'Scuse me. Fiona? Fiona Kavanagh? I don't mean to interrupt like, but . . ."

She knew that voice. She spun in her seat. She no longer could hear the sounds of background conversations, the mewling of the gulls.

A short man shot out his lower jaw, grinned, and said, "*It is*. It is, so it is. How's about ye?" He turned to Tim. "I didn't mean to intrude, like, but I've not seen herself there for about ten years and the missus says to me, so she does . . . she's over there in the smoking bit . . . Siobhan's with her. She's my daughter," he explained to Tim. Jimmy pointed to a table in the corner. "The missus says, says she, 'See you that there woman who's just come in? She looks a hell of lot like Davy's Fiona.' 'Away off and chase yourself,' says I, but the more I looked . . ." He held out his hand to Tim. "Jimmy Ferguson, by the way."

"Tim Andersen."

Fiona glanced across the room to where two women sat, one middle-aged, the other young, tall, with waist-length blonde hair. They waved. Fiona waved back.

"Jesus, Fiona, the things you see when you don't have a gun."

Gun. She flinched. Guns. Belfast. Jimmy Ferguson, housepainter and ex-Provo. The last time she'd seen Jimmy in Belfast, she'd run into him, quite by accident, in Smithfield Market, after she'd left Davy. She'd asked Jimmy to give her regards to Davy, and he'd phoned her. Asked her to meet him.

She took a deep breath. "Are you living in Vancouver, Jimmy?"

"Aye. Me and the missus emigrated to join Siobhan in Toronto. She sponsored us. She'd been out there for a while. You mind she'd been visiting us when . . . ? She went back after . . ."

After—after Davy had met with her, told her he *would* leave the Provos and come to Canada—and the feelings she'd had that night flooded back. She slipped her hands under the table, not wanting Tim to see how much they trembled. After—after he'd done one more mission, the mission that had blown up in his face as Jimmy's appearance here tonight had exploded in hers.

"Yes." Fiona's voice was cold. "I do." She could see Tim's brow wrinkle.

Jimmy's jaw flicked. "Aye, well, we'll say no more about *that*. Anyroad, I'd enough saved up for to buy a wee painting business in Toronto. But the winters was fierce, so they were. I tell you, when I go to hell, ould Beelzebub

won't be asking me to stoke the furnace. He'll hand me a snow shovel."
Jimmy tittered at his own joke. "I sold up and bought a partnership in a place
out here a couple of years back. And do you live here, too, Fiona?"

"I do."

"I'll be damned. Small world. I knew you'd come to Canada after us. Me
and Davy still write to each other. He told me you'd come."

He wrote to Davy.

Jimmy blethered on. "I'll tell you one thing: You've not lost your Ulster
accent."

"Nor you, Jimmy."

"Still thick as champ."

"That's creamed potatoes, scallions, and buttermilk, Tim."

Tim's frown had deepened. "Pay no attention to me. You two carry on."

"I'm sorry," said Jimmy, "but her and me and poor ould Davy go back a
powerful long ways."

"How's Siobhan?" Fiona did not want any more mention of Davy. Not in
front of Tim.

Jimmy's smile faded. He shot his lower jaw. "She's grand . . . now. It took
her a brave while to get over that bastard, pardon my French, Richardson
that called himself Roberts." He glanced over to his table, then lowered his
voice. "Sometimes I think she's still carrying a torch."

Fiona felt the lump start in her throat.

"If it hadn't been for him shopping Davy, you and . . ."

"Let the hare sit, Jimmy."

"Aye. Least said soonest mended. Anyroad, she got married to a Canadian lad. He does something in TV. They've two youngsters. He's working
in Montreal. He couldn't get away, so she come out here by herself for a wee
visit like. The youngsters are at home with a babysitter and . . ."

"Excuse me, sir." The waiter stood, balancing their starters on a silver
tray.

"Just a wee minute." Jimmy produced a camera.

The flash dazzled Fiona.

"I'll run away on. Tell you what, could we get together after supper for a
half-un in the bar?"

"Certainly," said Tim.

No. Fiona shouted inside herself.

"Right." Jimmy started to leave but turned to Fiona. "When I get this developed, I'll send one to Davy. He keeps on asking me if I ever run into you."

"Thank you, sir." The waiter served.

Fiona smiled at Tim with her mouth. Her eyes were lifeless. "Folks from back in Ireland. They *never* know when to shut up. You didn't have to agree to have drinks with them, you know." She toyed with her oysters, appetite gone.

"He seemed like a decent enough chap."

"I'm sure he did, but . . . Tim, I'd rather not talk about it just now." It wasn't fair. Her nightmare had brought memories of Davy McCutcheon surging back to her two nights ago. Since then, she'd thought more deeply about Belfast than she had for months. She didn't need another reminder from, of all people, Jimmy Ferguson.

"Come on," Tim said, a smile now on his face, "sounds like a bit of a mystery to me. 'That bastard Richardson that called himself Roberts'? 'Him shopping Davy'?" The smile faded. "I've never seen you look so rattled. Perhaps you should tell me about it."

She could hear his concern for her. Dear Tim. She would tell him. Sometime.

She laid her fork on her plate. "I will, Tim, but . . . not just now."

"Pity." His voice was level. "I was going to ask you about this Davy fellow."

CHAPTER 9

"*In nomine Patris, et Filii, et Spiritus Sancti, amen.*"

Davy and the men around him echoed the priest's final amen, the smell of the altar boys' incense heavy in the air. Another mass was over. He went not because of any deep faith but because there was a comfort in the service, the old well-remembered phrases learned as a skinny youngster at Saint Mary's Chapel just around the corner from his home on Conway Street.

". . . Holy Mary, Mother of God, pray for us sinners, now and in the hour of our death."

Going to chapel was something to do on a Sunday, a break from the everyday with its monotonous regularity.

Get up when you're told. Eat breakfast when you're told. Swab out the corridors and earn a little remission time. Eat lunch when you're told—and the food was always the same—grey meat that was so overdone you couldn't tell if it was pork, beef, or lamb. Soggy vegetables, hard, half-boiled spuds. Stale bread. Stewed tea. Back in your cell by two o'clock for the daily head count. The screws had become more insistent on that since 1981, when eight Provos had shot their way out of Belfast's other top-security prison, the Crumlin Road Jail.

Davy lingered in his pew, letting the other men push past him. The room was peaceful and spacious. Not like his eight-by-eight cell.

He watched the priest and his acolytes clearing away candles, crosses, and chalices, putting Communion wafers back in a pyx. They had to tidy up all vestiges of their brand of Christianity. There'd be a Protestant service starting here soon.

Any devout Protestant who was in jail for being a Loyalist paramilitary would think a crucifix was a sign that the Antichrist had been in the room. They were men who daubed the gable ends of the houses in Belfast's Sandy Row ghetto with slogans like "Home rule is Rome rule" and "Fuck the pope."

But this was a multidenominational chapel.

At least that's what the authorities called it. He knew bloody well that once the needs of the Republican Catholic prisoners and the, almost to a man, Free Presbyterian Loyalists had been catered to, there wasn't much call for the place to accommodate any members of other faiths like Jews or Buddhists or Hindus.

He smiled and remembered an old one-liner.

A Provo grabs a man on a Belfast street. "Are you a Catholic or a Protestant?"

"I'm a Hindu."

"Aye, but are you a Catholic Hindu or a Protestant Hindu?"

Black humour had always been part of the Irish way of dealing with disaster. The recipe for Potato Famine soup? "Take a gallon of water and boil it 'til it's very, *very* strong."

Davy enjoyed a good laugh as much as anyone, and, God knew, there wasn't too much to laugh at in this place.

He looked across the room and saw Eamon deep in conversation with three men. Davy had no doubt about what *they* would be discussing. After Mass was a good time for Eamon to meet inmates from other H-blocks.

One of the three, a short, dark-haired man, carried his left shoulder higher than the other. He wore spectacles. In the past, that wee shite Brendan McGuinness had not even bothered covering up his empty eye socket. The Brits had given him a glass eye. Taken him out of the prison for a couple of days to the Royal Victoria Hospital to have the job done.

Davy wondered if they'd cleaned the bugger's teeth while they were at it. Back before the Brits had stuck McGuinness in here, there had always been a greenish tinge to the man's smile. The unholy bastard. Davy hated McGuinness.

That turd had been the architect of Davy's last mission, the one that had got him in here, and he'd be one of the ones that Eamon would be going with when the attempted jailbreak happened. Davy had no doubt that if the men did get out of the Kesh, they'd be rounded up in no time flat. McGuinness and his like were going to land Eamon in the shite up to his nostrils.

Davy didn't want to share the same room with the bastard.

He genuflected to the altar, crossed himself, rose, and limped down the aisle and back to cell 16. He'd have one more try to persuade Eamon to give up the stupid notion but was certain he would fail. Eamon Maguire, for all his seeming good nature, was, deep inside, as fanatical as any man in the place.

· · ·

"*Tiocfaidh àr la*, Father Davy." Eamon bounced into their cell.

To Davy it sounded like "chucky air la." He knew that it was Irish for "our day will come" and was the standard greeting of one Provo inmate to another, so much so that they called themselves Chuckies.

"Right enough. That'll be the day we'll have to walk crouched over to avoid all the pigs that'll be flying about the place," Davy said.

"Don't be at it, Father. One day "—Eamon plumped himself down on his cot—"one day there'll be a green, white, and gold Irish flag flying over the Belfast City Hall instead of a Union Jack."

"And I suppose the Orange Order will have shamrocks and harps on their sashes and the Gaelic Athletic Association will switch from playing Gaelic football and hurley to rugby and cricket?" Davy sat on the chair. Symbols, he thought, shamrocks, harps, and orange sashes. Irish flags, British flags. Irish games, British games—symbols of the two tribes. But symbols as powerful as—as the Ark of the Covenant to a Jew, the Liberty Bell to an American, Mecca and Medina to a Muslim.

"You're in a great mood today, Father. Look. We're going to win. That's all there's to it." Eamon lay back on his cot and put both hands behind his head. "*Tiocfaidh àr la*."

Davy bent forward in his chair. "Eamon?"

"What?"

"I saw you talking to McGuinness after Mass."

"Aye."

"Would you not think again about what you and the other lads're up to?"

"Why?" Eamon sat upright as if he had a hinge at his waist. "We have thought about it. Thought about bugger all else for the last couple of years."

Davy rose and closed the cell door before lowering his voice and saying, "Ireland's a very wee country. An island. Every peeler and every soldier'll be on the lookout. The airports and the harbours'll be closed. You'd not be safe in England. The Brits would have Interpol after you in Europe. There's those who'd inform as quick as look at you. I wish you'd not do it."

Eamon laughed. "And I wish you'd come. Your stock's pretty high with the Officer Commanding since you done us that wee favour. I could still get you in on it. How is the paw, by the way?"

Davy held up his left hand so that Eamon could see the Elastoplast strip. "On the mend."

"Good." Eamon rolled off his cot to stand on the floor. "Davy, do you never feel as if some bugger had the walls of this place on some kind of ratchet and was squeezing them closer every day?"

"Of course."

"And do you not want to get out? Fight on? You've been in the struggle since before I was weaned."

Davy shook his head. "I'm done with it."

"So you say, but I'll bet . . ."

"I want no more of it."

"But you told me your da was in. He got you in."

"And I stayed in because of him." Davy limped to the wall, turned, stood and stared at Eamon. Should he tell Eamon about Da? Why not? Eamon was Davy's friend. Davy took a deep breath and blew it out through the hairs of his moustache. "Eamon, I killed my own da."

"You *what*?"

"You heard me. Back in the fifties. I was learning bomb making. One went off by mistake. Killed Da and three other men. Fucked up my leg." Davy massaged his left thigh. "It never healed right. That's why the bloody thing bust when I was trying to get away the day they caught me."

Was it because he'd just returned from Mass with all its talk of redemption, forgiveness of sins, that he thought the second breaking of the bone might have been God's retribution—yet his own absolution for the deaths of all the people his bombs had killed or maimed—for Ireland?

"Your own da?" Eamon put a hand on Davy's arm. "Jesus Christ, that's ferocious, so it is."

"Aye. Well." Davy moved away from Eamon, discomfited by his touch. "I miss him yet. Just before he died, he made me promise to go on fighting. And I did. For years. Because I promised Da and because I used to believe, the way you believe, but . . . Eamon, I've had enough killing. "

Eamon folded his arms across his chest. "Davy, that's quite a mouthful you've just told me, about your da and all . . . and . . . like . . . I'm sorry for your troubles. I really am." He walked away and turned under the cell's tiny window.

"It's not your problem, Eamon."

"I know that, but, Jesus, man . . . we're friends."

"Do you not think I know that?" Davy could still feel the warmth of Eamon's hand on his arm. "That's why I'm telling you not to go. Not with McGuinness."

"Brendan's not such a bad head."

Davy almost spat on the cell floor, but knew that if he had done he'd be the one who had to clean it up.

"Father Davy. I *know* you and him had your differences." Eamon let his arms fall to his sides. "And I know you think I'm daft. But neither you nor Jesus Christ Himself nor all the saints could talk me out of it."

"I tried."

"You did, but I'm going. And Davy?"

"What?"

"Do you remember that old Beatles song?"

"What the hell are you on about?"

"Come on. Let's get some lunch." As Eamon headed for the door, Davy heard his friend singing an old Beatles song. "It won't be long. It won't be looong."

CHAPTER 10

Sammy McCandless's confession and the act of contrition he'd been told to make had taken far too long. It had seemed like he'd never finish saying an Ave Maria and a Paternoster at all twenty-six Stations of the Cross. He was going to be late for his meeting.

He wheezed as he pedaled his bike up the hill to Point Alpha, a roadhouse on the outskirts of the town of Newtownstewart, smack in the middle of the area that the British Green Army, the regular, uniformed soldiers of the line regiments, called Bandit Country: territory so dominated by the Provos that troop movement was only safe by helicopter, never by road.

He'd returned the horse box to the O'Byrne's farm this morning, had a quick cup of tea with Erin and Cal and confirmed that the arms delivery had been made without any hitches. He was disappointed that no mention was made of the mysterious events that might happen at the Kesh, and Sammy had been smart enough not to ask questions. No point in arousing suspicion. He couldn't afford that. Not if he valued his life.

At that moment, as the rain sheeted almost horizontally against the raincoat that he wore back to front to keep the wind out, he didn't put too high a price on his existence. If he didn't die of fucking pneumonia out on a day like this, he'd be as good as dead if anyone saw him talking to the man he was to meet at the Royal Ulster Constabulary, E4A Special Branch (antiterrorist). Still, he tried to comfort himself, nobody in their right mind would go out today unless they had to, would they?

He crested the hill and saw the car he was expecting in the inn's car park. The battered old Lada was close to a fuchsia hedge. It was too thick for anyone to burst through on the left side of the car. Ahead, a tall brick wall blocked access to the car park where the summer's purple and scarlet fuchsia blossoms lay scattered on the tarmac like tiny, dying ballerinas. A cattle lorry hemmed in the vehicle on its right.

As Sammy propped his bike against the hedge, he could hear the lowing of the beasts in the transporter and caught a whiff of their barnyard smell. He bent and tried to look in through the car's windows, but they were obscured by condensation. His contact, code-named Spud, must have been here for a while. Sammy rapped on the window.

When the window was lowered, Sammy found himself looking into a pair of green eyes with a triangular brown segment in the iris of the left. The rest of the face was unremarkable. No moustache. His sandy hair was short, but not cropped like a soldier's. Sammy knew that a military cut stood out like a neon sign, even when the troops were off duty and wearing civvies. The Provos had a habit of killing off-duty soldiers and members of the Ulster Defence Regiment, civilians who worked as part-time soldiers and who had replaced the auxiliary police force, the B-Specials. In a small community, the UDR volunteers were well-known, easy targets, and very vulnerable to sneak attacks.

A cigarette drooped from the man's lips and jiggled when he said, "Get in." The door was pushed half-open. "You're late. You'd me worried."

Sammy climbed into the passenger seat and slammed the door. "I come as quick as I could. I fucking near didn't come at all." Sammy picked his nose.

"I was going to give you ten more minutes and then I'd've been off."

"You can fuck off anytime you like. I'd like to see the back of you for good and all. Six months you've had me at this. And haven't I given you good stuff?" Sammy wondered at his own bravado. The man in the driver's seat was built like a brick shit-house, and Sammy knew too bloody well that a word from him in the right place and he wouldn't be seeing Spud again. He'd not be seeing nobody never again. They'd find him lying in a ditch with a green bin bag over his bullet-smashed head and a twenty-pound note, his Judas money, clutched in his hand.

"Don't be like that, Sunshine. Here, have a fag." Spud pulled out a packet of Gallaher's Greens and offered one.

Sammy took it and accepted a light. He clutched the cigarette between nicotine-stained knuckles. His fingers were trembling. Maybe he shouldn't have said what he just had. Spud, not Jesus Christ, was going to be Sammy's sure road to salvation.

"Have a draw on that and take a grip on your knickers. I can wait."

"That's easy for you to say." When the Provos found out that one of their own had turned informer, they did not put much stock in a few acts of contrition by way of penance. They were more prone to blowing off an offender's kneecaps—or putting a bullet in his head after they'd wrung as much information out of him as they could.

He saw Spud glance in the rearview mirror. He was jumpy, too. Maybe all of these E4A men were trained to be careful. They'd need to be. They were the ones that worked with—Sammy hesitated over the word—informers.

"Here," he heard Spud say as he handed over an envelope. "Maybe that'll help you calm down."

Sammy took the envelope.

"You're not going to check it?"

"Nah." Sammy could feel the banknotes. "I trust you. I fucking well have to, don't I?"

"Sure, you know you can do that." Spud spoke softly, like a mother to a frightened ten-year-old. "You and me's got to be mates, haven't we?"

"Aye." It was true they had. Sammy's narrow shoulders relaxed. "I suppose so."

"Come on, Sammy. We *are* mates."

The hell they were, but who else could Sammy trust since he'd turned? Maybe this RUC man was just playacting. Sammy had heard that the E4A officers were trained to make friends with their sources—he preferred that word to "touts"—to gain their trust. Try to get into their minds. Was that all Spud's friendship was about?

"If we're such good pals, why won't you tell me your real name? You know mine." Sammy hadn't meant to sound querulous. He picked his nose. He always did that when he was nervous. And why wouldn't he be nervous? The envelope made a crackling sound in his hand. It wasn't the money he'd come for. It was the promise—

"Come on, Sammy. You know I can't do that. Still doesn't mean we're not . . ."

"Friends. Aye. I know."

"And friends tell each other things, don't they?"

"I've two things for you, but I'm not telling you unless . . ." He thrust the envelope at Spud. "I don't want your money no more. I want you to keep your promise. I want into one of them witness-protection deals in England. You promised . . ."

"And?"

"You fucking well promised," Sammy shouted.

There was a loud "Bang!"

Sammy ducked behind the dashboard. "What the hell was that?"

"There's beasts in that there lorry. One must've stamped a hoof."

Sammy straightened. "I near shit myself. I thought it was a gun."

"Come on, Sam. Don't be so jumpy. What's really bothering you?" He sounded like a mummy again.

Sammy's façade of toughness cracked. "I can't take it no more. I'm scared. I'm all on my own . . ."

"You've me. I look after you. Don't I look after you?"

Sammy nodded.

"'Course I look after you." He offered the envelope. "And the money's not bad. Twenty quid a week."

"I told you, I don't want the fucking money."

"Jesus Christ." Spud let an edge creep into his voice. "I thought you and me was friends."

Sammy's head drooped.

"Come on, Sam, are we not?"

"I'm fucking well petrified." Sammy's lower lip trembled.

Spud laid a hand on Sammy's shoulder. "I know." He forced a short laugh. "I get windy myself sometimes."

"Do you?" Sammy lifted his head. His black eyes darted from side to side like tiny trapped animals. Then he looked into Spud's. "Honest to God?"

"Your lot shoot peelers."

Sammy saw him glance in the rearview mirror. "Right enough."

"Takes guts to do what we do. I think you're a brave man, Sammy Mc-Candless."

"Honest to God?"

"Honest. Here." He reoffered the envelope. "Take it. You've earned it."

Sammy did. He fingered the envelope. "The money'll come in handy. I'm saving it up for when I get out of Ireland."

"Good idea. Mind you, the witness-protection blokes'll give you your pocket money . . . when we do get you out."

"They will, won't they?"

"You hang on to the cash. That's your regular weekly in there, and you didn't drag me out in the pissing rain just to get that. There's a bonus for good information. You said you'd two things to tell me."

"And I'll get the bonus?"

"Come on, Sam. You know the rules. You give me the information, and if it pays off, your next envelope'll be a damn site fatter than that one. Could be five hundred."

"And you will see about getting me into the witness-protection thing?"

"Tell you what, Sam. If what you're going to tell me is really good stuff, I'll try."

"Promise?"

"Cross my heart."

You're hearing what you want to hear, Sammy told himself, but where else could he turn? He tossed his cigarette butt out of the car. "Fair enough." His finger guddled in his nostril. "The first one's a sure thing. I brought in a shipment last night. Half a dozen ArmaLites and a wheen of Semtex from over the border. I stashed them in an old grave in Ballydornan churchyard." Sammy knew what the Security Forces could do once they'd got their hands on the weapons. They could fit one of the weapons with a miniature transmitter and use its signals to track the guns to their final destination. The British army called that technique jarking. Or perhaps they could nick the blokes that came to collect the cache.

"When's the pickup?"

So they did want to lift the collectors, and one of them might be Erin. Good thing Cal hadn't said when. Sammy fished in his raincoat pocket, produced a peppermint, and popped the white sweetie into his mouth. When he spoke, his words were indistinct and the inside of the car was filled with a minty smell. "I don't know. You just arrange to find them."

"Hardly worth the effort. When'll they be picked up?"

"Jesus, are you deaf? I don't fucking well know."

Spud took out his packet of smokes. He lit one for himself. He did not offer one. "And you want me to get you into a witness . . . You're doting if you think a few rifles in Ballydornan churchyard is worth that."

"Look . . . I'll phone you if I find out." And I'll make sure that Erin doesn't go, he thought.

"That's better." Spud drew on his cigarette. "Sorry. Want another one?"

Sammy grabbed the packet and helped himself. "What are you going to do?"

"Leave it to me, and don't you worry, Sam. If me and my lot think going after them and the blokes that come to get them would blow your cover, we'll just let the hare sit. You're far too good a man to risk."

"I am, amn't I?"

"You're bloody right. One of the best."

"Right enough. And you *will* ask about the other?"

"I might, but you said you'd two things for me."

"Aye." Sammy tripped over his words in his hurry to satisfy. "There's something big on. Really big. Don't know what it is. At the Kesh. Soon. I overheard things . . ."

"Like what?"

A shadow fell over the car. Sammy looked up. A man had moved between the Lada and the cattle truck. Spud's hand went to the glove compartment. Does he have a gun in there? Sammy wondered. He wasn't going to wait to find out. He whispered, "I'm off," and bolted.

As soon as he'd wheeled his bike to the exit from the car park, he looked back. The stranger was hauling himself into the cab of the cattle lorry, and the Lada was reversing. Sammy guessed the stranger had asked to be given room to get his big vehicle out.

The lorry driver finished reversing and ground the gears as he moved into first. He passed Sammy on his way out and took the road toward Strabane. Sammy remembered the abattoir where the occupants of the cattle lorry were going. He gave a little shudder and then cycled out of the parking lot, following in the muddy backwash of the lorry's rear wheels in the downpour of a Tyrone Sunday morning.

CHAPTER 11

There was hardly a cloud over English Bay, a mere ruffle of white on the water. The wind would be coming from the west at about ten knots. That should send *Windshadow* scudding through the water without heeling too much. In stronger blows, Tim reveled in storming along, but Fiona had to work to convince herself that the boat wasn't going to capsize.

Fiona strode toward Burrard Civic Marina, where Tim kept *Windshadow*, now known affectionately to both of them as plain *Windy*. She shifted her sports bag to her other hand. The bottle of Chardonnay, wrapped in a heavy sweater, should be safe enough. The wine was a peace offering for the way she'd behaved last night. An evening that had started so well had fallen apart when Jimmy Ferguson had appeared out of nowhere like a panto-mime demon. Dammit, she'd tried to persuade Tim not to join the Fergu-sons for that after-dinner drink, but Tim, typical of the man, hadn't wanted to hurt anybody's feelings.

As she crested the hill in Vanier Park, kites still flew, the smaller domi-nated by a massive contraption with a large, round head and great, long, skinny tail. It was often here. Tim said he thought it looked like a giant sperm. That was part of what she liked about the man. He had a delightful way of putting an eccentric spin on ordinary things.

She looked across False Creek to the city centre. Harsh, angular towers stood against the soft sky. She could make out the red bricks of Saint Paul's Hospital hiding behind the tall condominium blocks on Beach Avenue. Jimmy and his wife lived in one.

Last night, Fiona had tried to sound interested when, after insisting on buying everyone a drink, Jimmy had chuntered on about how smashing his apartment was—great views, lots of space, clean as a whistle. He said it was a hell of a sight different from the cramped terraces of the Falls Road. Mind you, he missed the *craic*, the cheerful banter so beloved by the Irish. His neighbours in the multistorey building weren't ones to stand and blether in the hallways. Still, there were no house-to-house searches by the Brits. She'd flinched when he'd said that.

He'd insisted that she make a visit, if possible before Siobhan went back to Montreal in another two weeks. "You two'll have a lot to talk about, so you will."

Fiona shuddered at the very thought of rehashing the past with Siobhan, particularly that part that still gave her nightmares, like the one on Thursday night.

Jimmy had given her his business card with his phone numbers and had taken Fiona's number in return. The last thing Jimmy'd said when Tim finally made their excuses was, "Give us a ring and we'll have the pair of you over for a wee bite to eat."

Jimmy was going to be disappointed. Fiona had no interest in maintaining that acquaintance—she had barely known the man in Belfast—their only connection was Davy.

And Davy *wasn't* in Vancouver. Tim was.

As she turned into the marina, she saw him taking off *Windy*'s navy-blue sail cover. She would make it up to him today. It had been cruel of her last night to brush him off with a perfunctory kiss and the excuse that she was really tired. But she'd needed to be on her own. She hoped he'd not bring up the subject today.

"G'dye." Tim stepped into the cockpit with the sail cover under his arm. "All set?"

"Just need to stow my bag. I've brought a bottle."

"There's ice in the cooler. Nip below, shove the grog in, and by the time you're back on deck, I'll have the engine running and the lines ready to cast off. Here," he handed her the sail cover, "stow that while you're below."

The clattering of the diesel engine was much louder in the boat's saloon. She felt the boat rock as Tim stepped onto the dock. He called, "I'm casting off."

She climbed back on deck and sat as Tim steered the boat out of False Creek.

Windy bounced to the waves of English Bay. Fiona felt her hair being tossed by the wind that blew away the diesel smell of the fuel barge moored beside Burrard Bridge and the never-quiet muttering of the city. To port the Vanier kites—all but Tim's giant sperm—swooped, soared, and rushed toward the ground only to race again to the heavens, their frantic movements in contrast with the granite immobility of the dark North Shore Mountains away to starboard.

Once the sails were hoisted, Tim stopped the engine. Without its clattering, her world became silent with only the gentle sound of water sluicing past the hull to intrude. She promised herself that the day would be perfect.

"A thing of beauty," Tim said. He sat ahead of her but close enough that she could feel the pressure of his body. Fiona held the tiller, feeling it tug in answer to the force of the wind on the sails.

Tim ducked to look under the boom. "We'll make Point Atkinson if you can hold this course."

"Right." She listened to *Windy*'s sharp bow cutting through the short chop, the occasional splat of a wave breaking over the foredeck, the singing of the wind in the rigging. The sun was warm on the back of her neck and her lips were salty.

She'd taken the helm the whole way across Burrard Inlet, tacking on Tim's command, back and forth across the sparkling water, slipping behind anchored freighters, sometimes changing course when an approaching boat had the right of way and a collision might be possible if *Windy* didn't yield.

Few words other than helm orders and acknowledgments had been exchanged. There had been no need. To Fiona, God was in his heaven and all was right with the world. No wonder Tim loved his sailing.

"You're getting the feel of her," Tim said. "I think I'll promote you from cabin boy to first mate." He leaned back and kissed her.

"Aye, aye, skipper."

He hunched one shoulder, rolled his eyes, and in a harsh voice said, "Aaar, Jim lad. Was you ever at sea?"

"You don't look enough like Long John Silver." She couldn't help laughing at him. "Anyway you don't have a parrot."

"But I have you, don't I?" She heard just the tiniest edge in his question.

"Of course, silly."

The sails started to flap. She looked up, grateful for the distraction. "Looks like we've run out of wind." She saw him stoop and start the engine. "We're in Howe Sound. The wind often dies here. Right. Hold her on that. I'll get the sails down and we'll motor up to Mannion Bay on Bowen Island."

She watched him, businesslike, competent, furl the jib and then lower the mainsail and fold it neatly on the boom. When the sails were down, she had an unobstructed view.

Tim came back into the cockpit and pointed at an island dead ahead. It had a high, rounded summit and a low, narrow peninsula that rose at its far end to a smaller hill. "That's Anvil Island. It always makes me think of a submerging dinosaur."

The island did look like a brontosaurus preparing to dive below the still, blue waters of Howe Sound.

"I'd never've thought of that, but you're right." He really did have a knack for seeing things differently from other people. "Let's call it Tim Island."

"Why?"

"Because you *can* be a bit of an old dinosaur sometimes."

"Shame about that," he said, pretending to scowl.

"What? That you can be a bit old-fashioned? I like it when you hold a lady's chair . . . like you did in Bridges last night." Why in hell had she brought up the very subject she was hoping to avoid?

"Oh, that sort of thing? Manners, they say, maketh the man . . ."

And he was a mannerly man. He must be good with his patients.

"Because if you'd meant it some other way"—Tim drew one finger across his throat—"I'd have made you walk the plank." He was grinning from ear to ear. He came toward her and hugged her. "I do love you," he said.

Windy swung to her anchor in Mannion Bay. Fiona lay back against the stern rail, arms spread to either side. Tim was below, refilling their wineglasses. She brushed the crumbs of her just-eaten ham sandwich from her T-shirt and watched the horizon swing past.

The green light marking the channel for the ferries that plied from Horseshoe Bay on the mainland to Snug Cove on Bowen Island slid aft. Houses dotted the shoreline of the bay, protected behind evergreen palisades. Inland, Mount Gardiner stood sentinel over the village. A family of Canada geese, mum, dad, and the kids, paddled past, gronking hopefully. Panhandlers.

She watched as a bald eagle soared on thermals, higher and higher until all she could see was a speck. No kite strings for him. Perhaps eagles didn't remember their pasts.

And it seemed that Tim hadn't been too interested in her past either. He'd not even batted an eyelid when she'd mentioned Bridges. His remark that he'd "wanted to ask her about this Davy fellow" seemed to have been forgotten.

Tim reappeared, plastic wineglasses in his hands. "Here you go." He gave her one and sat beside her. "Nice bit of grog, that. Reminds me of one from the Barossa Valley, back in Oz."

"Glad you like it." She snuggled against him, confident now that he hadn't been unduly upset last night. And anyway, what should it matter to Tim if she'd had other men before? There'd be something a bit odd about a forty-three-year-old woman who hadn't. Just to be certain that there would be no lingering rancour, she said, "I brought the bottle to say sorry about last night."

He didn't say, "No worries," which was Tim's usual way of accepting an apology.

"I didn't mean to get so bitchy."

She offered him a kiss, but Tim leaned back, looked into her eyes, and said quietly, "You weren't very polite to that friend of yours."

"He's not really a friend."

"But he's one of your mob. Irish."

"That's why I didn't want to go for a drink. There are some things about Belfast I don't like to have to remember. I've told you that." A gust made the rigging rattle. She shivered.

"It was more than that. Every time that bloke's name came up, you . . ."

"What bloke?" She'd been wrong. Tim hadn't forgotten.

"Who's Davy?" His voice was quietly serious. "Every time you heard his name, you shivered."

Typical doctor. They were trained to be sensitive to body language, and the signals she'd been sending must have been overpowering.

The wind was definitely freshening. "You really want to know, don't you?"

Tim nodded slowly, his gaze never leaving her eyes.

"I'm going below," she said. "I'm getting cold. I want to get a sweater." She rose. "Here. Hold this." She handed him her wineglass.

Her pullover lay on the bench. She hadn't bothered to repack it when she'd taken out the bottle of wine. Fiona hauled the heavy woolen pullover on, struggling to force her arms through the sleeves. What should she tell Tim about Davy? Nothing? A watered-down version of what had been between them? The truth? She clambered back on deck.

The wind was really blowing. Even in the sheltered anchorage, waves made *Windy* pitch. Tim was up on deck, bending over, doing something. Perhaps the freshening wind would distract him, give them both an excuse to drop the subject.

He came back to the cockpit. "Just fixing the anchor. *Windy* could drag if there's not enough rope between her bows and the sea floor." He pointed to waves breaking over a reef. "I'd not want us to go up on the rocks." He busied himself with some other ropes.

Nor would I, she thought, and I mean you and me, Tim, not the boat. Eight months they'd been seeing each other, and eight months had been time enough to get over the first purely sexual attraction, the tingling of knowing that she would see him and what they would do. The leaving of a restaurant early, the fumbling in the hall. Bed. And Tim was good in bed. Very good. They were practically on—and in spite of herself she smiled at the thought—"farting terms."

So, if they were going to go on seeing each other, he deserved the truth. If it was too much for him to handle, it would be very sad. She'd do anything to avoid hurting him, but better to get everything out in the open now. She knew that Davy McCutcheon was to her more than an old romance. More than a pleasant, fading memory. If Tim asked again—

"Let's get below," he said, picking up the two glasses and handing one to her. "Don't forget your wine."

She sat facing Tim, the table between. Through the port light she could see the shoreline speed by as *Windy* swung in an arc before jerking to a halt and swinging back the other way. The pitching increased.

"Are you sure we'll be all right?"

"As rain. That anchor would hold the *Titanic*."

"The *Titanic* was built in Belfast, and you know what happened to her. She sank."

"There're no icebergs here. We'll be fine." He sounded confident. He wasn't just saying that to reassure her. "These summer squalls blow over quickly, but we'll have to sit it out for a while." He leaned forward across the table. "Lots of time for you to tell me about . . ."

"Davy?" She felt her shoulders sag. She put her hands on the tabletop, stared at them, then looked him in the eye and said, "It's a long story."

"We aren't going anywhere." Tim settled back against the bulkhead. He looked as he must look when a patient launched into a convoluted history.

"You need to know more about me than I've ever told you."

Tim leaned forward and put his hands over hers. The warmth was comforting. He said nothing.

Fiona glanced down at her hands, covered by Tim's, and back to his face. She bit her lip. "All right. Davy McCutcheon was a man I was in love with. In Belfast. During the Troubles. Before I emigrated. We were meant to come to Canada together."

"Why didn't you?"

"He got caught. Put in jail." She saw one of Tim's shaggy eyebrows go up.

"No, he wasn't a criminal, at least not by his lights. He was in the Provisional IRA, the Provos."

"I thought they *were* criminals, murderers."

Fiona nodded. "So do most people, but *they* really do believe that they are freedom fighters at war with the English for Ireland's freedom. No more criminals than"—she searched for an analogy—"than the Allies in the Second World War."

Tim frowned.

"Tim, don't ask me to try to explain Irish history to you. We'd be here for weeks. Just take my word for it. Davy McCutcheon could no more be a thief than fly to the moon. He was a soldier, a volunteer."

"All right. I'll accept that . . . for the moment."

"So was Jimmy."

"The man at Bridges?" Tim whistled. "Good God."

"He was Davy's best friend. They made explosives for the Provos. Davy believed that he was working for a better Ireland. He was able to ignore what his bombs did . . . at least for a while."

"Did you live with him?"

"Yes."

"Fiona, I don't understand. You told me you were a civil rights worker. That you hated violence."

"I still do, but I loved Davy in spite of what he did. You can't analyze love, pull it apart, see how it ticks, and understand it. Once you start doing that, it would be like"—she thought about her biology class at school—"like cutting up a live frog. You'd understand its anatomy better, but the frog would be dead."

"I know." There was a hint of a smile.

Windy lurched, and Fiona had to steady herself with her hands on the seat. She looked questioningly at Tim.

"It's all right. Go on."

"I tried to leave him once." The smell of diesel fuel stung her eyes. "Everything sensible said I should, but I couldn't, until one day." Her eyes were filling. "One day one of his bombs killed a railway ticket collector. The man's daughters were in my class. I had to try to comfort them. What could I say to them?"

"It's never easy. I know. It goes with the territory in my job, and I hate it."

"That finished it for me. I told him if he didn't leave the Provos, I'd leave him. He wouldn't, couldn't, and so . . . I moved out. It's funny how you remember little things, but I left him my cat called McCusker."

"Is that why you called . . . ?"

"Probably." She shook her head. "It doesn't matter, but Davy doted on that stupid creature. He was a gentle man. Some people thought he was too fussy, a bit of an old woman for a man of thirty-eight. There were a hell of a lot of old, young men in Belfast in the Troubles. There were a whole lot of old, young men after Korea just like the ones in the trenches after the Somme and Vimy Ridge. War does that to you." She stared at Tim, and her voice cracked. "Davy didn't have many friends, maybe that was why he kept the cat, but he was close to Jimmy Ferguson.

"Belfast's a small place. A while after I'd moved out of Davy's house, I ran into Jimmy. He told me that Davy wanted to talk to me. That he'd made up his mind to go to Canada . . . Jimmy was all set to emigrate . . . and Davy had had enough, too.

"I didn't want to see Davy, but he phoned, and when I heard his voice . . ."

Windy lurched. Fiona's wineglass fell, and as she bent to pick it up, she saw the spilt wine flowing across the walnut and rosewood decking. "Give me a cloth," she said, straightening. At least she'd stopped crying.

"Leave it. I want you to finish."

"Finish? All right. There's not much more. We had tea together in the tea shop where we'd first met. He told me he wanted me back . . . and if you could have seen that man's face, crumpled, exhausted, your heart would have bled for him. He kept rubbing one fist in the palm of his other hand. He didn't plead, just came right to the point. He loved me. He would leave the Provos.

"I thought that it was Christmas and all my birthdays come at once . . . and I knew just how much I loved him. Then he told me there was a condition. He'd given his word to go on one more mission for the Provos. Davy was a terrible man for keeping his word. If I'd wait for him until the job was done, he'd come to Canada with me. That was in 1974."

"And after the mission he had a change of heart?"

Fiona thought that she could detect a hopeful note in Tim's voice.

"The mission was a failure. He was captured. Put in the Long Kesh Prison . . ." Tears welled and hung from her eyelashes. "That was when Jimmy's daughter lost her love . . ."

"Siobhan?" Tim stumbled over the pronunciation. "The blonde woman?"

"Siobhan. She'd fallen for a young man who called himself Mike Roberts."

"Jimmy talked about him last night."

"His real name was Richardson. Lieutenant Marcus Richardson. He was a British undercover agent. He was with Davy in a farmhouse on the last attack. The Security Forces knew about it. Richardson had told them. They set an ambush. Davy was in an upstairs room. There was a lot of shooting. Richardson was killed, but not by Davy, more probably by a random shot. Davy *had* killed a soldier, no question of that, but the British forensic people said that the bullet that finished Richardson couldn't have come from Davy's weapon. Losing the boy was very hard on Siobhan. She loved him very much."

She brushed away a tear. "Sometimes I think it would have been easier for me if Davy had been killed, too."

Tim drew the web of his hand from under his nose down below his mouth and chin and said, almost to himself, "Perhaps it would."

"Not Davy," she said softly. "I didn't really mean it like that."

"Look." He stared into her eyes. "Losing someone you love is like a death." He lowered his gaze. "When Carol and I were divorced, that's what it felt like."

Tim hardly ever mentioned his ex-wife.

"And what do people do when someone dies?" said Tim.

"Have a funeral? Bury them?" Where was this going?

"That's not all."

"I don't understand."

He reached out and took her hand again. "They mourn. They grieve . . . and in time they get over it."

It all sounded very logical. Very matter-of-fact.

"After my divorce, I used to find myself picking up things, like a drinking glass, and thinking, Carol used to leave lipstick on the rim, or looking in a mirror and remembering how she'd sit at it and brush her hair . . . and leave loose hairs all over the dresser. But after a while, the glass was just a glass with a clean rim. There were no loose strands on the dresser. It was like . . . like pulling apart a kid's LEGO construction, piece by piece, until they were all gone and back in their box . . . as if the construction had never existed except in a faint memory."

Fiona felt herself being jerked backward. *Windy* must have ridden up to her anchor and then fallen back to the extent of the anchor rope and been suddenly and forcibly pulled up short. The boat rocked as Fiona recognized Tim had rocked her.

"I don't think you've done that . . . and when you saw Jimmy at Bridges . . ."

The old wounds had opened. Wide. Tim was right.

"It's not just Davy. It's Belfast. You're right. I haven't—what did you call it?—grieved for him . . . or for Ireland. And they both come back to haunt me." She hesitated. "I had the dream on Thursday night."

"Dream?" Tim put his head to one side like a robin looking for a worm.

"It keeps coming back. I was nearly blown up by a bomb, and I see the blast and the hurt and dead people. I smell the explosives. Taste them. And I go home to Davy and . . ." She felt a tear slip down her cheek and moisten her lip. "I've never told anybody about it."

Tim stood.

She noticed that *Windy* seemed to be riding much more comfortably. The shrieking of the wind in the rigging had fallen to a muted piping.

He moved around the table and stood over her. Put an arm under her shoulder and lifted her to her feet. He held her, made no attempt to kiss her but stroked her hair and, with a finger, pulled the tears from under her eyes. He made soft noises in his throat.

Fiona held on to Tim. What had he said? "That anchor would hold the *Titanic*." Tim was like an anchor.

"The dream's awful when it comes," she said. "It leaves me shaking."

"I'm glad you told me," he said.

And she looked up at him and saw the truth of it in his grey eyes. "Kiss me, Tim."

He did, without heat, without passion, but with softness and comfort. She pulled away but remained in his arms.

He was smiling. It was a small smile.

She tried to smile back. "I've said a mouthful. You've given me an awful lot to think about . . . and . . . and you don't mind? About Davy?"

His eyes became very serious. He lowered his voice. "I love you, Fiona. As I see it, your Davy is hanging between the pair of us like a bead curtain between two rooms. Not blocking the way, but there. He . . . and Belfast . . . are ghosts we'll have to lay, but"—and his smile returned, broader than before—"between us I think we can manage."

"I'll try," she said. "I promise . . . but I'm going to need a bit of time."

His smile faded. "I'm afraid I'm going to have to give you at least a week. I have to leave tomorrow for a medical convention in San Francisco. But I'll phone you. And we'll talk about this when I get back."

"I'd like that."

Overhead, the rigging was silent. Sunlight coming through the port light made her screw up her eyes. The last tear fell.

Tim turned and said over his shoulder, "Feels like the squall has passed. I'll go and start weighing the anchor. You fire up the engine."

"Aye, aye, skipper." She managed to force a smile.

"It's two o'clock," Tim said as he climbed up the companionway. "Time we were moving along." The steps creaked under his feet.

CHAPTER 12

The broken springs of the sofa creaked when Sammy McCandless moved. He balanced a half-eaten plate of fried bacon, eggs, and soda farl, a late supper, on his lap. The eggs tasted like rubber and the bacon grease had congealed. No bloody wonder. His three-roomed labourer's cottage was always damp. The turf fire in the grate in the corner looked cheery but was bugger all use for heating the place. Sammy shivered.

He'd not be sorry to see the back of this place when Spud came through with that witness-protection business. Not if, but *when* he came through. He'd better get a move on.

From overhead came the sound of helicopter rotors. Bloody Brits. These days there were as many choppers roaring about over Tyrone as flies on a heifer's arse.

The nine o'clock news ran on an old black-and-white television, the newsreader's face blurred by horizontal lines that straggled in never-ending sequence from the bottom to the top of the screen. Reception was bloody awful tonight.

". . . The body of a man was found in a construction skip on Cupar Street in Belfast. He had been shot in the head. The police suspect foul play . . ."

Bunch of fucking Sherlock Holmeses. Did they think the poor bugger had crawled in there and done it to himself?

". . . A woman was admitted to the Belfast City Hospital with gunshot wounds to both knees . . ."

Sammy rose, shoved his plate into the sink, and switched off the television. He had to live with this shite every day, and the last thing he needed to be reminded of was the punishments handed out by the Provos to people they decided had committed a crime against the organization. That woman might have done nothing worse than have a bit of slap and tickle with a British soldier. The bugger in the bin? Had he been a "source"—like Sammy?

The folks round here said, "You can rape your best friend's wife and be forgiven, but if your grandfather informed to the British it would *never* be forgotten."

Sammy turned on the tap over the sink and waited for the warm water to make its way through the rusty pipes.

Memories were long in Tyrone. He'd been taught as a child about the history of insurrection against the British that went back centuries, to the times of the great Irish patriots, the O'Neills of Tyrone—*Tir Owàin*—the land of Owen.

And he'd learned the history of treason.

In 1681, Redmond O'Hanlon was betrayed to the British for one hundred pounds by his foster brother, Art O'Hanlon, who shot Redmond as he lay in bed; in 1744, Mollie MacDacker, for fifty pounds, sold Seamus McMurphy to the English constable John Johnston.

Mollie MacDacker had drowned herself because she could not live with the shame. He could understand how the woman must have felt, and he knew, too well, that today the Provos didn't rely on remorse to put paid to touts. The Provos took care of informers—permanently.

Maurice Gilvarry, Belfast Brigade, January 19, 1981, shot dead at Jonesborough—informer. Seamus Morgan, East Tyrone Brigade, March 5, 1982, found shot dead on the Carrickasticken Road—informer. Eric Dale, May 7, 1983. Sammy could recite the list of names—a list he did not wish to join—as well as he could say his Hail Marys. If he was found out, "Holy Mary, Mother of God, pray for us sinners, now and in the hour of our death" would be his last words—the Provos were very decent about letting a man make his peace with God—just before they "nutted" him.

Sammy *had* to get out of Ireland, and he wasn't going to do that on his fucking Raleigh bicycle. Spud had to deliver—and soon.

The water from the tap was, as usual, lukewarm. Sammy put the plug in the sink, squeezed in a few drops of detergent, and waited for the sink to fill before turning off the tap. The dishes could soak for a while. He needed a drink. Badly.

There was a nearly finished bottle of John Powers whiskey in the cupboard. He took it out along with a chipped glass and poured until the bottle was empty. The spirits were sharp on his tongue. Bloody drink. That's what had got him into this mess in the first place. Ever since the night he'd got into that stupid fight in a pub.

Sammy remembered how the peelers had lifted him and taken him to the Strabane police station. There wasn't a day that he didn't remember.

He fished a Park Drive out of a packet on the counter and lit up, returned to the couch, and sat.

The peelers had charged him with grievous bodily harm. They'd left him alone in a cell for hours, and then a man in plain clothes had come in. A big man. All smiles. Open packet of Silk Cut in one hand. He'd sat opposite Sammy. The plainclothes man had CID written all over him.

"Have a fag, Sammy."

Sammy had been well indoctrinated by Cal about what to do if he found himself being interrogated. You never said *nothing* to one of those bastards.

He refused to meet the man's gaze, and turned away.

"I'm having one." The man lit up, smoked the cigarette until it was finished, then crushed it out.

It seemed as if a lifetime passed before the stranger said, "You've six months coming."

Sammy stared at the ceiling. He stared at the floor, the drab green walls.

"I could get you off."

Sammy couldn't help himself. He didn't want to go to jail. He let himself look at the big man's eyes.

"Easy as pie. You'd be out of here in no time."

Sammy bit his lower lip. Say *nothing*.

The man offered the packet of smokes. "Go on, man. They won't bite."

Sammy knew he shouldn't, but he took a cigarette, accepted a light, and fixed his gaze on the acoustic tiles of the ceiling. He counted the holes. One hundred and ten. One hundred and eleven . . .

It was awkward trying to smoke with his hands cuffed. They'd handcuffed him after they'd taken away his jacket and shoes, and the belt that held up his trousers. The cell was cold and damp. The only warmth there'd been in that cell was in the big man's voice—at first.

"You don't have to go down, you know."

What was the bugger after? One hundred and thirty-one . . .

"Not if you'd do a wee job for me."

For a peeler? No fucking way. One hundred and fifty-six . . .

"Of course, if you don't want to . . ."

Sammy didn't. Six months with time off for good behaviour would soon be over. Once he got involved with the coppers . . . one hundred and . . . shit. He'd lost count. One, two . . .

"I could make things a lot worse for you than doing a bit of porridge."

What the hell was he talking about? Sammy glanced at his tormentor.

"Got your attention?"

"Fuck off. What could you do?" The words slipped out. Say *nothing*.

"You don't think it was just bad luck that you got picked up tonight."

Sammy did think that.

The big man laughed. "It wasn't bad luck, Sammy. I know you're a Provvie, so I wanted to have a wee word with you. I arranged to have you lifted."

Balls. If this fucker had any proof, Sammy knew he would have been nicked and charged. The big man was bluffing. Sammy folded his arms across his chest and smiled. Bluff away, you big cunt, you're getting nothing from me.

"You think it's funny?"

Sammy inclined his head as if to say, "What do you think, you Prod git?" but he reminded himself, *Nothing*, Sam. Say *nothing*. He stared up. One, two, three . . .

The man's words were slow. Measured. "Sammy, you've been in here for six hours. Your mates know you've been in here. We'd a young lad like you in here about a year ago. We knew he was a Provo . . . just like you. Kept his mouth shut. Just like you. It's a dead giveaway. Man up on a GBH charge? Offered an out and he says nothing? They teach you to keep your traps shut, don't they?"

This shite was on a fishing expedition. He didn't know that Sammy was a Provo, but the thick peeler thought he could trick him into confessing. Twenty, twenty-one . . .

"Pity about the young fellow. Nothing I could do would persuade him to work with us."

Good for him, Sammy thought, and you'll not turn me neither. He took comfort from the thought. Counting the holes had helped, but he didn't need to do it anymore. He *knew* this shite couldn't get to him, no matter what he said.

"Didn't matter. We used him anyway." The man lit another smoke. "Just put the word out that he'd turned."

You bastard. Sammy didn't need to be told what would have happened after that. "His friends interrogated him for seven weeks."

Sammy shuddered. The handcuffs bit into his wrists. He glanced back to the ceiling, but there was no solace to be had in telling his rosary of tile holes.

"He signed a confession . . . and the poor bugger was innocent." The big man inspected the lit end of his cigarette. "I suppose when they keep on hurting a man, he'll do anything to make them stop."

Sammy knew.

The man's voice turned cold. "Now you think about it, Sam. You can work for me, or we'll keep you here for another forty-eight hours, then let you go. That'd be long enough to persuade your mates that we might have got to you. They'll debrief you, Sam."

Of course they fucking well would. The Security Forces weren't the only ones with effective interrogation units. He'd be taken to a safe house, questioned, maybe for days, but, he reassured himself, his mates would soon see that he'd been loyal—wouldn't they?

"One of our blokes is round at your house now. He's leaving you a wee present."

The cell grew suddenly colder.

"Then a little birdie'll put out the word. Your mates pay a lot of heed to evidence that a man's working for us."

Despite the cold Sammy felt, his palms were sweating. Could the bugger do that?

"If they think that, Sam . . . and it won't be a kneecapping."

Sammy shuddered. In a barn, last year, he'd had to hold a young lout down. The youth had been convicted by the Provos of selling drugs. His howling as a Black & Decker drill had torn into his kneecaps had been masked by the screams of pigs being butchered in the barn.

"I'd not be in your shoes, Sam."

Sammy looked into the big man's eyes. They were cold. Unrelenting.

He lit another cigarette. "It'll be like the other fellow I was telling you about. It wasn't pretty what they did to him."

Sammy wanted to run, to get out of the fucking cell, to get away from the big, relentless man who sat back in his chair, smoking. But Sammy couldn't run, not from the cell, not from the trap the big man had set. He didn't want to listen. Tried to shut out the man's voice, but he couldn't put his hands over his ears. Not while he was wearing handcuffs. The man's words drove into Sammy's soul as viciously as the electric drill had ripped into the knees of the screaming youth in the barn. But the big shite was bluffing. He'd never set anyone up. Wouldn't be able to set Sammy up either. All that talk about planting evidence. Bullshite. It had to be.

The man let smoke trickle from his lips. Sammy would have killed for another cigarette. "You remember Finn McArdle?"

Christ Jesus. Finn. That fucking turncoat had got his last Easter. He'd been lifted for a petty crime—just like Sammy had. Been in the pokey for three days, then let go—like this bastard was saying he'd keep Sammy and then let him go. A few weeks after Finn got out, rumours started. Sammy had heard that the Provos' intelligence men had found money in Finn's mattress . . . telephone numbers . . . no one saw Finn for a couple of months.

"Friend of yours, was he?"

Sammy shook his head. He wasn't going to admit to having known anyone in the Provos.

"He's . . . no, he *was* the young lad I was telling you about. The one who refused to help me. I hear your lot found a stack of money in his mattress."

Sammy jerked back in his chair. How in the hell could the big peeler know that . . . unless . . . ? Holy Mother of God. Sammy knew how a fox must feel when the jaws of the leghold slammed shut.

The man stood, then walked round and stood behind Sammy's chair. He bent and whispered in Sammy's ear. "I told you, Sam, one of my lads is at your house now."

Sammy felt his tears start.

"If you don't help me out, Sam, your lot'll do to you what they did to Finn McArdle. I've a strong stomach, but I had to go out to the road where they'd dumped him. A .357 Magnum makes a hell of a mess of a man's head. I bloody nearly threw up."

Sammy did. The puke burned his throat. The stench filled his nostrils, stifling the stink of his fear. He heard the man's footsteps, felt a hand on his forehead, forcing his head back, forcing him to look into eyes that smouldered.

"You're stuck, Sammy, but if you work with us, there's a way out."

Sammy still said nothing. His eyes held pleading enough.

"Bit of information here and there. I'll look after you. If things get a bit dicey for you, I'll get you over to England into the Witness Protection Programme. They'd hide you. Give you a new identity. Money."

Sammy wiped his lips with the back of one shackled hand. No. He'd not turn. He'd not. He sat up straight, jerked forward, and spat at his tormentor.

The big man pulled out a hanky and wiped the spittle from his shirt front. "Maybe you need time to think it over." He tossed the handkerchief to Sammy. "Here, clean yourself up." He turned, left, and slammed the door behind him.

The crash sounded to Sammy like the closing of the gates of purgatory. The lights in the cell went out. He'd been left alone in the dark with only the stink of his own puke and his thoughts.

If he didn't go along with the CID man—Sammy's stomach heaved at the thought of what would happen to him if his friends thought he was grassing. He knew he couldn't face that. Couldn't. He was deathly afraid of physical pain. And he had no doubt that his police tormentor would carry through with his threats. He'd been the one who'd fucked Finn. He'd not hesitate to fuck Sammy.

But if he did grass, how would he be able to live with himself? It wasn't called turning for nothing. You had to leave everything behind. Friends of a lifetime. Erin. He'd have nothing—except the fear of discovery. He picked his nose, and his captive hand dragged over his chin.

Maybe—maybe he could pretend to cooperate with the peeler, get out of this hellhole, and go straight back home and make a clean breast to Cal. It would be like being an altar boy after confession. Sins absolved, ready for a fresh start.

But Cal O'Byrne wasn't a priest. Cal would report to Provo command, and Sammy knew that, even if he did tell everything, he'd never allay the suspicions of the senior men. They couldn't afford to take risks that anyone on the inside might be working for the British. The greatest threat to Irish revolutionaries had always come from within their own ranks. Once he'd opened the door to their thinking that they couldn't trust him, they'd want him out of the Provos—and there was only one way out. Sammy rocked in his chair. A keening sound slipped past his lips.

Could he run from the peelers *and* the Provos? Not a fucking chance. Where'd he go? He'd no money, didn't even have a passport. That only left England, and England . . .

He remembered something the big man had said, something about the Witness Protection Programme. Maybe there was a way, but if he took it he'd be no better than Art O'Hanlon or Mollie MacDacker. And he'd have to live with that—forever. It wouldn't matter to his friends whether or not he'd believed in the Cause, had taken risks for Ireland. All that would count would be that he'd been the lowest slimy shite in the world as far as they were concerned. A man had to have a crumb of pride.

Sammy started to pace, but in the dark, he blundered into the wall. His nose bled, and the blood and his tears made runnels down his lips on their way to join the vomit on his shirt front.

He groped back to the chair and sat, elbows on the table, head propped in manacled hands that spread like the supplicant hands of a pietà.

He was hardly aware that the lights had gone on and the door had opened and closed. He looked up and saw, blurred through his tears, a man standing across the table. Sammy sniffed, wiped each eye. It was not his previous tormentor. The newcomer had an open face and green eyes. There was something wrong with his left eye, a brown triangle in the green of the iris.

"Jesus, Sammy," he said softly, "you look a right mess. Did my mate belt you one?"

Sammy shook his head.

"You'd better clean yourself up. Gimme your hands."

Sammy obeyed and felt the handcuffs loosen and slip away. He chafed his wrists.

"There's a basin in the corner."

Sammy went to the basin, splashed cold water on his face. He hoped to God the cold would bring down the swelling under his eyes.

"Use the towel."

Sammy dried his face. The towel was blood-streaked when he hung it on a rail under the sink.

"Come and sit down."

Sammy sat. He felt like a spaniel obeying its master's every command.

"Let's have a look at you."

Sammy felt a hand under his chin, stared into the green eyes with the brown triangle.

"You'll live." The new man sat. "Fancy a smoke?"

Sammy nodded.

"Here." He gave Sammy a Gallaher's Green.

The smoke burned Sammy's throat, which had been rasped raw when he threw up. He coughed harsh, tearing hacks.

"Take it easy," the man said. "You'll strangle yourself." He sounded concerned.

Sammy looked up and saw a broad smile and, despite himself, responded.

"That's better, Sunshine."

"The name's Samuel."

The man laughed. "I know that. My mate . . . the one who was in here before . . . told me."

Sammy's smile fled.

"Bit rough on you, was he?"

Sam nodded.

"He can be like that. Pay no heed. He'll not be back."

"Thank fuck for that."

"So"—the man lay back in his chair—"did you get a chance to think over what he talked to you about?"

"About grassing?"

"About helping us."

"Aye?"

"And?"

"I dunno." Sammy picked his nose, clasped his hands, and stared at the wall, the floor, then the policeman. "Look. Tell me about that witness-protection thing."

"Sure. We've been running it for a while. When you get into it, we take you to England, give you a new identity, a whole new life . . . after you've done a few wee jobs for us."

Sammy hesitated.

"We'd look after you. We'd not throw you to the dogs, Sammy."

"Your mate said he would."

"Yes"—the word was drawn out—"but only if you don't cooperate. If you *do,* I'll look after you. Be your friend."

Sammy closed his eyes. God, he needed a friend, but not like the lads he went smuggling with or the Donegal men who helped them. They were all right to sit down with, have a pint, a cigarette, a few laughs, but they weren't real friends. Not like Cal or Erin O'Byrne—he *would* have to abandon her. He'd miss them both. A man couldn't live without other people he could trust and who could trust him in return. Friends. The kind who would leap into a swollen river if he was in it drowning. The kind who would jump over the fence of a bull pen and distract the animal when he'd fallen in the mud and the beast was set to gore him. The kind of friend a man only made in childhood—but kept all his life. He'd miss—but then, if the peelers carried out their threat, he'd miss them all anyway. Forever.

And he *had* to choose. One or the other.

He took a very deep breath, opened his eyes, and whispered, "All right."

"Great." The man put one hand on Sammy's shoulder and offered the other. Sammy accepted the handshake and was warmed by the contact.

"Now," the man said, "I'll tell you how it's going to work."

Sammy listened.

It took an hour to explain about dead-letter drops, safe meeting places, cover stories, the use of public telephones, how to spot a tail, how to listen for a bug on home telephones—all the hole-in-the corner details of informing.

They'd both need code names. The peeler laughed. "Why not what I just called you? Sunshine for you and . . . Spud for me?"

"Spud? You're not a Murphy, are you? You know as well as I do that every Murphy in Ireland's nicknamed Spud."

"Do you think I'd pick a code name that would give anyone a lead to my real name?"

"I suppose not."

"Bloody right. Now, do you understand all that I've told you, Sunshine?"

Sammy nodded.

"Come on, then," Spud said, rising, "let's get you out of here. You'll not have been in long enough for your friends to suspect a thing. You just tell them we had you in, 'to help us with our enquiries.' And do you know what?"

"What?"

"It's the truth."

"The truth?"

"Sure. That's exactly what you'll be doing. Helping us." Spud opened the door. "Let's get your clothes back."

Sammy scuttled to the open door, as anxious to leave the cell as a contrite sinner is to leave the confessional.

"Oh, and Sunshine?"

"What?"

"Just in case you think of changing your mind, don't forget about the wee present my mate said he'd put in your house. I think we'll leave it there. If you don't keep your promise and sing for me . . . my lot'll have to sing about you."

Oh, Christ.

"Don't worry, Sammy. I'll see you through the tough bits."

Sammy felt the heat as his Park Drive almost burned his fingers. He stubbed it out to keep company with a heap of butts in an old jam-jar lid. Just as easily as the Provos could have snuffed him out. But he had got away with the debriefing after he was released from jail. The senior Provos had accepted his story that the peelers had too much on their hands to be bothered with a pub brawl.

He had got away with his double life until now, but how long would it be until his mates twigged? The only hope for his future would be to get out, but Spud had made it a condition that Sammy give him something really big before he'd keep his promise about England.

And Spud would keep his word. As the months passed, Sammy had become attached to the peeler. He'd had to. Who else could he trust? Spud *would* keep his promise. He always did.

But Sammy knew he needed something more important to give. Something bigger than the word about the arms delivery that Sammy had been sure was going to be his ticket out. "That's great, Sam. We'll get you over to England now." But it hadn't happened, and he hadn't had a chance to explain that if the arms pickup *was* intercepted, the other members of the Provo cell would start to wonder how the Security Forces had found out.

Only a few people knew about the shipment. He was one of them. Had he cooked his own goose? He'd promised to tell the peeler when the arms shipment was to be collected. Would that be enough? It might.

He wished to God he knew more about Erin's slip of the tongue about Eamon not being in the Kesh much longer. If a jailbreak was planned and

Sammy could tell Spud, surely to God that would do the trick. Wouldn't it? Wouldn't it?

He lit another cigarette. The whiskey warmed him, soothed him. Maybe it would work out—the whiskey fueled his imagination—if the police could stop the jailbreak, Eamon would be stuck in there forever and just maybe Erin would get tired of waiting for him and Sammy could—he shook his head. He'd not have time for that before he was out of this fucking country for good and for all. That was what really mattered and, by Christ, Sammy was going to do whatever the hell it took to make it happen. He had to have a way out.

CHAPTER 13

"Hey on out, Tess," Erin shouted to her border collie, and gave a hand signal.

Tess, crouching low to the ground, scurried to the far side of the herd, snapping at the heels of a Dexter cow that was trying to stray back to the field they had just left.

"Hey on. Hey on." Erin turned, closed the five-bar gate behind her, and glanced down to where the sun's rays made the surface of the Strule River shine like molten copper.

Across the Strule Valley, the colours changed from the greens of the water meadows to the russets of bracken-strewn hillsides studded with yellow blooms of gorse and deepened to the purple, heather-clad slopes of Slieveard, where the mountain bulked against the eastern sky. Overhead, she heard the calling of a homeward-bound flock of green plover, their "pee-wit, pee-wit" a descant above the lowing of the herd.

Perhaps her brother and sisters were happy in their new countries, glad to be away from the Troubles, but they'd not have the chance to see the Strule, the Sperrin Mountains a craggy line to the north, hear the plover. They had all been a part of Erin's home for as long as she could remember. No wonder Da had loved this country. No wonder that she did.

"Push them in."

The dog obeyed, chivvying the milk-laden animals into the byre, the big beasts, rolling their liquid brown eyes in fear of the little dog, being driven where their tormentor ordered.

Just like, she thought, the way the mighty British Empire had been driven out of most of Ireland by the constant worrying of a small group of patriots nipping at their flanks. It only remained to chase England from the last six counties, here in the northeast. And she and those like her fully intended to see them gone, back to their home byre in the island across Saint George's Channel.

The weapons cache that Sammy had brought in on Saturday would be part of that, and Erin wanted the arms safely out of the churchyard before Eamon and the others made their break. Once that happened, the Security Forces would be so tied up, so single-mindedly focused on recapturing the escapees, that their guard would be down. She had an idea for taking advantage of that. And they'd need the rifles and the Semtex.

But that would have to wait for a little longer. She was still a farmer, and the work on the farm never stopped. Someone had to see to the cows, bring them in from the pasture, milk them.

The Dexter was a good breed. It had originated in the west of Ireland. The beasts were hardy enough to be driven outdoors year-round and equally prized for their beef and their milk. Da had built up the herd. He wanted Irish cattle on the O'Byrnes' place, none of the foreign English Friesians or Scottish Ayrshires for him.

Erin went into the byre, where the beasts, unbidden, had gone into their stalls and stood docilely, udders full of warm milk, contentedly chewing the cud, smelling of sweet clover and cow farts.

She hooked up the electrical milking machines as she'd done every day for years, grateful for the animals' doe-eyed patience—all except that bitch, Margaret. As usual, she kicked the side of the stall, bellowed as the cold steel nozzles were slipped onto her teats.

Being a cow must be pretty humdrum, Erin thought, as she walked from the last stall and switched on the power. Once in a while she'd not mind a bit of humdrum herself, but that would come—once the Brits were gone.

As the machinery hummed and the milk sloshed into the vat, she busied herself hanging up some loose pieces of equipment that should have been put back in their proper places. That brother of hers. She grunted as she lifted a heavy coupling for the mower; if he ever got through the pearly gates, Saint Peter would have to assign one angel full-time to keep reminding Cal to preen his wings and polish his halo.

Erin heard Margaret bellow. She always did that when her udders were empty. Erin switched off and moved along the stalls, unhooking the beasts. All she had to do now was wash the lines and nozzles.

When she was finished, she called to Tess, and together they walked across the barnyard. Erin carried a jug of fresh milk. She stopped and stared up at an outbuilding—that bloody roof. The slates were ebony black from the recent rain, overgrown with the moss of the years. Two—no three—were loose, and they were letting the rain through and onto the tractor in the outbuilding. The old rusting, red Massey-Harris had sounded as if it had bronchitis when she'd driven it yesterday. She'd have to chase up Cal to fix it. Or Sammy. He was a damn good mechanic.

She walked on to the farmhouse.

"Go to bed, Tess."

The collie looked up with porcelain-blue eyes and obeyed, slipping into her kennel.

Erin hauled off her muddy Wellington boots and tried to open the farmhouse door. As usual, it stuck, and, as usual, she swore at it, but she smiled as she swore. There *was* a comfort in familiar things, like milking the cows and the turn of the farmer's seasons—and an old sticking door that her big brother was too idle to mend.

She yelled across the barnyard. "Fiach. Supper."

The kitchen door jerked open. After the damp of the byre, the kitchen was turf-fire cosy. The smell of peat mingled with the aroma of roast ham.

She set the milk jug on the table.

"All done?" Cal turned from the range. Sammy sat at the kitchen table.

"Aye. Margaret acted up. That's your modern cow for you. No respect."

"Ah, Jesus, Erin, you've a quare soft hand under a duck, so you have. You could milk a rhinoceros with rabies."

"Bollocks," she said, grinning. "Get your hands washed, the pair of you." She moved to the range, slipped on oven mitts, and pulled the ham from the oven. "It's done to a treat." She set the roasting pan on the counter and lifted the ham onto a pewter plate, fashioned in the shape of a pig. "I'll carve."

Cal and Sammy washed in the kitchen sink and sat at the table.

Fiach came in, red-haired, broad-shouldered like his brother, his left eye closed and surrounded by a bruise that had started to turn yellow.

"It's a grand thing, that hurling of yours, Fiach," she said. "A real sport for gentlemen."

"The eye? Sure it's all in a day's work on the field. You should have seen me on Saturday. The fella that gave me this." Fiach pointed to the bruise under his eye. "I marmalized him, near killed him."

"I'm glad you didn't," Erin said. "They'd have chucked you in jail for murder, and Eamon in the Kesh is enough for us to worry about." She noticed Sammy swing toward her when she mentioned the Kesh. Was he still smarting because he hadn't been let in on the secret? Bugger him if he was. He'd live.

"Get washed," she said to Fiach, and as he passed her she tousled his hair.

"Here." Erin put a plate of ham on the red-and-white checked tablecloth and a tureen close by it.

She watched Cal help himself to colcannon. Nothing like it—creamed spuds and cabbage. He poured himself a glass of milk, waited for Erin and Fiach to take their places, closed his eyes, and bowed his head. Why was he saying grace to a God who had forsaken Ireland, a God that Erin had stopped believing in on the night of the failed ambush of a UDR man?

The bugger had seen them and fired first. That was the night when she and young Terry O'Rourke had stumbled off into the darkness, and she'd held the boy, lung shot, red froth on his lips, bleeding to death in a ditch as he cried to Mother Mary, whimpered for his own mother.

Her pray to God? Habit. Nothing more.

"Amen." Cal raised his head.

"Och, aye. God save Ireland," Erin said. "Pass the milk."

"You mentioned Eamon there, Erin. How is he?" Sammy asked, not meeting her eyes as he spoke.

So he *was* still smarting that something might be going on that he didn't know about. She wished she'd kept her mouth shut the other night. Or was he angry? Was there something else behind the question?

"He's fine, Sam. It's visiting day tomorrow. Will I tell him you were asking for him?"

Sammy nodded.

Conversation lapsed. Why, she wondered, shouldn't we tell Sammy about the impending break? They might need his help. But the peelers had lifted him. Could they have turned him? She glanced at the little man. He was picking his nose.

"Jesus, Sammy would you stop that. It's disgusting."

"Sorry." He blushed.

She knew he had a habit of doing that if he was nervous, but what had he to be worried about? Unless he thought that he was going to be asked to pick up the arms in the churchyard. Although he made a point of seeming to be courageous, she knew that inside he could be frightened of his own shadow. Sammy needn't be worried. She had other plans.

The ham was sweet and the milk warm. Erin ate silently. It seemed that after her telling Sammy to mind his manners no one had much to say. All right, she thought, to business.

"Fiach?" He turned to her. "Fiach, you've been agitating for a while now for us to let you help." She saw his good eye open wide, the half-chewed ham in his open mouth. "We've a wee job for you."

"Honest to God?"

"Aye."

"Dead on." A smile split his freckled face. "What have I to do?"

"There's a wheen of stuff in an old grave in the Ballydornan churchyard. We want you to pick it up for us."

"Now?" Fiach leapt to his feet.

"No, silly. Sit down and eat up. You've to do it on Friday night."

Fiach subsided, but his good eye gleamed.

Cal spoke slowly. "It's a one-man job. Use the tractor . . ."

"You'll have to take a look at the engine," Erin said.

"I'll do it tomorrow, or maybe Sammy could."

"I'll do it the night before I go home . . . Will you be wanting me to go out, too?"

"Not at all. I told you it's a one-man job."

Sammy was staring at her with a relieved look on his face. Maybe that's what had him worried. Not for himself. For her. The bloody man was besotted with her. Worried about her, was pleased that she'd not be doing the job herself. Why? It would be as routine as—as milking the cows.

"So," Cal said, "go out after dark . . ."

"Take Tessie and let her scout about first," Erin added.

"Sammy, tell Fiach exactly where the consignment is."

Sammy did, ending his explanation with a wry grin. "In with a poor ould dead Irishman."

"Aye," said Cal, "and it'll be going in with a clatter more dead Irishmen, but they've been gone for three thousand years or so."

"In the neolithic grave Da found?" Fiach asked.

"The very spot," Erin said. "The old tumulus. Nobody would ever find that place the way it's hidden under a mound, screened by brambles. Bloody good thing Da kept his mouth shut about it."

"That's great," said Fiach. "But . . . and I'm not scared to do the job . . ." He looked Erin in the eye. "Why move the things at all? Are they not safe enough in Ballydornan?"

"It's guns and Semtex," Erin said. "We've enough guns, but Semtex is bloody hard to come by, and"—she glanced at Cal—"it's about time we let the Brits know that there's Republican life in Tyrone yet."

Cal stopped chewing and set his knife on the plate. "What are you on about? I thought we'd agreed to lie low until after"—he looked at Sammy, who was staring at the table—"you know."

Erin laughed. "We did and we have, but I was thinking about it today. We've been quiet for a while now. It's time to go back into business again. There might be a chance very soon."

"Oh?" Sammy said.

Erin laughed. "And we *will* let you in on that, Sammy. Once Cal and I've had a chance to talk it over."

Sammy propped his bike against the public phone kiosk, went in, lifted the receiver, dropped his coins in the slot, and dialed.

"Hello."

Sammy knew that Special Branch men never gave their names or numbers over the telephone, but he recognized Spud's voice.

"It's me. Sunshine. I've the word on the pickup. Friday night. The stuff's in that big aboveground grave. Near the old Celtic cross."

"Good." Spud sounded disinterested. "Any news on the other?"

Sammy stumbled over his words in his rush. "No details . . . but there's something happening . . . at the Kesh. And they're going to get something going here, too."

"How do you know that?"

"Look." Sammy took a deep breath. "The arms are being picked up so they can get ready for another attack. They're going to tell me about it soon."

"Good." Pause.

"Hello?" Sammy wanted to be out of the box. "Are you there?"

"I was just thinking. This Kesh thing. You've no more details?"

"If I had, wouldn't I tell you?"

"It's pretty thin. Nothing for me to move on."

"I can fucking well put two and two together."

"And get three by the sound of it."

"For fuck's sake . . ."

"Sunshine, I'll think about the pickup. You'll get a few extra quid for that, but until you can give me the details about what you suspect . . . or maybe the gen on the attack you think's going to happen . . . I can't persuade anybody to get you into the Witness . . ."

"Christ. You've *got* to get me out of here. If your lot goes after the arms pickup, my lot'll suspect me. They already don't trust me. Not since I was lifted. They'll . . ." But he heard the click as the connection was broken, the buzz of the dial tone. Sammy slammed the receiver back into its cradle with such force that the Bakelite mouthpiece shattered.

CHAPTER 14

The final chords of *Don Giovanni* were ear-shattering. Waves of applause rolled through the Queen Elizabeth Theatre. The houselights came up, and the audience, Fiona and Becky Johnston among them, rose as one as the curtain closed only to reopen so that the cast could accept their accolades.

Fiona felt Becky tugging at her sleeve, turned, and saw her nodding toward the aisle. Becky had already started to move, and Fiona followed. Trust Becky. Once the curtain calls started, she'd mutter, "When in doubt . . . get out," and head for the nearest exit.

She was in the aisle, steaming ahead like a dreadnought battleship, ploughing through the growing crowd heading for the Dunsmuir Street doors. That was typical of Becky, Fiona's friend.

As Fiona followed in Becky's wake, she thought briefly about friendship. She believed that people would be lucky to make ten real friends in a lifetime—those to whom you could tell your deepest secrets, could rely on and who could trust you utterly in return. And most of those you made as a child or as a student. All of those friends, save Becky, were back in Northern Ireland.

As Fiona left the theatre, she saw Becky standing on the Dunsmuir Street sidewalk craning into the traffic. "Bloody taxis. They're just like policemen. You can never find one when you want one."

Fiona watched as a Black Top cab pulled into the kerb. Even before the passenger dismounted, Becky had grabbed the door and turned to a small man who seemed to be protesting that he had been first in line.

"My good man," Becky said in a voice that Fiona thought would probably carry as far as Granville Street, "remember the *Birkenhead* drill."

Fiona had moved to stand near Becky and the little man.

"The what?" he asked, stepping back.

Becky grabbed Fiona by the arm and hustled her into the back of the taxi. "The *Birkenhead* drill. Women and children first."

Fiona heard the door slam over the would-be passenger's protests and felt the warmth of Becky's presence beside her on the seat.

"Quickly," said Becky, "give the driver your address."

Fiona did, and the cab pulled away. She could feel her friend shaking with suppressed mirth.

"Did you see the look on that chap's face?"

"I thought, perhaps, we were a little rude."

"Rubbish. Charles Darwin was right. Survival of the fittest." Becky slid along the seat away from Fiona. "There's a bit more room for you."

"Thank you."

"So," Becky asked, "what did you think of tonight's performance? I must say *I* was sorry for the cat."

"What cat?"

"The one that started caterwauling every time the soprano sang. She *must* have been standing on a cat's tail."

Fiona smiled. The soprano *had* been a bit off-key. "It wasn't just the soprano, Becky. *Don Giovanni*'s a bit heavy for me. I prefer Mozart's lighter ones like *The Magic Flute* or *The Marriage of Figaro*."

The cab stopped at the traffic light at Helmcken Street. Becky peered past Fiona at the façade of Saint Paul's Hospital, grinned, and said, "Speaking of marriages, how are things with you and Doctor Tim?"

"He's in San Francisco."

The cab rattled on the rough surface of the Burrard Street Bridge. Through its latticework Fiona could see the lights of the ships moored in English Bay. The circles of radiance looked like a fleet of Chinese lanterns adrift on an ebony sea.

"That's not what I asked you, my gel. You've been rather quiet since the weekend. Is everything pukka with you two?"

Fiona held her hand palm down and rocked it from side to side. "He hasn't phoned."

"Mmm," said Becky. "It sounds to me as if I'd better come in for a night-cap when we get to your place."

"I'd like that," Fiona said, and was comforted by the light touch of Becky's hand on her own where it was resting on the seat. She turned to stare out of the window and said nothing until the taxi stopped outside her house.

Fiona paid the fare and followed Becky up the path. One of the things

Fiona liked about Becky, though English, was that she was not one of those overmannered Englishwomen who would turn a simple decision about who should pay for something into a prolonged battle to see who would have the privilege.

Fiona opened the door to her apartment and showed Becky into the living room. No flashing light on the machine. Damn. McCusker lay curled up on an armchair. He opened one eye and went back to sleep.

"What can I get you, Becky?"

Becky sat and kicked off her shoes. "I'd really like a cup of tea, actually."

"Right."

When Fiona came back from the kitchen, Becky was standing in front of the bookshelf. "Somerset Maugham, Graham Greene, Jane Austen, Simone de Beauvoir, Germaine Greer, W. O. Mitchell, Margaret Atwood . . ."

"You know I like to read." Fiona put the tray on a coffee table and poured.

"And that," said Becky, staring at what Fiona was doing, "that is further proof that the Irish are an uncivilized lot."

"What is? Reading?"

Becky shook her head. "You should *always* . . . and I do mean *always* . . . put the milk in first." She chuckled. "But it'll do." She accepted the cup and sat. "Come on. Sit down and tell Aunt Becky all about it."

"Could I put on a record first?"

"Certainly."

Fiona found what she was looking for. A man's soft tenor came from the speakers:

"My young love said to me my mother won't mind,
And my father won't slight you for your lack of kine . . ."

She turned the volume down until the song was just audible. "Sometimes I like to play the old Irish songs." She sat in the other armchair.

"Don't mind me. Nice voice, that chap. Who is he?"

"Liam Clancy. He's a County Tipperary man. From Carrick-on-Suir." Fiona glanced at the lightless telephone answering machine. Would Tim never call? She turned to Becky. "Thanks for coming in. I do need a chat with you. I think things are a bit . . . a bit . . ." She frowned. "Strained with Tim and me at the moment."

Becky pursed her lips, but said nothing.

"You remember what I said about forgetting our pasts? Well, mine caught up with me last week. Tim took me out to dinner on Saturday. It was supposed to be a lovely evening, but a man from Belfast was there and came over and spoke to me . . ." Fiona stood, walked to the mantel.

In the background, Liam Clancy sang

Last night I lay dreaming. My drowned love came in.
So softly she moved that her feet made no din . . .

"And?" Becky asked gently.

"It was just like the song. Jimmy, that's the Belfast man's name, Jimmy had been the best friend of a dear man I was in love with back in Belfast." Fiona swallowed and decided not to tell Becky *all* the details. She simply said, "He stayed there and I emigrated. I still do think of him sometimes, but Jimmy wouldn't stop talking about . . . about Davy." She could see Davy's blue eyes, tear-misted in the visitors' room of the Kesh. "And when Jimmy kept going on about him, I could see him, feel as if he was somewhere in Bridges with us."

Becky put down her teacup. "You must have been very much in love."

"I was . . . I think I still am."

"Have you told Tim?"

Fiona shook her head. "Not that I still care, but when we went sailing on Sunday, he asked me about Davy. I did tell him that we had been in love. Back in Belfast."

"How did he take that?"

Fiona allowed herself a small smile. "He was wonderful. He listened. It's good when people listen."

Becky said nothing.

"Tim thinks that I haven't let myself mourn for a lost love. He said I needed to grieve . . . that I'd need time. That he loved me."

Becky moved closer to Fiona. "I like your Tim. Very much. It sounds to me as if he has his head well screwed onto his shoulders and he *does* love you. I'm certain of that."

"Are you really?" Fiona stared at the Persian rug.

"It's not what I think that matters. It's what you think . . . and what Tim thinks but . . ." Becky put her hand under Fiona's chin and lifted her head. "Look at me, Fiona."

Fiona looked into Becky's green eyes.

"I think that Tim's right about one thing."

"What?"

"The grieving business. I once read a book by a woman called Kübler-Ross. She's a Swiss psychiatrist. She wrote *On Death and Dying* back in the sixties.

I'll wager Tim's read it. Kübler-Ross believes when someone finds out that they are dying, they go through a series of stages. The first is denial. 'It's not happening to me. It's not real. I don't believe it. I *won't* believe it.' There's a lot of other stuff in between, including the need to give way to grief before people can accept the finality. I suppose leaving someone you love can be a bit like that."

"So you think Tim's right?"

"He certainly could be. What else did he say?"

"He thought that Davy's memory was a ghost he and I would have to exorcise. That he'd help me do that."

"You, my girl, have a gem beyond price in that man. He loves you, he understands, and he wants to help. What more could you ask for?"

Fiona glanced at the answering machine. "I just wish he'd ring."

"He will. I'm sure he will. Don't forget *you* certainly need time to think things out, but so will Tim. Give him time." Becky took her hand from Fiona's chin, crossed to her chair, and picked up her teacup.

Fiona crossed her arms in front of her. Her right hand massaged her left shoulder. Becky *was* a good listener. She didn't beat about the bush, and, Fiona told herself, Becky's advice had been heartfelt—and straight to the point. She smiled.

"Thanks, Becky."

"Absolute rubbish. No thanks needed. None at all."

How English. Express thanks and they become embarrassed.

Becky bent, put on her shoes, and straightened up.

Fiona crossed the room and hugged Becky. "Thank you. I mean it."

Becky stiffened then relaxed. Fiona could see the faintest blush on her friend's cheeks.

"Well. Yes. Mmm," Becky said, glancing at the carriage clock. "You're going to be fine, Fiona, and I'm going to have to get going. Stay where you are. I'll see myself out." Becky surprised Fiona by returning a quick hug, breaking away and heading for the door. "I'll see you in the trenches tomorrow. Good God, I have to start with the grade sevens." She crossed her eyes, grinned, and left.

Fiona sat in the chair but jumped as McCusker sprang into her lap. "You startled me, silly." She fondled the cat's head. "It's a good thing to have friends isn't it, McCusker?"

Fiona could feel the vibration as McCusker purred.

Becky was a good friend, and it had been comforting to tell her about Davy, to listen to her advice. Fiona *had* tried hard not to think of Davy since Sunday. To take Tim's advice and understand that for her he no longer existed. That was pretty much what Becky had suggested. And yet—

In the background, she could hear Liam Clancy as he breathed life into "My Lagan Love," the most beautiful of Irish love songs.

"Where Lagan stream sings a lullaby, there grows a lily fair . . ."

If she hadn't stumbled on the banks of that very river, so long ago now, she would never have met Davy McCutcheon.

"The twilight gleam is in her eye, and the night is on her hair."

She could hear Davy's baritone as she sat on the floor, head on his knees, his hand stroking her dark hair while he sang those words to her.

Fiona sighed, rose, slowly went to the stereo, and switched it off.

CHAPTER 15

Davy switched off the electrical polisher he'd been using to clean the cell block's corridor. For some reason unknown to him, the inmates and screws alike called the machines, bumpers. "All done, Mr. Smiley."

"Right, Davy. Away on off and put that yoke in the closet."

"Right, sir." Davy limped along the corridor, pushing the bumper before him. Old Smiley wasn't a bad head—for a screw. Didn't mind having a bit of a blether with his charges. He'd only taken the job after he'd been laid off as a riveter at Harland and Wolff's shipyards. He'd once said that he reckoned he was a bit like an inmate himself. Serving his time until he could draw his pension. He wasn't like some of the other bastards in this place, who Davy thought were probably members of some Loyalist paramilitary group when they were off duty at the Kesh and who took delight in making the inmates' lives miserable.

Davy put his gear away and headed back to his cell.

Mr. Smiley yawned and looked at his watch. "I'll be out of here in another couple of hours."

"I'll not," said Davy.

Mr. Smiley tutted. "You keep up the good behaviour, keep getting remission, and the time'll go by, so it will. You never know. Maybe they'll declare an amnesty one day. Let you lot out. Maybe both sides'll see a bit of sense and pack it up."

"Aye. Did a leprechaun tell you that? Let us out early? Pack it up? Not at all."

"You never know, Davy."

"I suppose, Mr. Smiley, you don't just believe in leprechauns, you think there's fairies at the bottom of your garden, too?" Davy shook his head. He knew he'd not get away with a remark like that to any of the other screws.

"No, but while there's life . . ."

"There's hope. I know." Davy scratched his hand. The bloody thing itched like buggery.

"How's that paw of yours?"

"I had the stitches out today. The doctor'd not want to be coming in on Saturday to do the job. Linfield's playing, and he's a Blues supporter."

"Playing Celtic tomorrow?"

"Aye."

"I might take a run-race over and see the game myself. I've the morrow off, so I have. Back here on Sunday." Mr. Smiley looked at his watch. "Anyroad, time I was off."

"Fair enough. If you go, make sure and cheer for Celtic now."

Mr. Smiley laughed. "I'm a Blues man myself."

"Go on, you Prod git. Celtic'll beat the ears off them, so they will."

"And you think I'm the one that believes in fairies? Celtic couldn't beat the skin off a rice pudding." Mr. Smiley laughed.

Davy laughed with him, for a moment his imprisonment unimportant. He was a decent man, Mr. Smiley. Even if Celtic was a Catholic team and Linfield, the Blues, Protestant, the pair of them, sectarian differences forgotten, could be sitting over a couple of jars the way Davy and Jimmy used to do, pulling each other's legs. Davy shrugged and watched the guard walk away.

Davy returned to D-16. Soon be time for lunch. Eamon came in. He'd gone off to see some of his mates earlier in the morning.

"Here y'are, Davy." Eamon skimmed an envelope across the cell. "One for you in the post this morning."

Davy made an attempt to field the letter, but his wound made him clumsy and the envelope slipped through his fingers.

"Sorry about that." Eamon bent and picked it up. "Here."

"Thanks." The envelope had been opened. All the prisoners' mail was. Security. He glanced at the back. Canadians had a peculiar habit of putting a return address there. Sure enough it was from Jimmy Ferguson. Funny that. Davy'd been thinking about wee Jim just a few minutes ago. "It's from Canada."

"Canada? I hear it's not such a bad place. I've a cousin in Winnipeg. Says it's bloody cold in the winter and the midgies is something fierce in the summer."

"Right enough, when Jimmy was in Toronto he said the same . . . but he's out in Vancouver now. Not a mosquito in the place." And I wonder, Davy thought, where Fiona is?

"Are you not going to have a wee read of it?"

"Aye." Davy fished inside and pulled out sheets of folded blue airmail letter paper. As he opened them, something fell out and fluttered to the floor to be retrieved by Eamon.

"Have you a girlfriend out there, Father?" Eamon was looking at a photograph. "She's a right corker, so she is."

Probably Siobhan. Jimmy had written before to say he was expecting his daughter to come for a visit. "Give it here." Davy held out his good hand and took the snap.

"Oh, Christ . . . Jesus Christ . . ." Davy sat heavily on his cot. "Holy Mother of God." The letter slipped onto the cot.

"You all right, Davy?"

"Just a wee minute." Davy's hands shook. He felt his eyes fill. He stared at the picture. It was her. Fiona. He blinked. "It's . . . Oh, Christ . . ." He felt Eamon's hand on his shoulder and looked up to see the man's face, concern written in every line. Davy sniffed. "Look . . . if you don't mind, I'd like to be . . ."

"Fair enough."

Davy was hardly aware of the cell door closing as Eamon left.

Davy told himself to take a grip. It was only a fucking photo, for God's sake, but—he looked again. It was *her.*

She hadn't changed her hairstyle. It was still black and shiny, framing her face, the silver streaks that had always made him think of a stoat's tail tip in winter—there were more of them now. She looked surprised. Maybe Jimmy had caught her unawares when he'd taken the picture. Her almond eyes were open wide, her lips slightly apart.

Davy rocked back and forth. He held himself, picture forgotten. All the memories of her. Lord God, he could hear her voice, her laugh—the feel of her and the taste of her and the—the Fiona of her—and—fuck it. Fuck it. He stood, stared at the cell wall. She might as well be on the far side of the moon for all the good it did him.

He rose and started to pace. Three steps one way, three steps the other. His world. And she was in the world. But not in his world. What's the use? he asked himself. Don't look at the bloody picture again. He started to tear it apart, but his hands refused to obey. He tried to look at her again, but the light at that end of the cell made it difficult for him to see. Davy moved to where a thin ray spilled in through the little barred window.

"Lord, girl, but you've not changed one bit."

The way Jimmy had taken the picture, Davy could see that Fiona was sitting at a table. Knives, forks on a white tablecloth. A half-full glass in front of her had reflected part of the camera's flash and a split-second diamond of light sat frozen for eternity at the glass's rim. Was that water or wine in the glass? She only ever took a drink of sherry back here in Northern Ireland and only on special occasions. Of course she'd have changed. Nine years was a long time, and why shouldn't she have a glass of wine if she fancied one?

She was wearing a white blouse, open at the neck. He could see the shadow between her breasts—Davy closed his eyes—he'd not think of her breasts, of the night they'd made love on the old settee in the parlour of his wee house off the Falls Road. He'd often wondered if she'd known that the sofa anchored the rug over the secret place in the floor where he hid his detonators.

But the softness of her breast, the firmness, and the way she'd shuddered when he'd taken her nipple—stop it, he told himself. Stop it.

He looked at the cot, trying to banish the images, and saw Jimmy's letter. Maybe if he read that it would help. He picked it up and started to read.

Dear Davy,
   How's about ye ould hand?

Jimmy always wrote as he would have spoken. His penmanship was in very untidy scrawls.

You'll never guess who I seen last night. You will if you look at the enclosed snap. Ha ha. Me and the Missus and Siobhan, she's out with us on her holidays like I told you, was at this place for our supper and there she was bold as brass not five tables over—your Fiona. I took her snap. Siobhan says I shouldn't send it to you, it might upset you like, but I said not at all, Davy'd like to know.

Were you right, Jimmy? Davy wondered, looking at Fiona's eyes again.

So it's in the letter. I thought she was looking smashing so I did. We had a wee jar in the bar after with her and this Doctor fellah she was with. Calls himself Tim Andersen, some highheejin at one of the hospitals here.

Davy examined the snap. He'd not paid attention before, but there was a man's torso, cut off at the neck across the table in the background. So she had a boyfriend. Maybe a husband. So why was he getting himself all worked up? It was over. He knew it was over, but when he looked at her eyes on the glossy paper he felt as he had the first day he'd seen her when she'd stumbled on the old towpath beside the Lagan.

A stranger to him, she'd tripped on a root, he'd reflexively grabbed for her, been thanked, found out her name, and asked her to have a cup of tea with him. He'd loved her since that day.

Him and her's not married nor nothing, but they've been walking out for about six months or so.

So she hadn't married—yet—but six months?

She was a wee bit quiet when I tried to talk about the old days. Maybe she's like the rest of us out here and wants to forget all that shite, but I took a flier and I brought your name up, Davy, once or twice. She never said much but once I seen her hands and do you know? They were all quivery. I don't think she's forgot you.

So I got hold of her phone number. It's 604-555-7716. I don't know what you'd dial from Belfast to get Canada. Can you use a phone in there? Anyroad, she's living in Vancouver like us. I asked her to come over for her supper so maybe I'll be seeing her again. I'll let you know when I do.

Vancouver? Fiona was in Vancouver? Only eight thousand miles away and a jail sentence still to run. He knew it was stupid, but the thought made Davy smile. And by the tone of Jimmy's letter, she was well and that was good.

Anyway, that's about all my news, and I was never a great fist with a pen so I'll close now. Hope all is right with you there, Davy. We think of you often and I don't mean it in the old way, Tiocfaidh àr la. Your day will come.

> *Yours until pigs smell like violets, ha, ha.*
> *Jimmy*

Davy looked at her picture as a Dominican priest might stare at the Shroud of Turin: as if the shroud was mysterious, distant, but, in the mind of the priest, the face of the thing he loved best in this world and the hereafter.

"Fiona," was all he said. He forced himself to recognize the reality. She was there and he was here. As he slipped the photo inside the letter to put them back inside the envelope, he noticed the telephone number. Her telephone number. Shite. What the hell use was that? Davy could just see himself. "Excuse me, Mr. Smiley, could I make a telephone call to Canada?" The guard would give himself a rupture laughing, say something like, "Sure you wouldn't like me to book you a plane ticket while we're at it?" It would be different if he were out of here. He slammed his left hand against the side of the cot and instantly regretted it. The wound in his palm screeched in protest. Stupid bloody chisel. Stupid bloody Eamon and his stupid bloody escape. "When the boys get out, would you come with us, Davy?"

Davy unfolded the letter, took out the picture, saw her eyes, and thought, "Come with us, Davy?" If Eamon and his friends would have him, Davy'd go, all right. He'd ask Eamon as soon as he could see him.

CHAPTER 16

Moonbeams backlit the granite-block church and softened the outlines of the tombstones in Ballydornan churchyard. A Celtic cross supported by rusty iron braces leaned over the lesser grave markers. Its once deeply cut ogham script had been weathered by the centuries of cold Tyrone rains. Moss grew thickly on the cross's north side and covered the older, smaller headstones.

Jars of cut flowers, some fresh, most wilting forlornly, stood by more recent gravesides. Some of these headstones were half-obscured by plastic-encased, black-framed photographs of the young men interred beneath. Below each picture was printed, "Here lies [the man's name was given] a volunteer of the Tyrone Brigade, Provisional IRA. Murdered by the British forces of occupation."

The wind rattled in the branches of a blackthorn and whispered in the unkempt grass between the graves.

The moon's shadow of the cross slipped over a weed-grown gravel pathway and darkened a ditch. Sergeant Buchan of D Squadron, 22 Special Air Services Regiment (SAS), crouched beneath the bank of the ditch. At one time, he knew, the SAS had been commanded by an Ulsterman, Colonel Blair (Paddy) Mayne, from Newtownards, but that had been back in the Second World War, when Ulstermen could be relied on to support Britain. Not like the present lot. Half of them would be as likely to cut your throat as smile at you.

Sergeant Buchan grimaced as he tied the neck of a plastic bag and pushed the thing into a clump of ferns. He hoisted his camouflage pants, frowning at the rustling noise his movements made. He'd been huddled in this ditch since he and the rest of his "brick," the four-man tactical unit of the SAS, had been inserted by helicopter in the early hours of the morning.

The chopper had been one of a flight of three. The natives were inured to the constant coming and going of helicopters, and, with the clattering of so many rotors, nobody would have noticed that one of the machines had briefly touched down.

He and the other men had crawled for half a mile along the duckweed-scummed ditch so no trace of their entry would be visible near the target area. Once in place, he'd burrowed into a clump of briars and lain there, muddy, cramped, and damp for the remains of last night, today, and on into tonight.

That had been the second time on this mission that he'd had to shit into a plastic bag. Standard operating procedure for SAS men out on an "observation post/reactive," the regiment's euphemism for "ambush." Once in place, there was no nipping out to attend to the calls of nature. These waiting jobs could last for days, and without the bags, the "lurk" would become fouled, and the smell might give away its position.

This one shouldn't take much longer. His captain had briefed the sergeant yesterday.

"I want you to take your lot out tonight. We've just had word from Tasking and Coordination in Londonderry that the bad lads have an arms pickup tomorrow night. Some bloke in the Special Branch sent the word up from one of his touts. The brass in Londonderry seem to think the gen's reliable, so take your boys and put them in here." The captain indicated the position on a 1:250,000 scale map.

"Sir."

"We'd like prisoners."

"Sir."

"You'll have a Quick Reaction Force as backup in here. In that outbuilding."

"Any idea how many men will make the pickup?"

"Sorry. Probably not many. It's a small shipment."

"Right, sir."

"Do try to get at least one alive. We want to pump him. The brass need to know who's in the local Active Service Unit. They've a pretty good idea, but it has to be confirmed. Sometimes," the captain smiled wearily, "sometimes we can even turn a man. Have him work for us. HUMINT's bloody important."

Human intelligence? Sergeant Buchan thought, as he wiggled his toes in his boots. His socks were soggy, and his feet felt like blocks of ice. How intelligent was anyone who thought that shooting British squaddies was some kind of sport? Well, there'd be one or two less of the thick bastards after tonight was over, and they'd be short of whatever was under the lid of an aboveground sarcophagus that lay not ten yards from his position. With a bit of luck.

Luck was always important on jobs like this, but it was no substitute for good preparations. Sergeant Buchan had placed his men carefully. A trooper crouched in the ditch ten yards away. A corporal and another trooper were inside the church. The fields of fire from three ArmaLite AR-4 rifles and his own Heckler and Koch HK 53, 5.56 mm automatic would overlap in the "killing area" around the only raised grave between the ditch and the Celtic cross. It was the raised grave that the captain had stressed. He'd said that it was how the Special Branch man's tout had identified it.

Sergeant Buchan knew he should have posted "cutoffs" to intercept any of the terrorists who tried to make a run for it, but he didn't have the manpower. He hefted a small radio transmitter. At least he could summon the QRF, but hoped that he wouldn't have to.

A shriek cut through the night, sudden then dropping to a whimper before fading into the night's stillness. The sergeant shivered as though a goose had walked over his grave, then realized that he had heard a rabbit dying in the talons of an owl.

"For God's sake, Fiach, would you sit still? You've been going round all day like a bee on a hot brick." Erin O'Byrne shifted her chair at the kitchen table and grinned at the shape of her younger brother, outlined by the moonlight that spilled into the room. She had turned off the lights so his night vision wouldn't be harmed. She knew how excited the sixteen-year-old would be. She was excited for him.

Fiach plumped himself down in an armchair, muttering something about being pumped up, like just before the whistle blew at the start of a hurling match, that it was his first time, for God's sake.

"Aye, well," she said, "just you bide."

Cal, the idle skitter, had gone up to bed hours ago. Now, she told herself, she was being unfair. Cal and Fiach had been working like Trojans since she had come back from visiting Eamon on Thursday. Eamon had told her to get the old tumulus ready.

The men had spent all day yesterday running in underground electrical cables from the byre. The cables would power a couple of lightbulbs, a small convection heater, and an electric cooker. The neolithic grave was always musty and damp. Eamon had asked her to put in four camp beds and a small chemical toilet. The old tumulus would be a regular home away from home for Eamon and his friends. And the Security Forces could search the O'Byrne farm 'til hell froze over. They'd never find the hiding place. Nor would they find the guns and Semtex that Fiach would stash there as soon as he got back.

Fiach was asking her something.

"What?"

"I said, do you not remember your first time?"

"I do indeed."

"Go on then." Fiach badgered her. "Tell us about it."

Telling him would help pass the time. "All right," she told him, "I went out with Eamon."

Over the border into Donegal, halfway between Clady and Strabane, Eamon lay at her left shoulder behind a drystone wall close to the narrow B85, a road that a British patrol used regularly—stupid buggers. They hadn't recognized back then that consistency of troop movements was an open invitation to snipers or to the Provos to set remote-controlled bombs in culverts under a well-used road.

"Cal had had word that a platoon of Green Howards . . ."

"Green whats?"

"Howards. They're a British regiment."

"Green, by God. Are you sure they weren't Irish?" Fiach chuckled.

"Jesus, Fiach. Do you want to hear this or don't you?"

"I'm sorry. Go on."

"We went out as snipers. Just over the border."

"So the Brits couldn't shoot back?"

"That's right. They're not allowed to fire into the Republic."

"Seems daft to me. If someone was shooting at me, I'd bloody well shoot back."

"They couldn't. They still can't and that suits us fine. Anyway, there we were, me and Eamon hidden behind a wall. Just like clockwork, along comes the patrol. In the dusk."

She could still feel the weight of the rifle, the cold of the butt against her cheek, see the chevrons on the British corporal's sleeve as the crosshairs of the Bausch & Lomb telescopic sight moved across his arm to the centre of his chest.

"Twelve of the bastards, all spaced out, holding their rifles. Eamon had told me to take the wireless operator . . ."

"And did you?"

"No. I asked him home for a cup of tea."

"Away off. You never did."

"No, I didn't, but if you don't stop interrupting, I'll never get this story told."

She'd remember to her dying day the thump of the rifle's recoil into her shoulder, the man in khaki going down in a heap, and his mates scattering like scared rabbits.

"I got my man, and Eamon killed a second one who was trying to hide behind a whin bush."

Fiach whistled. "Good for you. I'd like to have a go at that."

"Well, you can't. They've stopped patrolling on foot now. It's too dangerous for them. They go everywhere by helicopter."

"I know," Fiach said. "Did you hear the racket last night? I wonder what they were up to?"

"Just patrolling. I'd not worry about it."

Fiach stood, walked up and down, and then asked, "How did you feel after? Were you not scared?"

Erin thought about the question and decided she'd not tell Fiach *all* the truth. He was too young to understand. "I was a bit," she said. "A couple of the soldiers ignored their rules and fired at where they thought we were. Ricochets going over your head make a hell of a row."

"Phweeeee." Fiach imitated the noises they'd both heard in the sound tracks of Western movies. "Like that?"

"More or less." Dear God. Sixteen and he was still only a wee boy at heart.

"I'll bet you kept your heads down."

"We had to stay behind the wall until it was dark enough to make a run for it." And that was all she was going to tell Fiach. He didn't need to know how, adrenaline running, all her senses honed to razor's edge, she and Eamon had slipped away after nightfall. They had found a dry hollow, and she'd gone at him, ripping the fly of his pants open, taking him in her mouth, hearing his cry as she had bitten too hard on the stiffness of him, the turf and bracken springy under her as he entered her, hot, determined, thrusting, the weight of him on her. And somewhere in the sky, clear and liquid, the song of a nightingale borne as Erin was borne, higher and higher on the rays of the rising moon.

She rose and looked through the window.

"Lord," she said, "is that moon never going to set tonight?"

The moon that she could see hanging above the barn roof would be fuller in two nights' time, when Eamon got here. Once he and his mates were safely ensconced in the old grave, she knew she'd still have to wait until the hue and cry had died down, but then she was going to hear the nightingale sing again.

Right, girl, she told herself, that's going to be then, but there's business to attend to now, and while a moon may be wonderful for lovers, it was a pain in the arse for anyone who wanted to move undetected at night.

Fiach stood beside her. "Is it not time yet?"

She thought he sounded like a six-year-old on Christmas morning. "Has Father Christmas come yet? Has he? Has he?"

"Just bide, Fiach. Look"—she pointed through the window—"see that big cloud bank?"

"Aye."

"We'll need to wait until the moon's behind it. That'll give you better cover."

"But I could get started now. The moon'll make it easier for me to see going across the fields."

"And what would you tell a Brit patrol if they stopped you? The O'Byrnes always spread slurry by moonlight?"

Fiach grinned. "There won't be any Brits out tonight. With all the sniping you and Eamon did, they'd be too scared."

Erin shook her head. "I'd not be too sure. Some of those bastards are hard to scare, I'll grant them that. But"—she crossed her fingers—"you're probably right. Now," she said, "be a good lad and sit down. I'll tell you when."

"All right."

She looked at him. His head seemed to be bigger because of the rolled-up balaclava perched on top of his head. "Jesus Christ, Fiach, you've a face on you like a Lurgan spade. Cheer up. It'll not be long now."

She wondered if she and Cal had been wrong to turn down Sammy's offer to go with Fiach. Cal thought the boy should go alone, said it would be his blooding, like the daubing of the face of a youngster out on his first hunt after the hounds had torn the fox to pieces. Decent of Sammy to volunteer, but she had seen the look of relief on the little man's face when his offer had been refused. Was Sammy losing his nerve? He'd have known that an arms pickup in the early hours of the morning would be simple, wouldn't it? Unless the Brits had got wind of something. And how could they?

The room darkened as the moon disappeared.

"Now?" Fiach leapt to his feet and rolled the woolen helmet over his face so that only his eyes and mouth showed. He headed for the door.

"Come here."

"What?"

"Give me a hug."

He turned and grabbed her. She felt the young strength of him as he squeezed.

"Jesus, I said a hug, not a crush." She kissed his woolly cheek. "Take care of yourself, boy."

"Don't you worry your head about me . . . Mammy."

"I'm not your mammy."

"You might as well have been."

And she knew the truth of it. She'd reared him when he'd been wee, dried his tears, wiped his snotty nose, put Elastoplast on his skinned knees, loved him.

"I'm off." He bolted for the door, opening both halves at once with a shove from his shoulder. "I'll be back in about an hour."

Erin heard the lower half of the door scratch along the tiles of the floor. The boy had been in such a hurry he'd not even bothered to close the upper half. She walked to the door and heard the clattering of the tractor's engine, watched the black outline of the tractor and the cart it was towing bounce down the farm lane, Fiach's silhouette dark against the skyline. He disappeared into the dip in the road.

She looked up at the stars, bright against the sky above the edge of the cloudbank. There was the handle of the Plough and its two far stars pointing to Polaris above the Sperrin Mountains.

She heard a questioning whimper from just outside the door, looked down, and saw Tessie.

Damnation. She'd told him to take the dog to scout for him. She should have made sure that he had. He'd been so damn impatient. It was too late now. The noise of the tractor's engine was nearly inaudible. Fiach was well on his way to the Ballydornan churchyard.

"Go to bed, Tessie," she said, and hugged herself. The night air was cold. Her breath hung misty and silvered. She crossed herself and whispered, "Holy Mary, Mother of God, watch out for my Fiach."

Another bloody wild-goose chase. Sergeant Buchan eased his cramped muscles and looked at the luminous dial of his watch. Three in the morning. "The brass think the gen's reliable." That's what the captain had said. How could anyone rely on information from a man who would inform? How did the tout's handler know that the Provos hadn't suspected, beaten the bejesus out of the snitch, and turned him into a double agent who'd feed nothing but a pack of lies to his E4A man? The Provos had done that before, and had themselves set up an ambush for their would-be ambushers. He'd lost a good mate like that south of here in Armagh.

The darkness since the moon had gone was like a shroud wrapping the graveyard. He scanned the target area through a monocular infrared tele-scope. Nothing but the grey-green outlines of the great cross, gravestones, the wall and gate at the far side. He stiffened, straining to hear. Yes. Yes. That was the engine of a tractor somewhere out beyond the wall. He waited. It was coming closer.

He squinted through the nightscope and saw the trooper farther up the ditch shift into firing position. So he'd heard it, too. The torch taped to the barrel of the man's ArmaLite was pointed directly at the sarcophagus.

The engine noises were much louder now, and the sergeant could smell the exhaust fumes. The engine stopped. The driver would be walking to the graveyard. Would he be alone?

Sergeant Buchan held his HK 53 ready and hoped to God his men would remember their orders. Bring 'em back alive. This was the first stakeout for the corporal and the trooper in the church. The soldier in the ditch was on his second tour in Ulster. He should know the ropes, and the rules of en-gagement. Every soldier in Ulster was issued with a Yellow Card, which said in no uncertain terms that, "opening fire is correct only if the person is com-mitting or about to commit an act likely to endanger life." Firing first was "likely to endanger life." So, in the sergeant's opinion, was pointing a gun.

He heard a metallic screeching to his front and focused the nightscope. A figure had opened the iron gate in the far wall, passed through, and was walking toward the sarcophagus. No sign of anyone else. Once the bugger opened the lid of the old grave and actually picked up a weapon and put his fingerprints on it, they'd have him cold—and the arms cache.

The sergeant heard the faint, metallic click as the trooper slipped off the safety catch of his weapon. The shadowy figure ahead paused, lifted his head as if scenting the air for danger, waited, then knelt beside the grave. Stone rasped on stone. He was shifting the lid. The sergeant heard the man grunt as he reached inside the sarcophagus. He straightened, a rifle held in both hands.

"*Now.*"

The beam from the trooper's torch slashed across the graveyard.

"Drop it. Get your hands behind . . ." But the figure slammed the rifle against his shoulder and swung to aim along the beam of the torch. A glance up the ditch reassured the sergeant that his man was not in any danger, hidden as he was behind the lip of the ditch.

"Hold your fi . . ."

A sound like ripping calico tore from the church doorway. Muzzle flashes rent the darkness. The Provo was slammed across the open grave, his weapon clattering as it hit the stone.

"Shit," Sergeant Buchan grunted, rising from his bramble patch and loping forward. "Keep that torch on him."

The Provo clutched his belly and whimpered.

Sergeant Buchan bent over the man and ripped a balaclava off his head. "Oh, Christ," the sergeant said, as he looked into eyes already milky with coming death. "It's only a kid."

"With a fucking ArmaLite," the corporal said from behind Buchan's shoulder. "And he fired first."

Sergeant Buchan lifted the ArmaLite. He sniffed the muzzle. Clean. The weapon had not been fired. He opened the breech. Empty. There was going to be hell to pay. Unless—

"Give me a round." He held his hand out to the corporal. The ArmaLite and the army-issue rifles were the same .223 calibre. He slipped the bullet into the open breech, closed it, pointed the weapon at the ground, and fired. "You're right, Corporal," Buchan said. "The bugger did fire first." He held the rifle for the corporal to smell the muzzle. "There's your evidence."

"What about your prints, Sarge? They'll be all over the bloody thing now?"

"Careless of me, wasn't it, to break procedure and pick up the weapon."

"Yes it was, Sarge."

Buchan heard the corporal snigger. He knew he could trust his men to back up his story. He knelt and felt under the angle of the boy's chin. No pulse. They'd get no HUMINT out of this one. He was dead. Dead as mutton. Pity about that.

CHAPTER 17

It was a pity that Erin hadn't made sure Fiach'd taken Tess. Should she have sent Sammy along with the lad? What the hell was keeping Fiach, anyway? Was the consignment heavier than he'd anticipated and was it taking more time to unload in the neolithic grave? But if he had gone there, surely she would have heard the tractor go by as he passed the farmyard. But Fiach *would* be all right. Of course he would.

Erin yawned. Her eyes were gritty, lids drooping, but there'd be no bed for her until Fiach was safely home. She stared through the window.

The greys of the false dawn had yielded to a pink glow that tinted the eastern hills like rouge on the face of a courtesan. The edge of the rising sun sliced into the sky above Slieveard. It was light enough to see that nobody was driving across the fields at the back of the farmhouse. He *must* be at the grave. Or had the bloody tractor broken down?

She heard the hall door open behind her and turned to see Cal, hair tousled, shirt undone at the neck, rubbing the sleep from his eyes.

"Is he not home yet?"

"No."

"He's taking a brave while."

"I'm worried, Cal."

"Och, he'll be grand." Cal turned to the range. "Tea on?"

"The kettle's boiled, but . . ."

"I'll make my own, have a cup, and if he's not home by the time I've drunk it, I'll take a wee run-race down to the tumulus. If he's not there, I'll head on over to Ballydornan."

"I'll come with . . ." Erin stiffened. "What's that?" She strained to hear. It sounded like an engine. She ran to the back door. It must be Fiach. It had to be. She threw open the upper door half and heard the noises of an engine—

more than one engine—coming down the farm lane from the main road. "Jesus, Mary, and Joseph."

The sounds of the vehicles were drowned by the roaring of a helicopter appearing over the crest of the hills. It swooped toward her and hovered overhead. She could see the British soldiers in the aircraft's open side doors, flak-jacketed, helmeted. They were pointing machine guns down at the house.

She spun to Cal. "Fiach's been lifted." Please, God, let that be all.

Cal moved toward her and put his arm round her shoulders. "We don't know that."

She watched a grey-painted Land Rover and a Saracen armoured car drive into the farmyard. Both halted. Tessie raced at them, barking as she did when any strangers came.

"Get in here, Tess." One of those trigger-happy bastards might shoot the dog.

Tessie obeyed, teeth bared, tail low, glancing over her shoulder at the intruders.

"Go to bed."

The collie slunk into her kennel. Erin could hear the dog's throaty growling.

Soldiers leapt from the open tailgate of the Saracen and took up positions surrounding the wall of the farmyard. Some knelt, covering the approaches to the farm with their self-loading rifles. Three faced her, SLRs at the high port.

A bottle-green-uniformed police inspector accompanied by a constable left the Land Rover. Both were flak-jacketed. Both were armed. The inspector who was carrying a beige envelope in one hand wore a holstered revolver. The constable carried a Sten gun.

She heard Cal whisper, "Don't tell them anything."

She peered inside the vehicle to where a man in plain clothes sat beside the uniformed driver. She knew that the ones in green were regular Criminal Investigation Department, CID, officers. The plainclothes man would be Special Branch, the antiterrorist wing of the police force. She could see part of his face. There was something wrong with his left eye. A triangle of brown in the green iris. She'd remember that.

The inspector and constable stopped outside the door. "Mr. O'Byrne?" the inspector asked.

"Yes."

"I'd like to have a word."

"What about?"

"Can we come inside?"

"Have you a warrant?" Cal moved to block the door.

"No."

"You can stay where you are then."

"We can do this back at the barracks, you know."

Erin knew under the Prevention of Terrorism Act the police could arrest anyone on suspicion—and refusing entry would be regarded as suspicious.

"You'd better come in," she said. "Just you. Leave that man outside. And tell him to point that gun somewhere else."

"Wait here, Constable."

"Sir."

The inspector looked down at his muddy boots.

"Use that." Erin pointed to a boot scraper beside the front step and waited while the policeman cleaned off most of the mud.

Why were they here? Was it just another routine raid? They knew about her and Eamon. Any associates, never mind girlfriends of known Provos, were kept under routine surveillance. But they'd never proved anything about the O'Byrnes. Never would.

Or was it about Fiach? She had to find out, right now.

"That'll do," she snapped at the inspector. "They're clean enough. Come in."

Cal wrenched the door open and stood aside. Erin preceded the inspector into the kitchen. Cal followed and stood beside her. She didn't offer the man a chair.

"What's all this about?" Cal asked.

"I'd prefer to speak to you alone, Mr. O'Byrne."

"I'm not leaving." Erin stared at the man until he looked away and said, "Suit yourself, Miss O'Byrne, but you may not want to hear this."

Jesus Christ Almighty. They must have lifted Fiach.

"Mr. O'Byrne, a man was shot this morning. Resisting arrest."

In spite of herself, Erin gasped.

The inspector swung to her.

"Are you worried about that, Miss O'Byrne?"

She steeled herself. "I am not. But I hate to hear of anyone getting shot. There's far too much of that round here."

"I agree." The policeman turned back to Cal. "We have reason to believe that the man in question was your brother, Fiach O'Byrne."

No. No. No. Erin screwed her eyes shut. She waited as the officer pulled a photograph from the envelope he carried. He showed it to Cal. "Can you identify this person?"

She couldn't bear to look. If it was Fiach, maybe—maybe—he was only wounded. She screwed her eyes more tightly and held her breath until she heard Cal say, "That's our Fiach." Cal's voice was leaden. "Is he . . . ?"

"I'm afraid so." The inspector shoved the photograph back into its envelope.

Erin opened her eyes. "You mean Fiach's dead?"

"I'm sorry, Miss O'Byrne."

Sorry? Sorry? You bastard. Standing there, mouthing platitudes, when it had to have been the Security Forces who'd murdered Fiach.

"What happened?" Her voice was level.

"I'm not at liberty . . ."

"What fucking well happened?" Something outside scared pigeons from the roof of the barn. She could hear their wings clattering as they took flight, rattling like a burst of automatic fire. She softened her voice. "Please. He's my wee brother. He's only sixteen. He plays hurley. He's not in the Provos." Erin knew she should have said, "He *was* my wee brother" but couldn't bear to. Not yet. She glanced at Cal. "None of us O'Byrnes is in the Provos."

The inspector coughed.

"Please." She leaned against Cal. "Och, please. What happened?"

"All that I can tell you is that one of our routine patrols"—

So they hadn't been lying in wait for him.

—"Saw a man acting suspiciously."

Jesus, why hadn't the young fool taken Tessie to scout for him? Why hadn't *she* made damn sure that he'd taken the dog? Why? Why? And yet, she tried to comfort herself, if the inspector was telling the truth, Tessie wouldn't have been much use. Granted, she could have sniffed out men lying concealed, but by the time she would have barked at a moving patrol, they would have had Fiach surrounded anyway.

"He fired at them. Our men returned fire."

Erin's eyes narrowed. "He couldn't have fired at them. The only gun Fiach ever used was a shotgun when he went wildfowling. Civilians aren't allowed to have rifles in Northern Ireland—you know that as well as I do. I don't believe he fired. You murdered him. Just because he's a Catholic."

"Miss O'Byrne, despite what Republican propaganda may say, the Security Forces do *not* indulge in reprisal killings. Not, may I say, like the Provos."

"Our Fiach wasn't a bloody Provo." That was technically true. Fiach had not made the declaration and been accepted as a volunteer. "He never fired that gun."

"I'm sorry, Miss O'Byrne. Ballistics have shown that the rifle he was carrying had been recently used."

"Liar."

The inspector pursed his lips, drew his shoulders together. "I can understand that you are upset, Miss O'Byrne . . ."

"Upset? Jesus Christ." She felt Cal's arms around her and looked up into his face, saw the frown and the almost imperceptible shake of his head that said, "Don't antagonize this man. They're bound to suspect us, too." Erin hung her head. "I'm sorry. I am upset." She hoped the bloody peeler couldn't see the fire that blazed in her eyes. Liar. Murderer. British bastard.

"I understand." The inspector turned to Cal. "Mr. O'Byrne?"

"Yes."

"Would you come to the mort . . . to Strabane Police Station to identify the body?"

She felt Cal's arms loosen. She clung to him and wailed, loudly, painfully, "Don't go, Cal. Don't leave me alone." She hoped that Cal knew she was playacting. She and her brother would need time to talk. Get their story straight before Cal went off to the bloody barracks.

His grip tightened. "Could it not wait for a wee while? Can you not see that she's all nerves? I'll need to stay with her for a bit."

"Well, I suppose . . ."

Erin keened, then begged. "Please don't leave me, Cal."

"Look," Cal said, "I'll come over this afternoon. All right?"

The inspector hesitated.

Erin thought about howling again but decided not to overplay her hand.

"All right. We'll expect you, and"—the inspector's voice hardened—"we may have a few more questions for you, Mr. O'Byrne."

"About what?" She heard the edge in her brother's voice.

"To try to clear up this regrettable business. We don't understand what your brother was doing out at night opening up a grave where we found arms and explosives."

Holy Mary. They'd found the shipment.

"Nor me," said Cal. "He may have heard something around. Went to have a look. Just curiosity, maybe? I dunno. I'll try to help." He put one hand on Erin's head. "But later."

"Fine. Then we'll be running along." The inspector turned to go. "I really am sorry, Miss O'Byrne."

"Bastard," she hissed at his departing back. She pulled away from her brother. "Shut the door." As Cal did she heard the engines starting, gears grinding as the two security vehicles pulled away. Overhead, the sound of helicopter rotors intensified and then faded into the distance.

"Look at that." She pointed to a set of muddy boot prints on the kitchen floor—just like the time, years ago, when the big RUC man had spat on the tiles. "The bloody British leave nothing but shite behind them."

"Do you reckon Fiach did try to shoot at them?" Cal asked.

"Not at all. You heard what I told the peeler. Fiach wouldn't have had a clue. One of their lot probably fired the ArmaLite after they'd shot him. They'd not want another enquiry, another 'regrettable civilian death' on their hands. Cal, they killed him. They murdered Fiach." She went to stand by the table. Her eyes were dry, her fists clenched. "Do you think it was a routine patrol, like your man said, or has someone grassed?"

"Who could have? Not you nor me. Sammy?" Cal snorted. "He'd be too bloody scared to. These things can just happen."

"'These *things*'? 'These *things*'? These bloody *things* are that Fiach's dead. Has that not sunk into that thick head of yours?" Erin glared at her brother. She saw his eyes shine, a tear run down his cheek. "I'm sorry. I shouldn't have said that. Come and sit down."

Cal walked slowly to the table and slumped into a chair.

Erin stood back as Cal rested his elbows on the tabletop and buried his head in his hands. She stroked his hair and watched her big brother's shoulders heave. "Och, Fiach," he whispered. "Why?"

Erin felt some of her anger subsiding, but not all. Not all. She'd give Cal time to pull himself together, and then the pair of them *had* to talk about what he'd tell the peelers this afternoon. Had to. But it could wait for a while. "Would you like that cup of tea?" she asked.

Cal lifted his head, shook it, sniffed, and dashed the back of his hand across his eyes. "How can you be so matter-of-fact? Are you not hurting, too?"

"Hurting? Of course I'm bloody well hurting. Fiach was my wee boy after Ma died. I reared him . . . but I reared him the way Da would have wanted. I brought Fiach up to love Ireland. The way the pair of us do." She felt a lump in her throat and whispered, "Fiach died for Ireland. Don't you forget that." She sat beside her big brother, put a hand on his arm, and said, "And he'd want *us* to keep on fighting."

"Not now, Erin. He's hardly cold yet."

"I know that, but never mind cold. The heat's going to be on us now. The Brits have always suspected the O'Byrnes . . ."

"They've never proved nothing."

"And they're not going to neither. You're going to see to that."

"How?"

Erin thought hard, then said, "They'll want to know two things. What was he doing out on the tractor last night, and why would he have gone to Bally-dornan."

"I dunno."

Jesus Christ. Cal O'Byrne, acting head of their Active Service Unit, sitting there like a lump of cold porridge, paralyzed with grief, unable to think straight. Erin knew she'd have to do the thinking for both of them. And she would have to do it fast. She couldn't give way to her own feelings. Not yet. She'd cry for Fiach all right. She'd cry rivers—later. "I have it," she said, "Fiach was sixteen."

"I know that."

"You need to be eighteen to get a driver's licence. But sixteen-year-olds can drive tractors over the fields. Tell them he'd gone off on it to a dance. That he must have been on his way home."

"What dance?"

"There's one every Friday night in the Parish Hall at Sion Mills. That's just a wee way past Ballydornan. He'd've had to pass the churchyard on his way back here."

"The peelers'll ask other folks who were at the dance if they saw him there."

Erin snorted. "And good luck to them. Tyrone Catholics wouldn't give the police the time of day, never mind information like that. Not about Fiach. They'd swear on a stack of Bibles he was at the dance. Even Father O'Driscoll would."

"I should have thought of that."

Yes, you should, she thought, before saying, "Now. What was he doing in the graveyard?"

"You just said that Tyrone folks don't talk to the police."

"You've lost me."

"They *don't* talk to the police . . . but they *do* talk to each other, even though we're supposed to keep things close to our chests . . . and the peelers know that bloody well. I'll tell them what I told the inspector—that Fiach must have heard something. He was only sixteen. Sixteen-year-olds are curious. He was just looking."

Erin let her hand fall onto Cal's shoulder. "Good idea. The only one who could tell them different would be Fiach . . . and he won't . . ." She choked on the next words. The enormity of what she was saying hit her like a rogue wave battering a rock. She shuddered but fought back her tears. No tears yet. Not yet. "Anyway," she said, "that should satisfy them for a while." She sat beside Cal. "And I'll tell you something else. I think the police and the army half-believe something like that already."

"Why?"

"That inspector was very quick off the mark to tell us that they've proof that Fiach fired first. I still don't believe he did, but they don't want an enquiry. You tell them what they want to hear, and they'll believe you."

"I think you're right."

"I'd better be because we've more work to do."

"What work?"

"Have you forgotten that Eamon and his mates are getting out tomorrow?"

"Of course not. Haven't I been breaking my back getting their hidey-hole ready?"

"And is it?"

"We'll need to put in some sleeping bags. You've to get the grub ready."

"I'll see to that." She hesitated. "And there's something else you and me and Sammy should be getting ready for when Eamon's out."

"What?"

She stood, took two paces from the table, spun, and paced back. "I want us to hit the Brits. I want them to die. For what they did to Fiach."

Cal stared up at her. "You're out of your mind, Erin. When the lads break out, the whole of Northern Ireland'll be buzzing like an overturned beehive. The Security Forces will be all over the bloody place."

"Yes," she said slowly, "they will, and the last thing they'll expect will be an attack right on their own doorstep, and I've a notion how to do it."

"Do what?"

Erin ignored her brother's question. "You take a good look round Strabane Police Barracks when you're in there today."

"You want us to go after . . . ?" She saw Cal's tear-reddened eyes widen.

"That's right," she said with ice in her voice. "And since the bastards lifted the Semtex we were counting on, we'll need Sammy to make the explosives."

Cal rose and grabbed both her arms. "You've taken the head-staggers. It's Fiach, isn't it? You've come unhinged because of him, haven't you?"

She lifted his hands from her upper arms and stepped away a pace. "Unhinged? I've never been more serious in my life." She paid no attention to the gormless expression on Cal's big ruddy face. "I told you we'd need Sammy, so you make sure you get him here tonight or tomorrow morning. I want to have a word with that wee man."

CHAPTER 18

"I want to have a wee word, Eamon." Davy caught up with his friend as he trudged round the exercise yard. "Have you a minute?"

"For you, Father Davy? All the time in the world."

"Not here." Davy led Eamon to a corner of the yard that he knew was out of earshot of the other men.

"Well?" Eamon raised one eyebrow and grinned through the gap in his front teeth.

"A while back you asked me if I wanted in."

"And you said no."

"I've changed my mind."

Eamon whistled. "Jesus, you've left it a bit late."

"I'm sorry."

"So am I. I'd've loved for you to be coming, but . . ."

"I understand." Davy turned but felt Eamon's hand on his sleeve.

"I never said it *can't* be done, but we're just about set to go." He lowered his voice until Davy had to strain to hear. "It's tomorrow."

Davy faced his friend. "And?"

"Look. I can ask Bic McFarlane. We all still owe you one for that wee thing you got for us . . ."

Davy glanced at his left hand, where a dirty strip of Elastoplast covered the healing wound.

"Bobby Storey's in charge of the . . . you know. I'll have to clear it with him, too."

"Would you?"

"Is the pope Catholic? Aye, certainly, but my ould da used to say, 'Never make a promise if you can't be sure of keeping it.' I'll not promise that I can do much."

"But you'll try?"

"Aye."

"I can ask no more."

"There's one wee thing." Eamon frowned. "It's only those who're going to fight on that's in on this. Are you ready to come back to us?"

Davy shook his head. "I'm done with the Cause, Eamon."

"Christ, you don't expect me to tell Bic that, do you?"

"You just said you all owe me."

"Aye, but . . ."

"You mind last week when you asked me for a wee favour and you said, 'Do it for me and Erin?' I'm asking you to do this for me . . . and Fiona."

"Fiona?" Eamon cocked his head to one side. "Fiona? Is she the one in the photo you got from Canada?"

"Aye. I never told you about her before."

"And if you got out you'd want to go to her?"

"She's in Vancouver."

"Have you been keeping in touch with her?"

Davy shook his head. "All I knew was that she'd gone to Canada, but wee Jimmy, my mate from the old days, met her in a restaurant. He sent me her snap . . . and her phone number."

"She must mean one hell of a lot to you."

"She does."

Then Eamon laughed.

"It's not funny, son."

"I'm sorry. I'm not laughing at you. I'm just thinking about what you'd need to get to Canada. It won't be easy."

"What'll I need?"

"You remember when you tried to talk me out of the thing? You told me that even if we got beyond the wall . . ."

Davy noticed a man's shadow approaching. "Wheest."

The uniformed figure stood close, rapping his truncheon against the palm of one hand. "What are you two up to? Planning to bust out? Ha. Ha." His laugh was forced and grating.

"Right enough, sir." Eamon gave the man a beaming smile. "The pair of us is off to the French Riviera for our holidays."

"Less of your lip, Maguire."

"Sorry, sir."

"Move along. You're meant to be getting your exercise, not standing round blethering like a pair of ould fishwives. Go on. Move it."

"Right, sir. Come on, Davy." Eamon started to walk to the track that encircled the yard, dusty, rutted from the countless paces taken by the countless feet during the immeasurable hours that the inmates had trudged round and round, like so many hamsters on treadmills. Davy fell into step beside him, glancing back to make sure that the screw wasn't following.

"That shite," said Eamon. "Thinks he's the fucking warden, so he does."

"Pay no heed to that one." Davy leaned his head closer to Eamon's. "What would I need?"

Eamon smiled with his eyes at a couple of inmates in the circuit behind Davy and Eamon. The men were loudly discussing Celtic's 2-0 loss to Linfield earlier in the day. Eamon's whisper was deadly serious. "Somewhere to hide, papers . . ."

"Papers?"

"Passport, driver's licence."

"Jesus. I hadn't thought of that."

"And you'll need money."

Davy silently walked on, head lowered. He *hadn't* thought about those things. Face it, he told himself, it was only a pipe dream anyway, but—his hand strayed to the inside of his jacket, where he'd tucked her picture. He could feel the gloss of the photographic paper, like the gloss of her hair. ". . . And the night is on her hair." His "Lagan Love."

"Fuck it." He glared at Eamon. "I'll think of something." He watched as Eamon's brow wrinkled.

"No . . ."

"What do you mean, no?"

"I've thought of something already."

Voices behind ranted on. ". . . That fucking goalie couldn't stop a bus at a bus stop . . ."

". . . And the centre forward? If goals was being handed out for free, he'd not know enough to stand in the queue."

Eamon dropped a slow wink. "I'll tell you later." He inclined his head in the direction of a man on the opposite side of the track. "You walk on, Davy. There's Bic McFarlane over there. I'll just nip over and tell him I need to have a word with him tonight. After the film show." Eamon started to move away, then turned back to Davy. "I'll bet you don't know what film they're showing us tonight?"

"I don't care."

"You should. It's *Escape from Alcatraz.*" Eamon grinned. "There's an omen for you."

"You're joking me." Davy had to laugh.

"No, I'm not," said Eamon. "*Escape from* fucking *Alcatraz.*" Eamon guffawed, then said, "Right. I'm off. I'll let you know what Bic says later, and I'll tell you what I have in mind for the other things."

"Thanks, Eamon."

"And don't forget, 'chucky air la,' ould hand."

Davy watched Eamon stride away. "Our day will come?" For the Provos? Perhaps it would, but Davy didn't think so. And anyway, he'd more on his plate to worry about now. Would Eamon be able to fix things? Would he be able to get to Canada? If he did, would she even want to talk to him?

He tramped on, watching the rise and fall of the shoes of the man ahead. Just like that Kipling poem Fiona had taught him, 'Boots—boots—boots—boots—movin' up and down again . . .' She'd been a great one for the reading, Fiona. And she'd taught him a lot.

At first, it had worried him that he was a man with no schooling since he was sixteen. She'd been far better learned than him. How could their wonderful thing last? One day she'd meet someone smarter than him.

Davy slowed his stride to avoid bumping into the two men ahead.

It had lasted because she was who she was.

He remembered the time she'd come home from school, her kids' exercise books under her arm, kissed him, and dumped the homework on the kitchen table.

"What's this?" she'd asked, picking up a book that he'd dropped on the table.

The picture was so vivid in his mind that Davy could read the gold print on the blue clothbound cover, *Treasure Island*. He could still see the outline of a man with a crutch, an eye patch. There was a parrot on his shoulder.

"A storybook." He felt himself blushing. It was one of hers that she used at school.

"It's a damn good story."

"Och, it's only for kiddies."

She sat on one of the kitchen chairs. "Sit down, Davy."

He sat, and she took one of his hands in hers. "It bothers you, doesn't it?"

"What?" He looked at her eyes, deep, full of softness.

"That you left school early."

"Aye, well . . ." He tried to look away, but her gaze held his. Her grip on his hand tightened.

"A lot of people did."

"You didn't."

"That's right. I got an education, and there's no reason *you* shouldn't."

That was one of the things he loved about her. She never beat about the bush.

"Me? Right enough. I can see myself up at Queen's University. 'Please, sir, I'd like for to study philosophy, so I would.'"

"It's, 'I'd like to study.' You don't need the 'for.'"

He tried to pull his hand away.

"No, Davy. Listen. Please."

"All right."

"You don't need to go to university. I can teach you. I'd like that. I really would."

He thought about what she'd said. She was a teacher. He wasn't stupid, just unlettered, and if he couldn't show his ignorance of books and things to Fiona, who could he trust?

"Maybe," he said.

She sat back, still holding his gaze. "Do you know what I say to a new class the first day I meet them?"

"No."

"I ask them, 'Are you here to learn?' 'Yes, miss.' 'Can you learn something you already know?' They always look a bit puzzled then, just the way you look puzzled now."

"Well, I . . ."

"So I tell them the answer. 'Of course you can't. So not knowing something is nothing to be ashamed of, if you want to learn the things you don't know.' And it's not, is it?"

He shook his head.

"Right then." She bent across the table and kissed him. "Will we start tonight?"

"I'd like that."

"So, tell me about Jim Hawkins."

"You mean"—he lifted the book—"in here?"

She nodded. "What kind of a boy was he? Why did he like Long John Silver at first?"

Davy started to answer her questions, hesitantly, but with more confidence as she gentled him along. They were still in deep discussion as dusk fell and the shadows filled the little kitchen. But it was only the fading of the daylight. In that evening, in himself, Davy felt a new dawn. He paid attention to every word she said.

He was not paying attention to where he was going. His foot tapped against the heel of the man in front.

The man stumbled. "Watch where you're going."

"Sorry." Davy shortened his stride. Watch where you're going? He knew bloody well where he was going. Out of here. To Canada. To Fiona. If Eamon could fix it.

The film ended. Davy walked back to his cell. Jesus, but it had been a great movie. That Clint Eastwood fellah was terrific. Funny they'd show it tonight of all nights. He wondered what Eamon thought about it.

Davy turned into cell 16. No Eamon. He'd said he'd have a word with the higher-ups after the movie. Davy started to pace. Come on, Eamon. Come on. The men who'd been selected were going to break out tomorrow, Eamon had said so, and Davy knew—he just knew—that he was going with them. What would happen after he'd no idea, but Eamon had said he'd worked out what to do. How he'd get things like a passport, Davy wasn't sure, but the Provos did have forgers. Maybe Eamon knew one. Maybe—

Davy felt someone come in. He turned. "Eamon?"

Eamon stood at the doorway, hands on the door frame.

"Well? What did he say?"

"What did who say?"

"Jesus Christ, Eamon. McFarlane."

"Bic?"

"*Eamon.*"

"Oh. Bic." Eamon moved into the cell, sat on his cot, and looked up at Davy. "Bic says . . . Bic says . . . you're in." He grinned widely, then started to laugh. "You're in, Father Davy. Tomorrow. After the two o'clock head count."

"Jesus, Eamon. You had me going there. I thought you were going to say no."

"It nearly was no. McGuinness didn't want you. Said you're too old and that bad leg of yours might hold us up."

"Bastard."

"Bic stood up for you. Bobby Storey wasn't so sure. He's worried about your leg, too." Eamon stood. "I told them I'd do a James Garner."

"What are you talking about?"

"You ever see that film *The Great Escape*? Your man Donald Pleasence went blind. James Garner took care of him after they got out. I'll be doing the same for you."

"If I remember right, Donald Pleasence got shot."

Eamon laughed. "Jesus, Davy, cheer up. We're going together. You stick with me, and we'll be in Tyrone before you know it." Eamon held out his hand.

"Holy Mother of God." Davy grabbed Eamon's hand and shook it, then Davy McCutcheon, that dour, taciturn man, laughed in his eight-by-eight cell and danced the steps of a jig, slipped his hand into his inside pocket, felt her photograph, and whispered, "I'm on my way, girl. I'm on my way. Tomorrow."

BOOK TWO

FUGUE

CHAPTER 19

Davy noticed a patch of rust on the frame of a .25 revolver that Eamon was deftly assembling from parts he had retrieved from under the tank lid of the toilet in their cell. A plastic bag of bullets lay on Eamon's cot. Davy hoped the lands and grooves of the rifling were clean. If there was dirt inside the barrel, the gun would burst when fired. Another good reason for Davy to hope that he'd never have to use the weapon.

"Gimme them bullets," Eamon growled.

Davy lifted the plastic bag and wondered why it was so slippery. He tipped six brass-cased, lead-tipped shells into his palm. They clinked in Davy's hand. How tiny they were, these .25 messengers of death. "Here y'are." He handed them to Eamon.

Davy remembered a line from a book of Kipling's poems Fiona had given him. "Two thousand pounds of education / Drops to a ten rupee *jezail* . . ." He'd had to ask her what a *jezail* was, and her vivid description of the long, brass-bound, Afghan musket had stayed with him. He'd had sympathy back then for the Pathan hill men who had been fighting the British occupation forces in their country just as he was in Ireland. She'd stood there in their kitchen, patiently explaining and smiling with her eyes as she talked. He loved her eyes—eyes that still shone from the photo he'd tucked into his inside jacket pocket along with Jimmy's letter.

He heard the "snick" as Eamon slid each bullet into the cylinder, the "click" as he closed the cylinder, the "whirr" as he spun it in the frame.

Eamon grinned. "Works like a charm. Now stick that there in your pocket."

Davy took the weapon. It was light in his hand.

"It's double-action. All you'll have to do is cock the hammer . . ."

"I've handled plenty of guns."

"We know that, Davy. That's why we're giving it to you. Shove it in your pocket."

Davy did and saw a bulge. "Jesus, Eamon, it's sticking out like the Cave Hill."

"Put on your cleaner's coat."

Davy took a brown nylon coat from a hook behind the cell door. He shrugged into it, and thank Christ for that, it did hide the bulge.

The revolver was cold against his thigh, but Davy knew it wasn't the chill of the metal that was giving him goose bumps. It was the prospect that in less than an hour he was going to have to stick the .25 in Mr. Smiley's face. He might have to shoot Smiley, not at long range like the Pathans had done, not in anonymity as he had killed people when others set the bombs he had made, but face-to-face with a man he knew and, in a funny way, liked.

Eamon said, "Remember the time I told you Erin was bringing me a wee present? That there's it in your pocket."

"How the hell did she get it in here?"

"Never you worry about that. I want you to tell me what you've to do with it."

Christ Almighty, that was why the plastic bag had been slippery. Erin must have hidden it the way he'd heard that other women smuggled things past the body searches and into the Kesh. She'd have had to put it right in herself. Just thinking of Erin hiding the gun brought back memories of Fiona lying naked on their bed. The gun pressing against his thigh and his balls, his certainty about where it had been, took his breath away. He felt the heat in his crotch, a stiffening . . .

"*Davy*, would you pay attention?"

Davy cursed himself for letting his mind wander, and was Eamon shouting because he was exasperated, or was he afraid about what was going to happen very soon? Davy looked into Eamon's eyes. They were cold and hard as a pair of agates.

"I'm sorry." Davy couldn't blame his friend for being frustrated with the wanderings of an older man's mind. Jesus, he wasn't that old, but at that moment he felt about ninety.

"'Sorry' be damned. Tell me what you've to do." Eamon's words were clipped.

"I was thinking about . . ."

"I don't give a shite *what* you were thinking about. *Tell me what you've to do.*"

Davy spoke like a child repeating a litany learned by rote. "Once head count's over, I've to go and clean the corridor. Get close to Mr. Smiley. Maybe chat with him."

"Right." Eamon could have been a priest at a Sunday school preaching to the boys about their catechism. "And you'll not be the only one doing that. There's others, and each one of them has an assigned guard. Five lads have guns like yours, and the rest have wood chisels."

"That's why you wanted the chisel?" Davy glanced at the still-red scar on the palm of his hand.

"You can kill a man with a chisel."

"I don't want *nobody* getting killed."

"What do you want more, McCutcheon . . . out of here, or a clear conscience?"

Eamon had called him, "McCutcheon." Not "Father Davy." At that moment, he wasn't Davy's friend; he was a Provo commandant issuing his orders, and expecting them to be obeyed.

Davy's old training took over. He came to attention and banished the last flickering images of young Erin O'Byrne pushing his gun into the damp folds of herself, of Fiona soft beneath his hands. It was laughable. Here he was minutes away from making the break and letting himself be distracted by those kinds of thoughts. Whether he liked it or not, whether he truly believed in it or not, once again he was a volunteer with the *Óglaigh na hÉirann*, a soldier, and he'd do well to remember that. "I'll do what needs done," he said, as much to himself as to Eamon. "I want to get out of here as much as you." More, he thought. Somehow—once he was safely away—somehow he would get to Canada, and to Fiona.

Eamon smiled, clapped Davy's shoulder. "I know you will, Father Davy."

The smile and touch comforted Davy, and he listened closely as Eamon explained the plan again, just as he'd done last night after lights-out. "You concentrate on Smiley. Some of the other lads'll be doing the same to every single floor guard and every single gate guard in H-7. There's twenty-six of them. One of the boys with a gun'll take over the central control room, the Communications Centre, so the screws can't lock themselves in there, slam all the electric gates, and activate the alarms."

"And the fellah in Communications'll be able to open the gates of H-7 from in there?"

"Right. The timing's going to be tricky, but as long as everybody does his part, it'll work," Eamon said. "And your part . . ."

"Is Smiley. I know." Davy hoped Mr. Smiley would cooperate. He was a decent enough man—for a screw. He was just doing his job, and he'd always been fair to Davy. He'd not want to have to hurt the man. There were enough deaths on Davy's conscience. "Don't you worry your head about me doin' what I have to," he said.

"I know that. D'you think I could have persuaded the Officer Command-ing to take you on if I didn't trust you?"

"Thanks, Eamon."

"Never mind thanks. What's the code word for it to start?" Eamon's smile had vanished.

"Bumper."

"Right. The screws are used to hearing 'Bumper' when someone needs the loan of a floor polisher."

"I've to stick the gun under Smiley's nose and get him into Sean Dono-van's cell. Sean and me'll get Smiley's uniform off. While I'm getting into it, Sean'll gag Smiley and tie him up."

"And then?"

"By then the lad in the Communications Centre should be in charge and have opened the H-7 gates so we can head for the main gate."

The main gate and then out of this fucking place. For good.

"You stay with me on the way out of H-7, Davy. You and a couple of oth-ers who'll be in guards' uniforms are going to have to bluff your way into the gate lodge and take over. We've to open the gates to the Tally Lodge from the control room in the gate lodge. The Tally's the only way out of the whole complex, and once we're in there, we'll get the main gates open and we're off." Eamon nodded toward Davy's pocket. "You'll maybe need to use the wee .25 there."

Davy shuddered and knew Eamon had noticed.

"Are you absolutely sure you can do it?" Eamon stared into Davy's eyes.

Davy squared his shoulders. "Aye. But only if I have to."

"Good," Eamon said softly. "Maybe you'll not. Maybe you'll just need to look as though you could, but, Davy? We *have* to get control and the timing *must* be absolutely spot on."

Would it be? Davy chewed on his moustache. Would it?

Eamon held out his hand, and Davy grasped it, warmed by Eamon's touch.

"Good luck to us all, Davy. I'm counting on you."

I'm counting on you. Maybe that "I'm" was what would keep him going. Davy didn't give a shite for the rest of the Provos, but Eamon was a friend, the only real friend Davy had, and getting him to his Erin was nearly as important to Davy as getting himself to Fiona.

He watched Eamon move to the shelf over the sink, take his dental plate, and slip it into his mouth. "I'd not want to forget them. I'll need to look my best when I see Erin." He grinned at Davy. "Don't you worry your head about nothing, oul' hand. We'll get you to your Fiona. That's a promise, so it is."

After three years in a cell together, Davy wondered if Eamon could read his thoughts. "Thanks, Eamon," he said as "Fiona, Fiona," ran in Davy's head like a chant. Like a prayer. Like, "Holy Mary, Mother of God, pray for us sinners, now and in the hour of our . . ." No, he told himself, strangling the familiar line. No. This wasn't going to be the hour of anyone's death and certainly not his own. He'd far too much to live for. Being on the outside and seeing the grin on a kiddie's face, standing in the drizzle in the terraces at a soccer game. He wondered, did they play soccer in Canada? Jimmy would know about that. It would be great to see wee Jim again, have a pint together. And Fiona. He was going to see Fiona.

Eamon used a finger to settle the plate. His next words were indistinct. "At least I'll not be using these falsies to chew my dinner in here tonight. Dinner's not getting here. We're going to hijack the caterer's lorry, and, Davy"—Eamon took his fingers from his mouth—"when we get that lorry, we'll be off like a bunch of lilties, over the hills and far away."

"Eamon?"

"What?"

"What'll we do if the lorry's late?"

"It won't be," Eamon snapped, then grinned. "But if it is, I don't know about the rest of the lads, Father Davy . . . you and me's going to run like the hammers of hell. There'll be a whole lot of very angry screws in the Kesh."

Davy grimaced. He'd not want to be one of the men who had volunteered to stay and keep the guards in H-7 quiet to give the escape party time to get away. Sooner or later, the guards would be released, and they'd be boiling for revenge.

Too fuckin' bad. The stay-behinds were all Provo volunteers. They were following their orders just like him. They knew what they were letting themselves in for. Did he?

Davy touched his coat where it covered the revolver's bulge. Was he going to have to use that wee gun? Could he honestly believe the whole bloody escape wouldn't turn into the same kind of fuckup as his attempt to blow up the bridge at Ravernet nine years ago?

Even if everything did go smoothly, how the hell was he going to get to Canada. And if he did, what gave him the right to believe Fiona would give him as much as the time of day? It had been all very well for him to have seen her photo and decide without thinking, after just one glimpse of her face, that he would take the chance he'd been offered. What was he going to say to her?

He'd had nine years to think only of her. She'd had the same nine years to meet other men. He couldn't bear to think about that. Davy tried to remember what Jimmy had said in his letter. She'd been having dinner with a doctor, but she wasn't married. At least that meant if she had been out with fellahs, they hadn't been important to her, except—except when Davy had asked her to marry him back in '74, she'd refused because—he could remember the words clearly—she "didn't believe in the bourgeois convention." Maybe she still didn't believe and was living with the doctor the way she'd lived in the wee house with Davy.

But he had to believe. He must believe as strongly as a Jesuit believed in his God that everything would be all right, even if he was deluding himself. He had to believe, and, he smiled at himself, if desperation was a great manufacturer of dreams and delusions, so what? He *was* desperate; as the whole of Northern Ireland, awash in its desperation for years, had nurtured its dreams and the delusion that it would be free.

"Cheer up, Davy. Everything's going to be fine."

Davy shrugged, glanced at Eamon, and gave a thumbs-up. There was too much water under the bridge, all of his bridges, to turn back now.

"Get a move on, for fuck's sake." Hughie Wilson pounded the steering wheel and peered through the open driver's window of his high metal-sided food lorry to see how far the tailback stretched. Not more than a hundred yards from the police checkpoint up ahead. Checkpoints were a fact of life in Ulster, but he didn't need one. Not today. This one had bloody well better not keep him too long.

It hadn't been his turn to drive, but his mate who shared the duty had phoned in sick. Hughie had been planning to go fishing. Still, the time-and-a-half money for driving on a Sunday would come in handy—bloody alimony—and if he could finish up reasonably early, he'd still have time to get down to Ballysallagh Reservoir near Bangor for the evening trout rise.

The traffic ahead inched forward. He followed. He heard the whicker of rotors and watched as a Wessex chopper hovered, veered, and headed toward Lisburn. It was probably going to Thiepval Barracks, headquarters of the British army's 39th Infantry Brigade. Helicopters were another fact of life in Ulster, like Saracen and Saladin armoured cars grumbling through Belfast: shootings, kneecappings, bombings, and still more bombings. Ireland, the "land of saints and scholars"? In a pig's arse it was, here in the charnel house of the Wee North.

The car behind him honked. Hughie engaged the gears, swearing as the worn clutch ground and the lorry jerked ahead until it was level with a grey,

armour-plated Hotspur Land Rover. He stopped and waited for a Royal Ulster Constabulary officer to approach, bulky in his flak jacket, Sten gun
menacing.

"How's about you?" Hughie said, resting his uniformed elbow on the edge
of the window.

"Sick of doing these fucking checkpoints, that's how I am." The constable
spat, but lowered the muzzle of his gun. "Prison dinners?"

"Aye."

"Off up the road?" The constable nodded to where the watchtowers of the
Maze seemed to gnaw at the skyline.

"I've the bad lads' grub in the back of this here. Feeding time at the fucking zoo. I don't want to be late."

"They'll hardly die of starvation for the want of a few minutes. Come on.
I've to look in the back."

"What the hell for? Do you reckon I'm a Provvie in a stolen uniform come
to bust my mates out?"

"I've my job to do."

"Yeah. Right." Hughie climbed down from his cab and walked to the back
of the lorry. He was not a patient man at the best of times. He could feel his
chances of getting a bit of peace and quiet on the water slipping away because this silly bugger had "his job to do." Could the peeler walk round the
truck any more deliberately? The shite probably trained racing snails for a
hobby. "Just get a move on, would you?" Hughie growled and rolled the
flexible back door up to let the constable climb inside.

Hughie paced. Short, angry steps. It would take another twenty minutes
to reach the barbed-wire fence that marked the perimeter of the prison
property, and then he'd to drive half a mile to the Tally Lodge, the main
and only entrance through the outer perimeter wall. He'd be held up there
and at two more security gates ahead of the final gate into H-7 itself before
he could deliver the 180 precooked Sunday dinners to the Fenian bastards.

The constable reappeared. "Away you go."

"About fucking time."

"Watch your lip."

"Right, Your Eminence." Hughie climbed back up into his cab, grunted
as the gears clashed, and drove off. "And fuck you, too," he muttered. It
wasn't his fault if checkpoint duty was boring. It wasn't his fault that wearing the green uniform was an open invitation to any Provo sniper with a
place to hide and an ArmaLite. The fucking peeler just, "had his job to do"?
Well, so did Hughie. Peelers weren't the only ones that the Provos might
target. They'd just murdered a couple of civilian contractors who'd been

doing construction work for the army. They could switch their attention to anyone involved with the Security Forces, and that included food-lorry drivers. He spat through the window.

He knew he was going to be late. He didn't give a shite if that meant the prisoners would have to wait for the meals that were congealing in their tinfoil containers behind him. Hughie wanted to finish the delivery, get back home and out of his fuckin' uniform, and escape to the peace of the reservoir nestled safely behind a wall of pine-scented trees, away to hell from Belfast. He could imagine the evening sun as it would glint from the dark waters, its reflection dappled by the rings made by trout that would rise as soon as the insects started to emerge and rest on the surface to dry their wings before trying to escape from the hungry fish. And the caddis-fly hatch wouldn't be held up by fuckin' checkpoints.

Inside block H-7, the prison officer, George Smiley, buttoned his dark-blue tunic and turned to the communications officer, John Adams. "I'm telling you, it's all right for you in here in the Communications Centre with all your switches and alarms, steel bars round the place, electric doors." He pointed past a solid steel door. "I've got to go out there, like Daniel in the bloody lions' den and do the head count. Some of them buggers scare the living bejesus out of me."

"Come on, George. You know as well as I do there's panic buttons all over the corridors. One sign of trouble . . ."

"I know. I know. One sign of trouble, I've to push the button and alarms go off like a bunch of banshees." George thought that John Adams looked just a shade too smug. No wonder. All *he* had to do was flick a red switch on his console and the whole block would be locked up tight, with sirens screaming and guards running to their emergency stations.

The communications officer would be in here behind as much armour plate as a Crusader tank while he, poor old George Smiley, would be locked in there with a bunch of men who were doing life for murder. Butchers who thought nothing of kneecapping some poor bastard and letting him writhe and scream before cutting his misery short with a head job. Not a day went by that he wished he'd not been laid off from the shipyards. If he hadn't, he'd not be in this bloody steel and concrete rat trap. Retirement couldn't come soon enough.

Bile burned his guts and rose in his throat. He stuck a hand in his pocket. Shite! He'd left his antacid tablets in his civvy pants in his locker.

He swallowed, tasting the sourness, regretting his carelessness and the remark he'd made about the banshee. He said, "I was just thinking I should never've said, 'banshee.' When do you hear her? Would you mind telling me that?"

"Before someone"—Adams made his voice quaver like Peter Cushing in an old B movie—"d-i-i-i-e-e-s-s." He rolled his eyes.

"Ha-fuckin'-ha," Smiley said flatly.

"I'm sorry."

Smiley saw how Adams peered at him before he said, a note of concern in his voice, "Are you starting to get the willies, George? After all your years on the job?"

Smiley crammed his peaked cap on. "I don't know. I've just this feeling . . ."

"Sure, we all get feelings sometimes. Cheer up. Don't let it get to you. Look on the bright side. It's not long to shift change, and we'll be out of here." Adams yawned and stretched back in his chair. "D'you fancy a jar on the way home?"

"A jar? Maybe." Smiley held himself more erectly. "You're right. I'm just being an ould worrywart." He wondered if he was reassuring Adams or himself, but said with a forced grin, "I would go for a pint or two, right enough." But whatever was bothering him would not go away. He muttered under his breath, "If the bad lads behave themselves." He was relieved to see that John Adams hadn't heard that remark.

He'd been too busy studying the clock above the control console. "A pint it is, George, but it's time you were on the go." He leaned forward and pushed a button. The steel door of the Communications Centre hissed open. "And quit your worrying. It's Sunday. The customers'll be quiet as mice. Just you think about us having a few and them buggers in here with their tongues hanging out for one."

George Smiley said nothing and walked to the door. A prisoner stood outside, broom and dustpan in his hands. Smiley recognized Gerard Kelly, whose job it was to clean the control room; Gerard Kelly, who in 1973 had been one of the team that had bombed the Old Bailey courthouse in London, killing one man and injuring 244. "Kelly," he said.

"Mr. Smiley." Kelly bobbed his head to Smiley and spoke to Officer Adams. "Permission to come inside and dust, sir?"

"Come on in, Gerard."

Smiley shrugged. Why should the guards be expected to work like a bunch of skivvies when there was plenty of free labour in the place? He let Kelly sidle past, walked away, then turned to look back along the corridor of the central bar of the H that housed admin offices and the Communications

Centre The Circle, as it was known, was the most secure part of the most escape-proof jail in all of Her Majesty's prisons.

He heard Gerard Kelly say to John Adams, "Boys-a-boys, Mr. Adams, but you've a brave power of electricals in here. What do they all do?" and Adams replying, "That's for me to know and you to wonder, Kelly. Just you clean the place like you always do. Now come by. I've to shut the door after Mr. Smiley."

As the door to the Communications Centre door began to hiss shut, George watched Kelly dust the console's countertop. The man's hands were huge. Powerful. Smiley frowned, but if John Adams was happy enough to be shut inside with a hard bastard like Kelly, that was Adams's concern, not his, but somehow it wasn't right. Not in the Circle. Shutting yourself in alone with a man like Kelly was about as sensible as locking yourself in a cage with a rabid pit bull. The burning in George's stomach nagged more fiercely, but he shrugged and headed for his area of responsibility—D wing.

CHAPTER 20

The hummingbird's wings flickered so rapidly that they appeared to be transparent. Fiona stood looking through her kitchen window at the tiny creature hovering beside her nectar feeder. She believed that fairies would have wings that looked like that but didn't think fairies in flight would make the same high-pitched, frenetic buzzing.

She belted her dressing gown more tightly. The kitchen was cool with no sun yet to drive away September's morning chill. She ignored McCusker's head butting against her bare shins and watched the bird in profile, its green back shining gently in the presunrise light. When it was full day, it would sparkle like a tiny, living emerald.

McCusker bit her shin. It was only a love bite, but she stooped to push the cat away. Her movement alarmed the bird. It gave a high-pitched "chip," spun to face her, and flared its tail feathers into a fan. She saw the orange of its chin and breast, a white collar between. That was very interesting. Only the male birds had such intensely orange chins and only a small percentage of them had green rather than orange backs. A flying metaphor for Northern Ireland, she thought. Orange and green together in one place.

The bird gave one more scolding "chip" and rocketed vertically. She watched the little dot soar over a tall pine that looked in the early light as if its ragged silhouette had been cut from dark cartridge paper by a child with blunt scissors.

She wished the creature Godspeed. The hummers that took up residence locally in the summer and came to her feeder and her hanging basket of fuchsia had all left three weeks ago, so he must be one of the last migratory birds from farther north stopping to feed before his long flight down to Mexico. She admired the stamina of the tiny bird and envied his ability to travel where he wished, when he wished. Not like someone she was trying to leave behind.

She'd not see the hummingbirds again until next spring, when the males returned to claim their territories, woo little females by sky dancing in great swooping parabolas, mate, and raise their families. She'd miss them in the dark winter months ahead.

She remembered Tim's remark about male rufous hummingbirds. "I reckon if there's any truth to this reincarnation business, I want to come back as one of those."

"Whatever for?"

Thinking of what he had said made her smile.

"Because all they do is drink nectar, make love, and spend the winters in Mexico."

She'd laughed and readily agreed when he'd asked, "How about you and me nipping down to Puerto Vallarta for a couple of weeks next year?"

"Only if you promise not to drink too much nectar."

"Well," he'd kissed her, "two out of three won't be bad."

McCusker's butting was more insistent. "All right," she said, "all right, cat, I'll get your breakfast." She filled his bowl, plugged in the coffeemaker, and poured cereal for herself.

She sat at the table. Tim would be back tonight. She hadn't realized how much she'd miss him until he had gone off to San Francisco last week. A trip with him to Mexico in the winter would be wonderful if it could be fitted in with the school holidays. Knowing Tim, he'd probably offer to pay. She'd certainly let him take care of the hotel room, but she mentally checked her last bank statement and was pleased that she should have enough to buy her own airline tickets.

She munched her flakes and listened to McCusker crunching his tuna-flavoured soy pellets. The light was stronger now, filtering in through the window, glinting off the chrome tap over the sink.

Outside, the pine's branches were more distinct, each one fletched with green needles. The leaves of the maple next door had looked grey, but now she could make out the yellows and ochres and the details of their dark veins, each leaf like a sheet of old parchment that someone had scrawled over with ancient ink. Beneath the tree, heaps of dead leaves lay on the lawn. Someone would have to rake them soon, and that someone was her, dammit.

She remembered neatly raked piles under the chestnut trees in Barnett's Park in Belfast. When she was a child, she and her brother Connor would take the bus from the treeless Falls Road to the Upper Malone Road and walk to the park. They'd go to collect shiny horse chestnuts and take them back home, drill holes in them, soak them in vinegar, and when the chestnuts were properly seasoned, they would tie each to a string so that after school they could play conkers.

She could feel the prickles on her palm of a chestnut's green outer shell, which had to be broken to release the nut inside; could smell the scent of the turf beneath as they ran laughing and squealing through crispy, crackling piles; could hear children's laughter as they rolled among the heaps, leaves in her dress, leaves in his hair.

The picture pleased her. She felt no sadness remembering her childhood. It was not the same as the way she often ached about her grown-up years, but she was ready to accept that Tim and Becky were both right; she should grieve and heal and put the misery of Belfast behind her. They were right, and she had resolved to take their advice, but she had no intention of letting the happy memories go.

She glanced at the leaves in the garden and thought about having to rake them. She could feel an ache in the small of her back at the prospect of the job. She understood now why the park keeper would run after them yelling, "Get away to hell out of that." They hadn't spent hours raking.

She and Connor would run down the hill to where the Lagan chuckled over the stones of the shallows below Shaw's Bridge. The river was clean up there, not the sluggish, scummy, debris-laden thing it became in the city under the gaunt gantries of the shipyards. Higher upstream it was hemmed in by the grey granite slabs of the Lagan embankment. The embankment where, thirteen years ago, she'd met Davy.

She heard the "ting" of the coffeemaker, rose, poured herself a cup, and went back to sit at the table. Davy. Davy. What had she just promised herself? No more unhappy memories? Well, now was as good a time as any to start working on that.

She remembered reading *Shōgun*, by James Clavell. He'd written part of the book in West Vancouver and, according to him, the Japanese could make compartments in their minds, put things they didn't want to think about in mental boxes and shut the lids. Perhaps that had been her mistake, trying to lock Davy in a box from which, try as she might to keep him in, he kept breaking out. Well, now he could stay out. Already she could understand that in the rest of her life she dealt with problems by facing them squarely, so she'd face Davy now.

McCusker mewed and distracted her. She looked over to where the cat had finished eating and was licking his paw. He yawned, mouth as wide as if he had dislocated his lower jaw, whiskers pointing stiffly forward.

"McCusker?"

The cat looked back at her, wandered over, tail erect, and jumped into her lap. She fondled the animal's head and felt the warmth of him, the comfort of his deep purring rumbling through to her thighs.

She smiled. Tim wanted to come back as a hummingbird? She'd prefer to be a cat. "I would, you know, McCusker," she said. "All you lot want is a peaceful home, regular meals, and someone to love you."

McCusker thrust his head against her hand.

A peaceful home, meals, love? She had them already.

Her apartment and Lord Carnarvon Elementary were her homes in Vancouver, and Canada was a damn sight more secure than Northern Ireland. She'd been right to get out of that country, even if she still did miss much about the place, always would miss it, and it didn't hurt to admit that to herself. She *didn't* regret leaving the violence behind.

She'd found the peace she craved in Vancouver except, she smiled wryly, for a small personal war that she must wage at Carnarvon Elementary. That little bugger Dimitris Papodopolous's resolve to behave himself had lasted for one short week, and he was playing his pins again. She'd have to meet with the parents next week, but even if she was going to let Davy out of his box, Dimitris was definitely going into one until then. He was going in right now.

McCusker jumped to the floor, and she smoothed her dressing gown over her belly, feeling the bulge. She wanted a home and regular meals? If that bit of extra tummy was any indication, she'd been eating too regularly and too much.

And as for having someone to love her, Tim would be back tonight.

As she savoured the thought of him, the room became brighter. She looked outside to where the shadow of the house had shortened. That meant the sun had cleared the North Shore Mountains and the morning was moving on.

She finished her coffee. Becky would be here soon. They'd planned to visit the aquarium in the morning and to have lunch in the Teahouse in Stanley Park. After lunch, they'd go shopping in Granville Market for the makings of the special dinner she wanted to prepare for Tim. And let the crunchy granola lot harp on as much as they liked about the evils of red meat. The steak she was planning to buy and cook for him wouldn't hurt Tim's blood pressure one bit.

After the Market, she'd ask Becky to drive to a little boutique on Granville Street. If the dress she'd seen in the window fitted her, she'd buy it and wear it tonight.

Never mind the steak, that dress would send Tim's blood pressure through the ceiling—she grinned wickedly—and she was looking forward to that—very much.

McCusker tried to jump back into her lap, but she pushed him away and rose. "Right," she said to the cat and to herself, "time to start getting ready."

CHAPTER 21

"Are you ready, Davy?" Eamon asked, pacing across cell 16, H-block 7.

"As I'll ever be." Davy fidgeted as he sat on his cot. The door was open, and through it he could see Mr. Smiley ambling past each cell, counting heads and marking his clipboard. Ordinarily, Davy would barely have paid attention, but today the routine seemed to be taking forever. Smiley was a bit of an old fussbudget, but did he have to lick his bloody pencil before every tick on the list? Get on with it for God's sake. Davy stood and limped past Eamon to the door of the cell.

Davy heard the click-clack on the concrete floor of Mr. Smiley's boots receding as he trudged to the gate, the man's voice calling the numbers to the gate guard. Davy tugged at his coat, and through the material pushed Erin's little revolver more deeply into his pants' pocket.

He heard Mr. Smiley shout, "Who's on cleaning today?"

Eamon whispered, "Remember, 'Bumper.'"

Davy went into the corridor. "Me, sir."

"Come on then, Davy. Get your stuff. The sooner it's started, the sooner it's over."

"Chucky air la," Eamon said, and nodded in obvious agreement with the guard's last remark.

It was all right for Eamon to grin. Davy felt as wound up as an over-stretched elastic band. He wished to hell that it *was* over. "Right, Mr. Smiley." Davy took one last look into the cell. Nine years in here. Nine years, three months, two weeks, and four days to be precise. This would be the last time he ever saw the place, and he was surprised that somewhere in him was a tinge of homesickness.

Mr. Smiley yelled, "Are we doing this today, Davy, or do you have other plans?"

Other plans? If Smiley only knew. "Sorry, sir." Davy swallowed, tugged on the hem of his coat, and limped along the corridor.

It was dark inside the broom closet, but he'd done this so often he could find his gear blindfolded. He took out a wheeled, galvanized bucket with rollers on its rim, put some detergent into the bucket and a capful of Dettol. The disinfectant's pungent smell would hang in the corridor for hours, mingling with the rank odour of infrequently washed bodies. God, but it would be good to breathe fresh air again. He grabbed a floor mop. "I'll need to get water, Mr. Smiley."

"We've not moved the tap since the last time you done this."

Davy filled the bucket, stuck the mop into the soapy water, and, pushing the bucket ahead of him, began to swab the corridor floor. The grey concrete, raddled with cracks like the strands of a spider's web, disappeared under the bubbles.

Mr. Smiley wandered over and stood beside Davy. Good. He'd been told to get close to the guard, keep him chatting.

"Did you get to the match yesterday, Mr. Smiley?"

"I did so. I took my boys. I thought you said Celtic was going to win." Smiley grinned. "They lost. Three to none."

"Och," Davy said, "you can't win them all."

"The way they're playing this year, they'll not win any. They'll not even beat Bangor next Saturday, and Bangor's been playing like a crowd from the home for the disabled." Mr. Smiley leaned against the corridor wall, one booted foot on the concrete.

Davy noticed that the lace of one of the guard's boots hadn't been threaded through all of the eyeholes.

"Linfield's at Glentoran next week, and me and my boys've tickets for that one, too, so we have."

Davy wondered if Mr. Smiley would ever get to that game. He'd be up to his neck in the post-breakout enquiry. He might even lose his job. That would be a shame, but when it came to Mr. Smiley's job or Davy's interests, there'd be no contest. What if the stupid bugger did try to put up a fight? Davy could feel the weight of the gun in his pocket. Could he use it?

George Smiley had a couple of boys. He was always going on about them. He'd chunter on about the mischief they'd got themselves into mitching apples, how the older one played inside-right for his grammar school's soccer eleven, how much they liked their da to take them to a game, kick a ball about with them.

Those boys would need their da, just like the two wee girls in Fiona's elementary class had needed theirs. But their father, a ticket collector at the Queen's Quay Station in Belfast, had been ripped apart by one of Davy's bombs, and it was no use telling himself that he'd only built it, that he hadn't set it. Fiona hadn't made any distinction. As far as she'd been concerned, Davy might as well have lit the fuse himself. She'd been right. She'd said, "I can't go on living with you, Davy. Not unless you leave the Provos," her voice as cold as that damp February night in 1974.

He shivered and rubbed his thigh, feeling the cold of the weapon in his pocket. Davy could see that Mr. Smiley was looking at him questioningly. Let him. Davy didn't want to come back to the present. He wanted to re-member how he'd talked her out of leaving, made gentle love to her on their old sofa. He didn't want to remember how, ever since that night, there'd been a new hardness in her, and how the thoughts of those wee fatherless girls had torn at something inside him, too. It was then he knew he'd started to question the rightness of the Cause, a question to which he'd found an answer shortly after being shut in this fucking place.

The Nationalists *were* right, always had been right in what they wanted. He'd never stopped believing that, but killing innocent people would never free Ireland. Not if a half a million died. Shooting people's relatives and friends wasn't going to make them more tolerant of the other side. You couldn't bomb folks into loving their neighbours. If that was what fighting for the Cause meant, he wanted no more part of it. He'd accepted responsi-bility for what he and his bombs had done, knew he could never wash away the stains. Him and Pontius Pilate. They made a right pair.

Davy glanced up and saw that Mr. Smiley had been keeping pace and was now directly beside him. "You're quiet the day, Davy."

"Och, there's days you don't feel much like talking." To anybody. Here he was, having spent the last nine years keeping his distance from the hard bastards like Brendan McGuinness, right up to his ears working for the Provos again and about to pull a gun on this man. What the hell was there to talk about?

"I hear you," Smiley said, softly. "The days can be hard on a man in here."

I don't want your shitty sympathy, Davy thought. He'd promised Eamon that whatever had to be done would be, but if things did get sweaty, he won-dered if in the heat of the moment his resolve might crumble, but if it had to be him or Smiley—Davy shook his head. He wanted no more deaths to his account, even if there were enough in his past to ensure that when he ap-peared before the judgment seat—if there was one, if there was an all-forgiving God, which he doubted—he, Davy McCutcheon, was already bound straight for hell. He'd not have to make the trip to purgatory. He was there already, because Eamon was relying on him again, just like the time he'd wanted a chisel.

Christ Almighty, Davy told himself, running the soapy mop through the wringers on the bucket, cursing as dirty water splattered his pants' legs, why had keeping his word always been so important to him? Still was important? Well, why shouldn't a killer have integrity? Davy had no difficulty thinking of himself as a killer, not since the ticket collector, not since the little girl he'd stood and watched being cremated in a car blown up by the bomb he'd made and planted with his own hands. He could hear her screams yet. The night he'd killed her and the rest of her family, he'd recognized that he wasn't a soldier, as much as he'd wanted to believe that he was. He'd been forced to accept that building bombs for others to use did not absolve him of responsibility for their use.

He stopped mopping and reminded himself his job was to talk to Mr. Smiley, not rehash all that was done and over.

What the hell was he meant to chat about? Would somebody for Christ's sake hurry up and give the code word? Say something, he told himself. Anything. "Do you know, Mr. Smiley," he muttered, "some days it's a good idea to take my oul' da's advice."

"About what?"

Davy mopped his way closer to the guard. "About some days it's better to keep your trap shut and let people think you're a bit thick . . ."

". . . Than open it and remove any doubt." Smiley laughed. "That one has whiskers."

And Davy would have a new crop of whiskers if the buggers running this thing didn't get a move on. In spite of himself, his hand dropped to his thigh and fondled the gun.

Smiley bent over, staring at where Davy's hand rested. The guard's voice was solicitous. "The ould leg playing up, Davy?"

"Aye. It gets a bit stiff now and again."

"I could ask the doctor for to have a look."

More bloody sympathy. Dammit, he liked Smiley. Davy forced a laugh. "Sure that fellah doesn't know his arse from his elbow."

"Do you want to take a wee breather?"

"That's very decent of you, sir"—Smiley was a decent man—"but I'll keep going." Holy Mother of God, he was going to pull a gun on this man, and all his kindness made the prospect more repulsive with every second. Killing strangers had been bad enough. Putting a gaping hole in the man he'd talked to nearly every day for nine years—Davy slammed the mop into the bucket, hauled it out, and swabbed on along the corridor.

He looked up to see Sean Donovan leaning against his cell doorway, arms folded on his chest. Donovan was a big man. He exercised in the prison gymnasium. Veins like small hosepipes ran down the fronts of his overdeveloped biceps. One arm bore a tattoo, an Irish harp and underneath the motto, "*Éireann go Brách.*" The other was adorned with a naked-breasted woman and the motto, "Erin go braless." He winked at Davy, who wanted to be as close to this cell as possible.

"If you don't mind, Mr. Smiley, I'll take that wee rest now."

"Go ahead. Do you want me to get Donovan there to finish up for you?"

It was the last thing Davy wanted. "Och, no, sir. I'll be all right in a minute."

"Fair enough."

Davy leaned against the cell wall, hand inside his trousers' pocket seeming to massage his leg as his fingers curled round the gun's butt. He heard voices yelling from somewhere.

"Jesus," said Mr. Smiley, "would you listen to that bloody racket? Just because some bugger wants a floor polisher."

Davy heard the shout by one man taken up and repeated by others. "Bumper," they were yelling. "Bumper."

CHAPTER 22

Judging by the way the brambles bent under the weight of fruit, there was going to be a bumper crop this year. Erin plucked two of the riper blackberries and popped them in her mouth. They were tart on her tongue and suited her bitter mood. She took little pleasure from the lack of breeze down here in the hollow behind the back gate of the farmyard or from the sun warming the back of her neck.

That sun would speed the berries' ripening, and in a week they'd be ready for plucking and she should make blackberry jam. The pounds of sugar she'd need were ready in a kitchen cupboard, but she had other plans for it now. Sammy would need them to mix with fertilizer to make the explosive ammonal.

If she had been going to make jam, she'd have boiled the fruit and the sugar in the same big pot that her grandmother, and her mother, and Erin had all used. Cal and Fiach loved her jams.

Fiach was dead, dead as the empty place inside where he had lived, laughing, and singing, and sometimes crying, growing to his young manhood. He'd only been sixteen. Sixteen with all his life ahead of him, until that life had been snuffed out by the British.

And for what, she asked, for what? For Ireland, that's what. Da would have been proud of his youngest son. Poor Fiach. Was it only a couple of weeks ago that he'd taken his shotgun here and Tessie with him to chase the rabbits out of these same brambles?

The bushes grew on a low mound in the hollow, and to the unsuspecting eye it was but one of several ordinary, low, bracken, and bramble-covered hillocks. What lay under the mound made it special.

She breathed in the scent of hay lying mown and ready for baling in the next field. From above she heard the sweet, sharp song of a skylark.

She looked up into the bowl of the sky and watched the bird climbing, higher, higher. Perhaps she had been wrong to dismiss the Christianity that had been drilled into her by the nuns at the parochial school. Perhaps there was a heaven and Fiach's soul had soared to it faster than the skylark was rising above her.

Erin wanted to believe in it, but in her heart she could not. She could remember the words, learned by rote so long ago, *Requiescat in pace*, Fiach; may he rest in peace. But her faith? Gone. Long gone. Fiach was dead and she had to face that squarely—and get on with preparing things for the living, for Eamon and the men he'd bring with him, and for the attack that would be her vengeance for her lost brother.

And it wasn't simply revenge she wanted. Hitting the Security Forces when they least expected it would drive home the message that as long as the Irish demanded their freedom, the British and the Loyalists could never win the fight to keep the Six Counties. She knew the raid she was planning wouldn't be the one to finish the war, but how much longer could the English go on suffering casualties, spending millions of pounds? One day they would be gone forever, and on that day, Fiach's sacrifice would have meaning, and in that meaning she would find a measure of peace.

She turned in a full circle, one last survey to make sure no one was watching her before she dropped to all fours and crawled along an animal track beneath the briars. She swore as a thorn pricked her hand. She heard something rustling through the undergrowth and listened intently. The noise wasn't loud enough to be caused by a large animal like a fox or a badger. It would be a rabbit scampering away, fearful for its life, white scut held high. That was the way she wanted the British to scuttle off, but she wanted them to go with their tails between their legs.

The light was dim under the thick bushes, the sunlight dappling the brown earth. Ahead, she could make out the low entrance to the old neolithic passage grave.

Erin squeezed through the narrow opening. The dark closed round her, and she waved her hand in front of her face until she felt a string dangling from the roof. One quick tug and a lightbulb glowed. Now she could see yellow cables coming out of the earth from where Cal and Fiach had run the electrical supply along a shallow trench from the barn.

The passage, the feature that gave the construction its modern name, was lined and roofed with stone slabs. The cables were fixed with staples to one wall. There was four feet of clearance between the earth floor and the roof. Erin felt the chill in the air, smelled the musty odour of damp and spiders. Despite the chill, her hands began to sweat.

She'd been terrified of insects as a child, felt hemmed in by enclosed spaces, but she stifled her fear and hurried forward on all fours, the light from the tunnel partly blocked by her body. Strands of gossamer stuck to her face. She ripped them away with one hand. She hated being in the tunnel, but she was doing this for Eamon. She offered a spoken prayer to the Madonna in whom she could not believe, "Mother of God, keep him safe and bring him back to me. Please."

She left the confined tunnel and stood upright in the grave's main chamber. A second string hung to the left of the entrance. When she pulled it, two sixty-watt bulbs illuminated the room. The light made her claustrophobia easier to bear.

She stood in a vaulted chamber from which two side rooms extended, and a smaller passage directly ahead made the whole structure cruciform.

She'd read about these monuments to a long-gone culture and knew that the grave had been built between 2,500 and 2,000 years BC, long before Saint Patrick had banished the Druids and brought Christianity to the Celts. Why, she wondered, had neolithic grave builders chosen to lay out their creation in the shape of a cross?

This passage grave was one of nearly three hundred similar structures scattered throughout Ireland. The largest was at Newgrange in County Meath. That one was much bigger, forty-five feet high, with a diameter of eighty-five yards. There were almost one thousand megalithic court graves and Bronze Age wedge graves. Court graves, so-called because of their oval or semi-oval courts from which galleries ran, had been built in the fourth millennium. There was one here, in Tyrone, at Ballywholan. Wedge graves were simpler, and triangular. The most famous was The Hag's Bed in Labbacallee, County Cork. Every one of those ancient burial chambers had been built on high ground, all except this one.

It was in a hollow, which was why it had never been found by the archaeologists who scoured the country for evidence of their forebears.

She looked all around and could still marvel, as she had done the first time Da had taken her here, at the work that had gone into building the place. The walls of the main and side chambers were huge vertically placed stones. In the gaps between these standing rocks, smaller pieces had been packed to provide stability. The vaulted roof was corbeled, the flat overhead stones neatly supported by the walls. Here and there, deep grooves in the walls glistened in the bulbs' light, and the packed-earth floor beneath the runnels was darker than the rest. Moss grew on the stones beside the ever-dribbling water, water that had dripped for centuries.

What had driven the builders to such efforts on behalf of their dead? The

Celts must have been making elaborate preparations for an afterlife. They must have believed in it devoutly.

Why, she wondered, couldn't she? Cal had pulled himself together after his initial fit of despondency, and she knew the solace he was taking from his trust in the hereafter.

She couldn't. She'd learned too much science in her years at university. She needed proof of the existence of a supreme being. There was no proof. Only belief, and belief required an act of faith. Her faith was in Ireland; in the land with its little fields and turf bogs, mallard in the bulrushes, snipe in the marshy hollows, brown trout in the streams, salmon in the rivers; in the golden sunsets over the Sperrins and the driving rains that swept down from those mountains; in her people, contentious brawlers who could sing and recite poetry, always on for a bit of *craic,* loyal, laughing in fun, ferocious in anger; in people who, like her, wanted nothing more than to rule their own kingdom, free from outside interference, people who wanted it so much they would die for it—as Fiach had died.

She had no faith, none at all, in a God who, if He had created man in His own image, must have a homicidal streak a mile wide, a God who could stand aside when Fiach was murdered. How could anyone believe that a caring deity, a caring, omnipotent God, could have let the human race slaughter each other for millennia—in His name, for Christ's sake?

The priests and the nuns had neatly dodged that question with their doctrine of free will. Man could choose, they said. Man was responsible for his choices.

Erin thought God, if He existed, was the ultimate lawyer who had written the Ten Commandments, then added the free will escape clause to the contract with humanity to absolve Himself from any responsibility for His creation.

So be it. She was responsible for her own life, and she would make those choices, exercise her free will gladly.

She'd broken the sixth commandment not once but several times, and— she shivered in the chill of the grave—she'd come here to make sure that everything was ready for Eamon and his friends so that they could rest and be safe—before they killed again.

Erin walked through the central chamber, moving to one side to skirt a folding, green-felt-topped card table and four wooden chairs that would make places for four men to eat the simple meals that she had prepared and put in an ice chest that sat beside one wall. It had made sense to put the food and its accompanying gallons of bottled water on the wall opposite the one where a ceramic convection heater and a one-ring electric element were plugged into an overhead light socket. Beside the heater, a box full of plastic plates and steel cutlery kept company with an electric kettle. Half a dozen car batteries that could be used in an emergency if the electrical power failed were lined up beside the kettle.

She paused to look into the side chambers. Two camp beds were crammed into each. All of the beds had sleeping bags and pillows. The accommodations, she thought, weren't exactly like the rooms of Belfast's Grand Central Hotel, but the men who would come here should be warm, dry, and fed.

She stepped into the room that was the extension of the passage beyond the arms of the cross. It held a chemical latrine close to one stone wall. Propped against the other wall were ten ArmaLite rifles, two old Lee-Enfield bolt-action .303s, and boxes of .223 and .303 ammunition, stacked beside the last weapon.

Erin ran her hand along the smooth metal of one gun. She sniffed at her fingers and rubbed her thumb across the pads of four fingers. The smell of gun oil and the smoothness of the film reassured her that the oil had done its work of protecting the weapons from corroding in the dampness of their hiding place.

Some of these automatic rifles had been in here for years, only being brought out for some specific mission like her first with Eamon and subsequent ones with Eamon or Cal and—dammit—there should have been six more and a load of Semtex. There would have been if Fiach hadn't—no more tears, she told herself. There was work to be done, and the arms in here would be more than enough for what she had in mind. As long as Sammy could manufacture the necessary explosives. He'd be arriving at the farm anytime now. And so—the thought pleased her—so would Eamon and, as he had told her, three other men. And they'd be safe in here.

Now she saw the old grave not as an archaeological curiosity but through Da's eyes as a sanctuary that the Security Forces would not suspect existed. A place where Eamon and the men he'd be bringing with him would be safe—and close. A place from which, with care, they could move under cover of darkness to the farmhouse—or farther afield.

Eamon had warned her that he and his mates would only stay in Tyrone until the hue and cry died down, and then they would have to get right out of the country. They'd be more men to add to the swollen ranks of the "Wild Geese," those who had been forced into exile from Ireland forever.

She understood why Eamon must leave Ireland, but she hated knowing that, although they'd be reunited after those three long years, he'd be taken from her again so soon. He'd said nothing more about his plans, but she could guess where his final destination would be. There were hosts of Irish sympathizers on the eastern seaboard of America in New York, Boston, Baltimore, Philadelphia. Hundreds of thousands of dollars annually flowed from them through NORAID, the Northern Ireland Aid Committee, into the Provisionals' coffers. The Irish-Americans who ran NORAID would keep Eamon safe in the United States and shelter him there, where she knew he'd be able to continue the struggle, raising funds, buying arms, succouring fugitives like himself.

He'd naturally expect her to go with him. Would she? She didn't know. Could she leave Ireland? Leave the farm? She swallowed and screwed her eyes shut. Could she abandon Fiach, cold and lonely in the soil of this land without her here to put flowers on his grave, with only Cal left behind to murmur, "*Ave Maria, gratia plena, Dominus tecum . . . ?*"

She hefted an ArmaLite, careless of the oil, and raised it to her shoulder, taking pleasure from how steadily her left arm supported the weight of the weapon. If she had to go with Eamon, it wouldn't be for a while, and at least they'd be here long enough to see firsthand that Fiach was not the only one in the ground. There was work to be done with this rifle, and soon.

She put the weapon back with its companions. Eamon had made his plans, and she would find out about them later tonight when he got here—and, by God, he'd find out about hers.

Eamon would fall in with her short-term wishes. He wouldn't have heard yet about Fiach's murder, but Erin had no doubt—none whatsoever—that, no matter what Cal might think about keeping their heads down, Eamon would want to mount an attack. He'd see the rightness of her decision about the timing of the raid. The struggle would only be won by hitting the Brits hard, again and again, until they were gone and Ireland belonged to the Irish, as it had when the Celts had built this grave to house their dead, never suspecting that one day it would hide the living.

She glanced at her watch. Two forty-five. If all had gone as planned, the escape would be well under way. She wished she knew what was happening but accepted that, for a few more hours, she'd have to bide patiently and wait as Irish women had always waited for their rebel men.

She sat on one of the wooden chairs, feeling the slats of the seat cold on her backside, and took one long last look around.

Cal and Fiach had done everything in here she'd asked of them. Fiach had done more. He'd given everything.

The Christ, the nuns had taught her, preached that, "Greater love hath no man than to lay down his life for a friend." But Jesus hadn't known about the men and women who'd laid down their lives for Ireland: Brian Boruma, Maeve, Macha, Silken Thomas, Pádraic Pearse, Eamon Ceannt, Bobby Sands, and, over the centuries, ordinary, nameless people in their hundreds. The list went on and on. Their love of their country had known no bounds.

Theirs wasn't a love like hers for Eamon, passionate, sensual. It wasn't a love like hers for Cal, comfortable, familiar, everyday. It wasn't a love like hers for poor Fiach—she felt the tears come and let them flow—a mother's love, all-forgiving, protective. Their love for Ireland was deep in the bone, as was her own. And perhaps she *was* going to have to leave the land she loved.

Erin rubbed the tears away with the heel of her hand. She glanced at the tabletop and the small vase of cut flowers that she'd brought with her earlier today. They were, she knew, of no practical value. They were just her way of saying "welcome home." And when they buried Fiach, she'd bring him flowers, too.

Erin stood and straightened her shoulders. She couldn't think of anything more that would need her attention. She crossed to the passage and turned off the lights. The central chamber was pitch dark with only a dim glow leaking in from the bulbs in the passage. She moved rapidly along the stifling tunnel and stuck her head out into daylight, pausing only to turn off the bulbs.

She passed through the bramble patch and gingerly parted the outermost stems. There was no sign of anybody who might be watching. Erin slipped out, stood, and dusted off her jeans. She looked across the farmyard and saw a solitary figure cycling down the farm road. That would be Sammy, and she and Cal had a lot to discuss with him before—and the thought warmed her—before Eamon arrived tonight under cover of darkness. By now, if all was going well, the men should be outside the walls of the Kesh.

She turned back to the briar patch and plucked a few more berries. She'd been right. This year there was going to be a bumper crop.

CHAPTER 23

"Bumper. Bumper." The words slammed along the corridors of H-7 and ricocheted off concrete walls.

Davy stifled his earlier misgivings, dropped his mop, and tugged at the gun in his pocket.

"Bu-u-u-u-mper."

The gun's butt slipped in his sweaty hand.

"*Bumper.*"

He tightened his grip, pulled harder, and—it snagged in the pocket's lining.

"What are you up to, Davy?" Mr. Smiley asked. "Can I give you a wee hand?"

Davy gritted his teeth and hauled, feeling the material rip as the revolver tore free. He raised his gun hand, and as he cocked the hammer he saw the cylinder revolve and carry a live cartridge into the breech. A .25 bullet is so small, he thought, and so very lethal.

"Freeze, Mr. Smiley," Davy said, aiming at the guard's middle jacket button. He noticed that the buttonhole was frayed and wondered why that should seem so important. He looked up and saw Smiley's eyes widen, his mouth fall open. Davy saw a tiny drop of mucus on a bristle in Smiley's left nostril. "Freeze . . ."

"For God's sake, Davy, don't be daft . . ."

"Don't make me shoot you." Davy's finger curled on the trigger. His hand shook. "Just do as you're bid. I don't want . . ."

Smiley grunted and moved to grab Davy, but he took a step back and shifted the gun's foresight to cover the spot between Smiley's eyes, where the guard's dark eyebrows nearly met. Davy was relieved to see that his hand was now steady.

"Fuck you, McCutcheon." Smiley pulled his truncheon from its holster. "You haven't the guts to use that thing."

Davy held his aim. A fraction more pressure on the trigger and the man's brains, his whole life, would be splattered on the wall behind him. Davy tried to squeeze, but his finger refused to obey, and in that second Smiley raised the ebony baton, grunted, and smashed it down on Davy's arm. The blow brought tears to his eyes. His grip on the revolver loosened.

"You Fenian bastard . . ." Smiley grabbed the gun with one hand and raised his truncheon with the other, aiming a slash at Davy's face.

"Oh shite . . ." Davy tucked his head into his shoulder and threw up his left arm to protect himself.

The blow never landed. Sean Donovan nailed Smiley in the small of his back. The gun spun away, but Davy caught it like a hurley player fielding a high ball. He ignored the throbbing in his arm and held the gun on Smiley.

"Mr. Smiley? Freeze . . . or I'll blow your fucking head off," and Davy knew that although seconds ago, when things *had* got sweaty, he'd baulked, now he meant every word, and he could tell that Smiley knew, too.

"You'll be sorry for this, McCutcheon," he muttered, but could not meet Davy's eyes. Davy could see the fight had gone out of the man and sensed that Smiley's life and his pension meant more to him than being a hero.

Davy hadn't realized that he had been holding his breath; he blew it out, relieved that he wasn't going to have to use the gun, but he thanked Christ that Sean Donovan had been as quick as he had.

"Get you into that there cell." Donovan pushed the man. "Keep him covered, Davy."

Davy pointed the revolver at Mr. Smiley, seeing the pleading in the man's eyes. Was he thinking about his soccer-crazy sons and worrying about how they'd manage without him? Davy uncurled his finger and laid it along the trigger guard. "Just do as you're bid, Mr. Smiley, and you'll be taking your lads to the match next Saturday," Davy said quietly. "You've my word on that." Somehow Smiley managed the tiniest smile. It pleased Davy. "Go you into that cell," Davy said, and motioned with the gun barrel.

Davy stood aside as Mr. Smiley lowered his head and followed Sean Donovan into the dark little room. Donovan snapped, "Get that uniform off."

Smiley hesitated, and Davy flinched as Donovan fetched the man a clout across the side of his head. "Get it off."

The guard glanced at Davy.

Davy let the gun's barrel point down to the concrete floor. "Come on, Mr. Smiley."

"Get a move on," Donovan hissed as Smiley slowly unbuttoned his tunic. "You're slower than a hoor in a strip club. Get off your pants, too." Donovan began stripping the bedclothes from his cot. By the time he had finished, the officer stood in his underwear, shivering, although the air in the cell felt warm to Davy. He watched as Donovan trussed the man like a Christmas turkey.

Donovan stooped and threw Davy the dark-blue serge pants. "Go through his pants, Davy. Get the bugger's keys."

The material felt rough against Davy's hands. He found a bunch of keys, held them up, and heard Donovan snarl, "Key to the lobby?"

Smiley shook his head.

"Shoot him in the kneecap, Davy."

Davy brought the revolver's muzzle up. He glanced into Smiley's eyes and saw the terror. Come on, Mr. Smiley, Davy thought, just remember your pension. "You'll never kick a ball again with your boys if I do kneecap you." Davy knew, only too well, what a permanently buggered leg meant.

"Don't shoot," Mr. Smiley begged.

"Shoot him, Davy."

So it *was* going to come to that. The poor, sorry bastard. Davy tightened his finger knowing that this time . . .

"No," Smiley yelled, "No. Don't. Please. I'll tell you. I'll tell."

"Which one is it, you stupid git?" Davy waved the key ring under the guard's nose, hearing the keys jangle, inwardly cursing the man for having nearly got himself shot.

Smiley pointed at one large key. His finger shook.

"That one?"

"Uh-huh." Smiley's head drooped.

Davy grabbed the key to separate it from the rest. He felt himself start to sweat. Christ, that had been a near thing.

He stood and watched as Sean Donovan used his pillowcase to blindfold and gag the guard. Sean offered Davy his hand. "You done good, Davy," and Davy knew it for the lie it was, but took the hand, amazed at its dryness. Donovan hadn't worried his head one bit about what they'd nearly had to do.

"Now, Davy, put on his uniform and stick the gun in the pocket. As soon as you're dressed, we'll take him down to the holding area."

Davy changed and pocketed the .25.

He could hear Mr. Smiley snuffling behind his gag.

Sean said, "Good. Some of the lads that have volunteered to stay behind can mind Smiley. We've to get a move on and get ourselves down to the lobby."

"Right." Davy turned to follow Sean, who was hustling Smiley along the corridor, hesitated, then turned back to pull Jimmy's letter and Fiona's picture from his old jacket and shove them into the inside pocket of his guards' tunic.

Inside the Communications Centre, Officer John Adams heard the ruckus outside the Circle. He got to his feet, walked to the bulletproof window, and peered through. "Holy Mother of Jesus . . ." He turned and tried to race to the master switch. Gerard Kelly, now holding one of the other smuggled .25s, blocked his way.

"Out of my way, Kelly." He lunged at the prisoner.

Kelly shot Officer Adams in the head, then bent over the console to activate the switches to open the gates in H-7. He thought it had been decent of the Brits to put a label on each one. He stepped over the crumpled form on the floor, slipped out of the control room, and pushed the button on the outside wall to close the steel door behind him.

The other screws inside H-7 heard the shot. They went quietly after that and were bundled into cells, stripped of their uniforms, and trussed up as Mr. Smiley had been. Some of the inmates selected to escape changed into discarded uniforms. Terrified officers were forced at gun- or chisel point to hand over their car keys, give the registration numbers of their vehicles, and the numbers of their places in the guards' car park—outside the perimeter wall.

The screws were handed over to the rear guard—Provo prisoners who had been ordered to stay behind to prevent the hapless warders from raising the alarm until the men going out would be well away.

As far as the staff of the Kesh outside H-7 knew, the only noise from that part of the complex had been the calls of "Bumper." Inside the H-block, the plan was going like clockwork, its timing down to the minute.

Outside the complex, Hughie Wilson stopped the lorry at the first of two security barriers he had to pass before he could finally deliver the meals to the lodge at H-7. He recognized the guard who was strolling from the gate lodge toward the barriers. Hughie pounded his fist on the outside of the driver's door and stuck his head through the window. "Can you get on with it, for fuck's sake, Archie?"

Archie grinned up at the driver. "Take your hurry in your hand, Hughie. Show me your pass."

"Here."

"Fair enough." Archie grinned. "Going fishing when you're finished?" He swung the first barrier up.

"If I ever get done here." Hughie forced the lorry to crawl after Archie. "I seen a clatter of cars in the car park outside, lads walking to the Tally Lodge. Some of the new shift coming on duty must be right keen buggers to arrive early for work."

"Not half as keen as the off-duty lads, me included, to get out." Archie strained to raise the second barrier. "This fucking thing's always sticking. Give me a hand, will you?"

Hughie jumped from his cab to lend his weight. "Aw, shite," he said, as he saw two guards leave the Tally Lodge behind him and walk toward the barrier. "I'm going to hit shift change. With them going off still here and them coming on arriving, there'll be more guards in here than fucking prisoners. I'm never going to get out of the place."

The barrier started to swing up.

"Go ahead," Archie yelled. "If you get in before they start giving the change-over reports, you'll get your papers signed and get away yet."

"Right." Hughie climbed back in and banged the truck into gear. He checked the time, two forty. He might make it, but now he was well and truly late.

In the holding area, the stay-behind volunteers kept watch over the screws. One Provo read from a prewritten document entitled "To All Prison Staff Who Have Been Arrested by Republican POWs on Sun 25th Sept.":

> What has taken place here today was a carefully planned exercise to cause the release of a substantial number of POWs. The block is now under our control. If anyone has been assaulted or injured, it has been as a result of his refusal to cooperate with us. It is not our intention to settle old scores, ill treat or degrade any of you, regardless of your past. Though should anyone try to underestimate us or wish to try to challenge our position, he or they will be severely dealt with.

As the man continued reading, a young, fair-haired guard whose left eye was bruised and swollen shut began to cry. Two of his captors laughed at him. One of them waved a chisel under the youngster's nose. "Just you be a good wee lad now. We don't want anything to fuck up the escape. You just listen to what your man with the paper has to say."

The man reading the document continued:

> Should any member of the prison administration ill treat, victimize,
> or commit any acts of perjury against Republican POWs in any follow-
> up enquiries, judicial or otherwise, they will forfeit their lives . . .

The sobbing of the young guard with the black eye drowned the rest of
the text.

Davy was breathing heavily when he and Sean Donovan reached the lobby.
Eamon; Bic McFarlane, Provo Officer Commanding; Bobby Storey, the
man in charge of the escape; and Brendan McGuinness, once Officer Commanding the 1st Battalion, Belfast Brigade, and Davy's immediate superior,
were all waiting. Despite his avowal to distance himself from the Provos,
Davy almost saluted.

Eamon grinned at Davy and held up one thumb.

"You got Smiley?" McFarlane asked.

"Aye," said Davy, "and I have his keys." He held them up. "I needed a bit
of help from Sean." A bit? If it hadn't been for Sean . . .

"Screwed things up again, McCutcheon?" Brendan McGuinness sneered.

Davy ignored him. This wasn't the time to settle old scores. The important thing was to get out before the screws in the rest of the Kesh twigged to
what was going on.

McFarlane said, "I heard a shot. Was that you, Davy?"

"No."

"I just hope to God the screws in the other H-blocks or in the guard
towers didn't hear it." McFarlane turned to Bobby Storey. "What do you
reckon?"

"If they had heard it, there'd be sirens going off, screws by the dozen running over to H-7, but the place is quiet. I think we're near home and dry."

Nearly home, Davy thought. He heard McFarlane bark, "Gimme the
keys."

Davy handed over the key ring. "That one there."

"Right. You lot wait here." McFarlane picked up his cleaning gear and
used the key to let himself out.

Davy waited and looked at the four men round him. They wore civilian
clothes, not prisoners' uniforms—the outward sign that the wearer was a
common criminal, not a political prisoner. The British government had
agreed to let IRA prisoners wear civilian clothes after the hunger strikes.

And a bloody good thing, too. It would make it harder for the Security Forces to track down the escapees.

Except—he looked at his dark blue tunic, blue shirt, and blue trousers—except for him and those other men who would be dressed like guards.

"Dead on," said Eamon. "If the buggers suspected anything, they'd never've let Bic in there."

Davy watched McFarlane disappear into the guard's office and reappear, heading back to the lobby, the Gate Lodge officer in front. The pair halted, and Davy could see the revolver pressed into the small of the screw's back.

"Right," said McFarlane, "the rest of you, into the Gate Lodge. I'll get this shite out of his uniform. Gerard Kelly'll be along in a minute. He's going to need it."

"What've we to do?" Davy asked.

"The ones without uniforms, hide. You sit up like the regular guard. The bugger driving our food lorry'll think you're a new man. He'll not suspect nothing. He has to check in at the H-7 Gate Lodge, and when he does, Brendan and Sean'll see to him." He turned to Bobby Storey. "Should that fucking lorry not be here by now?"

"It'll be here," Storey said. "The six of us had better get into the Gate Lodge before it is. Come on."

Davy followed the other five out of the lobby and into the Gate Lodge. They crouched on the floor. He sat in the guard's chair. Dear God, but he'd sweated like a pig in that tussle with Mr. Smiley and the rush down to the lobby. The arse of his trousers stuck to his backside, and he could feel large damp patches under his armpits. His smell was sour, and the other men stank, too, but at the moment that was the least of their worries. He ignored the stink and peered out through the window of the office. Half a mile away, the perimeter wall loomed, its gun towers manned by British soldiers.

Davy studied the Tally Lodge in the wall, a deep arch, its outer gate hidden from the view of anyone not looking directly inside. There was a gate lodge built into the thick wall beneath the arch, and the screws in there controlled the only gate in the Kesh leading to the outside world. There were other gates to pass, he knew, but the Tally was the last barrier between him and freedom. He saw two uniformed guards pass through and stroll across the open space between the perimeter wall and the H-blocks.

Where were they going? He'd no idea, but it didn't matter anyway, even if they came to H-7, because, according to Eamon, the plan called for another thirty-two of the most senior Provo prisoners to assemble here once their advance party had secured the food lorry. There'd be enough prisoners in the lodge by then to handle a couple of extra screws in H-7.

He just wished the lorry would get there. Davy and the rest would pile into it and be taken to the Tally Lodge. Once its gates had been opened, they'd all be driven away.

One hundred more prisoners would try to break out on foot from here. They'd have to cross open space under the eyes of the soldiers in the watchtowers. Groups of men in their ordinary clothes would be escorted by other inmates in stolen guards' uniforms. The organizers believed the troops would assume that these were more routine work parties. Davy hoped to God for the sake of those men that the leaders of the breakout were right.

He stared at the nearest watchtower. Two khaki-clad soldiers were on duty. One was leaning on the low parapet, watching the two guards cross the open space. As far as Davy could tell, the other was reading something. Their machine gun was unattended, its barrel in its perforated external air-cooling jacket pointing lazily at the sky above.

Those soldiers were bored. They must have pulled sentry duty a hundred times. Men like that would be slow to respond, and Davy hoped that when things started to happen they wouldn't suspect anything out of the ordinary until it was too late. He knew that even if they did, it would be to the advantage of the senior men in the lorry. It should be on its way, as it would be every Sunday. The sentries would ignore it and concentrate on what was happening *inside* the perimeter wall. That's what Eamon had said.

Davy felt disappointed by how cynically the senior officers planned to use one hundred of their own volunteers as live decoys, but inwardly blessed Eamon for arranging that he, Davy, would be in the lorry, not left to walk across the compound with the others. He comforted himself with the thought that if the walkers did manage to get outside the wall, there was a fighting chance that, as they'd been instructed, they would be able to steal cars from the guards' car park. That's why they'd forced the captured guards to give up their car keys and their parking spot and plate numbers. If they did succeed, they were to scatter through the length and breadth of Northern Ireland.

Davy heard movement behind him and turned to see Gerard Kelly leading a large group of men into the room.

"'Bout ye, Gerard," Bic McFarlane said. "No problems?"

Kelly scowled. "I'd to shoot your man Adams."

"You kill him?"

"Dunno. He was lying on the floor with blood coming out of his head when I locked him in the Control Centre."

Davy closed his eyes and pictured George Smiley with a shattered head.

It was a good thing it hadn't come to that. A goose walked over Davy's grave.

"Tough," said Bic, his voice matter-of-fact. "But you're OK?"

"Aye, certainly."

"Dead on. Now get that there uniform on you."

Kelly began to change.

Davy watched as Brendan McGuinness moved to the trussed Gate Lodge officer and kicked him in the ribs while saying, "You hear that, you shite? Adams got his. One peep out of you and you'll get it, too."

The guard grunted through his gag. His eyes widened.

McGuinness pulled back his boot.

Davy slipped off his chair and stepped between them. "Leave the man be."

"Who the fuck are you to be giving me orders, McCutcheon?"

Davy stood rock solid and stared McGuinness down.

A sound like a gunshot ripped through the room. Davy swung from McGuinness and stared through the window. A high-sided lorry was approaching. Behind it was a cloud of blue smoke. The bloody thing must have backfired.

"The lorry's coming," he said, his voice level, not betraying the racing of his heart. Davy wiped his palms on the legs of Mr. Smiley's blue serge pants.

Eamon called from where he was hiding, "See, Davy. I told you it would be grand."

Davy hoped to God Eamon was right. He looked out and saw that the two screws were strolling toward another block, H-6, as if they hadn't a care in the world. He wished he felt as carefree as they seemed.

CHAPTER 24

All the cares of the world weighed on Sammy McCandless's narrow shoulders. Not even watching Erin coming toward him could cheer him up. Fretting about being found out every waking hour, aye, and hours when he should have been asleep, was bad enough, but since Cal popped into Sammy's cottage this morning his nerves had been as stretched tight as the strings of an overtuned fiddle. Cal said Erin wanted to see Sammy this afternoon. Did she really want to talk to him about going after the Brits?

He propped his bicycle against the wall of the O'Byrnes' farmhouse, picked his nose, bent, and snatched off his bicycle clips. What the hell did she want to see him for on a Sunday? Was it about Fiach?

Cal had told Sammy about the lad's death. The news, terrible enough, had given Sammy one hell of a shock that had settled down to a nagging headache. It had hit him hard because he'd had no notion of what had happened on Saturday. Sammy had been keeping to himself lately. He'd stayed home all day trying to fix a leak in his roof. He hadn't even bothered going down to the pub on Saturday night. At least if he'd had a few, he'd have earned the ache above his eyes, but he'd not seen nobody since Friday, not until Cal had come and, without as much as a "How are you, Sam?" had said, as calmly as if he was remarking that it was nice that the sun was shining, "The Brits got the Ballydornan arms dump in the wee hours yesterday morning."

"They what?" Sammy bloody near shit himself. "You're having me on," he said, hoping to Christ that Cal was making some kind of stupid joke.

"No, I'm not." His eyes held no humour.

It was no joke. "Did Fiach get . . . ?"

"They got him." Sammy noticed the quaver in Cal's voice.

"They lifted him?" Pray God, for Fiach's sake, that was all. But if there had been an ambush, Cal or Erin would know someone had grassed. That fucking Spud had promised that he'd not go after the weapons if it might compromise Sammy.

"He's dead." Cal's voice was as dark and cold as a trout pool in the Strule.

"What? Dead? Mother of God." No. He couldn't be. At that moment Sammy reckoned *he* was dead.

"Och, Holy Jesus. I'm . . . I'm very sorry, so I am." For Fiach or for himself? And if he was sorry for himself, was it because now he must carry the guilt of Fiach's death along with his shame for having been turned, or was it because he was terrified that he might have been rumbled? "What happened, Cal?"

"The peelers were round at our place yesterday. They said . . . they said it was just a routine patrol."

Did Cal not believe them?

"They said they saw someone acting suspicious. He fired at them. They fired back. The suspect got himself killed." Cal's voice was as acid as unripe rhubarb.

Sammy stared at Cal's face. One of his eyelids twitched. His eyes were red-rimmed. "Do *you* think that's what happened?" Did Cal not believe the police account? If he didn't, and, more importantly, if Erin didn't . . . Sammy could see himself, head shattered, his Judas money in his hand. He shuddered. He had to know what the O'Byrnes were thinking. Sammy glanced at the open doorway. Try to sound natural, he told himself, and said, "It must've been something like that. Nobody knew about the arms but us and none of us would have squealed."

He knew it was risky even sowing those seeds in Cal's mind. Neither Cal nor Erin would have touted so that only left him as a suspect. It was chancy half-raising the subject, but he *had* to know what Cal believed. Sammy measured the distance to the door. One hint that Cal suspected, and he'd be out through there like a whippet. He hadn't a clue where he'd go, but he'd make a run for it. His headache pounded. He moved closer to the door and stared at Cal.

"I think . . ." Cal curled his lip. "I think for once maybe the buggers are telling the truth. Erin's not so sure."

"What's she not sure about?" Sammy started to sidle sideways. He could see the sunlight on the grass outside, desperately wanted to feel its warmth. He felt cold as a witch's tit in the cottage.

"Maybe she's right," Cal said, and his brows furrowed.

"Right about what?" Sammy felt a reef knot tighten in his guts. What was Erin suggesting? That it hadn't been a routine patrol?

"She says Fiach didn't even know how to fire an ArmaLite. He couldn't have shot at them, but they told us his gun had been fired . . . and they can prove that."

What had Fiach's shooting a gun to do with anything?

Cal clasped one big fist in the palm of his other hand. He squeezed and Sammy could hear the knuckles crack. He looked again at the doorway. He'd make a run for it, would he? Cal would be after him like a foxhound on a hot scent, and those big hands would snap Sammy's thin neck as if it were rotten kindling.

"Erin thinks it was a patrol all right . . ." Had Sammy heard right? "But that they shot Fiach and then rigged it to look like he'd fired the gun."

Sammy muttered, "Oh."

Cal let his hands fall loosely. "To tell you the truth, Sam, it doesn't matter to me one way or the other. Fiach's dead, and that's an end to it."

"I'd not put it past the peelers to do a thing like that." A half hitch was untied in the knot in Sammy's stomach. "They're a bunch of shites," Sammy said, thanking Christ that the peelers had had a good story ready. He'd no doubt that Fiach had been set up, but maybe Spud *had* kept his word about protecting Sammy after all. Fiach was dead. He couldn't tell anybody he'd been ambushed, and the story about a routine patrol was feasible—just. "Fucking shites."

"That's not the half of what Erin called them."

"Is Erin all right? She must be mortified, so she must." Sammy's concern for her now that it seemed the immediate threat to him was gone overrode his constant fear for himself. "It'll be hard on her, hard on you, losing a wee brother like that." Sammy tried to put his hand on Cal's arm, but Cal moved away. "I really am very, very sorry for your grief, so I am," Sammy said.

"I'll be all right. So'll Erin."

Sammy held his tongue, glad that they'd got away from the question of someone's having grassed. He watched as Cal straightened his shoulders and said levelly, "She says no amount of crying'll bring Fiach back. What we need to do for the wee lad is hit the buggers back. I agree with her."

"What?" Was she planning some kind of reprisal?

"She wants you round at the farm this afternoon about three."

"I'll be there." Bloody right he would. Maybe, just maybe, the details of whatever she was planning would be the big one that could persuade Spud to get Sammy out. After his Christ-awful scare in the last few minutes, the sooner that happened, the better.

"Good." Cal turned to the door. "I'll be running on."

Sammy walked Cal out into the yard. The sun was still shining, and Sammy let its radiance warm him. "I'm going to Mass, Cal. I'll say a clatter of Hail Marys for Fiach's soul." Sammy's voice faltered as he thought, and *I'll say a wheen more for Sammy McCandless,* as he crossed himself and murmured, "May he rest in peace."

"Thanks, Sam. I'd appreciate that." Cal walked to his van. "See you at three."

"You will."

And here he was, right on time, just like Cal had told him to be.

As Sammy waited for Erin to cross the barnyard, Tessie came out of her kennel, gave him a quick look, clearly recognized him, and without barking ran on to greet Erin. He watched her bend to pat the dog, the sun shining on her hair. She straightened, and Sammy wondered how she managed to smile at him, but that smile, as it always did, melted something in him.

"Erin," he said as she drew level, "I'm awful sorry for your troubles, so I am. Cal told me." He snatched off his cloth cap and bowed his head and, as he did, saw the dark shadow between the swell of the tops of her breasts in the *V* of the open neck of her blouse.

"Thanks, Sammy, but what's done's done."

"Aye. Well . . ." *Oh, Christ, with the light behind her, he could see her nipples, dark through the thin material.* He tried not to stare as she said, "Come on in. Cal's waiting for us."

Cap in hand, he followed her into the warm, familiar kitchen, seeing the old, dark ceiling beams, the copper saucepans on the Welsh dresser, smelling the peat burning comfortably in the range, half-expecting to find Fiach sitting at the table with Cal. Sammy would have forfeited his hopes of the life everlasting to be able to turn the clock back to before he'd been lifted after the pub brawl, before he'd met the only man he could trust now, that bloody Spud.

Cal rose. "Come in, Sam. Have a pew."

Sammy parked himself at the table opposite Cal and dropped his duncher on the table. He watched Erin walk over to stand behind her brother. Although light came through the windows, none shone through her blouse, and he was glad of that. He knew that he was going to have to keep his wits about him.

He'd been satisfied this morning that Cal didn't suspect anything, but Sammy knew how smart Erin was, and if she was worried about how the patrol had stumbled on Fiach, or that there had been a setup job, one slip by him, and she'd be on it like a Jack Russell on a rat. "Are you really all right, Erin?" he asked.

"Yes." Her eyes narrowed. "Quit going on about it."

"Look, I just want to say I am dreadful sorry, so I am." He put one hand on top of his cap. "I don't think I should be here at a time like this, but Cal told me to come." If there wasn't the chance he'd find out something useful, he knew he'd rather not be there at all. "I think it should be just the family, like."

"You're as close to being family as makes no odds," Erin said more softly than her earlier curt. "Quit going on."

Sammy wondered whether she meant that about his being like family or whether she just saying it to keep him onside. "Och, come on," he said, pleased despite his misgivings.

He heard the edge back in her voice when she said, "We've a couple of things to talk to you about."

"Oh?" What things? Cal had said she wanted to mount an attack, but still . . . Sammy sat upright, listening, waiting for the questions he was dreading.

Erin folded her arms across her chest. "You remember the other day I said something about Eamon?"

"Aye."

"He broke out of the Kesh about half an hour ago."

"He what?"

"Him and maybe a hundred other of the lads."

Sammy's jaw dropped. If only he'd known about the break and had been able to tip off Spud, Sammy would be in England today. They hadn't told him because they didn't trust him completely. Still, Erin hadn't mentioned anything about what had happened to Fiach. She was getting straight to the point of why she'd asked him to come over. The second half hitch of the knot in his stomach slackened.

"Him and a few of the others are heading here."

"Holy shite!" Sammy pushed his chair back. "He's coming here? That's stupid, so it is. It's the first place they'll look for him, and if they find him, anyone aiding and abetting a fugitive'll be going back to the Kesh with him."

He saw Erin smile. "He'll be safe as houses."

And Sammy knew, he just knew, where she'd hide Eamon and his friends. "In the old grave?"

"That's right."

Did her willingness to tell him mean that he really wasn't under suspicion, or was it simply because she knew that he was in on that secret and could work things out for himself whether she told him or not?

"That's great, Erin," he said, and saw her smile widen, and he knew what she was thinking. Her and Eamon and—och, Christ. The images made his groin ache, but the pictures he saw inside hurt more. Sammy inhaled and waited as she walked round the table to stand behind him. He could smell the woman of her. He felt her hands on his shoulders and turned to look up into her face, her smile.

"There's more to tell you, Sammy."

"What?" He felt himself grow tense. She must have noticed. Her hands kneaded his shoulder muscles.

"When Eamon and the boys get here, Cal and me and you and the lads are going after the Brits."

Sammy glanced at Cal, seeking confirmation. If it was true and he could find out the details . . . He saw Cal nod. "Where? When?" Sammy held his breath.

"Take your hurry in your hand." Erin stopped massaging his shoulders. Any other time he'd have been disappointed, but now he was relieved. He had to concentrate. Had to find out. "We need you to do things first."

If he was going to find out what the target would be, he knew he'd have to seem not to be too interested in it. He exhaled and said, "Like what?"

"Tell him, Cal," she said, and moved away from Sammy. The scent of her lingered even as she stood behind Cal again.

Sammy faced them.

Cal said, "We want you to steal a car and a tractor with a front-loading bucket."

"Wee buns. When do you want them?"

"As soon as you can manage," Erin said, and he heard the urgency in her voice. Show them you're eager, he thought. "I'll get onto it right away."

"Good. And Sammy . . . ?"

Dammit, she was smiling at him again.

"We need you to make the explosives."

"Explosives?"

"We'd not be asking you if we had the Semtex." He saw the smile leave her face, to be replaced by a look of sadness that had come to her as a summer rain squall comes to a sunlit meadow. "But the Brit bastards took it"—he heard the catch in her voice—"when they killed Fiach."

He saw Cal rise and put an arm round Erin's shoulders, heard her repeat bitterly, "When they killed Fiach."

Sammy's fingers crushed his cap. Was talking about her brother the sign she was going to start grilling him?

"Easy, Erin," Cal said softly. "Easy."

She pushed his arm away and snarled. "I'll not be easy until his murderers have paid for Fiach."

Sammy had once cornered a wild cat. He could remember how the animal had spat defiance. He watched her collect herself before she said, her voice controlled and level, "That's why we need you to mix up a batch."

"How much?"

The rain squall had passed, but Erin's returning smile was as feral as the wild cat's snarl as she said, with no more concern than if she'd been asking the village shopkeeper for a pound of nails, "Five hundred pounds."

Sammy whistled. Jesus wept. That was nearly a quarter ton. This wasn't going to be a wee culvert bomb. Not even a car bomb, and, his eyes widened, that's what they wanted the front-end loader for. To transport the device to wherever it was going. He had to find out what the target was. Dare he ask now? He decided to bide, not appear too curious. But if he didn't seem at least to be interested, that would be suspicious, too. What to do?

"That'll take a wee while," he said, deciding to wait before asking more. Besides, taking that while would give him breathing space to find out more. Time to get the information to Spud. Time to get the fuck out of Ireland. "I'll need to get the fertilizer from the barn."

Erin walked over to a wall cupboard and opened the door. Sammy could see a row of white bags of Tate & Lyle granulated sugar. "You'll need this, too. I was going to make blackberry jam . . ." Sammy wondered why her eyes had started to glisten. "But you'll put it to better use, won't you, Sam?"

"I will." Sammy rose. "Can I take the tractor, Cal, to carry the fertilizer?"

Cal shook his head. "No. The peelers have it." He glanced at Erin as if he was unsure about what he was going to say next.

"Fiach was driving it." Erin let the words hang. "Anyway, they're holding on to it. They say it's 'material evidence.'"

"Oh." The mention of the peelers made Sammy start. In just the last wee while, he'd been told about a huge breakout from the Kesh. Every fucking peeler in the country and every bloody soldier would be charging about all over the place looking for the escapees. And Erin wanted to attack something when all that was going on?

He frowned. "Can I ask you a question, Erin?"

He saw her tighten her lips and realized that she thought he was going to ask what the target was. "With the escape and all, the Brits are going to be madder than a bunch of wet hens. They'll be hunting all over hell's high acre for the lads."

"That's right."

"Well, no harm to you, but do you think it's a good time to go after something?"

"Couldn't be better. The last thing they'll be expecting is for us to hit back."

Come on, Erin. Hit back at what?

"And before you go getting your knickers in a knot, we're not going to tell you what we're going after just yet."

Shite. They'd told him so much already, opened the door to his hopes.

"And, Sam." She walked round the table to him. Her scent filled him. "It's not that we don't trust you, but"—she let her hand rest on his arm—"you could get lifted trying to steal the car and the tractor."

He tingled under her touch. "I suppose."

She squeezed his arm. "I hope to God you don't, but *if* you did, the less you know, the better."

He knew she was right but couldn't stop himself from saying, "I understand, but you will tell me one day?"

She surprised him by laughing. "Never you worry about that, Sam. You'd be no help hitting a target if you didn't know what it was."

She wasn't going to tell him now, and he daren't probe more deeply. The door had been slammed in his face. He forced himself to say, "Fair enough. And you'll not be attacking nothing if I don't get my skates on and get started."

"Good man, m'da," she said, and pecked his cheek.

He wanted to hold her, but he stepped away, lifted his cap, and headed for the door.

"I'll get the van loaded and come back for the sugar," he said. "And you want five hundred pounds?"

"Right," she said.

"It's not a van I'll need. It's a bloody lorry."

CHAPTER 25

Davy watched the lorry approach the Gate Lodge. Jesus, but it looked like a battered old banger, and the engine sounded rough. He didn't give a shite about its appearance as long as its clapped-out motor would keep going long enough to get him away.

It slowed and then stopped at the gate.

"Go," Bobby Storey hissed as he pushed the uniformed Gerard Kelly. Davy held his breath as Kelly sauntered to the cab, opened the door, and cheerfully said, "How's about ye, mate?" before climbing in.

Davy spared a thought for the driver. The poor bugger would be staring at the barrel of Kelly's gun, and if he'd any sense he'd do exactly as Kelly told him—wait until the men hiding in the Gate Lodge got in the back, then drive the thing to the Tally Lodge. He'd better be sensible. Kelly had shot one guard already.

Davy heard Kelly urgently saying, "Right. Get moving."

Davy ran to the lorry's rear, opened the doors, and clambered in. Eamon and three other men followed, and together they started hurling out the racks of dinners to make room for the rest.

The thing reeked of boiled cabbage, and as he worked up a sweat shoving the heavy, wheeled racks, Davy could smell himself, too. It was going to be dark and cramped and claustrophobic in here when everyone crushed in. But time was wasting, and the quicker they cleared space, the quicker they could get to the Tally Lodge and the last barrier, through it and well away from the Kesh and out of this lorry. Then, for the first time in nine years, he'd be able to breathe the fresh air untainted by prison smells and—Davy wrinkled his nose—the stink of other men.

Someone kept yelling, "Move it. Fuck it. Move it."

The last rack hit the ground with a crash, scattering aluminium-wrapped meals. Davy slipped on a pool of spilt gravy and nearly tumbled out. Eamon dragged Davy to his feet.

"You all right?"

"Aye." Davy's thigh throbbed.

Men piled in.

Bobby Storey roared, "Everyone's here. Shut the back door."

Davy could see nothing in the darkness, but he heard someone pounding on the metal back of the cab. The lorry backfired once, reversed, and lurched as the driver turned it. Davy would have fallen again but for the press of bodies.

In what seemed to Davy like no time, they stopped. He blinked as the door was opened and light streamed in.

"Lodge party out." That was Bobby Storey shouting. A group of men had been detailed to take over the Tally Lodge—there should only be four screws inside—and open the outer gates.

Davy was grateful there was more space now that those men had gone. He moved closer to the open rear door. He saw groups of prisoners wearing civilian clothes, men who would be making the attempt to get out on foot, accompanied by what would appear to any observer to be uniformed guards. The parties were crossing the open space between the wire of the H-block compound and the perimeter wall. It was perfectly normal after head count on a Sunday afternoon for escorted work details to be sent out to tidy up the open area.

Davy glanced at the nearest tower, where uniformed soldiers leaned on the parapet. They didn't seem to be remotely interested in the comings and goings below them. They must have seen and ignored the same thing every Sunday.

Could the soldiers see what was happening at the Tally Lodge? Davy didn't think so. The lorry was stopped in the lodge's narrow tunnel in the perimeter wall, blocking the troops' line of sight. He grinned, and, anyway, what Bobby Storey had called the lodge party was in the lodge and out of sight. Any minute now, they'd open the gates and the lorry'd be out of here.

Davy's smile fled when he saw Sean Donovan appear in the lorry's open doorway. There was blood trickling down Sean's face.

"More men, quick," Sean gasped. "We've hit shift change. The lodge's crawling with the buggers."

"Christ Almighty," Davy mouthed as he jumped out. The men behind the escape had no choice but to try to use the lorry to get as far away as possible before the hue and cry was raised. But there was a drawback. Its time of arrival every day was not much before shift-changeover time. The last thing the prisoners wanted was to be faced with twice the usual number of guards. But the thing *had* been late—held up no doubt by some unpredictable fucking checkpoint. Some of the early arrivals of the oncoming shift must have been in the lodge. Too many guards for a small group of prisoners to handle. Enough maybe to sound the alarm.

Davy glanced out through the still-closed outer gate to the guards' car park. Men were running across the grass. They must have suspected something was wrong. He'd no idea what could have tipped them off, but this place would soon be swarming with the buggers like flies round a heifer's arse. And more were coming.

Davy burst into the lodge. Pande-fuckin'-monium. Yells, curses, the crash of breaking glass, men wrestling, one guard on his hands and knees puking his guts up. The smell of vomit stung Davy's nostrils. He could see that the advance party was losing the Donnybrook, and unless he and the other men with him could turn the tide, the whole bloody thing would be over. One fucking gate from freedom.

Davy McCutcheon had never shrunk from a fistfight. He ignored the weight of the .25 in his pocket and waded into the nearest guard, feeling both the crunch of his knuckles on the man's chin and intense satisfaction as the man went down like a sack of spuds.

He looked across the melee and saw two guards trying to reach the control panel. If they made it, they would set off the alarms. Three prisoners stopped them, but more screws were nearing the console. One reached his hand toward a large red switch. Davy guessed it would be the one to activate the sirens and lock the gates. Was the little one beside it the gate-opening control?

Davy was swept forward against the console by a shove from a screw. "Fuck you, you Fenian bastard," the man screamed.

Davy slammed his knee into the man's crotch. The guard screeched, bowed forward, and clutched himself. Davy smashed both fists on the back of the man's neck and hoped to God he hadn't broken it.

Someone was shouting, "It's no fucking use. We'll have to give up." Davy recognized Bobby Storey, the escape commander. He must have lost his nerve. His words were hard to make out over the racket, but Davy heard him roar, "Leave the panel alone, McCutcheon. You're wasting your time. It's over. It's over."

"The fuck it is," Davy shouted back. He kept his eyes on the smaller switch on the console. One control—one—stood between him and getting out and all that meant to him. He knew the rest of the guards would be here in no time, no matter what, and the escape would be fucked in a few minutes anyway.

It wouldn't matter a tinker's damn if he set off the alarms. Davy thumped the button and flinched, waiting for the howling to start. Instead, he heard the hiss of hydraulics and, through the broken window, saw the gates swing open.

"You done good, McCutcheon. Dead fucking brill," Storey yelled. "Right. Everyone except the rear guard back to the lorry."

Davy glanced round. He was amazed by how, so suddenly, the prisoners had won the battle and cowed guards lay facedown on the floor. He had to step over one as he followed Bobby Storey to the door.

Davy'd time to feel sorry for those detailed off to keep the guards away from the alarm system. They'd be buying time, but the price would be high. They'd probably take a ferocious shite kicking when the new screws arrived, and, poor buggers, they'd not be getting any time off for good behaviour. Their sentences would be increased. Davy couldn't help but feel proud of their sacrifice.

He moved toward Eamon, who crouched behind the lorry. Both of them were panting as they waited their turns to scramble into the back. Eamon grabbed Davy's arm. "You're a fucking hero, Father. You really used your loaf. If you hadn't found that switch . . ."

"Bugger off," Davy said, surprised that, despite knowing his cheeks would be flushed from exertion, he seemed to be blushing.

He glanced out through the open gate to where he could see a low barbed-wire fence; past it, a road; and beyond, hedges and fields. Out there, half a mile away, was freedom. But . . .

He swore as a car jolted across the grass outside, slewed sideways, and slammed to a stop across the outer gateway, blocking the lorry as effectively as if the car were a brick wall. Its driver jumped out, leaving the door open, and Davy could hear him yelling for help as he ran back across the field.

Any minute now, someone would raise the alarm. Davy didn't know if guards carried walkie-talkies, but the fucking soldiers in the towers would have to be blind not to notice something. And the lorry couldn't budge because of the car in front of it. Shite. Shite. Shite. He could feel his scrotum tighten. He huddled against the side of the lorry and glanced behind, back to H-7.

The first groups of prisoners in stolen uniforms and the ones in civvies had reached the inner Tally Gate. There was no sound of shouted challenges, no small-arms fire, so Davy didn't think the Brit sentries were concerned—

yet. They must still assume that the men below them were working parties. But that couldn't—it just couldn't—last much longer.

He stared out to the far fence and the open ground between. Could they make it on foot across that half mile and past all the uniformed guards who were running from their car park across the weed-littered grass?

A cloud of thistledown drifted up from the grass where a screw's boot must have kicked a dandelion. The tiny parachutes floated on the light breeze toward the barbed wire. Davy wished he could fly off with them, but big men don't float, especially ones carrying extra weight like the revolver in his pocket. He could feel it cold against his thigh.

It was going to stay where it was. Even if Davy had the stomach to try shooting his way out, there were far too many guards, and they were much closer now, for him to drop more than one or two. The rest would get him. What would be the point of a couple more deaths? The odds were that anyone he shot would have kids, like Mr. Smiley has, and who—Davy managed a wry smile—would still be kicking a ball with his lads long after Davy was—was what? Back in the fucking Kesh?

He felt Eamon tug at his sleeve. "Davy. Davy."

"What?"

"All the other lads who was to get out on foot are here."

Davy turned to see a crowd, some uniformed, most in civvies, milling round the open inner gate.

"If everybody runs for it to the wire, some of us's bound to make it."

"You reckon?"

"Aye. Hang on."

Davy watched Eamon crab-crawl across to where Bobby Storey crouched next to Bic McFarlane in the doorway of the lodge, say something to Storey, and crawl back.

Storey stood, cupped his hands to his mouth, and yelled, "The lorry's fucked. We're going to have to run for it. Get going. If you've keys to a screw's car, steal it and take as many of your mates with you as you can." He and McFarlane started toward the outer gate.

Eamon grabbed Davy's arm and hustled him forward. He heard Sean Donovan call, "Wait for me."

Davy tried to follow Eamon, but his limp was slowing them down. "Go on without me, Eamon."

"The fuck I will. Move yourself, Father."

Davy squeezed past the lorry, saw its driver, shaking, huddled down in the cab, both arms over his head. He was sobbing. The poor bastard must be petrified. Davy could smell the hot engine oil of the car that blocked the lorry in.

Then he and Eamon were out in the open field, naked and unprotected as a couple of newborns. Davy half-hunched his shoulders as if that would somehow protect him when the soldiers started firing. The hell it would.

"Come on, Davy. You'll set the Belfast record for the half-mile dash yet and . . ."

Eamon's words were drowned by sirens' brassy voices, their wailing rising and falling regularly like ocean swells pouring into a narrow inlet. Davy glanced back at a watchtower, saw soldiers moving slowly as if they were confused. They'd not be confused much longer. He tucked his head further into his shoulders and ran as fast as his gammy leg allowed.

High on the wall, Corporal Bert Higgins heard the sirens. "What the fuck's that? Not another bloody drill? Christ on a rubber crutch. How many times do we have to play their stupid bloody games?"

Private Hamish McLeish shrugged. "Another FUBAR. Bloody officers."

"'Fucked up beyond all redemption.' You said it, mate. Just like this whole bloody tour in Ulster. Christ, I'm sick and tired of Paddy bashing." Higgins glanced down and saw nothing but a normal, escorted work party crossing the open space. "Take a shufti outside, Mac, just for form's sake."

Private McLeish moved to the outer parapet. Corporal Higgins peered across the ground between the perimeter wall and the H-blocks.

"Come here, Corp. Quick." McLeish sounded worried.

"What's up?" Corporal Higgins took the four paces necessary to cross the plank floor. "Blimey!"

Below him, he saw groups of men in civilian clothes running toward the outer wire fence. Uniformed guards were running with them, some grappling with the civilians. He watched one guard throw a low tackle that would have done an English Rugby International wing forward proud.

"Fuckin' 'ell." Higgins took one pace back, still staring outside the walls. Two of the prisoners were getting into a car. They started it and drove away. "It's no bloody drill. It's a breakout." This wasn't meant to be happening. Not on his watch.

He turned and moved rapidly to the other parapet. Without waiting to see if McLeish was following, Corporal Higgins started to drag the heavy general-purpose machine gun, GPMG, the "gimpy, from its mount on the compound side of the watchtower. He rested its barrel on the other parapet and pulled back the cocking lever.

"You going to open fire, Corp?" Higgins thought McLeish sounded doubtful, if he could make out what the man was saying over the incessant howling of the sirens.

Fuck the Yellow Card and its rules of engagement, if that was what was worrying McLeish. Corporal Higgins snugged the butt of the weapon against his shoulder and sighted on a group of men.

"Bloody 'ell." There was a guard in the middle of the scrum. Higgins knew he'd probably not get a bollocking if he stopped some of the escapees, even though there'd be a mountain of official paperwork to do, but pulling a blue on blue, shooting one of his own side, would bring down the wrath of God on his head. Maybe he should hold his fire.

If what their captain had told them was true when they were being briefed to work as sentries at Long Kesh, the bastards out there wouldn't get far anyway. Whoever had tripped the bloody siren had done a lot more than make a god-awful racket. Information would have been flashed to the Royal Ulster Constabulary, Army Headquarters, and the Northern Ireland Office. Already, troops would be pouring from their barracks to help legions of rozzers set up roadblocks on all the routes away from the prison.

He could just hear the distant roar of rotors, loud but muffled by the sirens' screaming. Choppers were being scrambled from Thiepval and nearby Aldergrove Airport. He knew to expect the first troop-carrying, twin-rotor Chinook to land here with reinforcements within the next ten minutes. If he remembered right, someone, probably that bloke Sir Jack Harmon, the chief constable, even had to notify the handbag lady. He'd seen in *The Daily Mirror* that Maggie Thatcher was on an official visit to Canada.

Maybe opening fire wouldn't be so smart after all, much as he'd like to nail one or two of the bastards down there. Nah. It wasn't his responsibility—but they'd killed enough squaddies in the last fourteen years, poor blokes who'd been posted here, just like him. And according to the politicos, the very shites that sniped at them and blew up their vehicles were the ones the army was here to protect. Provvie cunts. Never mind responsibility. He just needed an excuse to let rip.

He heard the staccato rattling of the GPMG from the next watchtower and jumped.

"Fuckin' 'ell," he said, smiled, and swung his sights onto an isolated figure standing at the wire. The man was some distance ahead of a civvy-clad prisoner, who seemed to be dragging a uniformed guard by the arm. The corporal lifted his aim to avoid the guard, held steady, and let go the regulation "tap" of four rounds. When the burnt-gunpowder-stinking muzzle gasses cleared, he was gratified to see his target writhing on the ground. Right. He'd slotted that one. Who would he take out next?

Sean Donovan had reached the wire, then been thrown to one side by God alone knew what and collapsed ahead of Davy. The man screamed like a gut-shot hare. Christ Almighty, he'd been hit.

Davy tried to make himself smaller and ran on, breath burning in his chest, thigh jarred by every step, ears tormented by the constant howling of sirens and the roar of helicopters. He wanted to rest, but Eamon kept hauling on Davy's arm, urging him to run faster. Machine-gun bullets whined as they ricocheted from rocks in the field.

Sean clutched his leg and moaned, the sound guttural from somewhere deep inside.

Davy broke free from Eamon's grip, ran to Sean, bent over, and saw the tears in his eyes. "I'm fucked, Davy. My leg's bust."

Davy hadn't enough breath to speak. He could see the rent in the man's blood-stained trousers, the jagged end of a shattered bone. He tried to lift Sean, but he screamed. "Put . . . me . . . down. Please."

Davy hesitated. He saw a man he recognized as Skeet Hamilton hurl himself full-length over the low barbed-wire coils and Eamon totter across the back of the human bridge. Davy was close enough to hear Eamon yelling above the racket, "Come on, Davy. Skeet'll wait for us. I'll give you a hand with Sean."

"Ah, Christ, Davy, for God's sake, run away on," Sean whimpered.

Davy looked into the big man's pain-clouded eyes, remembered that he owed him one for taking out Smiley when Davy had frozen, tried to tighten his hold, and flinched as another bullet slamming into Sean threw Davy off-balance. He lay on the ground beside Sean as his eyes clouded and the lids drooped. Davy didn't know if Donovan had been a religious man, but he made the sign of the cross and muttered a quick Hail Mary.

"*Davy,*" Eamon screamed. "Sean's done for. Get the fuck out of there."

Davy stood and limped to the wire. Eamon grabbed his hand and helped him across Skeet Hamilton's prostrate body.

Outside the wire, Davy stood, bent double, hands on his knees, hauling in lungfuls of air, and it was clean, gorse-scented air. He mustn't give up now, but he was almost at the end of his rope, and his weakness was holding Eamon back. It wasn't fair to Eamon.

"Go on . . . Eamon." Davy gasped. "Get . . . away . . . Erin's waiting for you." He watched Eamon help Skeet Hamilton tear himself free to gallop away.

Eamon hesitated, yelled, "I'll steal a car and come back for you. Find a place to hide," then raced off toward the nearby road, the road that should have taken Davy to Tyrone, to Canada, and to Fiona.

His breathing was easier now. He rubbed his thigh, thought of her eyes, and, ignoring the pain, hobbled toward the road as the sirens' wailing died, but the roar of helicopters and the clattering of machine guns racketed on and on through the Sunday afternoon.

CHAPTER 26

It was a lovely way to be spending a Sunday afternoon, Sammy thought, just bloody lovely. His headache refused to go away, and no wonder. It was heavy work in the outbuilding behind his cottage mixing ground-up ammonium nitrate fertilizer with Erin's sugar, then adding aluminium powder to make the explosive ammonal.

He'd been using a plastic shovel. One spark—and a metal shovel could make such sparks—and Sammy McCandless knew that he would have joined the growing ranks of Provo bomb makers who had scored own goals. Poor bastards.

He shivered and felt his vest clammy against his back. Despite the sweat generated by his exertions, it was chilly here in the big shed that Cal used to store farm machinery, but the place was well hidden from the road, a private place where a man could work undisturbed.

More importantly, the roof was watertight, not, he thought bitterly, like the roof of his bloody cottage across the lane. Water in the explosive mixture would ruin it, and although Sammy hoped to hell he'd be long gone before Erin had a chance to use it, he saw no reason not to take pride in using his skills to do a job right. God knew there was little else for Sammy McCandless to take pride in these days.

He was using a barley crusher plugged into the power shaft of a combine harvester to grind the granular fertilizer to a fine powder, then adding the sugar and aluminium until the mixture was a light brown colour. The dust clogged his nose and made his eyes run.

The combine's engine racketed on and on, its clattering worsening the pain behind his eyes. The couple of aspirin he'd taken as soon as he'd got home in Cal's van hadn't done a damn thing, and never mind keeping an eye to the job, he needed to be able to think.

He was fairly sure, even though he'd really sweated it out at the O'Byrne farm earlier today, that Cal and Erin hadn't got round to suspecting him of informing, yet. But they might start putting two and two together. How long would that take? *He* knew he was responsible for Fiach's death and would have to live with that, but—he blocked one nostril with his thumb and snorted down the other, dislodging a wad of dust and mucus—he'd rather live with the guilt for a long time than die very soon because of it.

He was sorry about Fiach, would miss the wee lad, but then he'd miss all the O'Byrnes. Jesus, Mary, and Joseph, he'd miss being near Erin, even if he could never have her. The way her hands had kneaded his shoulders this afternoon . . .

Forget about that, he told himself. When he was in England, he would still have his memories of her, might meet a nice English girl, and by God he was going to get to England. He wondered if he had enough information yet to satisfy Spud.

Would telling him where Eamon and his mates would be hiding do the trick? It might, and for a moment Sammy thought he could see his way clear, but on second thoughts . . . if it wasn't enough and Sammy had to stay in Ireland after the grave was raided, who would be on top of the list of suspects for having grassed? Sammy McCandless, that's who. He decided he'd say nothing about what he knew on that score. He'd be far better to wait and find out, or puzzle out, what the target was going to be for the vehicles he was to steal and the five hundred pounds of ammonal.

He looked into the barley crusher. Another batch was done. He turned off the machine, glad of the silence when its engine stopped, the gradual thinning out of the petrol fumes. He waited for the drum to stop revolving, held open the mouth of a plastic bag, filled it, then squeezed the bag into one of the sacks the fertilizer had come in. He tied baler twine at the bag's throat.

The filled sack and the other ones he'd finished now looked like a lot of harmless agricultural supplies. That's what the stencils on the sacks' outsides said. FERTILIZER. The plastic lining was to prevent the fine powder leaking through the coarse sackcloth weave. They might look harmless, although Christ alone knew the damage this lot would do when it blew. But that wasn't going to be Sammy's problem. He'd be long gone.

He humped the lethal sack over to its fellows and went out to the van to haul in a new sackful of unprocessed fertilizer. His thin arms ached, and he wanted a break. He'd told Erin and Cal that making the ammonal would take a wee while. He reckoned he'd earned a break.

He took his tweed jacket from a nail in the wall, shrugged it on, and felt in the pocket for his Park Drive. He was gasping for a smoke—but not in here.

He allowed himself a taut grin as he remembered a remark his father used to make. "I may be Irish, but I'm not that fucking stupid."

Sammy left the outhouse, closed the door behind him, stuck a cigarette in his mouth, and lit up. In the grass under his feet, he saw the sparkle of dewdrops reflecting the light of the sun. The air was crisp. And he'd been worried about the roof of the shed being rainproof? It wasn't even fucking well raining, but then, he worried about everything these days.

Sammy walked to his cottage. A cup of tea would hit the spot.

He paused before the door and stared at a spider that had been spinning under the eaves. The spokes and circles of the web shimmered like strings of diamonds. From the centre of the web, the spider scuttled toward a blue-bottle, which struggled, enmeshed, doomed.

Poor bastard, Sammy thought. I know how you feel. He picked up a stick from the ground, shoved it into the gossamer, and ripped a hole. The spider retreated back under the eaves. The bluebottle tore free. "Go on, bugger off," Sammy said as the fly buzzed drunkenly away.

From overhead, he heard the cries of curlew, liquid, plaintive. They'd be heading for the high moorland to keep company with the grouse that lived in the heather there. The rich bastards that held the shooting rights had been blasting away at the birds since August 12, the opening day of grouse season. Poor bloody grouse, minding their own business until they got chased from their hidey-holes by beaters or dogs and some shites killed them, just for sport. Did they not think enough things were getting killed in Northern Ireland?

And who was Erin going to be killing? He wished to hell he knew. Perhaps he could figure it out for himself.

He let himself into his cottage. It was dark, despite the brightness outside. Sammy opened the curtains, shoved the kettle on the stove, and waited for it to boil.

Erin's target had to be something close, and something big. If she intended to use the tractor, once he'd stolen it, and to fill its bucket with ammonal, they'd not be able to drive it very far from the shed here where he'd hide it. Omagh was too far away to the south. The nearest decent-sized town was Newtownstewart, but there was nothing there worth hitting.

Derry, Londonderry you'd call it if you were a Loyalist, was twenty miles to the north. It was the headquarters of the British army 8th Brigade and the Strand Road police station, the RUC's interrogation centre. Either of them could be a tempting target.

The kettle boiled. He made a cup of tea.

Sammy considered Derry but decided that, although Erin might be bound and determined to have her revenge, she was far too clever to let her grief over Fiach blind her to the lunacy of trying to hit something there. The city was too far away, and anyway the security there was as tight as that in Belfast ever since Bloody Sunday back in January 1972. That day, in Derry's Catholic Bogside district, soldiers of the Parachute Regiment had tried to break up a civil rights march. There'd been a riot, and the bloody Brits had shot and killed thirteen men and youths and injured seventeen others.

He frowned and tried to concentrate. What *was* she going after? There were army observation towers, great four-legged, menacing, spidery-looking structures built in a chain that ran from County Armagh south of here, but they were all on high ground.

Paying little attention to what he was doing, he burned his lip when he tried to sip his tea. That was bloody hot, so it was, and so were the towers as possible targets. The troops manning them could see for miles. They weren't going to let a tractor with a front bucket come within a mile of them without stopping and searching it. They were so security-conscious that their garrisons were inserted or extracted by helicopter. The Brits even used choppers to take the rubbish away.

Those buggers in the towers had machine guns and could call in Lynx, Puma, Wessex, or Gazelle helicopters. Or perhaps one of those bloody great twin-rotor Chinooks filled to the gills with soldiers of the Parachute Regiment, the same shites who'd fired on the march on Bloody Sunday.

The towers were all in South Armagh, where groups from the Special Air Service, the SAS, were stationed undercover. The British government protested that it wasn't true, but Sammy and every other Provo was fucking sure that those shites had orders to shoot to kill.

Christ Almighty, could he not stop thinking about people getting killed?

His tea tasted bitter, and he carried his cup to the sink, telling himself to stop brooding and concentrate. What was left that would be worth using five hundred pounds of explosives to take out?

Sammy nearly dropped the cup.

Strabane. It had to be Strabane. The town was only five miles away. It was quite small, but there was an RUC barracks. That was the police station where they'd taken Fiach's body. Strabane. It had to be; it absolutely had to be. There was nothing else close enough, nothing anyway that wasn't too strongly defended, and he knew there were no soldiers there. Nobody but peelers guarded the place.

Sammy left the teacup in the sink, grabbed his bicycle clips from a table, and slipped them over his trousers at the ankles. The sooner he got that information to his handler, the better. He knew now exactly what he was going to tell Spud. He'd give the Special Branch man half the information, where the attack would be, but demand, that was the right word, demand that he, Sammy, be sent to England before he'd pass on the day and time of the assault.

He opened the cottage door and hesitated, turning over a new set of ideas. Not only could he tell Spud there was a big attack coming, but Sammy had found out this afternoon that Eamon and some of the escapees would be part of it. Christ, it was fucking brilliant, so it was. Spud would be a hero with his superiors. Heading off a major attack, rounding up wanted Provos, and all because of Sammy. They'd have to get him out in exchange for that much information, wouldn't they?

And, Sammy grinned from ear to ear, even if he hadn't been able to give the E4A man the exact timing of the Kesh escape, the mere fact that it had happened and Sammy had been able at least to drop the hint something was up in the prison would be further proof that he was a reliable source of top-class information and that the new info he was ready to pass on could be trusted completely.

He closed the cottage door behind him, pausing only to notice that, already, the spider had repaired her damaged web and was waiting patiently in one corner for the next hapless fly.

CHAPTER 27

"If only those whales could fly, Becky, I think they'd soar out of that concrete pond and back to the ocean."

Fiona sat with her friend and a handful of spectators in the bleachers of the orca exhibit at the Vancouver Aquarium, watching two killer whales cruise round their enclosure. The animals' grey-white saddle patches shone beneath the surface. Their dorsal fins sliced through the water and left shallow ripples.

The male breached, hurling himself into the air. Sunlight sparkled from his glistening body. For a tiny moment, he hung suspended by some enormous force before slamming back to submerge, slowly waving a lonely pectoral fin. To Fiona, the gesture looked like a silent appeal for help.

The whales were magnificent animals, fascinating to watch, but Fiona was certain they didn't belong in captivity. She felt sympathy for all creatures that had been deprived of their freedom and remembered the rufous hummingbird. He was small but could go where he pleased; the whales were vast yet must live out their days penned in—like Davy.

Thinking of him hurt, but the feeling was less intense than it had been before Tim and Becky had both suggested that rather than try to make his memory sink, she should let it surface, even if, by coming into the light, it made her ache.

"I really think that orcas are just a tad on the heavy side for flight."

"Lord, Becky, you really can be a bit too literal." Fiona laughed, but said more seriously, "Don't you think they miss their pods, their families? I wonder if they remember the places they were taken from? If you were shut up in a jail like them, wouldn't you want to be able to escape, get back to your old, familiar haunts?"

"I rather think I would want to escape, in fact I certainly would, but I'm not imprisoned and 'England's green and pleasant land,' which I suppose is the place I was taken from, doesn't mean much to me now."

Fiona was surprised to hear Becky say that about England. She assumed all immigrants had ties to their countries of birth.

The waves made by the whale splashed against the pool's walls. Breaking water always reminded Fiona of the river Lagan chuckling over rocks in the shallows below Shaw's Bridge.

"You don't miss England?" she asked. "Not at all?"

"Not much. I was only seventeen when I left Henley-on-Thames, and I haven't gone back. I've no reason to, really." She chuckled. "It's been a long time, thirty-eight years since I came out here. I was lucky. My pod, the agèed parents, brought me to Vancouver, and it's as green and more pleasant here than England ever was. You know the folks're still living out in Abbotsford, bless them. I went out to see them last night."

"How are they?"

"It's a bit sad, but to use a word coined by one of my grade eights, they're slowly 'decrepitating.' Both in their eighties and getting very creaky, but they don't complain. Dad potters about in his garden. Mum still serves cucumber sandwiches. They never miss the Queen's message on Christmas Day. The pair of them are as English as ever. I suppose in a way it is comforting to keep up with a bit of your old heritage."

"You're probably right, but the only people I know from Northern Ireland who live here are a family called Ferguson." She hadn't thought of Jimmy since the night he'd appeared in Bridges. "They invited Tim and me to go round for a meal."

"Perhaps you should go. It never hurts to be reminded once in a while about what you've left behind."

"I'll think about it."

Perhaps she should give Jimmy a call. Despite his connection to Davy, simply hearing his and his wife's and Siobhan's Belfast accents had been pleasingly familiar.

Why not take Jimmy up on his offer and at least have a chat with Siobhan? Although Fiona had just met the girl, she was the only one Fiona knew who had faced up to the death of a man with whom, according to Jimmy, she'd been so deeply in love. At least Fiona assumed Siobhan must have managed to get over the young soldier because she was married now, with children. She wondered if Siobhan would be willing to talk about it, and, if she was, could that be taken as a sign that she had indeed weathered her loss?

A disturbance in the pool broke Fiona's train of thought. The orca was spy-hopping, pectoral fins on the water's surface, his entire head raised vertically above. She stared into his huge eye.

To Fiona, the orca's brown eye was full of ineffable sadness, like the misery in Davy's blue eyes the day she'd gone to the Kesh to tell him she was leaving him and leaving Northern Ireland. She knew that, try as she might, it was one particular scene she would never forget.

The whale slid soundlessly below, barely disturbing the waters as he sank, and she tried to let the memory of that day submerge and take the sadness with it. She leaned back on the wooden plank that covered the concrete, taking her weight on her hands.

She felt Becky's hand on her own and the warmth both of the wood beneath her palm and from Becky's hand above.

"Are you all right, old thing?"

Fiona heard the concern in Becky's voice, forced a smile, and said, "I'm fine. I was just thinking."

"Dare one ask what you were thinking about?"

How typical of Becky, to be sensitive to others' feelings and be desperately afraid of overstepping whatever inner boundary her inborn English politeness had drawn. "Of course," Fiona said. "I was remembering the day I told Davy I was going to Canada." It pleased her that she could say that without hesitating and without feeling too uncomfortable. "It was visiting day in the Kesh. I think that seeing those orcas captive in that tank"—she nodded toward the pool—"I think that's what brought the whole thing back."

"Is thinking about him still bothering you?" Becky's voice was soft.

"A bit. But not as much. He's fading like an old sepia-tint photo, except that one image. It's still clear as a bell." That one, she thought, and the nightmare in all its horrid clarity.

Becky's voice was soft. "It's going to hurt. There's no question of that, but"—she squeezed Fiona's hand gently—"I know the analogy is a bit hackneyed . . . but it's like lancing a boil and letting the pus out." She squeezed more tightly. "And it sounds to me as if you've had the courage to pick up the lancet."

Fiona looked down into the pool. The surface was flat, and through the aquamarine she could see the outlines of the two orcas in its depths. Wouldn't it be nice, she thought, and silently chastised herself for even thinking the word "nice." She spent hours trying to persuade her pupils to let "'nice' take a holiday" and find better synonyms. But it would be nice if her life could always be so calm as the pool was then.

A streak raced from the depths. White Wings, a Pacific white-sided dolphin who lived in the pool with the orcas, rocketed through the surface and curved in a high, graceful arc before returning to cleave the water with its blunt snout, reentering the pool as cleanly as an Olympic diver yet leaving expanding circles of wavelets to disturb the tranquility.

That, thought Fiona, was pretty much the way her own mind worked. She could still remember some of the psychology courses she'd taken at teachers' college. It was Jungian, that was the word. Whenever she believed everything was going the way she would like, thoughts of Davy or the damn dream would come roaring up from the depths of her unconscious, just as the dolphin had surfaced. And as he had left his ripples as mementos of his coming, so did they.

"I think," said Becky, "you've started something, wondering aloud about jailbreaks. I think the dolphin's trying to do a runner, too."

That made Fiona laugh. She squeezed Becky's hand. "Thank you," she said.

"Whatever for?"

"For listening. For making me laugh."

"You are, to use the expression of our Canadian cousins, entirely welcome." Becky stood. "Judging by the way my tummy feels, it's lunchtime. We should be moving along to the Teahouse."

"Right," said Fiona, "and it's my treat."

Becky chuckled in her turn. "Correct me if I'm misquoting Marlon Brando, but it's 'an offer I can't refuse.'"

The Teahouse was packed inside, the buzz of conversation deafening. Fiona was pleased when the hostess was able to seat them at a quiet patio table, where she could look over a low hedge and across Burrard Inlet. The sun, now that the autumnal equinox had passed, was lower in the sky. Great cumulonimbus clouds stood, puffed, white ramparts, ragged grey anvils over the North Shore Mountains to her right and above Point Grey ahead. Below her, the water's surface was a filigree of silver where the sun struck, dulled here and there by the clouds' tattered shadows.

"Isn't that lovely, Becky? The sea looks like a Turkish plate I saw in an antique shop once. The copper had been worn away in patches, and the brighter pewter shone through."

"It really is very pretty," Becky said. "Look how tiny the sailboats seem."

Fiona watched the boats heeling to a stiff breeze. "They're having fun," she said, remembering Bowen Island. "I do enjoy sailing with Tim."

"The good doctor's back tonight, isn't he?"

"I'm going to make him supper at my place."

Becky raised one eyebrow. "Good for you, girl. Trite though it may sound, the way to a man's heart is definitely through his stomach; and speaking of stomachs, I'm famished." Becky picked up her menu. "And I could murder a glass of something white, dry, and *very* chilled."

A waitress came and took the drink orders.

Fiona sat forward in her wrought iron chair and rested her forearms on the glass tabletop. She watched how intently Becky studied her menu. Her friend certainly enjoyed her—what would Becky call them? "Vittles."

Fiona was glad that she'd met Becky: someone who would listen, someone who put Fiona completely at ease, someone to whom she could open up as she had done at the aquarium earlier, a woman with the knack of being able to say the right thing and, more importantly, one who knew when to say nothing.

Some of Fiona's Canadian acquaintances, knowing of the Troubles back in Ireland, thought that it was odd that an Irishwoman and an Englishwoman could be so close. Why the hell shouldn't they?

They had a lot in common: teaching, the opera, books, an ability to find the same things hilarious, often to the confusion of their Canadian acquaintances, and something that Fiona knew she had taken time to recognize—a shared background, even if they had come from different sides of Saint George's Channel, which separated England from Ireland.

The ten-year gap in their ages made no difference. As girls, they had read the same Bible (although as taught by clergy of different persuasions); studied the same books at school, the same works of Shakespeare; been taught the same history, even if—as Fiona recognized years ago—the history had been slanted in favour of the English. They'd listened to the same pop groups, watched the same television programmes, probably read the same newspapers. They spoke the same language, though with different accents, different nuances, but each understood the other's subtleties. Their sameness was what had brought them together in the first place, and from that coming together a friendship had grown. She wondered if Becky was of the same opinion? She looked questioningly at her friend, who must have misunderstood the look.

Becky pointed at the menu. "Are you having trouble deciding, Fiona?"

"Not at all. I'll have a Caesar salad. I told you, I'll be cooking a big dinner tonight for Tim."

"Indeed. Lucky Doctor Tim. I'm having sardines on toast for my tea, so if you don't mind, I'm going to tuck in now, and the scallops meunière sound absolutely delicious."

The waitress appeared with their drinks. Fiona ordered their meals, then raised her glass to Becky. "Cheers."

"I think," said Becky, "we can do better than that. Let's drink to home-comings."

Fiona thought of tonight and Tim. "To homecomings and, Becky"—Fiona looked across at her companion—"to friendship."

"I'll certainly drink to that." Becky took a healthy swallow, then stifled a tiny burp.

Fiona sipped, glanced out toward the road past the Teahouse, and watched two joggers running past, Lycra-clad, grimly determined, never smiling, ignoring each other, oblivious to the sea, the mountains, the billowing clouds above. On they ran, conscious only of their individual pulse rates, the miles covered, their improved cardiovascular status, toned thighs, and selfish hopes for everlasting life.

They thought they were running *to* something. Fiona knew she had fled from Northern Ireland and still ran from her memories, and she believed that inside every jogger there was something *from* which they were running. Everyone did that in their own way, she supposed. Some drank or used drugs, some shopped, some were workaholics, some hid in a religion.

She looked across the table to where Becky sat, seemingly contented in the sunshine, and wondered what, if anything, chased after that most placid of women. It was none of Fiona's business, she knew, but realized that if something were troubling Becky deeply, she'd let down her reserve and tell her friend Fiona.

And Fiona smiled because she knew that, unlike the self-contained joggers, she and Becky each had a friend to run with.

CHAPTER 28

How much longer would they have to keep running? Davy stared at the darkness through the side window of the car racing along the country road to Castlederg, where a bridge spanned the Derg. Eamon, who was driving, said the river was the last obstacle between them and the safe place in Tyrone—if there wasn't a roadblock on the bridge.

Davy hoped to God there wouldn't be. He'd had enough close calls since he'd got outside the wire at the Kesh, but now they were on the last lap, and he had nothing to do but sit with his thoughts.

Although his heart rate had slowed, he moved restlessly in the backseat. Perhaps, he thought, it's just the darkness that's unsettling me. He was used to Belfast and its streetlights. One or two always managed to survive the glass-shattering street riots. Corridor lights had burned all night in the Kesh. Even the flare of Molotov cocktails hurled by the Loyalist mobs as they rampaged through the streets of the Falls in the early days of the Troubles would have been preferable to the impenetrable gloom outside the car.

The last time he'd experienced the utter nothingness of the countryside at night was way back when he'd been training as a boy in the Tyrone Sperrin Mountains.

The Sperrins weren't very far away now, and it struck Davy that there was a certain symmetry in his being taken back to Tyrone, where the whole bloody thing had started for him when he was sixteen.

Da had enrolled Davy and Jimmy Ferguson in the old Official IRA. They'd been sent down here from Belfast. Someone senior in the organization had decided that Davy would be trained as an explosives expert.

Back then he'd believed in the Cause, and, when one of his devices had gone off prematurely, killing Da and wounding Davy, he had strengthened his resolve to fight for a free Ireland.

After the explosion, he'd had to lie in a crude shelter, nursed by wee

Jimmy. God, even if Fiona wouldn't see him when he got to Canada, and Davy couldn't believe that was true, had to believe it wasn't true as fervently as he used to believe in the struggle, it would be great to see Jimmy Ferguson again. Him and his quoting William Butler Yeats.

In the long, dark nights, with only the cold, distant stars for light, Jimmy would sit by Davy and recite: "O'Driscoll drove with a song / The wild duck and the drake / From the tall and tufted reeds / Of the drear Hart Lake . . ." or, "Two girls in silk kimonos, both / Beautiful, one a gazelle."

When he'd first met Fiona, he'd thought of her as a gazelle, and he'd kept that thought through the last nine weary years. He knew that lovers could part, that often after a time they found someone else. Davy smiled wryly. Who the hell was he meant to meet in the Kesh? Eamon? Poor Sean Donovan? As his smile faded, he knew that, had he been on the outside with every woman in Christendom, waiting and willing, not one of them could have taken Fiona's place.

But she must have had other men. Davy flinched when he realized what "had" could mean. He didn't want to imagine her in bed with a stranger, with anyone but him, but he couldn't help himself, and the images tore at him.

Nine years was a hell of a long time to stay celibate, and to distract himself he thought back through the long years since he'd last been in Tyrone. He could remember one more line that Jimmy was fond of, from Yeats's "Down by the Salley Gardens," "She bid me take life easy, as the grass grows on the weirs; / But I was young and foolish, and now am full of tears." And he *had* been foolish back then. They all had, believing they could get rid of the British.

Was he full of tears? He'd only shed them the day after she'd left the Kesh having told him she was going to Canada. All of his other tears, for the people his bombs had killed or maimed, were buried somewhere deep inside him along with the ones he should have shed for Da, killed by the bomb that had shattered Davy's thigh.

He tugged his pants away from his thigh, feeling their dampness, smelling the stink of the ditch where he'd crouched after staggering across the road outside the Kesh and smashing his way through a blackthorn hedge. He imagined he could still hear the racket of choppers clattering over his hiding place, the drone of a high-winged monoplane, the whining of tires on tarmac as Saracen armoured cars and Land Rovers sped past him toward the prison.

The relief when Eamon had hauled him into the back of a black Mercedes that they'd stolen from a nearby farm had been replaced by a feeling that came close to despair when the bloody car ran out of petrol.

The surge of hope again when the ambush that Eamon had arranged paid off, even though it had seemed to take a lifetime. Davy had sprawled on the road pretending to be injured. Eamon flagged down a motorist, asked for help with Davy, then overpowered the man and hijacked his Hillman. The details were blurred, but the picture of the victim's wife sitting on the road, her skirt rumpled above her fat white thighs, shaking her fist and screaming, "*You Fenian bastards*," would stay with Davy.

He took comfort from knowing that, although they'd lost their car and she'd lost her dignity, they were both still alive and unhurt. And a bit of her dignity was a small price to pay for the Hillman. Being on the move again had given Davy reason to believe he was going to make it, and everything that had passed was going to be worthwhile. It had been crowded in the small saloon.

There had been five other men in the Mercedes when Eamon had come back for Davy, and squeezing them into the Hillman had been a tight fit. Now there were only three in the new car. The others had headed for Belfast in the Hillman after Eamon had pulled into a lay-by and stolen an old Ford Prefect from an elderly couple who'd been having a picnic.

Davy felt his head bang off the roof and heard Brendan McGuinness, who was sitting in the passenger's seat, mutter, "Take it easy, Eamon."

Just my luck, Davy thought, to be stuck with that shite McGuinness.

The group had split up. Three men from Andersonstown, a Republican ghetto in the city, had wanted to head for home, and Davy had assumed McGuinness would also want to get back to his own familiar territory, but no such luck. It seemed his plan was to head for Dublin and the headquarters of Provisional Army Council, the Provos' governing body. It suited him to make the attempt to cross the border from Tyrone.

Davy stared at the outline of the man's bullet head. What was it that made him such a bitter little shite?

Davy had felt sympathy when the old gentleman pleaded with Eamon not to take the Ford, explaining that his wife was diabetic and had to get home for her insulin. McGuinness had asked Davy if he still had the .25 and made no bones that he thought they should shoot the old folks and dump the bodies in the bushes so it would take much longer for the Security Forces to find out what car some escapees were using.

Fuck you, McGuinness, Davy thought, glad he had lied, said he'd dumped the gun. He dropped his hand to his pants' pocket. The little revolver was hard against his hand. He hoped the old pair had managed to get help.

The car started to slow down. Had they arrived at the sanctuary Eamon had promised? Davy craned forward and tried to see what the headlights were showing. He could just make out the rear end of another car. Eamon braked and stopped the Ford. Davy could see that they were in a built-up area with lighted shop windows on both sides of the road. They hadn't reached safety yet. Was this Castlederg?

"The bastards. The bastards." Eamon pounded his fist on the steering wheel. "There's a fucking roadblock on the bridge."

Christ, it was like being on a roller coaster, up one minute, down the next. Davy stared through the windscreen to where, by the Ford's headlights and the dim glow of streetlights, he could see a tailback before the bridge. He glanced behind through the rear window. There was a great big petrol tanker nearly up their arse.

The queue was creeping inexorably to the checkpoint. As they moved along the main road, Davy could see Land Rovers and Saracens blocking every side road. Peelers and helmeted soldiers, weapons never still, covered the vehicles moving toward the bridge. How the hell could they get out of here?

Eamon said, "We're going to have to run for it. I can see the roadblock ahead and they're making everybody get out of their cars. If they see your uniform pants, Davy . . ."

McGuinness growled, "Leave McCutcheon. We can make it while they chase him."

Eamon ignored McGuinness. "There's a bunch of peelers in the street off to our left, then there's a gap up ahead and a bit of dark. As soon as we're into the shadow . . . everyone out."

Davy could understand why Eamon was well regarded by the Provos. That was the second time today in a moment of crisis that Eamon had taken charge. No fuss, no bother—he simply got on with what had to be done.

Davy followed Eamon and Brendan as they kept in the shadows and slid toward a tobacconist's shop, its lighted windows protected by a metal grille. Beside him, the line of cars jerked forward, and from behind came the honking of a horn. It must be the driver of the petrol tanker, impatient because his path was blocked by the abandoned Ford.

He saw Eamon and Brendan vanish inside the shop. As Davy shut the door behind him, he heard a small bell jangle. There was a notice hanging from a suction cup stuck to the door's glass. Davy turned the sign so to any passerby it would read CLOSED.

The shopkeeper, beefy in a collarless shirt, stood behind a glass-topped counter. Shelves behind him on the wall bore packets of cigarettes. Glass-stoppered bottles of unwrapped Gobstoppers, brandy balls, midget gems, and liquorice comfits jostled for space. In a better time, Davy would have bought quarter pounds of all three to give to the youngsters on his street.

A bead curtain hung from an arch at the back of the premises. Was that another way out?

"Can I help you, gentlemen?"

Eamon said, "*An bHfuil Gaeilge aGat*?" It was about the only Irish Davy knew. The citizens of Belfast had given up the ancient tongue generations ago—Gerry Adams had had to take Gaelic lessons when he was in the Kesh—but many Republicans from the country were still fluent. Loyalists were not. Despite city folks' general ignorance of Gaelic, one phrase, "Do you speak Irish?" was still a handy password in any Republican area. Da had taught Davy that, years ago.

He saw the shopkeeper's eyes, piggy slits in his jowled face.

"What?"

"*An bHuil . . .*"

"Fuckin' Fenian hoors' gits." The man's face turned puce. He lifted a horizontal wooden gate at the side of the counter's glass and forced his bulk through. He had fists like hams. "Get the fuck out of my shop, or I'll . . ."

"You'll what?" Eamon said. He stood in front of the man. Davy and Mc-Guinness flanked him, forcing him to back up against the counter. "You'll what? There's three of us."

"I'll . . ." He swung at Eamon. Missed. Eamon grabbed the arm, and Mc-Guinness kneed the man in the balls.

Davy heard him howl and his breath wheeze like air draining from torn bellows. The fat man's face crumpled, and he sank to his knees, clutching himself.

"See if we can get out the back, Davy. Brendan, lock the front door."

Davy shoved the bead curtain aside. He was in a storeroom. Cardboard cartons and crates of soft drinks were stacked to the low ceiling. An aisle between the supplies led to a door. He hurried to it, found the lock, opened it and tried to pull the door open. It wouldn't budge. He jiggled the lock and tried again. Not an inch. Davy put both hands on the handle and hauled until he could feel the veins standing out on his forehead. He paused to take a breath before he put his shoulder down and charged the thing. As he leaned forward, he noticed a sign on the doorframe. PUSH.

Push, for fuck's sake.

He did, and the door opened onto a concrete-paved backyard huddled between low red-brick walls, half-lit by the glow from the street lamps in front of the shop. Davy took one step and froze when something metallic crashed ahead of him. He saw a dustbin lid, still jangling as it settled on the concrete, and a cat leaping to the top of the wall.

"Christ." He ran back to the shop.

The shopkeeper lay on the floor, struggling to take off his trousers.

"There's a way out," Davy said.

"Great," Eamon said. "Get those guard's jacket and pants off you. Take your man's trousers."

Davy undid the waist button and zip, ripped the dark blue serge down. When he hauled on the shopkeeper's corduroys, he felt as if he had climbed into a tent, but at least the pants were dry and didn't yell, "Escaped prisoner." He peeled off his jacket, only pausing to retrieve Jimmy's letter and Fiona's picture and stick them in his pocket.

A shadow fell across the floor. Davy glanced to the window and saw a helmeted head and the outline of a self-loading-rifle. Their owner pounded on the locked front door.

"Open up."

The shopkeeper tried to slide across the floor. McGuinness booted him in the guts. His grunt was smothered by the sounds of pounding on the glass and a yell from outside of, "Open the fucking door." Glass shattered, and a hand slid though the broken pane, its fingers groping for the lock. There were more troops outside.

"Out the back," Eamon said quietly.

Eamon, followed by McGuinness, led the way through the storeroom. Davy hesitated, bent and pulled the .25 from his discarded trousers, and stuffed it in his new pants' pocket. He had no intention of using it, but unless things had changed radically since his day, the Provos had always found arms hard to come by. The least he could do was give this one back to its owners.

He ran into the next room, turning cartons and crates into the aisle behind him. Out the door and across the yard. He could hear the soldiers swearing as they struggled with the cartons in the storeroom.

Eamon and McGuinness were up ahead, and Davy pounded after them, trying to ignore the ache in his thigh.

"Halt or I'll fire."

A muzzle flash tore the night apart. The report echoed across the yard's walls. The bullet struck brick close to Davy's head, and the ricochet whined away to oblivion. Those fuckin' soldiers were given what the British army called Yellow Cards, rules of engagement that said troops could open fire only if fired upon. What the fuck did I fire at them, Davy asked himself, brandy balls?

He ran after Eamon. They were in a back alley between rows of terrace houses. Davy limped on as fast as he could, not daring to look back.

"*Halt.*"

Another shot. Eamon went down.

Davy ran up to the fallen man, grabbed him by the shoulder, and hauled him to his feet. There wasn't time to ask Eamon if he'd been shot. "Can you run?"

"Aye," Eamon managed to gasp.

"Come on, then." Davy pulled on Eamon's arm, relieved that he was following. If he hadn't been, Davy had already made up his mind to carry his friend.

The alley turned sharply to the left. That would protect them until the soldiers reached the corner.

Davy knew that he was flagging. His breath seared his lungs. He peered ahead. Where the hell had McGuinness gone?

Four more steps. It was only a matter of time before the soldiers . . .

"Get youse in here, quick," a woman yelled from where a gate stood open.

Davy hauled Eamon into another concreted backyard, heard the gate scratch over the surface. "Into the house."

He was in a kitchen, recently washed dishes stacked neatly in a draining board, laundry hanging from a pulley-operated rack overhead. The smell of boiled cabbage made him think of the Kesh and the back of the food lorry.

The woman, fluffy pink slippers on her feet, plastic Spoolies curlers in her hair, shut the kitchen door. "Your other fellah says you're out of the Kesh."

"Right."

"Me and my man heard the shooting."

"God bless you." Davy was able to breathe more easily.

Eamon supported himself on the kitchen table. "You folks in the . . . ?"

"We're not all bloody Prods here in Castlederg. You lads that was in the Kesh was fighting for the likes of us. Now, come on next door."

Davy helped Eamon across a hall and into a small parlour. A man in a dressing gown held out his hand. "Dermot Donnelly."

Davy took the hand. "Davy . . ."

"I don't want to know. Take the end of that sofa. Shove it back."

Davy pushed, and the sofa slid toward a wall, where three china mallards flew up to God alone knew where.

Dermot hauled the rug free, knelt, and lifted a section of floor. "Your other fellah's up in the attic. There's room for you two in there. Get in."

Davy climbed in, and Eamon followed. Dust, mouse shit, joists, and enough room for the pair of them to lie down if they curled up.

The floorboards above were refitted, and the hidey-hole plunged into darkness. Davy stifled a sneeze. He felt Eamon wriggling.

"You all right, Eamon?" Davy whispered.

"I'll live. I tripped over something."

"Jesus, I thought they'd got you."

"They might as well have. I knocked the wind out of myself. If you hadn't . . . I owe you one. You should have left me."

"Don't be daft. I've already left Sean Donovan behind. I wouldn't want it to get to be a habit."

Eamon laughed. "Back in the Kesh, when I first was put in, Gerry Adams told me not to pay any heed to what McGuinness said about you, Mc-Cutcheon, that you're a sound man. Gerry was right." Davy felt Eamon squeeze his arm. "But sure I've known that for years, Father."

Davy tried to shrug, but his shoulders were jammed against a joist. "I'd not be here if you hadn't come back for me outside the prison."

"But you are here, Davy, and I'm bloody glad that you are. I want to get home to Erin." Eamon said it as a monk might tell a fellow cleric that he was heading for the Holy Grail.

"So do I. Want to get home, I mean." Davy wondered why he'd said that. Canada wasn't his home. But Fiona was there. Had he ruined her photo when he'd crammed the revolver into the same pocket in his trousers? What the hell? It was only a snap; but it was that snap that had made him resolve to join this escape. Even if it was crushed and Jimmy's letter crumpled up, he'd still be able to read her phone number.

Davy laughed softly. A wee laugh was like the safety valve on a steam engine when the pressure built up. "I'm going to get there . . . somehow."

He heard Eamon shift position before he said, "You'd need papers. A passport, driving licence, National Insurance Number or whatever they call it in Canada, money."

"Aye. I might as well ask for a magic carpet while I'm at it."

"Don't be so sure about that. We've some bloody good forgers. I'll . . ."

"Would you?"

Eamon laughed. "I told you I owe you one. When we get out of this, back to Tyrone . . ." He let the promise hang.

But the promise half-spoken was enough to make Davy forget that he was thirsty, dirty, tired out—no, he was exhausted—and crammed in a dark hole under the floor of the house of a couple of Republican sympathizers. He hugged the promise to him.

His stomach rumbled. Dear God, but he was hungry. As he drifted off to sleep, Davy wondered how long it had been since he'd been in the back of a lorry with enough meals in it to feed 180 men.

CHAPTER 29

The meal was all but ready. On the kitchen table, two glass goblets held cold, freshly peeled, boiled prawns supported by beds of iceberg lettuce. On the counter, a pair of recently husked corncobs kept company with a panful of mushrooms and the makings of a green salad. Two Idaho potatoes were tinfoil-wrapped, ready to be popped into the oven. A bottle of a California Merlot stood uncorked, "breathing," Tim called that, and a Chardonnay was chilling in the fridge.

All Fiona had to do was mix the olive oil and vinegar for the salad dressing. If Tim's plane from San Francisco was on time, and when she'd called Air Canada they'd told her it would be, he'd be in a taxi on his way to Whyte Avenue.

When he phoned on Friday night, horribly apologetic that he had been unable to call sooner, Fiona had been surprised at how relieved she was to hear from him. They'd chatted about inconsequential things, the weather in Vancouver, the great Irish pub, Harry Harrington's, Tim had found on Jones Street. He'd told her—told her three times—that he loved her and suggested that she meet him at Bridges on Sunday night. She had said, emphatically, that she'd cook dinner.

Neither one had mentioned her "ghosts," as they now called her old painful memories, and she was grateful to Tim for that. Only one person could exorcize them, and that was her, and, she smiled, she was certainly starting to do that.

She was pleased with her decision of a week ago, strengthened this morning at the Aquarium, to let Davy back into her life so she could face him head-on, pleased to have recognized that by avoiding folks from Northern Ireland, she'd been trying to deny her heritage, and it was a heritage that she knew mattered to her.

Was she now ready to follow through on her new plan to phone Jimmy Ferguson and perhaps have a chat with Siobhan? Damnit, she asked herself, if she wasn't ready now, would she ever be?

Fiona walked through to the living room, took a deep breath, hunted in the back of her address book, took out the card Jimmy had given her, and dialed his home number.

Even after eight years in Canada, Fiona still found the single ringing tone odd. She waited to see if anyone would answer.

"Hello? Vancouver 555-2996."

She'd know Jimmy's voice anywhere. "Jimmy? It's Fiona."

"Fiona? Fiona Kavanagh? That's great, so it is. How're you doin'?"

"I'm fine thanks, Jimmy." And so far she was, if she ignored the way her fingers were drumming on the top of the telephone table.

"Dead on. So are you and your doctor going to take a run-race over?"

She hesitated. Was she ready?

"Hang on." She heard Jimmy shout, "Jessie, have we enough for five the night?"

Jessie was Jimmy's wife. Fiona had learned that the night in Bridges. Jessie's reply was indistinct.

"I've just had a word with the missus." Jimmy sounded excited. "Can you and Doctor Tim be round about eight?"

She laughed and could guess Jessie Ferguson, like most wives from Northern Ireland, had probably snapped at her husband but, having had hospitality bred into her, had ground her teeth and said she'd whip up something.

"Whoa, Jimmy. We can't make it tonight." And be honest, she told herself, she was glad about that, and not just because tonight was for her and Tim alone.

"Och! That's a shame, so it is." She heard him shout. "They're not coming, dear."

She could hear the disappointment in the man's voice and could imagine Jessie's relief.

"I'm sorry, Jimmy, but I did want to call and say it was great to see you last week. I'd not realized how much I've missed hearing people from Belfast."

"'At's all right. Maybe some other time, like?"

She hesitated. Hearing Jimmy's Belfast accent, knowing what he had meant to Davy, she had thought that even talking to him would have made her uncomfortable, but it hadn't. Well, not very. "I'd like that." She knew that she was nearly ready to face Jimmy and the part he'd played in her own past, but perhaps not quite yet. To forestall Jimmy suggesting a date, she said, "I'm really busy this week. Could I give you a call next weekend?"

"Could you not make it a wee bit sooner? Siobhan's away off back to Montreal on Friday, and I know she'd like for to see you, so she would."

Damn. If she wanted to meet Siobhan, Fiona could see that she'd have to stifle her fears of the past. She'd done pretty well plucking up the courage to phone Jimmy, hadn't she? Go the next step, she told herself. Meet the Fergusons. "Could I call you back in a day or two?"

"Aye, certainly."

"Thanks, Jimmy."

"It'll be great to talk about home with someone, so it will . . . hang on a wee minute . . ."

Fiona waited and tried to make out what Jimmy was saying to someone.

"Siobhan's here. She'd like to have a wee word with you."

"Hello, Fiona?" Fiona heard the same soft contralto she'd heard in Bridges. "Dad says I may not get a chance to see you before I leave."

"I'd like to see you, Siobhan."

"Look, Dad and Mum have to work during the day, but can you get free in the afternoons? Maybe just you and me could have a cup of coffee."

It was important for her to talk to Siobhan, ask her about her Marcus, the British soldier who'd been sent in to infiltrate the Provos. Perhaps Siobhan wanted to talk about Davy and Fiona. "I've a free afternoon on Tuesday."

It wasn't true. She'd no classes that afternoon but was meant to be meeting with Dimitris Papodopolous's family at two. She could reschedule. The principal and the bearded mathematics teacher had called a meeting for three. She felt guilty about missing these terminally boring affairs, but, damnit, Carnarvon Elementary could function for one day without her.

"Terrific. I still don't know Vancouver very well. Could you come here?"

"What time? I have the address on your dad's card."

"Two?"

"That would be lovely . . . and, Siobhan . . . I hope you don't mind but . . ." Her voice tailed off.

"You want to ask me about . . . Davy."

She looked at her watch. "Siobhan, someone's coming for dinner, so I have to run. But I will come to your folks' place on Tuesday . . . and we'll talk."

"I'd like that."

"Two on Tuesday." Fiona didn't wait for an answer as she hung up, congratulated herself on how she'd handled the conversation, and, humming gently, walked into the bathroom to make sure that she was ready for Tim.

She wanted him to get the full benefit of her just-bought-this-afternoon Diane von Furstenberg dress. She admired herself in the mirror. Makeup? Very little—a tiny touch of eyeliner and mascara and a pale pink lipstick. She patted her freshly shampooed hair back into place. Her black patent leather pumps, the high-heeled sneakers that Tim liked, pinched a bit, but he was worth a little discomfort. The new dress, cream with a superimposed, subdued paisley pattern in reds and browns, was simply cut. Knee-length and wraparound, it was held closed by a single tie at the waist. She fiddled with the V-neck, pulling the edges just a little more to the side so that the upper curves of her breasts were visible. She cupped them and offered a silent prayer of thanks that she was still firm enough to go braless. All that she wore under the dress was a pair of black silk bikini panties. She put the tiniest dab of a musky perfume at the hollow of her throat.

Fiona went back to the living room. It was a bit nippy, so she lit the propane fire. McCusker marched to the front of it, sat, threw his head back, and stared fixedly at the cornice between the wall and ceiling. The cat always did that when she lit the fire. McCusker, Fiona was convinced, had adopted the flames as a feline deity, and his stance and upwardly fixed gaze were a prayerful attitude, as if the animal were attempting to attain a state of grace.

She selected a record, Kiri Te Kanawa's Mozart arias, turned the volume low, and as the first notes of *Voi che sapete* whispered from the speakers, the intercom buzzer rang.

"G'dye."

"Come on in, Tim." She opened her door and watched him stride along the hall carrying his briefcase in one hand and pulling a small wheeled suitcase behind him. She hadn't realized fully until that moment just how much she'd missed him.

He stopped in front of her, let go of his suitcase, and, still hanging on to his briefcase, hugged her. She felt his lips warm on hers and the briefcase bumping her backside. She was breathless when they broke apart.

"Welcome back. Here, let me take that."

Tim handed her the briefcase, tugged his suitcase into the living room, and flopped into a chair. "Strewth," he said, pulling off his suit jacket and tie and chucking them over his chair back, "it's nice to be home."

"Nice to have you back," she said, putting the briefcase beside the telephone table. "I've missed you."

"Give us another kiss."

She bent before him, knowing that he couldn't help but be peering down her cleavage—that was why she'd bought this dress, wasn't it?

He tasted salty.

"Now," she said, still bent at the waist, "let me get you a drink. I've opened a good Merlot."

"Later," he said. "Right now I need a cold beer. I'm as dry as . . ."

". . . A dead dingo's thing-a-ma-bob." She laughed. "I even know what you're thinking."

She could see him staring down the front of her dress.

"Do you, by God?" he said. "In that case, I should be blushing." He reached for her, but she moved away.

"Yes, you should, but don't bother. I'm thinking the same thing myself"—she took another step back—"but later."

"Aaaw."

"Later." She left for the kitchen. "I'll get you that beer."

She returned in a moment, a glass of Chardonnay for herself in one hand and a cold glass of beer in the other. No one back in Ireland would think of drinking beer straight from the tin the way Canadians did.

"There you are," she said, handing him the glass, "Foster's Lager."

"Best grog in Oz." Tim demolished half of the beer in one swallow. "Now that's what I call taking care of a bloke."

She sat in the other armchair, crossed her legs, not minding that as she did so, the hem of her dress rode up, exposing half of one still-tanned thigh. "Cheers," she said, sipping her wine. "And again, welcome home, Tim."

He reclined and stretched his long legs, feet crossed at the ankles. "Sometimes I wonder why I bother going to these conventions. Dull lectures, rubber chicken dinners, and a lot of blokes polishing each other's egos, and," he said, arching his back, "I'm the wrong size to fly in the back of the bus. I swear to God Air Canada has the seats on a ratchet system and move them closer to each other every hour on the hour."

"You poor thing." She smiled at him.

"Nah," he said, and she heard the serious note in his voice, "it's worth it, just to come home and see you, love."

"Thank you, sir," she said, inclining her head and smiling.

"And it's worth it to see that smile on your face." Tim stood and moved in front of her. Only a shadow of his smile remained. "How've you been?"

"Me? Fine." But she knew what he was really asking. "Fine. Honestly."

"No more nightmares?" He laid one hand on her shoulder.

She shook her head. "I did have a chat with Becky about . . ." She didn't want to say the word.

"Good," Tim said. "And what does Becky think?"

"About me and Northern Ireland and . . . ?" She couldn't look at him.

"The Davy fellow," Tim finished her sentence.

She looked up at him and nodded.

"Well?"

Fiona sighed. "She said pretty much what you did, that I have to face up to it all, stop pretending none of it ever happened, get over it, and get on with life." She looked him directly in the eye. "You're both right. And, Tim, I'm trying. I really am. I . . ." She hesitated. "I thought about . . . Davy . . . a lot today." She glanced at Tim to see how he was taking that.

He cocked his head to one side, "And?"

"And you were right. I do have to face it."

"Good lass," he said, bending and kissing her gently. "It's all I can ask. That you try."

"I am," she said. "Really." And inside she thanked him for his understanding and his patience. "I even phoned Davy's old pal Jimmy just before you came. I'm having coffee with Siobhan next Tuesday."

"Jimmy's daughter? And you're not worried it could bring back too many memories?" She heard concern in his voice.

"To be honest? Yes, I am worried, but if I'm ever going to get over it, I *have* to see her, and—don't get cross—one day soon you and I will have to have a meal with Jimmy and his wife."

"Why would I get cross? He seemed a decent enough chap. I can certainly stand an evening with him if it's important to you." He kissed her gently. "I do love you," he said quietly.

"I know," she said, and only briefly hesitated before whispering, "and I love you, Tim."

She stood and hugged him not with passion but as a sister might hug a brother, and, bless him, Tim responded just as a brother might and softly stroked her hair.

She moved away from him but held on to his hand. "Come on," she said. "The prawn cocktails'll be getting soggy," and she led him through to the kitchen.

Tim burped. "'Scuse me." He laid his knife and fork neatly across his plate between the empty skin of the potato and the now-stripped corncob. "Feast fit for a king."

Fiona chuckled. "I'm glad you enjoyed it, your majesty."

"Too right, and this is very good, too." He drank the last mouthful of Merlot from his glass and refilled it from the bottle, now half empty.

Fiona picked up their plates and took them to the counter beside the sink, opened the fridge, and took out her Chardonnay. She had been more abstemious than Tim, but as she moved back to the table and topped up her own glass, she recognized that inside her was a gentle warmth, and she wondered if it was the wine, or simply having Tim back that gave her the glow. "I'll pop this back in the fridge," she said. As she returned to the table and picked up her glass, she was conscious of Tim's gaze moving over her from the tips of her pumps to the top of her head. She raised her glass. "Right," she said, "what'll we drink to?"

Tim glanced at the neck of her dress then back into her eyes.

She noticed how grey his eyes were, pale yet deep.

"How about"—Tim's voice was soft and serious—"to us?"

"To us," she said from across the table, and drank.

"To us," Tim said, and winked at her.

The wink surprised her. Made her giggle. Some of the glow she felt was definitely wine-induced. And the feeling pleased her. She moved around to him and heard his chair legs scrape on the floor as he pushed it back and stood. She looked up at his face. Felt his lips on hers, his tongue on her tongue, his arms round her, strong but gentle. She laid her head on his chest and murmured, "Welcome back. I've missed you."

Tim stroked her hair. "You smell good," he said.

She felt his hand at her waist.

"What does this line do?" he asked, tugging at the dress's tie.

She took two paces back, her own hands dropping to the bow. "Watch," she said, as the knot slipped free. "I'll show you." She unwrapped the folds of cloth and held the dress apart, feeling the coolness of the evening air on her breasts. She saw Tim's eyes narrow, heard his breathing quicken, as did her own.

She knew, as women had known from the beginning of time, that men were so easily aroused by what they saw. She pouted, moistened her thumb and one index finger between her lips, then used them to grasp her left nipple, feeling it stiffen. She closed her eyes and pulled in one long breath. She let her nipple free and, using both hands, slipped the dress from her shoulders, feeling the light material slip to the floor to lie crumpled round her ankles.

She heard Tim gasp. "God," he said, "you're lovely."

She smiled at him, and when he smiled back, she felt heat between her thighs and an urgency that would not wait. "Love me, Tim," she said, softly. "Love me."

His shirt was rough against her skin, his hands warm and soft on her back. She felt the hardness of him and his hands on her buttocks pulling her against him. She felt the heat of him and her own heat and the dampness of her. She kissed him, softness on softness. She tasted the bouquet of his wine. His hand cupped her breast and his mouth found her nipple, and the softness of his kiss on her breast was matched by the hardness of him.

"Love me, Tim," she whispered, taking his hand, feeling the one callus that she knew was the result of hauling lines on *Windy*.

She squeezed his hand. "Love me, darling." And like a mother leading an eager child, she brought him to her bedroom.

"Go away," Fiona muttered, half awake. Beside her, Tim's breathing was soft and regular. His hand still held one breast.

The telephone in the living room jangled again.

She glanced at the alarm clock on her bedside table. Who the hell would be phoning her at eleven thirty? "Go away."

She vaguely heard her own recorded voice telling the caller to leave a message. Why, tonight of all nights, must she be woken from the best sleep she'd had in weeks, sleep that had stolen on her as softly as the autumn fog rolls into Burrard Inlet while she lay spent, nestled against the safety of Tim, the pair of them curled up like two spoons?

The answering machine beeped.

She heard a voice—a man's voice with a thick Belfast accent. It had to be Jimmy, but she couldn't make out what he was saying, didn't want to make out what he was saying. The wee Ulsterman was too keen by half, what they'd call "pushy" here in Canada. She felt her lips curl into a soft smile. Take your hurry in your hand, Jimmy. Whatever it was could keep until the morning. She pushed back against the warmth of Tim and, knowing that he held her safe from her dreams, slipped into an untroubled sleep.

CHAPTER 30

Erin huddled in the kitchen armchair. She'd been awake all night. How could she possibly sleep? Eamon should have been here in the late evening, should have been but wasn't. It was now 7:00 A.M., and there was no sign of him.

It was seventy-five miles from the Kesh to the farm. She'd driven those roads often enough to know them as well as she knew the lane from the farm. It shouldn't have taken more than three hours for him and his friends to reach the nearby woods, where he'd told her they'd wait until dark before finally crossing an open field to the tumulus.

The breakout had happened at 2:30 yesterday afternoon, and she'd marked every hour on the hour since then, hoping, wishing. She'd been able to pass the early part of the evening doing routine chores. She'd finished milking the dairy herd. Even dealing with that bloody cow, Margaret, had been something distracting to do. She'd made an early supper and taken pleasure from the way Cal, as usual, tucked in. She'd picked at her food.

Needing something to occupy her mind after supper, she'd talked with Cal to refine their plans for the attack on the Security Forces.

After she'd cleared the dirty plates, she'd laid a large-scale map of Strabane and the surrounding countryside on the kitchen table. Cal and she had gone over the details of the raid and the all-important getaway. As she explained the finer points to Cal, he'd become more and more enthusiastic. All that time she'd listened for any unexpected sounds from outside, despite knowing that there'd be nothing to hear. Eamon and his friends were to go to ground, and she was to make her way to the grave after dark and greet them.

She'd waited until Cal had gone to bed, telling herself she was giving Eamon and his friends plenty of time to be safe in the tumulus. And, she admitted, if he had to wait that hour or two longer to see her, he'd be all the more glad when she came to him.

She'd crept to the neolithic grave only to find it deserted, told herself that it served her right for trying to play silly games with Eamon's emotions, reassured herself that the men would be here soon.

She'd gone back twice: once at 10:00 to hang a thick blanket as a blackout curtain over the inside of the entrance, because on her first visit she'd noticed that light from the passage could be seen through the brambles. There was no sign of the men.

In the wee hours, when a sudden gale had rattled the shutters and hurled rain against the windows like bursts of machine-gun fire, she'd put on her oilskins and battled against the wind to deliver a heap of bath towels wrapped in a plastic bag. The men would be soaked. But there weren't any men, just damp and spiders and the ghosts of long-dead Celts. She'd left the towels on the table, turned out the lights, and struggled back to the warmth of the kitchen.

Now, fearful that someone might notice her going and coming in the daytime, she knew she must wait, as indeed the men would, until darkness fell again. They were somewhere out in this bloody awful weather. She shivered.

Wait. She'd done nothing but wait in this kitchen; waiting on Friday night for Fiach, who would never return to her, waiting now for Eamon, who would. He *would*, damnit.

She walked to the kitchen door, opened the top half, and stared out into a steady downpour so heavy that the nearby hills were hidden behind curtains of rain that slashed across the farmyard, the sheets of water blown nearly horizontal by a bitter northeaster. She hoped that Eamon and his friends were somewhere sheltered.

She wished she could see the familiar landscape, the fields, the valley, the Strule, and the hills, because in the not too distant future they would have to live only in her memory. The long early morning hours had given her time to consider her future.

She could see clearly that once they were committed to bombing the Strabane Barracks, and she had every intention of doing so, there was a risk that if any one of the attackers were taken or killed, the Security Forces would be able to identify their other assailants and come after them. The prospect of her own dying caused her little concern, but the thought of a long prison sentence, locked in a cage like an animal, miles from her home, her Tyrone, made her shudder. Once they had attacked, it would be safer to run. She was sure of that.

They *could* call off the raid, but she'd still have to face the fact that Eamon couldn't stay here. He'd have to get away, and he'd expect her to go with him. In her heart she knew that yesterday afternoon in the tumulus she hadn't been sure what she'd do. After the long night just gone, worrying about him, aching for him, she had made the decision to go, and she'd tell him—when he arrived.

So, if it were inevitable that she would have to leave all this, leave the farm, leave the Ireland she loved—Erin smiled thinly as she thought of the five hundred pounds of ammonal Sammy was making—she might as well go out with a bang.

She heard the hall door open. It would be Cal, and, damnit, he'd be wanting his breakfast. She wished that her brother had taken the trouble to learn how to fry bacon and eggs for himself.

"Morning, Cal."

"How are you, girl? No word yet?"

She shook her head and walked to the fridge. She heard the wind slamming the top half of the outer door with the same finality with which she had closed her mind to any possibility of staying in Tyrone.

"Bacon and eggs?"

"If you can be bothered."

"Whenever couldn't I be? It's my job." She tried to keep bitterness from her voice, clattered the pan onto the range top, stripped three rashers of Galtee bacon from their package, and lifted two brown eggs from their carton.

The bacon spat and sizzled in the pan, and the smell of its frying made her stomach heave. She'd drunk so much tea last night, she'd not room for one more cup, never mind bacon. "There's tea in the pot," she said.

"Thanks."

She watched Cal fill his cup before saying, "Will I turn on the news?"

She hesitated. The story of the break would be all over the headlines. What if they said Eamon had been recaptured? She closed her eyes. She knew, she just knew, that he hadn't—but—but if she were wrong? The truth would be better than her present uncertainty. She opened her eyes, feeling them gritty, knowing they would be bloodshot. "Go ahead," she said quietly.

Cal turned the knob on the TV that sat among the copper pots on the Welsh dresser.

> Roadblocks have been operative in a series of concentric circles at five-mile intervals on every road leading from the Maze. Many escapees have been stopped and detained. One inmate, Sean Donovan, was shot and killed while attempting to escape.

Erin flinched. Donovan was one of the men Eamon had said he'd be bringing to Tyrone, and if he'd been killed . . . She held her breath as the newsreader continued:

> Some of those still at large are senior members of the Provisional IRA. Among them are Brendan (Bic) McFarlane; the Old Bailey bomber, Bobby Storey, who, it is believed, was the mastermind behind the jailbreak; and Brendan McGuinness and David McCutcheon, who were imprisoned together in 1973 following an attempt on the life of the then prime minister Harold Wilson.

Erin moved closer to the screen. Eamon had mentioned a Davy Mc-Cutcheon as his cell mate and friend. McGuinness was coming with Eamon, so perhaps McCutcheon was, too, and if they were still at large, Eamon had to be. He had to be. "Do you think that means Eamon's still out?" she asked Cal and was reassured by his, "I'm sure of it," even though she knew he had no more reason than her to sound so certain.

Pictures of army and police vehicles flickered on the screen. The image changed to an aerial view of the Kesh as the camera panned slowly over the perimeter wall, zoomed in for a close-up of grim-faced soldiers in one of the watchtowers, and switched to a wide-angle shot of the H-blocks and the deserted compounds. Erin listened carefully.

> The guards who were held captive by the prisoners have been released, but the prisoners have barricaded themselves in their cells and are refusing to come out until assured that there will be no reprisals. The guards are understandably angry. Six of their number were injured in fights, two seriously. We are taking you now to the Royal Victoria Hospital.

Erin crossed her arms, leaned her head on her shoulder. Eamon had said there wouldn't be any violence, not that she gave a shite about the Brits, but if guards had been hurt and Donovan shot dead, there must have been more injuries among the prisoners.

A shutter banged, and she twitched as if she had heard a gunshot. Was Eamon hurt—bleeding—hiding in a ditch somewhere in this god-awful gale?

She stared at a young woman reporter cowering under a golf umbrella in front of the red brick entrance to the Royal. Wind in the microphone distorted the words.

Of the six injured officers, three have already been discharged after receiving treatment for sprains, cuts, and bruises. Officer John Adams, who was shot in the head, is in the Royal on ward 21, the neurosurgery unit, and is in serious but stable condition. He is expected to make a full recovery. Officer George Smiley has been admitted to hospital with what is thought to be a perforated duodenal ulcer. One guard, whose name cannot be released until the next of kin have been notified, was stabbed with a wood chisel and has subsequently died, not, we are informed by a hospital spokesman, of his wounds but of a heart attack. In addition, Hugh Wilson, the caterer's lorry driver, is under observation for "nervous exhaustion."

Erin could smell something, something wrong. Christ, the bacon was burning. She grabbed the pan, roasting her hand on the metal handle, dropped it, found the oven cloth, lifted the pan and shoved it in the sink, turning on the hot tap and stepping back as the pan hissed and bubbled and a column of greasy smoke rose to the roof beams. "I'm sorry about that, Cal," she said, and inwardly thanked him when he put his arm round her shoulder and said, "Never worry. I'll make myself some toast."

She turned off the tap and faced the screen, where the newsreader in the studio was saying, "Members of the public are warned not to approach any suspicious-looking men, as they may be armed and dangerous. It is hoped that the crisis will not last long. We have been informed by RUC headquarters that the Security Forces have mounted Operation Vesper, involving thirty thousand security personnel. The airports, harbours, and all train stations are under surveillance. The border with the Irish Republic has been sealed." He gave his most reassuring smile. "The dragnet is being drawn closed. It is unlikely that the escapees will remain at large for long."

Erin felt Cal's arm tighten about her. She'd had to stand on her own two feet since Da died, but she was not too proud to let her big brother comfort her now as he'd done when she was a wee girl, crying because someone had broken one of her dollies.

In the background, the television droned on. ". . . Turning to the sports news, Linfield have signed an exciting new German striker . . ."

Erin pulled away from Cal's protection. She was worried, worried sick about Eamon, but in her, her concerns wrestled with rage, the pain of Fiach's murder, her disgust with the great mob of people in the North who couldn't care a shite about Ireland and Irish freedom.

"Listen to that. A bloody soccer player. That's more important to half the idiots here than the breakout. People in Northern Ireland want to pretend that nothing's happening here. Jesus wept, Cal. Turn that bloody thing off."

Cal switched off the set.

"They think if they go to their soccer games, close their eyes, then we'll go away. Well, we won't. Not here in Tyrone." She stood, arms tightly folded across her chest, fire in her green eyes, knowing that of all her anger the fiercest part was reserved for the root cause, the British occupation of the Six Counties.

"Sit down, Cal," she said. "We need to talk."

He sat at the table, making toast forgotten. "About Eamon?"

She shook her head. "We can do nothing about him. I just hope to God he's all right . . ."

"He will be."

"Maybe, but if he's still out, and I have to believe he is, he'll not try to get here until after dark, and the pair of us can't sit here all day like a couple of broody hens worrying ourselves sick. Can we just try to put him out of our minds for a minute or two?" Erin knew why she was suggesting that. The matters she had to discuss with Cal would occupy her thoughts completely.

She stood facing her brother, looking directly into his eyes. Her voice carried all the seriousness in her. "Cal, just so I'm certain, are you sure, absolutely sure, that you want to go ahead?"

"With . . . ?"

"Aye. The attack on the barracks."

She waited for him to speak, waiting for the least suggestion that he couldn't meet her gaze.

His eyes never left hers. "No," he said, "I'm not sure . . . but I'll do it."

At least he was being honest.

"Why aren't you sure?"

Cal took a very deep breath. "What we've discussed *should* work. You've me persuaded it *will* work, running the tractor down the hill into Strabane, through the wire-mesh fence outside the barracks. That chicken-wire contraption is only meant to keep out Molotov cocktails. You're right that snipers at the street corners can deal with any peelers who survive the blast if they run onto the street. We've hashed and rehashed the details of the getaway. It should be OK."

"Then why aren't you sure?" His uncertainty was rattling her. Cal might be a procrastinator, but once he made his mind up to do a job, he did it.

Cal covered his mouth with one hand, glanced at the tabletop and back into her eyes. "I don't know," he said quietly, rubbing the web of his hand over his chin. "It just doesn't . . . feel right. Don't ask me why." He stood, clenched fists, which hung loosely by his sides. She saw his jawline harden. "But . . . and it's a big but . . . them's the buggers that got Fiach, so to hell with my feelings . . . superstitious drivel, anyway. If Eamon and his mates are on for it, and you're still on for it, we'll do it."

She moved to him and hugged her big brother. She knew, after thinking about it throughout last night, that her choice had been easy to make. Cal was willing to overrule his feelings, even if in Ireland such premonitions should be taken seriously, no matter what Cal might say about superstition.

Although he hadn't said it, Cal was willing to go ahead not because of how he felt about Ireland—although he was Irish to the bone—and only partly because he wanted revenge for Fiach. Cal had always fallen in with her plans because he loved his family, and she was his sister. And Erin loved him for that, and, because she loved him, she forced herself to tell him the thing that he didn't seem to have considered.

She let him go, walked a few paces, and turned.

"You know that if we go ahead, me and Eamon and likely you too'll have to go to the States?" She smelled the peat in the range, saw the old wooden table, and in her mind saw Da sitting there, pipe lit, singing old rebel songs. "We'll have to leave the farm."

Cal surprised her. He nodded. "Aye. I've thought about that. I'd not want it to fall into strangers' hands."

"Who'd . . . ?"

"Who'd look after it? Sammy. For a while."

"Sammy?" She heard her voice rise. "Sammy?"

"Aye. When we talked about it, planned it, we reckoned we'd need a team of seven. I think we could manage with six. Sammy can't go on the run with us, so he has to have a foolproof alibi if he does go out on the attack. He's sure to get lifted afterward, because the peelers know he works for us."

"Why would Sammy get lifted?"

"Come on, Erin. If we run, it's the next best thing to a confession. I reckon the police would be smart enough to work out who the attackers were. They'd be bound to go after Sammy. We can't take him with us, and if we make him come on the raid and he hasn't got a watertight story for afterward, we'd be dropping him in the shite."

She recognized immediately that Cal was speaking the truth. She might not like the wee man, but it was a long Provo tradition to protect its volunteers. "You're right, Cal. And if he doesn't go and has a cover story, even if they do lift him, they'd have to let him go."

"Exactly. And then he could keep an eye to the place, aye, and look after Tessie and the beasts when we're gone, at least until the rest of the family decide what to do. I think one of them would come home to take over. Maybe Turloch would come back from Australia."

Erin took a step back. Why hadn't she thought of that? She'd never even thought about the border collie, or any of the other animals for that matter. And what Cal had just said about Sammy was brilliant. If Cal could have his feelings, so could she, and she didn't trust Sammy.

She knew she had no real reason not to trust him, but she'd seen him staring at her breasts yesterday. She shuddered. And something else still worried away at her. The police had been very quick off the mark to tell the O'Byrnes that Fiach had been killed because a routine patrol had spotted him. How often did the Security Forces patrol out here in the wilds of Tyrone? Practically never, because they were scared to. They *could* have had a tip-off, and the only one who could have touted was Sammy. She knew she couldn't prove that. To try to do so would drive him away, and they still needed him to make the explosives, steal the vehicles.

She had already decided not to tell him about the exact target until the very last minute. He'd accepted her explanation that he shouldn't know until after he'd stolen the vehicles—just in case he got lifted. Now, if they did what Cal suggested, then they'd never have to tell Sammy, and she was pleased about that.

"I hadn't thought of that," she said, then hesitated. "It's a great notion, but do you think we could manage with five?"

"Why five?"

"Because we just heard that Sean Donovan was killed."

Cal crossed himself. "God rest his soul."

"Never mind his soul. He was meant to be coming here with Eamon."

"That's right. So maybe we will need Sammy after all."

No. She wanted him kept in the dark, and she knew that once she and Cal were gone, there must be a caretaker for the farm until one of the other O'Byrnes came back.

"I think," she said slowly, "five could do the job, but we'll need to talk to Eamon . . . when he gets here. I'd like to have Sammy able to stay and"—the realization hit her—"if one of the rest of the family comes back and runs the place, it'll be waiting for us to come home to when . . ."—and it would be, it would be—". . . when Ireland's reunited and the Brits have gone."

She wondered why Cal was looking at her as a father might look at a child who'd just claimed she'd seen a leprechaun. Let her brother doubt. She had no doubts, none at all, that Irish independence would come.

CHAPTER 31

Irish independence. Sometimes Sammy had to remind himself what the fuck he was supposed to be doing this for. And what the hell did that mean: independence? A free shamrock on Saint Patrick's Day for everyone, singing "The Soldier's Song" instead of "God Save the Queen," and every signpost in Gaelic, which he couldn't read anyway. Sammy sneered and tugged his raincoat tightly round his skinny chest. It was fuckin' well freezing in the stolen tractor's unheated cab, so it was, with the rain driving in through badly fitting Perspex side panels that flapped and rattled in the wind. The gusts were so strong that every time he'd tried to light a Park Drive, he couldn't keep the match lit long enough for the tobacco to take. He was dying for a fag.

The only good thing about the gale was that it was keeping the Security Forces' helicopters grounded. There seemed to have been more of them in the air than a swarm of gnats yesterday, hunting for the poor buggers on the run from the Kesh.

Jesus, but the ones that were still free must feel great, just being out of their jail for a while. Sammy knew all about prisons and that being behind bars wasn't the only sort of prison a man could be in. He knew that only too bloody well.

If only his telephone conversation with Spud yesterday afternoon had gone better. Did the bugger not recognize the risks Sammy had to take just to phone? Could he not at least have congratulated Sammy for having been right that something *was* up at the Kesh? All the E4A man had said was that the new information about an attack on Strabane Barracks *could* be interesting, but not right now, Sunshine, I'm desperately busy with the breakout. Get hold of me in a couple of days. Good-bye.

Fuck that. A couple of days? Had that bloody peeler any notion of what each day stuck in Tyrone meant to Sammy McCandless? Spud said he was Sammy's friend. The only man he could trust. All he could be trusted to do was bugger Sammy around—but there was no one else to turn to, and, anyway, with a bit of luck in the next day or two, Sammy might have all the information he needed. If he could really be sure that it was Strabane and, most importantly, *when*, he could hand the lot to Spud on a plate, but only, only, when the E4A bugger had kept his word about England. Maybe waiting wasn't such a bad idea.

And it wasn't Sammy's fault that Spud was busy. He wasn't the only one. Erin had said she wanted to get the job done as soon a possible.

Sammy was doing his best about that. This freezing-cold tractor and the dusty five hundred pounds of ammonal he'd worked at making until late last night were the proof. He just wished it was like the old days, when he'd have been doing his work to please Erin. Now all he could think of was how soon he could find out more, could get Spud to agree to Sammy's plan, and maybe, just maybe, very soon, for the first time in six months, could get a decent night's sleep without having to wonder who might come hammering on his cottage door.

Christ, but he'd like to see his way ahead.

Sammy hunched forward but could hardly see through the squalls. As if that wasn't bad enough, the weight of the front-loader bucket made steering nearly impossible.

He had to wrench hard on the steering wheel to prevent the machine slewing off into the ditch. He slowed down because he knew that there was a hairpin bend coming up that would be a bugger to get round.

Once he got onto the straight after the bend, it was less than a couple of miles to the outbuilding at his cottage. He'd be there in another five minutes, and then, by God, he was going to get this bitch of a thing inside and cover it with a tarpaulin. The repainting job and fitting false number plates could wait. He was going to run into his cottage, chuck a heap more peat on the fire, get dry, have the cigarette he craved, make himself a fuckin' huge, hot John Jameson's whiskey, even if it was only about noon and he normally didn't take a drink before six o'clock, and then put his fuckin' feet up. He'd earned that. Bejesus he had.

Up half the night finishing making the explosive. When the storm had started, he had been truly thankful that the outbuilding *was* waterproof—a huge, cold raindrop was blown in and dripped down inside Sammy's collarless shirt—unlike the cab of this bloody tractor. He was tired, soaked, foundered with the cold, and wanted to get home.

The machine rocked and bounced over the pothole-pitted road. Christ Almighty, could the Tyrone County Council not send out a couple of men with shovels and a load of hot tarmac to fill in the craters?

Sammy had never in his whole life been farther from Tyrone than into County Donegal across the border. He'd heard about the motorway from Belfast and that England was crisscrossed with first-class roads. He'd like to see one of them, if they existed. Aye, if. Irish folks were powerful good at believing what they wanted to believe. Them as had fled Ireland on the coffin ships when they'd been evicted by English landlords after the Great Hunger had believed that the streets of America were paved with gold. The Irish back then would have believed anything.

They'd soon found out which end was up when the men, who hadn't a word of English among them, were met at the docks by an interpreter, offered an immediate job, three square meals a day, and a new suit of clothes if they'd just make their marks on pieces of paper.

Maybe the sidewalks of New York weren't golden after all, but getting a paying job right off a boat where half the passengers had died of dysentery or typhus must mean America was the promised land after all. Leaving their homes forever and facing the perils of the Atlantic crossing had been worth it.

Those that signed got the job all right, and the new suit. The suit was navy blue with a leather-peaked kepi and a .50 calibre minié musket as accessories. Most of the poor bastards who had, in all innocence, signed up for the Union Army never came back from the U.S. Civil War.

And that, he thought, came from trusting someone who seemed to care about you. The damnable thing was that even if Spud really didn't give a shite about Sammy, he was bloody good at giving the impression that he did. And Sammy had come in an odd way to like the policeman. He'd miss him when he delivered on his promise and Sammy was away to hell and gone from Tyrone, its fuckin' miserable weather, its rutted roads with hairpin bends like the one he was crawling round, knowing that the cottage, the fire, the cigarette, and the whiskey were almost in sight . . .

Fuck it. Fuck—it. There was a Saracen armoured car parked on the verge just after the crown of the bend, and a soldier in a flapping waterproof cape standing in the middle of the road waving at Sammy to stop. What had Erin said? We'll not tell you the target in case you get lifted. He was stuffed.

Yet Sammy was surprised to feel a sense of relief. If he was done for stealing a tractor, at least he'd be safe in a civilian prison for a couple of years. Maybe if they let him have a word with Spud, the peeler could get him off the criminal charge, just like the last time, listen to what Sammy had to say, and . . .

He braked and pulled the tractor to the side of the road just in front of the armoured car. He took out his wallet, started to remove his forged driver's licence, and recognized the uselessness of doing so. If the soldiers had the tractor's plate numbers, he was buggered and that was all there was to it.

He undid the catch, holding the side panel shut, making sure it was the one in the tractor's lee. He was wet and cold enough as it was without taking an unnecessary soaking. That Brit was dressed for the weather in his army-issue waterproofs. Let him get drenched.

Sammy waited for the soldier to draw level before lifting the side panel. He noticed that the man, although carrying a Belgian FN self-loading rifle, did so with its muzzle pointing to the ground. That would keep the rain out right enough, but Sammy knew from too much experience that getting the barrel wet didn't usually stop these shites from covering a suspect.

"Very sorry to bother you, sir, so I am."

Holy God, the man had a thick Belfast accent. Sammy knew it wasn't unusual for Ulstermen to volunteer to serve with the British Forces. They'd done so for centuries. Old man O'Byrne, when he'd been alive, God rest his soul, was forever going on about England fighting her wars off the backs of the Irish.

"We've run into a wee bit of bother, sir. Maybe you could help us, like?"

It wasn't an arrest. Sammy didn't know whether to be relieved or disappointed, and as for helping the British, he was an expert at that. "What can I do for you, Sergeant?"

"I'm only a buck private, sir," the soldier said, hunching his shoulders against the driving rain. "It's right fuckin' embarrassing, so it is. I'm driving that yoke there"—he gestured to the Saracen—"and I'm lost."

"You're what?" Sammy nearly smiled. "And you an Ulsterman? My God."

"Aye, well. I'm from East Belfast . . ."

Protestant bastard.

". . . I've never been out of Belfast in my puff until I went to England for to join up."

Sammy did smile. Just like himself, who'd never been out of the country, but at least the soldier had been to England. "Where're you trying to get to?" Sammy knew only too well where he was trying to get to.

"Portadown, and then it's only a wee doddle on to Thiepval Barracks in Lisburn. I tell you, mate, I'll not be sorry to get in out of this fuckin' rain."

"Me neither," said Sammy, thinking of the big hot Jameson's. "Right," he said. "Go a ways the way you're headed. About two miles."

"Right."

"Take the first right at the crossroads."

"First right?"

"Aye. Onto the A5, and that'll take you to Omagh. Follow the signs from there to Ballygawley. Left there'll get you to the M1 Motorway."

"That's great, so it is. Never mind Portadown. I can find Lisburn once we're on the M1."

Sammy hoped he had given the man the right directions. He was simply repeating the route that he'd heard Erin say she used to go to the Kesh to visit Eamon.

"Thanks, mate," the soldier said. "Sorry to hold you up."

"Never worry. I wasn't going anywhere important."

"Take you care now, oul' hand. There's all kinds of the bad lads on the run, so there is."

Sammy watched the soldier jog back to the Saracen and climb in. He waited for it to pull out and pass the tractor, and it left a cloud of exhaust fumes to be torn apart by the wind. He put the tractor in gear and started to drive to his cottage. Easy as that, by God. The soldiers had just wanted to be told how to get home.

And Sammy had got himself all worked up over nothing. But maybe it wasn't nothing. Maybe he was like those soldiers, looking for guidance. Maybe, he thought, maybe those lost soldiers could think of a barracks in a hostile country as home. How the hell could he ever think of his wee cottage, Tyrone, Ireland, as his home? He could find his cottage, right enough, but was he safe there? No fuckin' way. He just wished he had someone to give him simple directions that would get him out of here.

CHAPTER 32

"We'll be out of here once it's dark. We'll juke across that there hayfield, through the hedge, and then we're home, Father Davy," Eamon said from where he and Davy and Brendan McGuinness lay at the edge of a pine wood. They huddled beneath a tarpaulin camouflaged by heaps of sodden, earth-smelling bracken.

Davy looked straight up into the branches of a solitary rowan tree, its clusters of red berries dark from the rain that splashed from them and pattered on the dripping leaves. "Home," he said through chattering teeth. "Home . . . and dry." He smiled at his weak pun. He was frozen and wet, and knew that the other two men were as well.

"Nice one, Davy," Eamon said, grinning. "I'd not mind getting myself dry on the outside, but a wee hot wet inside would go down wheeker, so it would."

Davy's smile broadened at the thought of having a hot Irish whiskey, sweetened with sugar, spiced with a couple of cloves, made piquant with a squeeze of fresh lemon juice, the mug filled to the top with boiling water. It would be his first drink in nine years, and it might just bring a bit of heat back into his bones, which, at that moment, felt as ancient as the skeleton of a dinosaur he'd seen in the Ulster Museum on the Stranmillis Road.

Davy glanced at McGuinness. The man was ignoring them both.

Fuck you, McGuinness, you wizened-up wee git, Davy thought, and rolled onto his side, turning his back. At least Eamon and myself can squeeze a bit of humour out of the situation while we're waiting for the last lap. It would be dark by seven, so they'd about four more hours to wait here in the woods.

He stared ahead through the rain, over straight rows of mown hay, to a blackthorn hedge at the far side of the field. Eamon said their hidey-hole was down in a hollow behind that hedge. Beyond that was the back gate to a farmyard, in which Davy could see the glistening slate roofs of a farm-house and its outbuildings.

A dog barked twice, and Davy enjoyed the sound. He'd never once heard a dog while he was in the Kesh, and it had been little things like that he'd missed.

He watched a curl of smoke rise from a chimney and slowly drift away, showing him that the gale-force winds had died almost as quickly as they had screeched in overnight.

Eamon's Erin would be in that house, maybe sitting by the fire. Davy imagined he could smell the peat smoke, and his picture of her close to the glowing turf warmed him. The poor girl must be frantic with worry. Eamon was meant to have got to her last night. She'd have no idea what had happened to him but wouldn't be human if she didn't imagine the worst.

Davy glanced over at his friend and saw how Eamon stared at the farm-house. He was bustin' to see Erin, tell her everything was all right, and fair play to him for that.

Davy accepted that it could be weeks before he could get to Canada. It was about three o'clock here in Tyrone, 1500 hours as all armies, including the Provos, measured time. Vancouver was eight hours behind Belfast, so it would be . . . 1500 minus eight equals seven. Seven in the morning. Perhaps she'd be waking up beside the doctor fellah and making breakfast before the pair of them went to work.

Would Tim Andersen make Fiona a cup of tea the way Davy used to?

God Almighty, knowing the man's name made the whole bloody thing too immediate, too personal. Too real. Maybe if the doctor was important to her, seeing her was all Davy'd be able to do, just see her, talk to her for a wee while.

Then he might have to walk away, but Davy couldn't believe she'd be able to dismiss him so easily once she'd seen him. Once he'd kissed her. If she'd let him. But she would. He knew she would after all they'd meant to each other—and nine years apart wasn't all that long, not really.

Leaves above sagged under the weight of water and spilled frigid drops onto his head. He shook himself like a soaked dog, slipped farther under the tarpaulin, and silently blessed the now-dying gale for the cover it had provided when they'd made their break from Castlederg.

He thanked their saviours back there, the Donnellys. If it hadn't been for them, he'd be in the Crumlin Road Jail or back in the Kesh by now. He shuddered, and it wasn't from the biting cold. He'd be a lot colder but for the tarp Dermot had given them, and that wasn't all he and his missus had done.

Davy stretched out his legs to their full length, enjoying the luxury of that. He'd no idea how long he and Eamon had been forced to lie curled up under those floorboards, hardly daring to breathe.

They'd only been in the hiding space for twenty minutes when he'd heard doors being hurled open, the crash of hobnailed ammo boots, the shouting of foreign English and Scottish voices, of British soldiers on a house-to-house search.

He'd felt Eamon beside him tense as Davy had stiffened and frantically stifled a sneeze when footsteps thundered overhead and paused for what had seemed like an eternity until the clumping had moved away and finally vanished.

Neither he nor Eamon had dared to relax until Davy'd heard the front door slam and Mrs. Donnelly, who must have slipped in silently in her carpet slippers, call from overhead, "It's all right, they've gone, but youse'd better stay there 'til the morning."

He wriggled farther to one side because the wee .25 in his pocket was digging into his hip. He'd rather have that discomfort than suffer the cramps he'd had through the long hours under the Donnellys' floor. When Mrs. Donnelly had come to let them out, it had taken Davy half an hour to get his legs to work properly, and by the way Eamon had groaned and massaged his calves, he wasn't in much better shape.

Davy glanced over to where Eamon lay. Good God, the man was asleep. Davy could hear him snoring, envied his friend's ability to snatch a nap, and wished that he, too, could drift off, but after the excitement of the last twenty-four hours, he knew he was far too keyed up. At least he wasn't hungry.

Mrs. Donnelly had made sure the fugitives were well fed. She had a huge pot of tea ready and must have been up for hours frying bacon and eggs, soda farls, potato bread, tomatoes, and black pudding.

Davy slipped a finger into his mouth and used the nail to dislodge a shred of bacon from between two teeth. He could taste its saltiness.

Dermot hadn't joined them for breakfast but had come in through the back door, wringing wet, dripping puddles on the lino floor. Mrs. Donnelly had scolded her husband for making a mess, clearly more concerned about the puddles than the fact that her tidy kitchen held three escaped Provos. She'd reminded Davy of *Under Milk Wood,* an oddly written book by the Welshman Dylan Thomas. Davy'd found it in the prison library. One character, Mrs. Ogmore-Pritchard, wouldn't let the sun into her parlour until it had "wiped its shoes."

Dermot had told his wife to wheest because he'd been out for a couple of hours getting things ready to get Eamon and his friends away to hell out of Castlederg. It was bucketing down outside, and how did she expect him to come in and not bring some of the rain with him? Davy could still hear her exasperated sniff as she'd grabbed a mop and cleared up the wet patches. Just about this time yesterday he'd been mopping. He spared a thought for Mr. Smiley and hoped he was all right.

Davy stared across the field ahead. There was so much space to enjoy after so many years of his tiny cell, and being able to see it and feel the openness was thanks to Dermot Donnelly.

While Davy and the others had been feeding their faces, Dermot had been out and confirmed that the army still had a roadblock on the Castlederg Bridge. He'd borrowed a builder's van and made room in the back for the three men to hide behind heaps of construction supplies. It had been his idea to drive them, hidden in the lorry, to Spamount, a small village a few miles away. There was a bridge over the Derg and it was usually only protected by a small RUC detachment.

In Dermot's opinion, they should leave in broad daylight while the gale was still screaming through the streets of Castlederg, sending dustbins bowling and clattering down the back alleys, ripping slates off roofs to crash and shatter on the concrete of the backyards. The peelers at Spamount would rather stay in their hut than struggle out into the downpour to search the lorry thoroughly.

Eamon had agreed.

They'd piled into the lorry. Davy wondered who McGillivray and Sons were. That was the name painted on its sides in fancy gold script inside curling red bars. He hoped Dermot wasn't going to catch any shite for borrowing it.

They'd huddled into a small space behind laths, bricks, and bags of plaster, then Dermot had shoved sheets of plywood over the narrow opening. Davy shuddered. It had been too bloody much like the back of the food lorry, and look what a cock-up that had been.

He needn't have worried. Dermot was right. There'd been a momentary hold-up before the Spamount Bridge, then, in what to Davy had seemed like no time, the lorry stopped, and Dermot hauled the supplies out of the way and told them to get out.

Davy'd blinked in the sudden light and slipped out of the lorry to join Eamon and McGuinness as they hunched their shoulders against the wind and rain. He waited, looking at a wood that reached the verge of the narrow country road; watched as Dermot gave Eamon a package. "A wheen of ham sandwiches and a couple of bottles of lemonade. The missus put them up for you."

The sandwiches had been eaten hours ago. Davy could still smell the mustard. He was sorry the lemonade was gone, but he could put up with a bit of thirst now that safety was so close. He slid farther under the tarp, Dermot's parting gift. If it hadn't been for the big sheet of canvas, Davy reckoned the three of them would have frozen to death waiting for nightfall.

He moved and accidentally nudged McGuinness.

"Watch what you're doing, McCutcheon."

Davy pulled his legs away, rolled onto his side, and found himself face-to-face with McGuinness's scowl, his one good eye almost as lifeless as his glass one. "Can you do nothing right?" McGuinness spat. "You never fuckin' could."

All right, Davy thought. All right, you shite, you want to have this out now, once and for all? "What exactly do you mean by that, McGuinness?" He kept his voice low and steady, not wanting to alarm Eamon.

"You know bloody well what I mean. I'd not be in this fuckin' wood, half-froze, but for you."

"That's right. If I'd not found the gate switch in the Tally Lodge, all of us, you included, would still be in the Kesh."

"You think you're quare and smart, so you do. You're not. I'd not have been there in the first place if you hadn't let a British agent into the Provos. You asked a stranger for help with Semtex without telling *me,* your senior officer. I got you the stuff, and you were too fuckin' proud to let on you hadn't a clue how to use it, so you got advice from a man *you* thought was an explosives expert from Canada who wanted to join the Provos. He was a Brit, you fuckin' cretin."

"Christ Almighty, McGuinness, tell me something I don't know."

But McGuinness was right about the bare facts. Davy hadn't known how to use Semtex. Jimmy had met a young man who called himself Mike in a pub and found out that he worked with plastic explosives in the oil fields of Alberta. It hadn't hurt Mike's case when Jimmy had said that his daughter, Siobhan, was daft about the young man. When Jimmy introduced Davy to him, his expertise had seemed like the answer to Davy's problem. He would help Davy use the Semtex, so Davy could keep his promise to his senior officers.

"You don't know your arse from your elbow, you never did, you stupid old shite . . ."

Davy's hands, unbidden, curled into tight fists. His breathing quickened.

". . . You thought the youngster was an Irish expat, just because he had a Bangor accent and said he'd come home to help in the struggle. You arsehole."

"He was an undercover Brit. I know that."

"You didn't know it then, and he tipped them off and put them onto me. You got me put in the Kesh." Spittle flecked McGuinness's lips. "*Me,* for Christ's sake, who's done more for the Provos in a week than you did in twenty fuckin' years."

Christ, McGuinness had confronted Davy with all this rubbish on the very first day they'd bumped into each other in the jail. He'd been feeding off his poison for nine years, bearing a grudge, still probably wanting some kind of revenge. Davy wasn't going to ask for forgiveness, and McGuinness wasn't going to back down, so what was the point of rehashing it all over again? "Have you finished?" Davy asked, struggling to keep his voice level.

"Fuckin' right I have. I've finished what I have to say." McGuinness rolled away from Davy and snarled over his shoulder, "And I've finished with you, McCutcheon, you useless old bastard. Once we're out of this mess, I never want to see you again."

Davy let his fingers uncurl, his rapid, shallow breathing slow. There was no point arguing with McGuinness. The man's mind was too closed to understand how someone like Davy had his pride, and because of that pride had been too ashamed to admit when he'd been asked to do a proper job against a legitimate military and political target that he lacked the skills for. He'd hardly even heard of Semtex, much less ever had the chance to use it, and, he smiled grimly, the orange Czechoslovakian plastic explosive hadn't come with a handy instruction book.

It had made him happy then to feel that he could pull off one more real attack and, in a way, by doing so, salve his conscience for the unnecessary civilian deaths that he, no one else, had caused. He'd been determined to make that important ambush his swan song before, with the full permission of his old commandant, Sean Conlon, bidding the Provos farewell and going to Canada with Fiona.

At least Fiona had made it to the promised land, and he sincerely hoped she was happy there. Davy consoled himself by arguing that if she still loved him—and she must, she must—as much as he loved her, then everything would be all right when he saw her.

A small part of him could feel sorry for this Tim. If Fiona liked him, he must be a decent chap, and if she left him for Davy, Tim was going to get hurt. Maybe leaving him would upset Fiona, too. But, he asked himself, what was the point of trying to puzzle out answers to those questions, here, eight thousand miles from Vancouver? The important thing was to wait for a few more hours and get to the safe haven across the hayfield and the hedge. If he didn't, if he was recaptured, he'd never need to face any problems in Canada.

Davy glanced at Eamon, who was still deeply asleep. His friend had promised that he'd take care of all that was necessary to help Davy get there and that he'd do that as soon as possible. Eamon and Davy were two of a kind. Once they had made a promise, they'd keep it, no matter what.

And that shite McGuinness? Christ, he wasn't worth arguing with. He never wanted to see Davy again? He was going to get his wish, and that, as far as Davy was concerned, was all the revenge he needed. McGuinness could carry on his futile fight for his useless "Cause," go to hell in his own way and in his own good time. Davy would be far away from the likes of him, from the Provos, from the bloodshed, and from—the last thought made him pause—from Ireland.

He would miss some things about the place, like the football, even if his team, Celtic, were having a horrible season. He'd miss the pubs with their smoky fug and beer stains on the tables and the *craic* of the lads. But what else really important to him was he leaving? Cramped, dirty streets; cramped, dirty houses; no jobs; city people with minds as narrow as their tenements, where the gable walls were painted with slogans and tribal flags.

King Billy on a white horse. Orange lilies. Union Jacks. The Red Hand of Ulster set in the middle of the cross of Saint George of England. "Remember 1690." "Not an inch." "No surrender." "This we will maintain."

Kathleen ni Houlihàn, with her green cloak, her long chestnut hair. Irish harps. Shamrocks. Green, white, and gold tricolours. "You are entering free Derry," "Brits out," "*Faugh à Ballagh.*"

Taunts of "Fenian gits," "Croppies lie down," "Fuck the pope." "Orange bastards." "Black and Tans," "Remember the martyrs of '16."

The songs "The Sash My Father Wore," "The Green, Grassy Slopes of the Boyne," "The Augherlee Heroes," on one hand; "The Wearing of the Green," "The Foggy Dew," "The Patriot Game," on the other.

And what did the pictures, the flags, the slogans, and the war cries mean? That those who used them were devout adherents to a particular brand of religion?

They might think they were, but Davy had come to see and now believed that the Protestants and Catholics in the Six Counties, in their poverty and unemployment, had more in common than they realized. Both sides, in their own warped way, and with their deep attachment to what was in reality a very tiny piece of real estate, were so very much alike. Why couldn't their commonality bring them together as it had done in April 1941, when the Nazis had blitzed the Belfast docks and Protestant families had taken in and sheltered Catholics made homeless by the bombs?

The badges and emblems they clung to were nothing more than symbols of an ingrained tribalism as primitive as the family bonds of chimpanzees, bonds that drove the primates to stick together and defend their territory against all other chimps and their families. Sometimes he wondered if that was all the human race was, a brighter, more lethal primate, and he knew full well he'd been as primitive in the early days as the rest of them.

Their tribalism had driven them into futile sectarian conflict that had gone on for eight hundred years, and as far as Davy could tell would still be going on long after he was in the grave.

And when he *was* in his grave (and the thought didn't bother him), it would be under a foreign sod like generations of the Irish before him; in the quarantine camps on Grosse Isle in the Saint Lawrence, in America by their hundreds on the banks of canals dug by Irish navvies, along the embankments of railroads laid by Irish labourers, in the outback of Australia, where men and women transported for crimes as trivial as poaching a rabbit had scrabbled to exist in the penal colonies.

Irishmen lay in their thousands in France after the Battle of the Somme, in which most of the fallen soldiers were from the Ulster Division, five thousand in the first July day in 1916, three months after the leaders of the Easter Rising had been executed in Dublin. Dublin Fusiliers slept in the rocky soil of the Gallipoli Peninsula at Sed el Bahr and Suvla Bay.

When they got round to planting Davy McCutcheon, all he would ask for was to have Fiona say an Ave for him, "Hail Mary, full of grace, blessèd art thou among women . . . pray for us sinners, now and in the hour of our death." And when her time came, and he didn't want to dwell on that thought, she'd be laid down beside him, and if the flag overhead was a maple leaf, which one of them would care?

God, he told himself and smiled, sometimes, McCutcheon, you really can be a morbid old bugger.

The silence that, until that moment, had been broken only by the soft rain, the dripping of the leaves, and Eamon's snores was shattered by the deafening whicker of rotors. The leaves above him trembled in the downdraft. A Puma helicopter, mottled in dark green and khaki dazzle paint, swooped out over the wood, across the field, and hovered low over the farmhouse, its slipstream shredding the chimney smoke.

Davy could see a collie in the farmyard, frantically leaping. It must have been barking its brains out at the intruder, but he couldn't hear that, only the roar of the rotors.

He hated the sound. The last time he'd heard it so close was when he'd been trapped in that farmhouse near the Ravernet Bridge while trying to send Harold Wilson to *his* maker.

Davy could still see the soldiers piling out of their aircraft and running toward him. Sweet suffering Jesus, was a platoon going to be disgorged now and fan out, rifles ready as they ran across the hayfield to where he lay?

The helicopter made a complete circle, rose, and headed in the direction where, Davy knew, the Sperrins would have their craggy peaks shrouded in the low clouds. It would serve the buggers right if their chopper slammed into one of those mountains.

He waited and listened as the racket grew softer and softer, until it finally faded and all he could hear was the rain and the barking of the collie.

Davy felt Eamon stir beside him.

"Jesus," Eamon said. "The noisy buggers won't even let a man get a nap in peace."

"They've gone," Davy said.

"Good thing, too." Eamon shuddered. "Jesus Christ, but I'm foundered." He forced a grin. "Mind you, Father, if them buggers come back in their helicopters tonight and they have sensors on board that would pick up a man's body heat in the dark, they'll have as much chance of detecting us as they would of finding an ice cream van." Eamon grunted and smiled at Davy. "Cheer up, Father. It'll not be long now until we're out from under this soggy tarpaulin, away from the stink of dead bracken and into somewhere warm, dry, and safe."

CHAPTER 33

She was warm and safe and pleasantly drowsy when the alarm clock jangled. Fiona pushed the off button, squinted at the dial, noted it really was 7:00 A.M., and snuggled against Tim's back. She saw a tiny smear of her lipstick on his neck. She didn't want to get up and leave the cosy bed and the comfort of having Tim so close.

She didn't want to get up but knew she must. So must he. He'd told her last night that he had a committee meeting first thing this morning. He'd told her that sometime before—she stretched and wriggled and smiled, thinking of their next lovemakings, not once but twice again in the early hours. She threw back the duvet and saw Tim's back, where scratches from her fingernails had left a red tracery from his shoulders to the hollow above his tight buttocks. God, but he'd a lovely arse. She bent and kissed one cheek, feeling him stir.

He rolled on his back, yawned, opened his eyes, rubbed them with the backs of his hands, and mumbled, "Morning, darling."

He'd never called her "darling" before, and she liked the easy familiarity of it, as if they had been together for years, not a few short months.

"Time you were up." She watched his hand slide along his belly and stroke his penis. She chuckled. "Not that kind of up, idiot. We've both to go to work." And she kissed him before saying, a little breathlessly, "but it would be nice."

"Aw." He fondled her breast, "I hate committee meetings." He put his lips to her nipple, and she felt his tongue flickering, swiftly, lightly as an adder's, and she wondered if, like the little snake, he was sensing her through his tongue.

It would be marvelous to reach for him, love him, spend the day in bed with him, fill herself with him, and—she felt the heat between her thighs—not just down there for the tiny eternity that came with having him inside her. She wanted to talk and explore the Tim of him, and the "them" of them both, and now, as her past receded, a future that she felt could open for her with Tim.

His hand, warm and soft but for its single callus, fondled the inside of her thigh. She drew one leg up, closed her eyes, and waited for his touch. Then she realized that the very thought of their having a future together meant that they wouldn't have to cram all their lovemaking into a few short hours like a couple of randy students and that the pleasure could come from the anticipation, the imagining of what was to be as much as from the act itself.

She shuddered as his fingers found her, grasped his wrist, pushed his hand away, rolled over, and held him to her, feeling his penis hot against her belly. "Not now," she whispered.

He dropped a kiss on her hair. "All right," he said, his voice husky, "I do love you. But I can wait."

"I love you, Tim," she said, loving him for his body but more for his patience, his understanding. "You go and shower. I'll get breakfast on."

"Right." He rolled out of bed.

She watched as, naked, he walked to the bathroom, his buttocks flexing as he walked, and he did, he certainly did, have a lovely arse. She almost called him back. Perhaps she should take a cold shower. The sisters at the convent school had been very keen on them for dulling the lusts of the flesh. The poor celibate nuns. They didn't know what they were missing.

Fiona chuckled wickedly, left the bed, slipped on her dressing gown, and went through to the kitchen. She tutted to see her von Furstenberg dress crumpled on the floor, where she'd left it last night in her eagerness for him. Passion was all very well, but dresses like that didn't grow on trees. She lifted it, took it back to the bedroom, and hung it in her wardrobe.

She could hear the shower and Tim's tenor voice, horribly off-key, singing, "We're a band from a land down under . . ." the words of some Aussie rock group called Men at Work. Doctor Tim Andersen was no Plácido Domingo. He might play on her body as Casals bowed his cello, but the poor man couldn't carry a tune in a bucket.

Breakfast, she told herself, and headed back to the kitchen. As she plugged in the coffeemaker, she heard the cat flap rattle. McCusker came in, tail erect, rigid as Tim's—she tried to concentrate on the job at hand.

"Tim," she yelled—realizing she'd never made him breakfast before and that she was going to enjoy doing it, not just today but in the days to come— "what do you take for breakfast?"

"What?" She heard the water stop.

"Breakfast. What do you like?"

He came round the door. He was wrapped in a bath sheet. "The coffee smells good, darling. If you've a slice of toast and bit of marmalade . . . ?"

There was that "darling" again. "Your word is my command, sir," she said, popping a couple of slices of whole grain in the toaster.

"I'm skipper. Just like on *Windy*."

She bristled, just a bit. "It was a figure of speech. I've been pretty good at running my own life for the last nine years. I'm not very good at taking orders."

He held up his hands, palms out. "I know. I think it's one of the things that makes me love you . . . that and the way you taste."

She laughed. "Gloria Steinem says that women shouldn't be sex objects."

"You mean," he said, looking puzzled, "that you object to sex? You could have fooled me."

"*Tim*. Idiot. Here." She poured his coffee. "Now, if the great skipper can manage to get his own milk from the fridge, he'll find the butter's in there, too. When your toast's ready—I presume you *can* take it out of the toaster yourself—the marmalade's in that cupboard. I'm off for my shower."

"Right," he said, still leering. "Sure you don't want me to come and scrub your back?"

She was still laughing as she went into the bathroom. And nothing would have given her more pleasure than to have him scrub her back, and her front, and all of her. She knew he would have scrubbed gently.

When she came back, coiffed, lightly made up, wearing her navy-blue suit over a demurely buttoned white blouse, Tim was dressed and waiting for her. She thought that he looked very much the head of a hospital department.

"More coffee?"

"No thanks, love. I've had my second cup. Time to get going. I'll call a cab. It'll be here in a few minutes." He stood and let his hand fall onto her shoulder. "Can I give you a lift to the school?"

"It's all right. Becky's picking me up in fifteen minutes."

"Well," he said, grinning again, "if I were you, I'd try to get that utterly satisfied look off my face before she gets here. Might shock the poor old thing if she guesses what we've been up to."

"Becky? I don't think she's so easily shocked, Tim." She squeezed his hand. "She'd be happy for us."

"Good for her." Tim's voice became soft. "I certainly am."

"So am I, Tim. Honestly." She hesitated, then asked quietly, "When can we do it again?"

"Right now, if you really want to. Right here on the table, and if Becky walks in, that might really shock her "

"Stop it, you randy old goat. I mean, when am I going to see you again?"

"Oh," Tim said, looking crestfallen, "I'm not absolutely sure. I've been away for a week . . ."

I know, she thought, and it seemed like a month.

"I'll have to check my hospital diary. Tell you what. I'll call you tonight after work."

"I'd like that," she said. "Very much."

"Right. Give us a kiss."

She stood and kissed him.

The buzzer rang.

"That'll be my cab," Tim said, starting to leave. "And when we do get together, wear the creation you had on last night. It bothers me on a boat if I don't know how to work all the lines." He dropped a slow wink. "I'd like to have a go all by myself at undoing the one that holds that dress shut."

"Get out," she said, laughing and relishing the thought of Tim undressing her.

"I'm off," he said, hesitating at the door. "By the way, I forgot to tell you. You've a message on your machine." He blew her a kiss. "Bye."

A message? Now she remembered. Jimmy Ferguson had phoned last night, and she'd let it go into the machine. She'd had better things, much better things, to do. She wondered what he could have wanted. Well, she told herself, walking into the living room, she'd already made up her mind that she wasn't going to avoid facing reminders of her past. Listening to whatever Jimmy had to say couldn't hurt now. Not after last night with Tim.

She paused in front of the flashing red light. Somewhere within her, she remembered that red was the universal danger signal. Stuff and nonsense. She pushed the play button.

A metallic voice said, "You have one message." There was a pause.

"Get on with it," she muttered.

"Message one. Sunday, September twenty-fifth, eleven thirty P.M."

She heard Jimmy's Belfast brogue. "It's me, Fiona. Jimmy. I'm awful sorry to phone so late, so I am, but there's been a breakout, so there has."

A what? She sat heavily in the armchair.

"A bunch of the lads has got out of the Kesh. The man on the CBC gave a list of names. Look, Fiona, I know this'll upset you, but . . . Davy's out, so he is. He could be headed here. Will you give me a call? 555-2996."

The machine clicked off.

Fiona's hand covered her open mouth. Her nightmare always started with an explosion, but she was wide awake, and this was no bad dream. What Jimmy Ferguson had just said hit her with greater force than any imagined bomb burst.

Fiona blinked at the morning sunlight bursting through the trees, hardly understanding how she had moved from her flat to Whyte Avenue to wait for Becky. Branches of the old maples swayed gently. There were no maples in Ireland, she thought, but Davy McCutcheon was free there and, according to Jimmy's message, heading to Vancouver. She'd replayed the recording again to make certain she'd not misunderstood. Dear God, there'd been no mistaking the voice's bald statement.

She was trying to make sense of her feelings now, but in the seconds after she'd heard what Jimmy was saying, she'd not taken time to think. She'd rejoiced in Davy's freedom, inwardly cheering as enthusiastically as a fan whose team had scored the winning goal in overtime.

In that millisecond where conscious, cold, intellectual analysis of the facts was pushed aside, what she had felt deep within her had been instinctive—and absolutely honest. She wanted him to come.

Now she'd had time to digest the reality: a man she'd not seen for nine years might show up on her doorstep. Her doubts had started, along with the first grumbling of a migraine, still distant but ominous as the growling of an over-the-horizon thunderstorm. She'd taken a couple of Tylenol ten minutes ago and hoped they'd do the trick, at least for the incipient head-ache. No tablets, no potions could help her decide what might happen if and when Davy appeared. And if she was so sure she loved Davy, what was she going to tell Tim?

If ever Fiona'd wanted Becky's advice, it was now. She wished her friend would hurry up.

What if she left Tim, Davy showed up, and she found that what she thought she was feeling was nostalgia, not love? Was thinking she loved Davy a subtle way of making him a symbol for the good things she could recall about Ireland: chestnut trees, the Lagan River, her brother Connor before he was killed, the people, the *craic*? That Ireland had been torn up forever by the Troubles. "All changed, changed utterly" when the "terrible beauty" was born.

She wasn't the woman she'd been back in the North. She'd embraced a wider world. Could Davy have changed as much as she had in the last nine years?

She'd been free to face what Becky called the "dreadful tyranny of limitless choices here in Canada." But Fiona had embraced those choices freely.

In Ireland, it had taken all her courage to hew to her decision to get out of the ghetto of the Falls Road by refusing to accept her station in life as a Catholic woman, a position preordained by centuries of tradition. Despite the objections of her family, and defying them had cost her dearly, she'd pursued her goal, finished her teachers' diploma, even taken up with a Protestant in teachers' college. That had been the last straw for them. They hadn't spoken to her since.

It had been hard to accept at the time, but by their intransigence they had left her unencumbered by family ties and free to chart her own course in this new country.

It was 1983. Women had demanded, and now had, the right to attain their potential. Canada was a country where people of every nationality were arriving daily, and no one cared tuppence if they went to chapel, church, shul, mosque, or temple. She *had* been right to challenge her parents' assumptions, and the way she was now free to live her own life made their stubbornness over a Protestant boyfriend seem almost comical.

Her regrets about leaving her parents, the North, her friends there had faded. Only the lingering sadness about losing Davy remained. The choice she'd made nine years ago had seemed like a good one then. It had been. She'd been right to emigrate, to put behind her the mayhem that was Northern Ireland, the mayhem that Davy had been a part of.

God knows, she'd tried to understand him then, to forgive him, and would have if he'd not been arrested. She was certain of that, as certain as she was that she could forgive him now, provided he had foresworn his allegiance to the Cause. He must have. She'd watched his disenchantment grow, accepted his promise that after one last mission he would turn his back on the Provos—forever.

She knew full well that a committed man wouldn't be coming to Canada. He'd be going underground in Ireland and fighting on. Jimmy seemed certain Davy was heading here, and surely that alone was proof of his intentions? It had to be.

In his rejection of the violence, a rejection begun back in 1974, Davy had already started to change. She wondered how he would feel when he began to understand how different she had become.

He'd been a simple, ill-educated man; it hadn't bothered her back then, but it might now. Her own life had moved on, but she doubted if Davy's could in the confines of a maximum-security prison. Would he feel she was too good for him? Worse, would she? Her temples throbbed as she looked at her watch. Where was Becky?

She was starting to feel imprisoned herself, constrained by an utterly un-reasonable yearning for Davy, yet knowing that Tim loved her and, by his love, had a hold over her. Once she told him about Davy, about how she felt, she'd lose Tim, just as she'd had Davy taken from her. And it had cost her sorely.

Perhaps part of her old attraction to Davy had been in the way she could live vicariously through him. In her young years, she had embraced the civil rights movement as her way of striving for a better Ireland. It hadn't worked. Davy, in his way, had continued the struggle, and for all her deeply embraced pacifism, she must have harboured a hope that the Provos would win, the Ireland she wanted so much would materialize. Was that why she'd been able to turn a blind eye to what Davy did?

If he made it to Vancouver, there'd be risks ahead. He would be in the country illegally. They would never be free from a nagging worry that one day an immigration officer could show up and she'd lose him again. Plan-ning to wait for him made no sense, no sense whatsoever, but when the heart ruled, sense flew out the window.

The logical thing to do, the sensible thing, was to put Davy away and stay with Tim. There'd be no risks to be taken if she chose that path. It could be a horrible mistake to let Tim go, but unless she stopped feeling the way she did now, it would be unconscionable to keep him hanging on like some kind of romantic insurance policy.

She rubbed her temple. For all the good the Tylenol was doing, she might as well have rubbed her head with vegetable-marrow jam. That was one of Davy's old cracks. Where in God's name had it come from?

She saw Becky's car coming, and as soon as it pulled up, Fiona slipped into the passenger seat. "Morning Becky. I have to . . ."

"Sorry I'm late," Becky said tersely and drove off.

Fiona didn't bother to fasten her seat belt. She blurted out, "I had a phone call from Jimmy Ferguson. Remember I told you about Jimmy . . . ?"

"I'm late because I was on the phone with Mum. She's pretty upset. Dad's being admitted to hospital. He was full of beans when I was out in Abbots-ford on Saturday, but she couldn't waken him this morning."

Not this morning of all mornings. Not when Fiona wanted to—she was being selfish. Her own troubles could wait. "What's wrong with him?" She wished she'd sounded more sympathetic.

Becky didn't seem to notice. "The local doctors think he's had a stroke. A big one."

"I am sorry. I really am." Fiona turned to look at Becky and saw the moisture in her eyes, how her hands gripped the wheel. "When will you know for sure if it is a stroke?"

"They're sending him to Vancouver General. To the neurology unit."

"You must be worried sick."

Becky tried to smile but failed. "I'm worried about Dad, but he's eighty-two. He's had a fair innings. I'm much more concerned about Mum. If he goes . . ."

"He won't. I'm sure he won't."

"It's kind of you to say so, but we have to be realistic. If he does, Mum's going to be utterly lost without him. They've been married for fifty-six years."

"That's a very long time." The four years she'd been with Davy, even the nine they'd been apart, were nothing. Her few months with Tim seemed like a one-night stand compared with this lifetime's commitment.

Davy, Davy, why did you have to go on that mission? If you hadn't, the pair of us would be here, growing old together like Becky's folks. I'd never have met Tim, wouldn't have any decisions to make.

Becky drove ahead. "I'm not sure she'll be able to manage without him."

Fiona knew what being alone was like, having someone you loved taken away, and remembered how lonely she'd been in her first years in Vancouver. Poor Mrs. Johnston would be devastated.

"What are you going to do?" Fiona asked.

Becky changed gear to slow down behind a dump truck. "What am I going to do?" She blew out a long breath. "To tell you the truth, I'm not entirely sure. There's probably not much I *can* do until we know what's really wrong with Dad." She stopped the car and waited for the truck to turn into an alley. "I'll have to have more to go on, so I'd like to get to the hospital as soon as I can." She moved ahead.

"Unless you can speak to one of his doctors, the staff'll probably just tell you he's 'comfortable' or 'critical,' or some other meaningless line."

"I know." Becky sighed. "But I still have to try."

"Would you like me to give Tim a call? See if he can use his connections to find out exactly what's happening to your dad?"

"Would you?" Becky pulled into the school parking lot. "Would you really?"

"Of course," Fiona said, although she already regretted having made the suggestion. She didn't want to talk to Tim. Not yet. Not until she'd had time to think. "If I call straightaway, perhaps I can catch him before he goes into his meeting."

"I'd appreciate that," Becky said as they left the car for the short walk to the school.

Fiona strode along the corridor straight to her office. As Becky flopped onto a chair, Fiona dialed Tim's number and was surprised to hear his voice. It was usually his receptionist who answered the phone.

"Tim, sorry to bother you, but I've got an emergency. No. No. I'm fine. It's Becky's father." She explained the situation to him, and he promised to call right back. "Tim's going to phone the chief of neurology at VGH. They're sailing friends. He says he knows how bloody awful it can be hanging about waiting for the phone to ring, so he'll call us right back either with the information or at least with some idea of what time he will have some news."

Becky nodded and hunched forward, staring at the telephone.

Fiona sat behind her desk, fidgeting with a pencil, searching for words to comfort her friend, but there didn't seem to be any. Poor Becky. It must be terrible having a parent so ill.

It was something Fiona hadn't had to face—yet. Earlier this morning, she'd been thinking of her parents. She hadn't spoken to them in all these years, but her sister Bridget occasionally wrote. One day she'd phone to say one of the folks was ill, or had died, and family was family, so she'd have to go back to Belfast. Perhaps she should try to heal the old wounds before it was too late. Perhaps she should go back there soon and see if she couldn't persuade them that what was done was done and over?

The phone rang.

Becky stiffened and stared up at Fiona.

Fiona picked up the receiver. "Hello? Tim?"

"Yes, it's me, love."

"Right," she said. Just like the man. Punctual to the second. "And . . . ?" She heard him sigh. "And . . . ?"

"I'm afraid it doesn't look too good."

"I see." Fiona deliberately kept her voice flat. "Would you like to speak to Becky? She's here."

"Christ, I hate this, but, yes, put her on."

Fiona passed the receiver over and watched her friend's expression change from hope when she said, "You did get hold of your colleague," to sadness as she muttered, "I see. I see. It is a stroke. Thank you." Becky sniffed and swallowed before saying, "I appreciate your honesty, Doctor Andersen . . . Yes, I'll put her on." She held the receiver to Fiona. "He wants a word."

"Hello, Tim?"

His voice was very businesslike. "I have to run. I'm late for the meeting. Becky can explain about her dad. I have to tell you, my on-call's been buggered up; one of my colleagues is sick, so I can't get free until Saturday. I'll call you tonight, and I'll see you then." He whispered, "Love you," then hung up.

So she'd not have to face Tim until Saturday, but she needed to set that aside, think about it later. "What does Tim say about your dad? Has he had . . . ?"

"Not good, I'm afraid. Yes. It's a massive stroke. He's on life support." She turned, stared at the drawn curtains, and said very quietly, "They're not sure if he'll live."

Fiona rose and hugged her friend. "I'm so sorry, Becky. Is there anything I can do to help?"

"I don't know." Becky looked bemused, drifting, lost, shrunken. "Mum's with him." She clasped one hand with the other, then said, "I must get up to the hospital and see how Mum is."

Fiona took Becky's hand. "Of course you must. I'll rejuggle the others' assignments, see if I can get a substitute teacher, so you can have the rest of the week off." She smiled grimly and let Becky's hand go. "It's one advantage of being vice principal. I can do that."

"I'd appreciate that. Mum's going to need me."

So do I, Fiona thought, but once she'd worked out a new timetable, she knew she'd be lucky to see Becky for at least a week, and it wouldn't be right anyway to ask for her help when Becky had a crisis of her own.

"I'm sorry to be putting you to so much trouble, Fiona. I really am."

"You get along to VGH right now and don't worry your head about me," Fiona said. "I'm quite capable of sorting things out." And how she wished it were true.

CHAPTER 34

Davy shuddered but was glad they'd soon be getting on. He'd grown even colder since the light had faded. When it still was bright enough for him to see his fingertips, they'd been slate grey. They were probably purple now. He blew into his cupped hands. For all the good it did, he might as well have dunked them in ice water.

Eamon had managed to drift off shortly after the Puma helicopter burst out from over the trees, but now he was going to have to be wakened. It was time to get moving.

Davy glanced to where McGuinness lay. If the bastard had frozen to death, tough titty. The arrogant little prick and his, "I've done more for the Provos in a week than you've done in twenty years." Och, for Christ's sake, if it suited him to believe that, then fuck him. Davy knew *exactly* what he'd done, and what he was going to do, and that was of no concern to the Provos or to McGuinness. But if Davy was going to get out of Ireland, the first step had to be leaving this wood and finding shelter. Soon.

Davy shook Eamon's shoulder. "Wake up, Eamon. Come on. Up."

Eamon stirred, yawned, rubbed his eyes, and sat up. "Jesus Christ, I'm foundered," he muttered. "Have the screws turned the heating off?"

Davy managed to chuckle in spite of the cold. "We're not in the Kesh anymore."

"Unh?" Eamon stared around. "Right enough. For a minute there . . ."

"Are you wide awake now?"

"Aye." Eamon stood. "It's blacker than the hobs of hell out there." Davy heard the excitement in his friend's voice. "Time we were on the move, Father, before the moon rises."

Thank God, Davy thought. He wanted to be somewhere, anywhere, dry and warm. At least the rain had stopped and the clouds had drifted off. He heard Eamon say in a low voice, "Are you ready, Brendan?" and Mc-Guinness's grunted, "Aye."

"Right," Eamon said, "give us a hand to get this tarp hidden. I'd not want anyone to find it and wonder what it's doing here."

Eamon could always be trusted to consider the details. Davy helped fold the canvas. "Should we not take it with us?" Davy asked.

"Nah," Eamon said. "It would just get in the way."

Davy gathered armfuls of bracken and spread them over the tarpaulin. The effort brought a tiny bit of warmth to his chilled body. He sniffed. Jesus, but that rank, pungent smell was ferocious. God, but it was strong. "What's that stink, Eamon?"

"That? It's just a fox. A vixen used to have her den near here. She probably still does. The O'Byrnes never let the gentry hunt on their lands."

"Oh." No wonder Davy hadn't been able to recognize the odour. There had been no foxes on the Falls Road.

He could make out Eamon as he stood, flapping his arms across his chest. Davy heard squelching of boots hitting damp vegetation and reckoned McGuinness must be stamping his feet.

Somewhere to Davy's left a shriek tore at the fabric of the night. He felt the hairs on the back of his neck rise. "What the hell was that?"

"Barn owl," Eamon said. "Out looking for mice or rabbits."

And who, Davy wondered, is out there looking for us, wandering round in this bloody awful darkness like—like the three blind mice?

Davy sensed rather than saw Eamon stride forward. "Follow me. We'll be there in no time," he said.

Davy limped to the edge of the wood, leaving McGuinness to bring up the rear. In the distance, Davy saw a glow from farmhouse windows. Eamon was heading in that direction. The going was heavy. It must be muddy, and, by the weight of his feet increasing with each step, Davy knew that he'd be clabber to the knees by the time they'd left this field.

Once they were away from the trees, Davy could see the sky. He wondered if Eamon knew the names of any of the multitude of stars that glittered like bright tinsel on a black velvet-felt board. He could only recognize the Plough, hanging its handle to the earth, its pointers there to lead a man's gaze to Polaris.

He hesitated, trying to see the North Star, the constant, fixed point for navigators since the dawn of time, just as Fiona was his lodestone, drawing him to her.

He was nearly knocked sprawling when McGuinness blundered into him.

"Get the fuck out of my way, McCutcheon." McGuinness lumbered past.

Davy plodded on. McGuinness had turned, and Davy followed, walking at an angle across the swaths of mown hay. His foot snagged in the sodden harvest, and he stumbled, landing heavily on both hands. Jesus Christ, the last time he'd fallen in a field, a ploughed field, had been on the night he and Mike Roberts had carried sixty pounds of Semtex to the Ravernet Bridge.

Davy shoved himself back to his feet. He'd not forget that earlier fall. He'd been carrying fulminate-of-mercury detonators. A sudden jar could make them go off. Anyone who'd watched *Lawrence of Arabia* wouldn't forget the scene where Lawrence's Arab friend, young Faraj, had done just that with a detonator in his shirt.

Davy had no detonators this time. Only a small .25 revolver in his pants' pocket.

He limped on, stared ahead, and could barely make out Eamon's shape, which was limned by the welcoming glow from the farmhouse. Davy had earlier imagined he could smell peat smoke. He wasn't imagining it now. It would be great to be going to that fireside.

By the light of the stars, he could make out his breath as it hung in little clouds. There was condensation in the hairs of his moustache. Surely to God they didn't have to go much farther?

Eamon had stopped. McGuinness was nowhere to be seen. As Davy approached, he saw that Eamon was standing beside a tall hedge.

"Not far now, Father." Eamon showed Davy a gap between the plants. "Go on ahead. There's only room for one to get through. Watch out for the thorns."

Davy sidled through the hedge, pricking his palm near the scar of the wound he'd made with the chisel. Had that only been ten days ago? Ten days in the past seemed to be as far away as the Ice Age. He heard branches being forced apart.

As he waited for Eamon, Davy watched a waxing moon slide up over distant hills, its cold, silver-shining light etching the dark crests against the ebony sky. He could make out the loom of moving headlights coming from somewhere between the hills and where he stood. Would that be locals in a car—or Security Forces in an armoured personnel carrier?

Eamon arrived at Davy's shoulder and pointed. "Down in there, Davy, and we'll've made it."

Davy looked ahead to a hollow, where he could see nothing but a tangle of bramble bushes, snarled and intertwined like the coils of barbed wire outside the Kesh. There was no Skeet Hamilton to flatten them this time.

Davy'd thought they were heading for the farm and its turf fire. He couldn't stifle his disappointment. "Christ Almighty, we're going to hide in more bloody bushes?"

Eamon simply laughed, said, "Come on," and started down the hill.

Dear God, not another night out in the open. Davy wished they'd brought Dermot's tarpaulin instead of leaving it in the wood. He took a deep breath and followed Eamon, who had walked round the side of the bushes and stood waiting.

"You're going to have to be a rabbit, Father," Eamon said as he knelt and carefully parted bramble stems. "Brendan'll've gone in already. I explained it to him before I sent him through the blackthorn. Can you see that there path?"

Davy peered in and could just make out a narrow animal track. "Aye."

"Get in under here and follow your nose. I'll be right behind you."

"Right." Davy dropped to all fours and scrambled under the briars. He could hardly see where he was going and had to feel his way. He drew a rapid breath and pulled his hand back as bramble thorns pricked it. He could hear the noises Eamon made as he followed.

Davy nearly crawled headfirst into a large rock. To its left he saw what might be an opening. Was that the entrance to something? He stretched out his hand. There was nothing in front of it, until he felt some coarse material. He pushed it aside and blinked as pale yellow light shone from the entrance to a narrow tunnel.

"In there?"

"Aye, and get a move on. We don't want that bloody light shining out over half of Tyrone."

Davy rose to his feet and looked around. The light coming from a couple of overhead bulbs was much brighter in the stone-walled chamber, and, thank God, it was warm. He could hear a low hum that had to be coming from a heater. He blessed whoever had thought to put the thing in here. He barely took notice of the crouched form of McGuinness and hoped they'd not have to stay long with the man. McGuinness was planning to head for the Republic, wasn't he? The sooner he went, the better. The space was smaller and mustier than Davy's cell in the Kesh. It was going to be a tight fit for three men.

He felt movement at his shoulder, stepped aside to let Eamon enter, and watched as he glanced round the room.

"Here we are, Davy, home sweet home for the next wee while. We'll do rightly in here. Look"—Eamon pointed to a heap on a table—"towels." He nodded to the elements against one wall. "A cooker and"—Eamon bent and opened an ice chest—"grub." He stood and grinned. "Not badly equipped for an old Celtic grave. Erin's done a grand job."

So that's what this was. An old grave. Davy was glad he wasn't a super-stitious man. When the lights were put out, it would be easy to imagine the ghosts of the original inhabitants being angry with whoever had disturbed their peace.

"Your Erin set it up?"

"Aye." Davy could hear the pride in Eamon's voice. "And she'll be here soon, wait 'til you see." There was more pride there than longing, and that didn't surprise Davy. Not one bit.

"I see Brendan's already made himself at home," Eamon said.

"Too fuckin' right. I thought I'd never get warm 'til I got here. You give your Erin a big kiss from me, Eamon. She has done a grand job, so she has."

Davy stared at McGuinness, surprised to hear the man praise anyone. Perhaps even that hard bastard had a soft side. He might have, but tidiness didn't seem to be part of his makeup. A crumpled towel lay discarded at his feet. His clothes were carelessly thrown over the back of a wooden chair be-side a folding table. Mud from his pants had made dirty marks on the table's top.

The man himself was draped in a blanket that must have come from one of the camp beds Davy could make out in two side alcoves. McGuinness was crouched over the heater, but again surprised Davy when he moved to one side and said, "I won't hog all the heat."

"Right," said Eamon, picking a towel from the heap and passing it to Davy, "get you out of those sodden clothes and get yourself dry." He turned back to the ice chest, pulled out a plastic container, and opened the lid. "Great," he said, "chicken soup. I'll get this heated up."

"Are you not going to get yourself dried off first?" McGuinness asked.

"Nah," Eamon said. "We all need something hot inside us. It'll only take a minute."

Davy, silently admiring Eamon's toughness, put his towel down and peeled off his soaked shirt and vest. As he took off his shoes and pants, he noticed that his arms were covered in goose flesh. He laid his clothes, except for his pants, on a chair and, ignoring how cold he was, reached into the pocket and left the .25 there but pulled out Jimmy's letter and Fiona's picture. Both were soaked. He smoothed them with his hand. Some of the writing where the ink hadn't run was still legible, and, praise be, that included the phone number.

Her picture was a soggy mess of crumpled paper. All he could make out was the brightness of her eyes. No matter. He'd be seeing her whole face soon. He put the papers on the table, noting as he did that someone had left a vase of flowers. A nice touch, he thought.

He grabbed the towel and began to dry himself, his hair, his face, chest, and belly, and as he dragged the terry cloth across his back, the chafing began to warm him. He closed his eyes, toweled harder, and reveled in the feeling.

He inhaled the vapours from the soup pot. "Jesus, Eamon, that smells good."

"Right enough," Eamon said, "but I'm sorry it's not the wee hot half-un we were thinking about."

Davy laughed.

"Come on, Father," Eamon said, "get you one of the blankets like Brendan."

Davy hesitated. He didn't want to do anything like McGuinness and realized that he was being childish. He glanced at the two men. Both were intent on their own business, Eamon stirring the soup, McGuinness rubbing his palms together over the heater. Davy slipped the .25 out of his soggy pants' pocket, wrapped it in his towel, and walked to a bed in the alcove opposite to the one from which McGuinness had taken his blanket. He might have to share the accommodation with the man, but he'd be damned if he'd sleep next to him.

He slipped the revolver under the bedclothes, wondering why he hadn't simply given it to Eamon. Davy had no intention of using it. And yet—

He pulled off a blanket to wrap round himself and noticed an alcove ahead. In it he saw ArmaLites and Lee-Enfields. He'd wear a blanket like McGuinness, but if the bugger had any notions of Davy using one of those rifles, he had another think coming. Davy walked to the table and hung his trousers over the back of a chair.

"Fuck it, McCutcheon, you look like one of the blanket men back at the Kesh," McGuinness said.

Davy spun on his heel, one big fist tightly clenched, but relaxed when he saw that McGuinness was smiling. Good God, he'd been making a joke.

"Right enough," Davy said, "but don't you worry, I'm not going to smear my shite all over the walls."

He was surprised to hear McGuinness chuckle, a dry, harsh sound. If it was a sign that he wanted to call a truce, that was all right with Davy; he'd play along. Maybe he'd not needed to hold onto the .25, but he still couldn't bring himself to trust the man.

Davy heard noise coming from the tunnel. He glanced to where he had left the little gun, then to Eamon, who was staring at the entrance.

A young woman with chestnut hair scrambled to her feet, her green eyes fixed on Eamon's face. By the narrowness of her lips, Davy could tell that she was angry.

"Erin," Eamon whispered. "Dear God. Erin." He grinned like a moon calf.

She took two paces across the floor and stared at him. "What kept you?" she demanded. "What the hell kept you? I was up all last night, worried sick. You were meant to be here *then*, damnit. I nearly went daft with the worry."

Davy saw a single tear spill from one of her green eyes and heard Eamon say softly, "It's all right now, love. It's all right," as he moved to take her in his arms.

To Davy's amazement—they'd been apart for three years, after all—she stepped back, put a hand on her hip, dashed the tear away with the other hand, forced a smile at Eamon, and said, "Don't you come near me in those filthy, soaking clothes. Jesus, and the stink of you." She wrinkled her nose.

"You've not changed," Eamon said. "Have you?"

"No," she said, "but the sooner you change your clothes, the better."

"I will," he said, "but I'd like you to meet a couple of friends of mine first. Erin O'Byrne, Brendan McGuinness and Davy McCutcheon."

She smiled at them, and Davy felt welcomed by it. "Miss O'Byrne," he said.

"Pleased to meet you." Her smile faded. "We were expecting four of you. I . . . I heard about Sean Donovan."

"Aye," said Eamon. "That was bad luck."

"There's been a bit more bad luck," she said, quietly.

"What?" Eamon frowned. "Tell me."

She shook her head. "It'll keep." She turned to Davy. "Look, I'm very sorry, but it wouldn't be safe for all three of you to come up to the house. Tyrone's up to its ears in peelers and soldiers. We had a patrol here earlier tonight."

"Looking for me?" Eamon asked.

Davy heard the soup bubbling on the little stove and moved to take the pot off the ring.

"Aye, and your mates." She smiled. "I don't think the peelers'll be back tonight, but I'd rather be safe than sorry, so I want you to come up to the house by yourself. You can have a bath. Your mates'll have to stay here. I'm sorry."

Davy would have killed to have a bath, but he could smell the soup and feel the warmth of the blanket and the heater. That would satisfy him for now. He glanced at what would be his cot and ached to crawl into it. "Never you worry about that, Miss O'Byrne," he said.

"Thanks, and it's Erin, Davy." She smiled at him again, and behind her eyes he saw Fiona's smile. She turned to Eamon. "When we get up to the house, Cal and me have things to talk to you about, and"—she moved close to him and took his hand—"I want to get you out of those stinking clothes."

Davy heard more in her words than the simple statement, and by the way Eamon was grinning, he'd certainly got the not-too-subtle message, too.

CHAPTER 35

At last her wishes had come true. Eamon was here on the farm in Tyrone. His shirt, vest, and socks were in the dryer, along with the other men's clothes. Erin listened as shirt buttons rattled on the dryer's drum. Eamon's jacket and the trousers she'd sponged clean hung steaming on a clothes-horse in front of the range. They kept company with another pair of pants and a jacket that she'd bundled up before she and Eamon had left the grave and walked to the farmhouse. She hadn't bothered to see to the trousers Davy had given her. They were far too big for him. Some of Cal's should fit. When she'd asked him, he'd told her to take her pick. She'd take a pair of them down for Davy with the rest of the men's dry clothes. Cal wouldn't be needing them much longer anyway.

He'd been waiting for them, but after he'd greeted Eamon, had made an excuse to go out. She'd not thought that Cal could be so understanding. She knew bloody well that the milking machine didn't need mending at this hour of the night.

Eamon was upstairs having a bath. He'd said, eyes twinkling, that she should come up and scrub his back, but she'd told him she'd other things to do.

She lifted the lid of the range and shoved in more peat. The flames from the opening made her flinch. She was warm enough, and it wasn't from the heat in the kitchen; it was having him home. She'd thought he wasn't com-ing. She'd seen him dead, recaptured, a dozen times over. As if she hadn't had enough to worry about in the last few days.

She heard the hall door open and turned to see Eamon, barefooted, wrapped in Cal's dressing gown, hair wet and shining and slicked back.

"That," said Eamon, tipping his head to one side and poking at his ear with one finger, "that was great." He moved closer to her. "I had a shave, too. Feel." He took her hand in his and rubbed her fingers along his cheek.

Erin held back. Dear God, she wanted him, but they'd hardly spoken since leaving the grave, and she *must* tell him about Fiach—and about her plans. That was why she'd let him bathe alone. To have seen him naked would have distracted her. Even now, the very thought that he was wearing nothing under the dressing gown made her shiver. She ignored his puzzled look and said what she knew she must. "Eamon, look, I'm sorry I snapped at you back there, but I *have* been worried sick about you . . ."

"Well, you needn't worry now." He moved nearer.

She could feel his breath. No. Not yet. "There're some things, very important things, I have to tell you . . ."

"Sssh," he said, and bent and kissed her, pulling her to him.

She felt the strength in his arms holding her, his body warm and hard, his tongue on her tongue, and she slipped her hands inside his dressing gown, put her arms around him, her hands on his back, her nails raking gently. She tried to tell herself not yet, not now, but his hand had found her breast. She gasped. Telling him about Fiach's death and about the raid would have to wait.

"God, I've missed you," she murmured, and bit his lower lip. "I do love you, you daft bugger."

"I want you," he said, voice husky, hands fumbling with the buttons of her shirt. "Now."

"Yes." She helped him with the buttons, pulled the shirt apart, her breasts burning where his tongue flicked over her nipple. "Yes, but . . ." She held his head between her hands and forced him away. "Not here. Cal might . . ." But his hand was under her skirt, under her panties, and she remembered telling him, the day she'd given him the gun, that she'd not be wearing any when he came home. His fingers probed, and she opened for him and stood gasping, wanting.

Her own hand groped inside the dressing gown and she held his penis, felt him fierce and stiff. She knelt and took him in her mouth, gently biting, tasting him, hearing his groan. She slipped her hands behind his buttocks and pulled him into her. His hands went behind her head, holding her on him as she tried to rock back and forth.

She felt his hands entwine in her hair, pulling her head back.

She stared up along his flat belly, along the line of hair to his navel, past his muscled chest to his thrown-back head, mouth wide—he was wearing his dental plate—eyes closed.

She rose and kissed him, followed as he led her to the kitchen table, bent over it, hands behind her lifting her skirt. She thrust against him as he entered her as a stallion mounts a mare, her thoughts of Cal and Fiach and raids and the Cause gone to oblivion as if they had never existed.

She whimpered, bit the back of her forearm as he drove himself deeper. She heard him groan, felt his hand on her breast and the weight of him as he fell forward on her back.

Her breath left her in one, long gasp, and her body convulsed as if struck by an earthquake and—"O sweet Mother of Jes-uh-us . . ."—its aftershocks. Her curled fingers clutched at the edge of the table as each tremor passed.

She felt Eamon push her hair aside and kiss the nape of her neck. "Christ Almighty," he said softly, "it's been a long time."

She tried to turn to kiss him, but his weight held her down. For a moment all she wanted to do was lie there, held by him, until he was ready to take her again, but Cal could walk in at any minute.

Erin looked round the old, familiar kitchen that she loved, the one she must leave, along with the farm, along with Ireland if he asked her to run with him. But at that moment, she was spent and at peace and old, half-forgotten words came to her, "whither thou goest, I will go."

She noticed the tiled floor and saw the cracks where so many years ago peelers had stamped their booted feet and Ma had scrubbed her hands red-raw. The memories brought Erin back to the real world, where love and passion would have to take their turns with the killing that must be done. But Eamon's loving had been so sure, so familiar, so powerful, yet so comfortable that she wished the dying and the Troubles would go away forever. But they wouldn't, and there were things Eamon must be told.

"You're crushing me," she said, trying to push herself up.

"Right," Eamon said, and she felt his weight and his warmth leave her, and her eyes grew moist because she wanted him back. She straightened, half-turned, and smoothed her skirt.

Eamon stood looking at her. "I love you," he said, and stretched out one hand to her breast.

She pulled her shirt closed and began to button the front, tucking the tails into her waistband as soon as the first buttons were closed. She tried to ignore his disappointed look and continued buttoning.

"Aaw," he said, but she could hear the chuckle in his voice.

She glanced down to where his dressing gown still hung open and saw how shrunken he was. She smiled at him, pointed at his limp penis, and said, "You're like the cow in the kids' poem, "The House That Jack Built."

"You mean I've got a 'crumpled horn'?" Eamon laughed. "I've not heard you say that for three years." He pulled his dressing gown shut and belted it.

"After that long, I can make the wee bugger stand to attention anytime you like."

She smiled and kissed him. "I'd like it well enough right now."

"Well . . . ?" He tried to hold her, but she stepped back.

"We can't, Eamon. I've things to tell you."

"Like what?"

"Come and sit down," she said, rearranging her hair as she sat at the table.

Eamon sat opposite. "Like what?"

"The Brits murdered Fiach early on Saturday morning." Her tone was flat, matter-of-fact, and she was surprised by how easily the words came.

"They what?" Eamon's voice rose. "They what? Fiach? They killed your wee brother? The shites." He stared at her. "I can't believe it."

"It's true. I sent him to pick up an arms delivery and bring it back here." She looked at him to see if he were blaming her for sending a youngster out, but there was no anger in his eyes, only sadness. "An army patrol shot him."

"Jesus Christ. The poor wee lad." Eamon rose. "You must be hurting like hell."

She knew he was going to come to her, to hold her, to comfort her, and she loved him for his compassion.

"Are you all right?" he asked.

"I'm fine. Honestly. And just sit you where you are. There's more."

Eamon sat slowly, never letting his gaze leave her eyes.

"Cal and I have been thinking about what to do."

"What the hell can you do? You can't bring Fiach back." He sounded puzzled.

"Hit the bastards. Hard."

Eamon sat back. "Are you serious? Attack the Brits?" He shook his head. "I just don't see it. Right now? The place is crawling with the buggers." He rose and walked across the floor, arms folded, head bowed.

She waited. Give him time. Eamon was clever enough to work out the rightness of what she was suggesting.

He turned and stared at her. "You think they'll not be expecting an attack?"

"They'll be vulnerable," she said quietly.

She saw his eyes narrow. "I'm not so sure. I'd have to think on it." He moved to her and cupped her face in his hands. "I'd other plans," he said.

"Like leaving the North?" No matter what she'd thought about that, moments ago, it was still hard to face. She swallowed. "I knew you'd have to." She stepped back.

"It's not just me. Brendan has to get to Dublin. To Army Council. Davy wants to go to Canada." She wondered why Eamon's eyes had a faraway look. "Davy has a girl called Fiona there. He hasn't seen her in nine years."

Erin knew how much she had pined for Eamon, and that had only been for three years. Nine? Davy McCutcheon must love the woman very much. Did she still love him? Erin remembered the day she'd nearly thrown up in a ditch because she'd been bound and determined to leave Eamon in the Kesh. "Nine years is a long time," she said.

"I know, but Davy's going . . . and I promised to help him."

"You promised?"

Eamon nodded. "I've got to know him well. He's a sound man. He did us a favour in the Kesh, and if it hadn't been for him opening the last gate, I'd not be here now."

Not here? She couldn't bear the thought. Not after what had just been. And if Eamon felt he owed Davy McCutcheon and had promised him something, to Eamon a promise was never made lightly. "I understand," she said. "What help does he need?"

"Papers. Money. Out of here and down to the Republic. Airline tickets."

She moved to him, put her arms round his waist, and looked up into his eyes. "So will we."

"We?"

She smiled. "You said you've got to run. You're not going without me."

"Do you mean that? You'd leave Ireland?"

She kissed him, then said, "You left me once for three years. I'm not letting go of you again." And she squeezed him more tightly.

"I love you, Erin."

"I know," she said, "and I'm not going to play silly games like, 'well, if you really loved me, you'd help with the attack Cal and I've planned.'"

Eamon sighed. "You've your mind set on it, haven't you?"

"Cal's is half made up, but"—she knew she had to be honest with him—"but he says he'll only do it if you agree."

"I can't agree . . ."

"Why not?" Erin knew there was anger in her voice.

"Because," Eamon said levelly, "I never agree to anything until I know the details." He sat at the table. "I think," he said, "you'd better sit down and tell me all about it."

Erin heard his curiosity. She knew he was as committed to the Cause as she was. Eamon was like a trout rising to a fly, suspicious but hungry, and if she let the bait dangle a little longer, he'd take it and she'd have him hooked. She sat, looked him in the eye, and said, "Strabane Barracks."

He whistled on the intake of breath. "The police station?"

"Yes."

Eamon ran a hand over his head and frowned. She knew he always did that when he was concentrating. He looked at her. "When?"

"As soon as we're ready."

"And when'll that be?"

"There's a few things to do first."

"Like what?"

"Get papers for your Davy and the rest of us. That'll take a few days."

"Will we use the forger from Newtownstewart?"

"Aye." Although Eamon hadn't said so directly, Erin sensed that he was already beginning to sound like a man who was ready to take part. "Cal'll have a word with him."

"Right."

"Sammy's working as fast as he can making ammonal. Stealing a car and a tractor."

"Sammy McCandless? He's still here? I'd not mind seeing the wee fellah again." He laughed. "Even if he does fancy my girl."

"Pay no heed to Sammy," she said, and smiled. "He's harmless, and he's a bloody good armourer." Her smile faded. "And we need him. The Brits got our new supplies when they killed Fiach."

"Bastards." Eamon said, and looked at her. "Is it because of Fiach you want to get back at them?"

"That's part of it," she said levelly. "But there's a lot more to it. When we run five hundred pounds of ammonal through the fence at the barracks, shoot the peelers that survive the blast, we'll have shown them that the Tyrone Provos don't roll over and play dead, that we still want the Brits out."

"I'm glad you said that. I'll tell you a thing, Erin. If I thought this was a simple reprisal raid, I'd not go. I'd not have you taking risks just for the sake of revenge."

This man of hers thought clearly, loved Ireland, loved her. She leaned across the table and kissed him. "You'll be taking risks, too." And for a fleeting moment, she had second thoughts. Why risk anything?

Her doubts vanished when he said, "All right. How many men do we need?"

"Five." She leaned forward so he could see down the front of her blouse. "And one of your men's a woman in case you hadn't noticed."

"I noticed all right," he said, and covered her hand with his. "So that would be you and me and Cal and the two lads from the Kesh?"

"Aye."

"Fair enough, and there's plenty of rifles in the grave."

Erin waited to hear what he would say next.

"I'll have a word with Brendan and Davy. See what they say." He frowned. "I may have a wee bit of difficulty with Davy."

"Why?"

"He gave up on the Provos years ago. He says he wants no more killing."

She lifted his hand to her lips, and when she raised her head, said quietly, "I'm sure you can talk him round. All you'll have to do is tell him he'll be doing it for Ireland."

CHAPTER 36

Sammy hawked and spat. Bugger Ireland. The only thing he cared about the place was to get the fuck out of it as soon as possible, but that wasn't going to happen until he'd got these bejesusly jobs finished. Erin had told him what the target was, and he'd passed the information to Spud.

Sammy dragged on his cigarette as he walked along the path from his cottage to the outbuilding. He would finish up everything today, and he'd not be one bit sorry.

He hauled the doors of the big shed open. A sunbeam shone past him, its light washing over the sacks of ammonal piled against the back wall. They'd be a million times brighter in the millisecond of their explosion, and Sammy wished he knew exactly when that would be.

He dropped his Park Drive on the muddy path, ground the butt out with his heel, and went inside, leaving the doors half open.

He'd prefer to close them but this evening the place must be well ventilated when he started the tractor's engine to recheck the hydraulics. The station wagon he'd stolen in Derry yesterday was still to be repainted.

The red tractor with its new plates, HKM 561, stood to one side, the station wagon to the other. He climbed into the tractor's cab and started the motor, cocking his head to listen to the engine note. There was nothing wrong there. He worked the levers controlling the front bucket and watched it rise smoothly until he stopped its progress, waited, and lowered it back to the ground. He switched off the engine, coughing as the exhaust fumes irritated his throat. He'd load the sacks of ammonal after he'd finished with the paint job. Why anybody would want a powder-blue wagon was beyond him, but the light colour would be easy to disguise.

He walked round it to make sure the newspaper was firmly taped in place over the headlights and radiator grille, windscreen, windows, and taillights. He tutted when he had to retape a loose page of *The Belfast Telegraph* over the rear window. The headlines yelled, "Nineteen senior Provos recaptured. Nineteen still at large." Lucky buggers, the ones still out.

He felt for the poor shites who'd been stuck back in the Kesh. They were as trapped as he was, but he had a key to his cell. All he needed was to be told the date the raid would happen and have his suspicions about the target confirmed.

He poured black paint into a paint sprayer, slipped a scarf over his mouth and nose, flipped on a switch, and directed a fine spray of paint over the bonnet of the wagon. The electric motor hummed, and the paint hissed out. It wouldn't take long to disguise the vehicle.

He wondered how long it would be before the Brits changed his identity once he got to England.

The blue vanished under a coat of wet, shiny black. Perhaps he'd have to dye his hair a different colour. Grow a beard. He'd always fancied having a beard. It was bother enough to shave, anyway. It cheered him to think about those kinds of details now that he was so close to getting away.

The O'Byrnes'd have to let him in on everything soon. Erin was right to be cautious about telling him the details. It was the way the Provos worked. If a volunteer was at risk in the early part of an operation, the less he knew, then the less he could tell if he was arrested.

There had been a real danger Sammy could be lifted stealing the vehicles. A peeler nearly got him in Derry when he'd been trying to feck a car before he went to Ballybofey to pick up the arms. Jesus, it seemed like a year ago. Look what had happened when he'd been driving the tractor home. He'd been stopped by the bloody army. He might have been arrested and interrogated—but he hadn't been.

Now that those kinds of risks were over, Sammy could go to Erin and tell her he'd done his job. She'd have to come clean with him then. Maybe she'd smile at him. He'd had few enough people smile at him in his whole fucking life. These days, nobody gave a shite about him except the O'Byrnes and Spud, and all Spud and Cal really cared about was using him. Erin was different. She would smile at him, didn't seem to mind much when he looked at her, never refused to look him in the eye. A while back there, she'd told him he was like family and he'd liked that.

Family? He'd no fucking family, no brothers, no sisters, no Ma since he was five. His oul' bastard of a da had been a vicious drouth and beat the living bejesus out of Ma every Friday night after he'd drunk his wages. She'd fucked off, and Sammy couldn't blame her, even if she had abandoned him to the oul' shite's rages. The day Da'd been crushed to death under a tractor, fifteen-year-old Sammy hadn't wept one tear.

Nor hardly a one since, except maybe when he got stocious himself and had maudlin thoughts about Erin, his shining girl, his star, his unreachable star. Well, in England he'd have to forget her, or at least try to forget her.

He knew he wouldn't, nor would she forget him. He couldn't find a way to keep her from mounting the attack. She'd be arrested, and she'd know who'd grassed. She'd hate him. Everyone here would hate him just like they hated Art O'Hanlon and Mollie MacDacker.

His hand trembled, and he misdirected the spray of paint, splattering the newspaper over the windscreen. He told himself to get a grip. If he wanted out, he couldn't turn back now, no matter what anyone would think of him. It wasn't, he told himself bitterly, as if anyone thought much of him anyway.

As soon as he knew everything, he'd get hold of Spud. It was better Sammy hadn't gone off at half cock when he'd tried to phone the E4A man on Sunday. Spud had said to get in touch in a couple of days. Sammy'd let Spud wait a while longer until, he hoped, he knew everything. He'd go to the farm tomorrow to tell them he was ready, hear what he wanted, and then—then one phone call, and he'd be on his way to England. It was all that really mattered, and it was going to happen. As he worked, Sammy whistled "The Irish Washerwoman" off-key.

Now that he felt more cheerful, the job went smoothly, and in an hour he was able to turn off the paint sprayer and admire his handiwork. It wouldn't take long for the paint to dry, and then he could strip off the newspaper, put on the false plates.

Now for the ammonal. He manhandled the first heavy sack across the floor and heaved it into the tractor's bucket, returned to the row of great bags labeled FERTILIZER, and repeated the task, feeling his sweat start.

When the last sack lay with its fellows in the tractor's bucket, Sammy's spine ached and his arms felt as if they had been stretched by six inches. He put a hand in the small of his back and took a deep breath.

He was sick to death of the smell of paint, sick to death of the whole bloody business, but he still had work to do on the station wagon before he could leave the shed.

After that, he'd go home and finish the last job, connecting two fulminate-of-mercury detonators to a timer and getting the batteries ready. Whoever was going to drive the tractor would have to connect the batteries to the circuit and put the fusing device in the ammonal just before they wanted the thing to go off. It was an absolute rule that you never transported the charge with the detonator wired in. Fulminate was unstable stuff. Only a fucking idiot would make a bomb live before the very last minute. Some buck-eejits had got their wings and halos or maybe horns and pitchforks a damn sight earlier than they'd expected.

He wished he had some RDX or PETN. They were fantastic accelerants, the best and most stable detonators available, but they'd been taken when—when—the soldiers shot Fiach. He told himself not to think about Fiach or anyone else getting killed, but the thought of death refused to go away.

Who, he asked himself, was the most likely to end up getting shot during the raid? The poor bugger driving the tractor, that's who. Fuck that for a game of soldiers. Even if by some weird cock-up Sammy had to go out on the attack, he'd make bloody sure he wasn't driving. He was only the armourer. It was his job to make final adjustments to the bomb. That was all. What the hell was he worried about anyway? By the time the O'Byrnes headed to Strabane, he'd be well away. In England.

Sammy wanted a smoke. Badly. The plates for the station wagon and taking off the newspaper masking could wait.

He left the building, closing the door behind him, pulled out a Park Drive, and lit up. His nostrils were clogged with the fresh-paint stink of the place. He sat on a bale of straw beside the building's plank wall, closed his eyes, and let the sun warm him.

The noise of a distant engine roused him. It was probably someone out on a tractor, but the engine note was wrong. He listened. It was a motorcar, and—he opened his eyes—dear God, he could see it coming down the lane to his cottage. Holy fuck. He glanced behind and took another quick pull on his fag. Thank Christ he'd shut the door. He'd not want any stranger to see what was in there.

The car kept coming, bouncing over the ruts in the lane, then stopped close by. Sammy jumped up, trying to see who was inside, and when he recognized the driver, Sammy dropped his smoke. What was Spud doing here in broad daylight? Sammy crouched as he neared the car and wrenched the driver's door open. "What the fuck are you doing here? If anybody sees the pair of us together . . ."

"Nobody's going to see us, and if anyone does, it won't matter, Sunshine. I'm just making routine enquiries." Spud smiled. "Eamon Maguire's still out. He's not at the O'Byrnes'. We've checked . . ."

Aye, but you've not checked in the old grave, Sammy thought, and if I've guessed right, he should be there by now.

"You've known Eamon for years. It's only natural the police would pop in to see you. Make sure he's not here." The E4A man lowered his voice. "After you phoned on Sunday I wanted to have a wee chat."

"Out in the fucking open with your car sitting at my place? Why don't you just put an advert in *The Newsletter*?" Sammy scrabbled in his pocket for his packet of Park Drive.

"It's not my Lada. We never use the same car long. Too much risk of your lot recognizing it and wiring a wee surprise to the ignition. It's happened before."

When Sammy opened the cigarette packet, it was empty. If ever he'd wanted a fag, it was at that moment. "For God's sake," he begged, "come into the house. Out of sight."

"Get in the car."

Sammy hesitated, then shook his head. If anyone was watching, this had to look like a routine visit. He'd walk to his cottage and let himself in. As he headed slowly up the potholed tarmac of the path, he heard Spud park the car. Sammy pushed open the cottage door and waited for the policeman to enter.

He slammed the door behind Spud. He gathered up dirty clothes from where they lay scattered on the old sofa. "You're going to get me killed, coming here like this, so you are." He dumped underpants and shirts in a heap on the table among the unwashed breakfast plates. "Sit down." Sammy heard the springs creak as Spud sat, then he dragged a chair from the table and sat facing the policeman. "Can we get the fuck on with this?"

"What have you to tell me, Sunshine?" His tone was all business.

"You told me if I gave you a really big one, you'd get me out."

Spud nodded.

Sammy stood up, paced, and thought, this is it; I'm sorry, Erin, but it's you in jail or me in England. "Like I tried to tell you on the phone, they're going after the barracks in Strabane," he said with as much certainty in his voice as he could muster. The peeler had no way of telling it was only Sammy's best guess, but he had to know that this information would be the stuff that would do the trick.

Spud whistled softly. "Strabane." Sammy knew the policeman could taste commendation and promotion. "Tell me when."

"I don't know exactly, but soon. I had stuff to get ready in a big rush."

"It's not much use to me if I don't know when."

"Look, I'm right about this. Haven't I always been right? Ballydornan and the arms dump? The Kesh? I tried to tell you, but you wouldn't listen. It *is* fuckin' well true, and I'll find out when tomorrow."

"Let me know."

"Of course I'll fuckin' well let you know, but *I* need to know now, are you for getting me to England? If you go after the ones who're going to attack, I can't stay here in Tyrone." Sammy picked his nose and gnawed a nicotine-stained knuckle.

"Why not?"

"Because if you lift them and don't get me away, the same senior Provos up in Derry that debriefed me after your mate lifted me and got me into this shite in the first place, them senior men know who I am, who I work with. They'll come after me. They don't trust nobody." Sammy could still smell the stench of flesh burned by an electric drill when they'd punished the young lad who'd been selling drugs, still hear his screams. Sure, the Provos dealt in drugs to finance their operations. They did, but they took a very dim view of anyone who tried to go into business for himself.

"I'll be regally fucked," Sammy said, remembering Finn McArdle, the poor bastard the peelers had set up the way they'd threatened to do to Sammy. After weeks of interrogation, Finn'd been forced to confess, even though he was innocent, and he'd got a .375 Magnum slug in his head. "You'll not get any help from a dead tout."

"True." Spud shrugged.

Was the man not listening, was he not going to promise to get him out of this God-forsaken country? Sammy felt his eyes fill. He sniffed, then shook his head. He had another card to play. He clenched his fists and said, with a hint of disgust, "Once you take my friends, I'll be no fuckin' use to you anyway. Can you not see that?"

"Why not?"

"Jesus, how many Provos do you think I know? Just one Active Service Unit, that's all. Do you suppose the senior men'll assign me to another Active Service Unit? As far as I know, there's not one for miles, and me with nothing but a bicycle to get about on. If you get my people, who the fuck else do you think I'll be able to find things out about? I'll have nothing left to tell you."

"But you've other things for me now, haven't you?"

"Like what, for Christ's sake?"

"More details."

"Like what?" Sammy sat heavily on the wooden chair. "Like what?"

"You said you'd been ordered to get stuff ready. What stuff?"

"Christ. Do you want me to take you out to the big shed and show you?"

"No. Just tell me. I'll believe you, Sunshine."

"Five hundred pound of ammonal . . ."

"How much? Holy shite."

"Five hundred, and I'd to steal a tractor to carry it."

"Had you, by God?"

That made the bugger sit up and take notice.

"And a station wagon. I've just been painting it black." He showed Spud paint-stained fingers.

The policeman fished in his inside jacket pocket and produced a note-book. "What's the plate numbers of the tractor and the wagon?"

"HKM 561."

"And the wagon?"

"LKM 136."

Spud scribbled, blew out his breath, patted Sammy's knee, and said slowly, "Jesus, Sammy, but you've done good. It is going to be a big one all right."

"I told you, didn't I?" There was a hint of pride in Sammy's voice, and that wee bit of praise went a long way. Sammy had needed someone to tell him he'd done well, and more; he wanted Spud to reassure him that promises would be kept. "I've kept up my end. It's up to you now."

Spud stood and offered his hand. Sammy looked at it suspiciously. The peeler had never offered to shake hands before.

"You get me the date, Sunshine, and you're on your way. That's a promise."

Sammy took the hand, knowing that to an Ulsterman a bargain sealed with a handshake was as binding as one stamped and sealed before a High Court judge. "I told you. I'll know by tomorrow."

"Phone me." Spud released Sammy's hand. "And if you can't get through, do you remember what I told you about the dead-letter drops?"

"Aye. Them secret places I can leave you a note."

"Use the one under the Celtic cross in Ballydornan churchyard."

"Why won't I be able to get through to you?"

Spud rose. "I'm going to be just a wee bit busy for the next few days." He walked to the door. "I'll see myself out—and, Sammy, if anyone has seen me, you tell them it was a routine visit . . . looking for Eamon."

"I will," Sammy said. "I just hope nobody did."

"Another wee thing."

"What?"

"You're getting out. You've my word on that . . ."

"I should fuckin' well hope so."

"After the Strabane raid."

"*What?*" Sammy knew he sounded like one of the altar-boy trebles in his chapel on a Sunday at Mass. "*After?*"

"If you vanish before, do you not think your friends'll suspect, call the whole thing off?"

"I suppose."

"And we want your Active Service Unit, Sunshine. We know who they are."

"You what? Away off and feel your head." The policeman was bluffing, trying to trick Sammy. He wasn't going to fall for it.

"We've known about the O'Byrnes for years. Their da was in the IRA. Cal and Erin went into the family business with him. We nearly got them when we nailed Eamon Maguire, but we've never been able to pin anything on them. Nothing that would stand up in court. We want them badly, so we have to get them committing such a serious crime that a hundred lawyers couldn't get them acquitted. This raid's our best shot. We can't afford to scare them off."

Sammy's hands trembled, but to his surprise he felt a kind of relief. If what Spud said was true, that he already knew about the O'Byrnes, then Sammy wasn't really grassing about them. Not really. And the bit about no lawyers getting them off? That meant an arrest for sure. Erin's life would be spared.

"Get me the date and go on the raid with them. I'll get you out."

"Look"—Sammy scuffed his feet on the linoleum—"just say it is the O'Byrnes, and I'm not saying it is, so I'm not . . ."

"You don't need to, Sammy. We know." Sammy heard the absolute certainty in the man's voice.

"Why not lift them as soon as they come here to pick up the stuff in the shed? Nobody'd get hurt." And that included Sammy. Better Erin alive in jail than—

"It's not what the higher-ups want. I've talked to my bosses since you phoned. Told them there was likely a big one coming. They're embarrassed as hell about the breakout. They want to send a message. It's not up to me."

Sammy understood only too clearly what the E4A man was saying. Corpses didn't need lawyers. He could see Erin, bloody, torn, dead. Had he the guts to confess what he'd been doing to the O'Byrnes so they'd cancel the raid and she'd be safe?

"Sunshine, I've taken a chance telling you this, and I'm telling you because we're friends. I trust you, and I don't think you'll try to play the double agent and tip them off."

Shite. Could the bloody peeler read Sammy's mind? Friends. He'd come to rely on Spud's friendship for the last six months, and now they were so far down this road that the E4A man was Sammy's only hope of staying alive. Telling the O'Byrnes would be great for his conscience, but he'd be signing his own death warrant.

"I'd not be that fuckin' stupid," he said.

"And I'll look after you, Sammy. All you'll have to do is tell one of the officers you're Sunshine."

"How can I tell anyone anything when you buggers start shooting?"

"Have you a green scarf?"

"Aye."

"Wear it. I'll have my people well briefed."

"You'd fuckin' well better."

Spud clapped Sammy's shoulder. "I will."

Sammy grunted.

"Right," Spud said. "I'm off." He grinned at Sammy. "I've a lot to do . . . and that includes getting a ticket to England for a friend of mine."

Sammy barely heard the door close or the car pull away. England. He'd done it. He was going. As he waited for his breathing to slow, he savoured the thought. England. But, fuck it. At what price? He'd sold his soul. He'd sold Erin. He was a fuckin' Judas.

But even if he had exaggerated his certainty about Strabane, he'd forced Spud to commit himself. And he had, by God, he had. Sammy was convinced he was going to have his suspicions confirmed tomorrow, and if he had guessed wrong, one phone call would soon set that right. What the policeman was interested in was a big raid and who was going to make it. The O'Byrnes.

He didn't want to think about it now. At least he'd be alive to feel guilty if he survived. He'd hoped he could get out before the attack, hadn't foreseen the one snag that Erin might cancel the thing if Sammy disappeared. Spud had been onto that like a flash. Sammy was going to have to go, knowing the Security Forces would be waiting.

He saw a long butt in an ashtray, lifted it, and struck a match, seeing how the flame shook as his whole body shuddered. He inhaled, took no pleasure from the smoke, but he was going to finish it before he went back in the shed to complete the job on the station wagon.

Was there no way to stop Erin from going? None at all? An idea began to form, but he couldn't quite understand. It had something to do with him having to take part. He worried at the thought, but his mind refused to focus.

The cigarette was nothing but a tiny stump, the burning tobacco hot on his lips. He chucked the butt back in the ashtray, not bothering to crush it out. Fuck it, he'd go and see to that bloody wagon.

He let himself out to walk back to the shed, pausing to look round in a full circle to see if anyone was near. Anyone who could have been watching.

From above his head, he heard a plaintive "pee-wit, pee-wit" and looked up to see lapwings slowly straggling across an eggshell-blue sky. There was something dark higher than the flock, hovering, head to the wind, tail feathers fanned.

It was a kestrel waiting in ambush.

Sammy watched as the hunter closed its wings and stooped, plummeting down the sky. "Look out," he called, as if his warning could do a damn bit of good. Sammy heard the "thump" and saw the burst of green feathers as the kestrel struck. Royal Ulster Constabulary uniforms were a darker shade of green. The poor bloody lapwing couldn't have known what hit it. Locked together, hunter and prey fell into the next field, and from there he heard the falcon's shrill, "kek-kek-kek," the predator's cry of triumph, and he pictured the victim, body broken, its blood already congealing on the warm ground.

CHAPTER 37

The blood where he'd nicked himself shaving had clotted hours ago. Davy touched the scab under his nose and peered in a mirror hanging from the back wall of the tumulus. He frowned at his reflection. Deep lines from the sides of his nostrils ran down to the outer corners of an upper lip, which seemed to be shorter now that his moustache was gone. He'd had the thing for thirty years. Taking it off this morning hadn't seemed so difficult to do, but now he felt as if he'd lost an old friend.

"You look about ten years younger," McGuinness said from where he sat on his cot.

Davy grunted and ignored the remark, although there was some truth to McGuinness's words now that Davy's thinning hair had been dyed auburn with Clairol. When he put on the plain-lens granny glasses to complete his disguise, he looked his forty-seven years again.

It didn't matter a damn how old he looked as long as the photographs taken by a young man Eamon had brought from Newtownstewart at noon would do the trick. Davy's forged passport and Canadian driver's licence were to be delivered on Friday.

They'd better be here by then, because before he'd left with the photographer, Eamon had said that on Saturday they'd all be heading for Dublin and the shelter of the Provos based there. Davy'd be only a plane flight away from Fiona. He hoped he could phone her from Dublin. Hearing his voice would unsettle her, but not be as big a shock as turning up in person, clean-shaven, auburn-haired, and hardly looking at all like the man she'd known.

Maybe that wasn't such a bad thing.

He wasn't the man she'd known years ago. Back then, when they'd first met, he'd been sustained by his rigid faith in the Cause, embarrassed in her presence by his lack of schooling. Even before he'd been jailed, that faith had faltered, tottered, and collapsed, leaving a vacuum in his soul that no religion could fill. He'd only had Fiona and her unshakeable belief that he could change to sustain him.

She'd been willing to understand why he'd fought and had never wrapped up her disapproval but didn't keep harping on about it. She'd been able, at least at first, to forgive him. Had she forgiven him for insisting on the one, last raid at Ravernet? He believed with all his heart she had and would tell him when he saw her—soon, very soon.

From the mirror, his blue eyes stared back and told him, despite his repudiation of the violence, some of the old Davy lived on. Some of him would never be altered. He still believed in Irish freedom, but not at the cost the Provos wanted to exact; he believed in friendship, he believed in keeping his word, and he believed in his devotion to the only woman he'd ever loved.

She'd been certain he could change, and—he smiled at his bare lip and auburn hair—he had, and not just in his appearance. He had a skill, carpentry; he'd built on her early tutoring and had read just about every book in the Kesh library—novels, biographies, some philosophy, Irish history. One of those books had said that a man's attitudes could only be altered by some shattering experience. Watching a little girl burn had torn at him and forced him to see the havoc he was creating, and not just for the victims of the bombings and shootings. He couldn't be the only one of the hard men who was revolted by what they were doing, who carried their guilt like millstones.

There must be men who felt the way he did, but they didn't include his friend Eamon or—Davy glanced over to where the man sat on his cot, arms folded, shoulders hunched one higher than the other, his good eye fixed on the stones of their sanctuary—Brendan McGuinness.

He must have seen Davy's questioning look. He stood, arms still folded. "If you've finished admiring yourself, I'd like a word with you, McCutcheon." The man's voice had its usual harsh edge. He walked toward Davy.

Davy waited.

"You and me's had our differences."

"We still do, and no amount of you preaching at me's going to change that. You and I are never going to agree."

"We both agree Ireland should be free."

Davy hesitated and then said slowly, "I'll grant you that."

"Whatever way you cut it, we're both on the same side."

Davy shook his head. "Not anymore. Not since you sent me out to blow up an army patrol and I killed a farmer and his family."

McGuinness shrugged. "Accidents happen. If we're going to get the Brits out, we have to hit them and keep hitting them."

Davy wondered what, if anything, drove the man other than hatred and an overweening lust for revenge. He'd not rest until Northern Ireland was a heap of corpses, and even then he'd not be satisfied. Davy said, "Maybe *you* have to. I've had enough, and in case you've forgotten Sean Conlon trusted me. He gave me permission to quit after the Ravernet attack."

"I didn't want you to go out on that one. I didn't think you were up to the job, and I was right. You let us down and got the pair of us arrested."

"Do you think I don't know that? I've had nine bloody years to think about it." And, he thought, nine years to ask myself, why did I go to Ravernet when Fiona didn't want me to, nine years to try to work out who I was then, who I am now? Some kind of Mr. Hyde becoming a gentler Doctor Jekyll? He hoped to God she would see the transformation when he got to Vancouver.

McGuinness snapped, "You're not the only one that's been stuck inside, but some of us have the guts to go on fighting now we're out. You don't."

Davy tried to let the accusation that he was a coward pass and made to push by, but McGuinness stood in his way. "Fighting?" Davy said, his voice low, "do you want to fight with me?"

"Fuck it, no." McGuinness took a pace back. "No. I want you to keep on fighting the Brits."

"The Brits? In my day, we fought soldiers, the police, not little girls, not railway-ticket collectors. Fighting? Even if your 'fighting,' as you call it, brings a united Ireland, what the hell kind of a country do you think it's going to be?"

"It'll be ours again."

"Filled with a legacy of death and bitterness, all the hatred of the centuries fueled by the slaughter of the last fourteen years. Some bloody country."

"Do you see any other way to get what we want, the freedom Ireland has earned through the blood of her martyrs?"

Oh, Jesus, not the bloody martyrs again. In lieu of mother's milk, Da had fed Davy the stories of the heroes who'd died, and look where that had got him. He shook his head. "No," he said wearily, "no I don't, but I want no more of killing for it. Ever." He knew this was a fruitless debate and wondered why McGuinness had brought the subject up in the first place. "Why don't we just drop it?"

He expected McGuinness to start ranting and was surprised when he said, "All right. It wasn't what I wanted to talk to you about anyway."

Davy frowned. He'd detected a note of—it couldn't be—conciliation in McGuinness's voice. "I'll listen," he said.

McGuinness shifted his weight from one foot to the other, glanced at the floor, focused his good eye on Davy, and said, "I've no intention of kissing and making up, but the pair of us, and Eamon when he gets back, are stuck in this wee place for three more days. It's like being cell mates back in the Kesh."

"I don't see what that's got to do with anything."

"Just listen. I know you don't like me." I've never liked you, McGuinness, Davy thought as the man continued. "I don't like you either, McCutcheon. I think you've let us down, and I know you're wrong not wanting to fight on."

Davy shrugged. This was pointless. They were heading off again down the old well-ploughed furrow. He'd not bother to argue.

McGuinness scratched the socket of his glass eye with one finger. "I could have been wrong about something else, too." He stopped scratching. "I'm trying to say . . . och, fuck it . . . I'm trying . . ."

By the way McGuinness was fidgeting, whatever was on his mind was difficult for him to spit out. "Look, just say your piece and leave me alone. All right?"

"You done good back in the Kesh."

"What?" Davy jerked back. "What did you say?"

"I said, you done good when you got that chisel for us, and if you hadn't found the right switch in the Tally Lodge, we'd all've been fucked."

Christ Almighty, it must have cost McGuinness dearly to say that. "Eamon asked me for a favour with the chisel," Davy said. "And I wanted out as much as everybody in the lodge. I got lucky."

"Maybe, but . . ."

"But what?"

"We've to put up with each other in here. We'll have to work together getting to Dublin."

"So?" Was the man trying to call for a truce, like the one the Provisionals had called with the British back in 1972? It had only lasted for a few months.

"I'll let bygones be bygones if you will." McGuinness folded his arms across his chest.

Davy was glad the man hadn't offered to shake hands. He wasn't sure he could have returned the shake, but he said, "Fair enough."

"Good." McGuinness spun, stared at the tunnel, and whispered, "What the fuck's that?"

Davy heard scrabbling. He glanced at his watch. Four. Eamon wasn't due for two hours. Christ, could the police have found the grave?

His hand slid under his pillow, grabbed the cold metal of the .25, and let it go. If there were a couple of peelers in the tunnel, there'd be a squad of the bastards outside. He couldn't hope to shoot his way out. He slipped off the cot and stood waiting, fists clenched, feeling his pulse quicken.

A man appeared, crawling on his hands and knees, stood, and dusted off his pants. "Hiya, Father. Brendan," Eamon said through his gap-toothed grin.

"Jesus, Eamon." Davy's heart rate slowed. "You'd me near petrified."

"Sorry about that," Eamon said, peering closely at Davy's face. "My God, Father, I'd hardly recognize you."

"Aye," said Davy. "As long as the people in Canada don't, I'll do rightly."

"Never you worry about that." Eamon plumped himself down in one of the chairs. "Come over here and sit down, the pair of you. I said I'd explain what I was up to today. I've been sorting things out with Erin and Cal . . . I've had some bad news."

"About us getting to the Republic?" Davy thought his heart would stop.

"No. That's still on . . ."

Davy closed his eyes and muttered a silent thank-you.

"But I haven't had a chance to tell you sooner . . ."

Davy couldn't decide if Eamon sounded sad or angry.

"The Brits killed Fiach O'Byrne, the youngest brother last week."

"Och, dear," Davy said. "I'm sorry, Eamon." He glanced at McGuinness. See what your fighting gets you? Another useless death.

"Erin and Cal want to do something about it before we get out of Tyrone."

"I should bloody well hope so," McGuinness growled. "Count me in whatever it is. British Bastards."

"Fair enough."

Davy was making no promises until he understood exactly what Eamon meant. Was he thinking about some kind of reprisal? That would be stupid when freedom was so close. Davy stood and tried to walk away. If Eamon wanted to coerce Davy into being part of whatever he was planning, he'd better think again. Hadn't he just finished telling McGuinness he'd fight no more? Hadn't he just finished convincing himself he was a changed man, a man Fiona could respect, could still love? She'd never forgive him. He'd promised her Ravernet would be his last raid, and by God it would be.

Eamon stood, laid a hand on Davy's arm, and looked him in the eye. "I want to ask you a wee favour, Father."

"Have you no chisels of your own here?" Davy glanced at McGuinness. He was the one who'd reminded Davy about the last favour he'd done for

Eamon. It was because of it Eamon had arranged for Davy to join the escape. Maybe he still owed Eamon for it. "What is it?"

"Can you drive?"

"Aye, certainly."

"Good. I need you to do a bit of driving for us."

Davy stuffed his hands into his pockets and said, "My oul' da used to say, 'never make a promise unless you know you can keep it.' I'll make you no promises until I hear what I've to drive for."

Eamon said softly, "Erin has a plan to take out Strabane Police Barracks."

No, damnit, no, a voice screamed in Davy's head.

"Tell us about it." McGuinness leaned forward. "How? When?"

"In a wee minute, Brendan. I need to hear what Davy thinks."

"You know bloody well what I think. I told you often enough back in our cell. I'm out. I don't even want to drive you. I'm finished with all that shite." Davy was hurt that Eamon would ask.

"I'm sorry, Davy, but we need you." An edge had crept into Eamon's voice.

"You can need away. I'm not doing it."

"Are you scared, McCutcheon?" He could see McGuinness scowling, him and his blether about letting bygones be bygones. Some truce.

"No. I'm not scared. I'm not killing anyone, that's all. And that's final." Davy turned his back on the others, strode over to his alcove, and sat on his cot. Christ, would Eamon not leave him alone? The man had followed him and stood in the opening.

"I'm not asking you to kill anyone, Father. Brendan and the O'Byrnes and me'll take care of that."

"Can you not get it through your head? As far as I'm concerned, I want no part of it."

Eamon ran one hand through his hair. "Can I tell you how it's going to work? Please?"

"I owe you that much. You got me this far. I'd still be in . . ."

"That's over and done. You owe me nothing, except to hear me out."

"Go ahead. I'm listening."

"Right. I'll give you the bare bones. We've to use the farm van to get the attack team from here to a big shed about four miles away. They'll pick up the explosives there and a tractor and an escape car. We'll go into Strabane. The driver . . . that's you, Davy, has to get the van back past here, across the border at Clady, and on into Lifford in the Republic, just over from Strabane."

Davy frowned. He was caught up already in trying to understand the details, and if he let himself get interested, the next thing he knew he'd be agreeing to help. "I don't see why you need me," he said. "Get somebody else to drive to your shed. Leave the van there."

Eamon scratched his cheek. "We could, but how would you get down to the Republic? We've only the van on the farm."

"I've no idea." The words slipped out. "I thought you were going to take care of that."

Eamon laughed. "I'm trying to. Look. Once we've hit the barracks, the four of us will take the escape car across the wee bridge between Strabane and Lifford, but we'll have to dump it there. The RUC and the soldiers can't follow us into the Republic, but they're bound to give the description to the Gardai. We'd not get ten miles in it. The idea's for us to ditch it in Lifford and use the van to get to Castlefinn in Donegal. It's only about ten miles from Lifford."

"Why Castlefinn?"

"Sean Conlon's sending a car there to meet us. It'll take us all to Dublin. I had a yarn with Sean on the phone today. He sends his regards."

"Is he well?" Davy remembered his old CO with affection. "He's still there with Army Council?"

"He is."

"I'd not mind seeing Sean again, but why doesn't he send the car to Lifford, then you'd not need the van nor me?"

"He could, I suppose, but the Gardai will have the getaway car's number, and there's an off chance someone could spot us making the transfer from it in Lifford. There'd be an all-points bulletin out for that vehicle all over the Republic. We can't take a chance Sean's car would be spotted like that. It won't matter if the van's seen. We'll be in Castlefinn in five minutes. No one will notice anything there. If the Gardai do get the van's number, by the time they find it in Castlefinn, we'll be well away in Sean's car."

That made sense to Davy. He put the web of his hand up to stroke his moustache, forgetting he no longer had one. The action pulled the scab free, and he felt a tiny trickle of blood.

Eamon moved closer. "Davy, I'm not asking you to make a bomb. I'm not asking you to carry a gun. All I want you to do is give us a lift, bugger off to the Republic, and pick us up when everything's over."

It didn't seem much to ask. "Well, maybe . . ." Davy hesitated because, try as he might, he couldn't see any difference between delivering a lethal weapon, the attack squad, and furnishing the bombs he'd made in the past for others to plant. In both cases, he was distanced from the killing but no less a part of it. "What'll you do if I say no?"

Eamon scratched his chin. "Davy, if you won't drive, we'll have to take the farm van, dump it at the shed, get Sean's people to come to Lifford, and take our chances."

"I'd rather you did it that way."

Eamon looked straight into Davy's eyes. "What about you? If we take the van, you'll have no transport. We can't come back for you. How're you going to get to Dublin? You'll not get there on foot."

"What?" Eamon was right, and Davy'd been so self-righteously concentrating on keeping his hands spotless, he hadn't considered these implications.

Eamon put a hand on Davy's shoulder. "The Republic's no safe haven for Provos on the run. Most of the ordinary people there couldn't give a shite about what goes on in the North, want nothing to do with the likes of us. The government officially cooperates with the Brits. You'll get lifted by the Gardai and stuck in jail while the Brits apply for extradition, unless, of course, you do what I'm asking."

Jesus Christ Almighty. Davy looked all around. Was he never going to get out of some kind of cell, like the one in the Kesh, this prison of a hiding place, and now the vice Eamon had him in? Carrot and bloody stick. Eamon wanted another favour, and Davy always found it hard to refuse a friend. But surely to God a friend wouldn't use blackmail? That's what it was. Drive the van, and Dublin was within reach; refuse, and Dublin and Canada— and Fiona—were out of the question.

He had to choose. Fiona had said she loved his integrity. What price his precious integrity now? Every man has his price, Davy thought bitterly, and if he wanted her, he was going to have to pay.

He looked Eamon straight in the eye and said, "Fuck you, Eamon, I've no choice, have I?"

"I'm sorry, Davy, I really am."

No one spoke. Davy felt the ties of friendship breaking. "You've not the right to ask this of me."

"I know," Eamon said. "But I have."

"And you'll do it, McCutcheon." McGuinness rapped. "You're still a Provo volunteer whether you like it or not, and you'll obey orders."

Davy spun on the man. "Fuck you."

McGuinness ignored Davy and spoke directly to Eamon. "You've had your word with McCutcheon. He'll do as he's bid. Now I want to hear the details."

Eamon looked long and hard at Davy, who could see the sadness in Eamon's eyes. Eamon understood bloody well what he'd done. Davy knew it should have come as no surprise. He shouldn't be feeling betrayed. Those committed to the Cause would sacrifice everything on the altar of their dreams; their lives, their loves, and their friends. Eamon looked away, took a deep breath, and said, "I told you the target. The Police Barracks in Strabane . . ."

"Fuckin' aye," McGuinness said.

"But you'll need to hear the exact details, so the three of us'll"—Eamon tried to look at Davy again, but Davy saw the glance and turned away—"go up to the farm after dark. I want everyone . . . including you, Davy . . . to hear the plan. The plan for Saturday."

CHAPTER 38

Saturday was four days away, Fiona thought, as she hurried along Beach Avenue toward Jimmy Ferguson's apartment. She hunched her shoulders against the wind, which churned the sea to foam and hammered whitecaps against the seawall. The gale growled and hissed and spat spume across the road.

A gust screeched in from English Bay and tore past her to batter the Sylvia Hotel and blocks of low-rises. The apartments seemed to be cowering. She could taste the brine in it, and—she put a hand to her head—her hair must be a mess. Her umbrella had been blown to tatters. Its pale ribs looked like the bones of a long-dead fish.

Beach Avenue was deserted; it had none of the usual cyclists and joggers, no walkers, no dogs, only cars, windscreen wipers thrashing, tires spraying sheets of water. She had not felt so isolated since her first year in Vancouver, before she'd made any friends, when she couldn't stop thinking about Davy. As if she could stop thinking about him now.

He filled her thoughts, and she needed a friend to talk to, but Becky wasn't there to help. She'd called this morning to say that it looked as if a decision might have to be made soon, and it was going to be a difficult one. The doctors were already wondering aloud about whether the family wanted to keep her dad on the ventilator. It wasn't going to be easy for her friend.

Fiona leaned against the wind and kept plodding along the deserted street, wondering if she'd been right to arrange to meet with Jimmy's daughter, Siobhan.

Screwing her eyes against the wind, she peered at a wooden sign on the sea-wrack-strewn lawn of a cold, concrete, and glass low-rise. Nineteen fifty Beach.

She pushed the button beside an address plate reading 407. MR. AND MRS. JAMES FERGUSON.

A man's voice came from a speaker. "Fiona?"

"Is . . . is that you, Jimmy?" She'd been expecting to hear Siobhan.

"Aye. Siobhan's here, too. Come you on up out of that bloody awful weather."

A buzzer whirred.

Fiona pushed through the door. When she'd gone to the Kesh to tell Davy she was leaving him, all the gates had been electrically controlled. Last Sunday, Davy and the other escapees must have opened them somehow.

She crossed a tiled hall into an elevator and pushed the 4 button. She'd hoped to avoid seeing Jimmy. She'd hardly known the man in Belfast, even though he'd been Davy's best friend. When Davy'd been captured, she'd debated going to see Jimmy to ask him about what had happened, but soon the story had been all over the media.

"An attempt on the life of the British prime minister has been foiled, although the bridge at Ravernet near Hillsborough has been destroyed and several soldiers killed."

She'd been sitting alone at her sister's house eating supper and watching the six o'clock news on April 18, 1973. Her forkful of beef stew had stopped halfway to her mouth.

"An IRA terrorist has been arrested. David McCutcheon . . ."

No.

". . . of Conway Street, Belfast, was injured while attempting to escape. He has been taken to hospital and remains under observation and under police guard."

She'd tried to visit him in the Royal Victoria Hospital, but an army major had refused to let her see him. By then, she'd steeled herself to read the news accounts.

It seemed Davy had been waiting in a farmhouse to detonate a bomb under Harold Wilson's car as it crossed a bridge en route to Government House in Hillsborough. She'd learned how Wilson's convoy had been turned back before it reached the ambush and how Davy, trying to halt the pursuing soldiers, had set off the explosives, but to no effect. He'd been captured, and from the Provo point of view the operation had been a disaster.

Davy would have succeeded, according to the story, but for the heroic sacrifice of a Lieutenant Marcus Richardson, Royal Army Ordnance Corps, who had uncovered the plot and alerted the Security Forces but been killed during the operation to protect the prime minister.

She'd bumped into Jimmy several days later. He'd explained that the young army officer had been working undercover in the Falls Road district. Posing as an expatriate Ulsterman, he'd claimed to be an explosives expert from the oil fields of Alberta who had returned to Belfast to help in the struggle.

Jimmy'd been angry that day. He blamed himself for introducing Richardson, who had assumed the alias of Mike Roberts, to Davy and, worse, as far as Jimmy was concerned, to Siobhan. Davy had recruited the young man to help in what was to have been Davy's last attack. Siobhan had fallen deeply in love with him.

Meeting Richardson had led to disaster for Fiona and Siobhan.

The lift doors opened. The fourth-floor hall was carpeted in nondescript brown, the walls papered in a lighter shade. It smelled of apartment, veiled cooking odours, and the nose-irritating fumes of carpet cleaner. Fiona saw Jimmy waiting in the doorway of 407.

"How's about ye, Fiona." His lower jaw twitched as he stood aside to let her in and closed the door. "Here, gimme your coat and that oul' umbrella."

Fiona shrugged out of the sodden garment and gave it and the battered brolly to Jimmy, who hung the coat in a hall closet. He looked at the umbrella. "I think this should probably go out."

"So do I."

"Leave it in the hall. I'll see to it later. Come on in and take the weight off your feet."

"Thank you." Fiona followed Jimmy along a hallway into the living room, where Siobhan stood waiting. "Hello, Fiona," she said. "Have a seat."

Fiona sat in a comfortable armchair, one of a sectional suite, and glanced round. One whole wall of the apartment was a rain-streaked picture window overlooking Burrard Inlet. On another wall, the Ferguson's had hung a couple of Irish scenes, a watercolour of a mallard at Lough Sheelin and a pretty pastel of the Mourne Mountains, small reminders of home.

"It's a ferocious day, so it is," Jimmy said, parking himself in a second chair. "Even the ducks is flying backwards." He laughed, a high-pitched hee-heeing noise. "You must be foundered, so you must."

"I've certainly been warmer." She shivered and rubbed both hands together.

Jimmy clucked sympathetically. "Would you like a wee cup of tea in your hand? A hot Irish?" Jimmy asked.

"Tea would be grand." Fiona smiled. She'd almost added, "so it would." She could feel herself wanting to slip back into the Belfast dialect. The harshness of Jimmy's speech reminded her of Davy's deeper brogue, and it was comforting.

"Coming up." Siobhan left.

Fiona saw the grace of the younger woman. As she walked along the hall, she seemed to glide in a gentler version of a model on a catwalk. Her blonde hair fell to her waist. It was quite gorgeous.

She heard clattering from the kitchen. "Please don't go to a lot of trouble on my behalf."

"It's no bother. I'll just be a wee minute." There was a hint of a laugh in Siobhan's contralto. "Do you want one, too, Dad?"

"No thanks, love. I'll need to be running away on soon."

They sound so easy with each other, Fiona thought, the way it used to be with her own parents before they'd turned their backs on her. She looked at Jimmy, who shot his jaw sideways. Hearing his laugh, seeing the little man's nervous tic, brought her back to the Falls Road, where for a while she'd tried to rebuild a little family with Davy.

"Look, I know you come to have a yarn with Siobhan, and I don't want to get in the way, like, but I just, I just thought I should have a wee word with you. Maybe I should've never phoned and upset you?"

"It's all right, Jimmy. I'm not upset." Liar, she scolded herself. "It's far better to know now than to have Davy suddenly appear."

"Aye. It would've given you a hell of a shock. I near took the rickets my-self when I heard." Jimmy smiled. "I hope he gets here soon. I reckon he's still out, you know."

She felt as she had yesterday morning after she'd turned on the machine: caught hopelessly off-balance, confused, upset that the life she'd thought was finally settling down had been thrown so far off course—and wanting so much for him to be out, to be coming to her.

"Why do you think that, Jimmy?" she said quietly.

"I seen the news on the telly this morning. The reporter said some lad called Bobby Storey, he's one of the Provo highheejins, and four of his mates was picked up. They was hiding in the Lagan, underwater, trying to breathe through hollow reeds, but the telly never said nothing about Davy."

"Why would they mention him? Davy wasn't an important Provo."

Jimmy rolled his eyes. "I tell you, a man what tried to off the British prime minister would've his name in the headlines if they'd got him. They'd be crowing it from the rooftops. I'll bet you he's still out, and the longer he stays out, the better the odds he'll get here. You mark my word."

Jimmy was watching her, gauging her reaction. He must wonder if she still cared for Davy. It was none of his business, but she'd find it difficult not to tell him how she felt if he was blunt enough to ask. She mightn't know the man well, but he *had* been Davy's best friend, and somehow talking to Jimmy was like talking to Davy by proxy.

"I'd be quare pleased to see him again, so I would. Him and me was mates, and you don't make that many good mates in a whole lifetime." Jimmy hee-heed. "I'd love to take oul' Davy out for a jar. The pair of us hasn't had a pint together for donkeys' years."

"It has been a very long time, Jimmy." She tried to keep her voice level.

She saw how Jimmy was looking at her, his head cocked to one side. "You'd not be too sorry to see him yourself, would you, dear?"

"Dear." If a Canadian had called her "dear," she'd have bristled, but coming from Jimmy it was only Irish affection. "You're right, Jimmy." She smiled at him. "Not one bit."

"Great, I thought I might have dropped a right clanger."

"To tell you the truth, it was a bit more than a clanger."

"I'm sorry." Jimmy flicked his lower jaw to one side. "The missus always says I never know when to keep my trap shut, so I don't."

She smiled. "I was going to say it was more like a bombshell, but it is all right. Honestly. I *was* rattled when I heard your message first." He opened his mouth to speak, but she carried on. "But I'd've found out anyhow, and you've given me time to think about things. Thank you."

Jimmy rubbed his hands along the tops of his thighs. "Aye, well. Now look, what's between you and Davy's your own business, so it is, but . . . but I just wanted you to know that me and the missus is always here. Sometimes the likes of us immigrants need some of our own kind to have a bit of a blether with."

She felt a lump in her throat as she recognized the truth. "I hear you, Jimmy, and I promise I will take you up on the offer."

"Anytime. Anytime at all." Jimmy turned and shouted, "Are you picking them tea leaves in China, Siobhan?"

"Coming, Dad." Siobhan appeared carrying a tea tray. She set it on a low coffee table. "I've just a few scones to butter and I'll be back."

Jimmy rose. "I'll need to be running away on."

"Thank you for being here, Jimmy," Fiona said.

"Not at all. My pleasure." He started to walk down the hall, then turned. "Do you know," he said, "there's another wee thing I was thinking about."

"Oh?'

"Aye. I'll bet you're all worried about what Davy'd do for work in Vancouver."

"Well, I did wonder . . ."

"He's been learning to be a carpenter in the Kesh. He told me in his letters, so he did."

"A carpenter? Davy's taking woodworking lessons?"

"Aye. And with Expo coming to Vancouver in '86, there's more work for chippies than you could shake a stick at. And me a painter. Don't I know half the job foremen? I'd get him fixed up in no time flat."

"That would be kind of you, Jimmy. I'm sure he'd appreciate it." She pictured Davy's big, square hands touching her. She could feel the roughness of them, hardened by manual labour. Davy'd been no stranger to unskilled work, shoveling, pushing wheelbarrows, carrying hod loads of bricks—when he hadn't been making bombs for the Provos. She could see him now, proud of his new skill, using it to build instead of to destroy. He would like that.

"Kind me arse . . . I'm sorry, Fiona, that just slipped out. If I'm for having a pint with my oul' mate, he's going to have to pay his whack, so he is." Jimmy hee-heed again. "There's only one wee snag about him and me going down the pub, though."

Fiona frowned. Was Jimmy going to tell her not to get her hopes too high, that Davy might never get here at all?

"Aye. I just hope I'll be able to understand him now he's a very learned man."

"He's what?" Her left eyebrow rose. Davy? Learned?

"You'd not know, of course. My God, if you could see some of the big words he puts in his letters, and it's all your fault. You started him on the reading away back . . ."

The kitchen in Conway Street, her standing over Davy as he asked what a certain word might mean.

". . . I doubt if there's a book our Davy's not read in"—Jimmy hesitated—"in the Kesh place."

She liked that, "our Davy." "Yes," said Fiona, "our Davy." And she laughed for the first time since she'd learned the news, and Jimmy laughed with her.

"There you go," he said. "You'd a face on you like a Lurgan spade when you come in here, and now you're having a wee chuckle. I told you, us folks needs to stick together." He bent and picked up his cap from the top of a coffee table. "Anyroad, I've to be off. The missus is at her work so you and Siobhan can blether away in peace." He headed down the hall. "Now mind, don't you be a stranger. Do you hear me?"

"I won't, Jimmy. I promise."

"And the minute I hear anything, I'll give you a call . . . if that's all right with you?"

"Of course it is, Jimmy. I'd appreciate it if you would."

"Never you worry," he said. "One of these days, Davy's going to turn up, right as rain. You wait and see. And I'll tell you another wee thing. He'll be shot of the Provos, too." He opened the door. "I should've shown you what he said about *that* the last time he wrote, but I can't find the letter nowhere."

"Dad, would you come in or go out? There's a draft in here that would blow your hat off."

"Right. I'm away on," Jimmy said, closing the door behind him.

Fiona blew out a long breath. She'd badly misjudged wee Jimmy Ferguson. She smiled. If he ever gave up house painting, the man could get a job in the diplomatic corps. It had been decent of him to wait to see her and try to allay her fears.

"Just a few scones," Siobhan announced, as she carried a plate into the room and set it beside the tea tray, smiling as she said, "That dad of mine would talk the hind leg off a donkey."

"I was happy to have a chat with him. In the North, they'd say your dad's a 'sound man.' I will be seeing more of him and your mum after you've gone home."

"He'd like that. He misses Belfast and the Belfast folks." Siobhan glanced at Fiona's empty cup and tutted. "He may be a sound man, but he hasn't a clue about entertaining. You've not got a cup of tea." She poured. "Milk and sugar?"

"Just a bit of milk, please."

Siobhan handed Fiona a cup and saucer with a buttered scone balanced in the saucer, the way all hostesses would do in Belfast, settled comfortably in one armchair, and crossed her legs.

They sat opposite, neither quite meeting the other's eye. Fiona wondered what the next step was in this ritual getting-to-know-each-other dance of women who were virtual strangers. "I'd love to hear about Montreal and your kiddies," she said.

Siobhan smiled. "I've snaps here." She opened a handbag that Fiona had not noticed in the chair. "That's Rory; he's three, and Caitlin will be two next month."

A tall dark-haired man pulled a toboggan load of two laughing children across a white field with dark, snow-dusted pines in the background.

"They're lovely," she said. "The youngsters, I mean. And that's your husband? He's a handsome lad."

"Jean-Claude's a sweetheart," said Siobhan, with the whisper of a sigh.

Fiona wondered if the younger woman's marriage might be under some strain or if Siobhan still harboured feelings for the young British lieutenant. "Your Jean-Claude's French Canadian?"

"*Pur laine.*"

Fiona frowned and tried to remember her schoolgirl French. "Pure wool?"

"It's Québécois. It means his family go right back to the original settlers of New France."

"That's what, three hundred years?" Fiona set her cup on the table. "It certainly makes you and me a couple of newcomers."

"That's what his mother said." Siobhan grinned. "I don't think she was too impressed when her boy brought home an immigrant Anglo. Mind you, it did help that I'm Catholic."

"Not like back in Belfast. It wasn't an advantage back there." Fiona kept the bitterness from her voice but could feel it in her throat.

Siobhan stood, walked to the window, and stared down. The glass rattled as a stronger gust battered the low-rise.

She turned back to face Fiona. "Poor old Belfast." She folded her arms across her chest. "I don't know how you feel, Fiona, but I'm well rid of the place. Dad does miss it, but he's better off here."

"We all are. I don't miss the violence, who would? But I can understand your dad, too. There *were* good times. I really miss some of the people."

"You mean Uncle Davy."

Fiona nodded. "You and your brother called him that when you were little, didn't you? He was a great man with children. He used to love to meet me at the school, kick a ball around with the bigger boys." And back in their terrace house on Conway Street, he'd never held it against her that she'd refused to start a family. Not as long as the Troubles went on and on.

"When he'd come round to take us to a soccer game or the cinema, he always had a bag of sweeties. I think there was a bit of the kiddy in Uncle Davy and that's why he got on so well with the wee ones."

"Do your youngsters like dinosaurs?" Fiona asked, remembering an afternoon when she and Davy had visited the Ulster Museum on the Stranmillis Road.

"Do they?" Siobhan picked up the snaps she'd left on the coffee table. "Rory won't go to bed without his stuffed brontosaurus." She looked at the snap. "God, I miss them."

"I took Davy to see a dinosaur's skeleton once. You should have seen the look in his eyes. He said, and you could hear the wonder in his voice, 'Boys-a-boys, but there's a brave bit of architecture about that big lad. I never knew nothing about them animals.' He shook his head when I told him they'd been wandering all over the North millions of years ago. Then do you know what he said?"

"No."

"He looked so serious, but he'd a twinkle in his eyes. 'There's still the odd one about the place. Just you think of that Reverend Ian Paisley.' As they say back home, I laughed like a drain."

"Oh dear, oh dear." Siobhan chuckled. "People who didn't know him often thought he was dour, but Uncle Davy wasn't. I know that."

"And you're right about him still being a bit of a child. Can you imagine what he'd say if he went to see the orcas at the aquarium?" And Fiona knew his delight would be tempered by sadness. Davy was a sensitive man, and if anyone could sympathize with a creature's captivity, it was Davy McCutcheon. "He's a lovely man," she said.

Siobhan plucked at the cuff of her sweater, then said, "Fiona, we hardly know each other, so if I'm being a bit tactless, tell me. But the way you talked about him just now . . . you still miss him, don't you?"

"Yes. Yes I do. Very much."

"I know," Siobhan said. "I know because I love Jean-Claude . . . I really do . . . but I miss Mike."

"I understand," Fiona said softly.

There was a tear on her lower lashes. "Mike won't go away, and that's not fair to Jean-Claude or the kids."

"You must have loved him very much."

"I did, and it's crazy. I hardly had a chance to get to know him properly." Siobhan wiped away the tear. "One night, not long after we started going out together, Mike took me to the cinema. The Loyalists had booby-trapped the place, and we all had to get out in a rush. The explosion wrecked the place. Mike saved a girl who was too shocked to move." She looked into Fiona's eyes. "Poor old Belfast. There seemed to be nothing but bombs in those days. Were you like the rest of us and tried to ignore them?"

Fiona shook her head. "How could I? Your dad must have told you what Davy did for the Provos," she said, thinking of the fatherless daughters of a railway-ticket collector and the explosion in the Abercorn restaurant she saw in her nightmare. "Sometimes I still can't get away from them."

"Bombs, I hate them." Siobhan hesitated. "But I think it was after the one in the cinema . . ." She looked into Fiona's eyes. "I think . . . I think that's when I started to fall in love with Mike."

"A stranger grabbed my hand when I'd tripped and was going to fall." Fiona smiled. "I fell for him, for Davy, when he took me to a tea shop."

"Tea?" Siobhan managed to smile, and sipped from her cup. "It sounds very ordinary."

"It was. But it was very special, too."

Siobhan frowned. "Fiona, do you ever wonder if maybe people fall in love more quickly, more deeply when their world's going to hell all around them?"

"I'm sure they do."

"It's what happened to Mike and me," Siobhan said. And her voice became very soft as she whispered, "Then he was killed."

Fiona hurried to say, "It wasn't Davy who . . . who shot him."

"I know, but we both lost someone we loved that day." She lightly touched Fiona's arm. "I'm sorry for you. I really am."

Fiona felt the warmth of the young woman's hand and patted it with her own.

"But at least your Davy's still alive." Siobhan stood and turned away.

Fiona saw the girl's shoulders tremble, and as she would if one of her pupils was upset, rose and hugged her. "It's all right. It's all right to cry." She could feel Siobhan's body shake, heard the sobs. "Wheest. Wheest," she murmured, feeling Siobhan's pain as her own, comforted that she was not alone; Siobhan, like her, still ached.

"I'm sorry, Fiona, but I've had this bottled up in me for all those years. Dad says we should put it all behind us. Mum, bless her, does what Dad says. They won't talk about the Troubles anymore. There's been nobody . . . until today . . . who understands, who'll listen."

Fioana stroked Siobhan's hair and then took her hand. "Come and sit down." She led Siobhan to the armchair, waited for her to sit, and stepped back.

Siobhan looked up and tried to smile. "I'm sorry about that. Sometimes. Sometimes . . ."

"Sometimes it just hits you. I know." And Fiona pictured dolphins streaking from the depths and the ripples left on the water in an aquarium tank.

"Do you think . . . ?" Fiona saw pleading in Siobhan's eyes. "Do you think I'll ever get over him?"

Fiona paused. The truth, at least *her* truth, so clear to her now, would hurt both the tearful young woman and herself. "I've tried to forget Davy. I really have," she said. "But I can't." She rubbed her upper arm with one hand, tucked her head toward her shoulder. "You know he's escaped and your dad thinks he's coming here?"

"Yes. I hope he makes it for your sake."

"Oh, Lord, so do I. I need him to come. I need him so much. I want him back, Siobhan. God help me, I want him back." And the saying of it aloud made the truth of it shine.

Fiona wondered why Siobhan was smiling. "I thought you'd say that, Fiona, just because of what Dad's told me about you and Uncle Davy, how much he loves you, the way Mike loved me. I think . . . I think you're lucky he's alive." Siobhan clasped her hands in front of her. "I envy you," she said quietly.

"Perhaps you shouldn't."

"Why not?"

"You have a husband who loves you, and the wee ones. You just said how much you miss them. Just suppose your Mike could come back. What would you do?"

"I don't know. I honestly don't know."

"Could you live with yourself, knowing the hurt you'd cause if you left them?"

Siobhan shook her head.

"Well, I'm going to have to, because"—the words rushed out—"because I'll have to abandon someone, and I'm going to have that on my conscience for a long time."

"The doctor with you in Bridges?"

"Tim Andersen. That's right. It'll be hard." She swallowed and bowed her head, but looked up when she felt Siobhan's arms round her.

"Wait for Davy, Fiona," Siobhan said. "Do what you must with Doctor Andersen . . . It'll be hard for you, I know, but do it . . . and pray. Pray hard for Davy."

Fiona nodded and, over Siobhan's shoulder, saw through the window to where a sudden hole had been torn in the storm clouds and a ray of light forced its way through to flash and blaze on the tangled waves below.

CHAPTER 39

Flames danced from the top of the range as Erin fed in pieces of turf. They vanished when she dropped the cast-iron lid with a clang. Davy savoured the unfamiliar smell of burning peat. It wasn't like the well-remembered, eye-watering fumes of a coal fire banked with damp slack.

It was cosy in the farmhouse's big, comfortable kitchen, but for him the atmosphere was as chilly as the air in the neolithic grave they'd left at eleven o'clock.

He'd kept to himself while Cal and Erin told Eamon about the arrangements for Fiach's funeral on Thursday. They would be attending, Eamon couldn't, and it was family business, none of Davy's, but poor wee lad, he thought. The boy had only been sixteen, practically a child, but youth had never been a hindrance to the Provos. Davy well remembered the snotty-nosed ten-year-olds on the Falls Road, screaming and chucking Molotov cocktails at armoured cars. They should leave the kiddies alone. The cause was a grown-ups' war.

He sat in an armchair as Eamon, McGuinness, Cal, and Erin huddled round the table discussing their plans for the attack on Strabane. Let them. Davy knew exactly where he stood. He'd not had any doubts since Eamon had coerced him into agreeing to drive the van to the shed, back to Clady, and on to Lifford. He'd have to do that much, but when it came to the bombing and the killing, he'd leave it up to the O'Byrnes and Eamon and McGuinness. If they thought they could force him to do more, he'd not give an inch. The thought made him smile wryly. "Not an inch. No surrender," was one motto of the Orange Order. He wasn't supporting the Provos anymore, true enough, but he'd not gone as far as embracing the ideals of the Protestant side, even if he had, for a second, stolen one of their catchphrases.

Davy had become too realistic in his appraisal of all that had been achieved, or rather had not been achieved, by both sides in the years since the Troubles started. The raid that his companions were so enthusiastic about, the probable deaths of some RUC men, the possible deaths of some of the attackers, wouldn't bring a united Ireland one inch closer.

His commitment was to keep his promise to himself and to Fiona never to kill again, to get to Canada and to her. If he must live with feeling resentful of Eamon, be stuck at close quarters with Brendan McGuinness for a few more days, so what? Davy'd managed to survive nine years in the Kesh. A few more days were nothing.

He felt drowsy but forced himself to stay awake. Surely to God they'd finish soon and he could get back to his cot?

Eamon called, "Come here, Father, and take a wee gander at this."

Davy shook his head.

"Please?"

"Shite," he muttered, but wandered over to stand behind Eamon, who sat beside Erin. Davy noticed how they held hands under the table, out of sight of Cal and McGuinness at the other side. "Take a look at what?" He craned forward.

"Erin's sketch map of Strabane." It was marked on the back of a sheet of drawer-lining paper held flat by four empty jam jars, one at each corner. "Her and Cal and me's gone over how we can make this work, but I want everybody's opinion and that includes yours, Father."

"I'll not have much to say, except maybe to try to talk you out of it."

"You won't," McGuinness snarled. "So save your breath." He put one finger on the corner of the map. "Go on, Eamon."

Davy looked at the map as Eamon used a pencil to point out the features.

"That there road runs down a hill into the town, and the square at the bottom of the hill's the barracks," Eamon said. "It's a big, three-storey building sitting about twenty-five yards on all sides behind a weak wire fence. Cal'll drive the tractor along the road to the top of the hill. Erin and Brendan and me will be in another car just behind. Brendan'll drive it."

"It's not how we do it in Belfast," McGuinness said. "We should have a car in front *and* one behind the tractor so if there's peelers anywhere, the leading or trailing car can fuck them up while the rest get away. That way you don't lose as many men. Why not get McCutcheon to drive the van through Strabane and get across the border there to wait for us?"

"No," said Eamon. "We've asked enough of Davy already."

Bloody right you have, Davy thought.

"Cal'll park the tractor at the top of the hill for a wee while. We'll drive past the barracks a couple of times, make sure there's no extra police outside or any soldiers."

"Why the hell would there be soldiers?" McGuinness demanded.

"No good reason, but with them all over the North looking for us and the rest of the lads, there might just be a patrol in Strabane."

"And it's better to be safe nor sorry," McGuinness agreed.

So did Davy. He straightened for a moment. The angle he was leaning at had given him a crick in his back. He massaged it with one hand.

"A bit stiff, Father? Jesus, but old age and decrepitude are terrible things, so they are." The others laughed, and Davy knew there was affection in Eamon's teasing. You'll not get round me that easy, Davy thought. He said nothing, didn't smile, but bent forward. In spite of his resolve, he was becoming interested.

"Right," said Eamon, "now look at this. See those streets and that there lane in front of the police station?"

Davy studied the map.

The square depicting the barracks and its enclosure lay at the foot of the hill road. It branched immediately in front of the centre of the building into a T-junction that ran to right and left. Two streets met the crosspiece of the T at right angles. Those road junctions faced the police station compound at its corners. A lane ran between the hill road and the right-hand street.

Eamon said, "Once we're happy the coast's clear, Brendan'll drop me at the corner of the left-hand street there." He pointed with his pencil. "Erin, you'll get out at the foot of the hill, and Brendan'll take the car to the corner of the right-hand street. We'll all have ArmaLites under our coats. They have collapsible stocks. Folded up, they're only two feet long, so we can keep them hidden until we need them. Is that clear?"

Davy heard the murmur of assent.

"Good. Now, Brendan'll park the car close by the right-hand corner, stay in it, and keep the engine running. If you see we need backup, get out, get cover at the corner, and use your rifle."

"Right."

"When Erin sees I'm in position and the road between the tractor and the barracks is clear, she'll take out her hanky and blow her nose. That's the signal for Cal to set the fuses and get the tractor moving down the hill and through the wire."

Davy noticed how Erin looked at her big brother. He saw all the concern of a sister in her eyes. He could imagine the tractor charging down the hill and battering through the fence surrounding the barracks. Before the explosion, Cal would have to leave the cab and make a run for it. Until he reached cover, he'd be vulnerable. Was she picturing the same scene, perhaps having second thoughts? She was going to bury one brother on

Thursday. How in the name of all that was holy could she even consider losing another?

"You keep your head well tucked in, Cal, when you jump out of the cab and run to me," Erin said.

"She's right," Eamon said. "But with two ArmaLites to lay down covering fire, no peeler in his right mind'll risk exposing himself to take a shot at you."

Davy saw Erin nod in agreement. She's trying to reassure herself, Davy thought.

"So? What do you think so far?" Eamon asked but looked directly at Davy.

Davy reckoned it was a good plan. The trouble with plans, and he knew from bitter experience, was that they didn't always run smoothly. He decided to keep his counsel, save his breath as McGuinness had said.

"What about the getaway?" McGuinness asked.

Davy noticed Erin letting go of Eamon's hand and how intently they all leaned forward, especially McGuinness. Killing for their cause was one thing, but none of them really wanted to die for it, despite all their bravado about the nobility of sacrificing oneself for Kathleen ni Houlihan. Davy wondered why he felt compassion for them all, even McGuinness.

"We'll have the charges on a timer," Eamon said. "So we'll have five minutes before the ammonal blows. Erin thinks we should take cover until it does and then kill any peelers who survive the blast and come outside." He glanced at her before saying, "I'm not so sure."

"If we're going to go to all this bother, we might as well go the whole hog." Erin looked straight at Eamon. She did not smile.

Davy waited, sensing the tension between the two. He had no doubt that Erin very much had a mind of her own and wouldn't take kindly to Eamon overruling her.

"If we wait like Erin wants, or if we run for it *before* the explosion, we still have to get to Lifford in the Republic. That's where you'll be, Davy."

"Huh." Davy stared at the map.

Eamon carried on. "Lifford's close, I know, and the crossing's not well defended, but the longer it takes us to get to the bridge, the more time the Brits have to send in reinforcements."

"From Derry or Omagh?" Erin asked. "Sure they're both twenty-odd miles away. The soldiers'd take forever."

"By chopper? No more than ten minutes after the alarm's raised. Now when the peelers see the tractor crash through the fence, they'll be surprised. They'll likely take a minute or two to wake up and try to phone. They might even wait until it goes off, but you can bet that unless the blast wrecks every telephone, they'll be yelling blue murder for help by then."

"Before or after they've changed their underpants?" Cal's first contribution made Eamon and McGuinness laugh.

Davy saw Erin smile. He didn't. He could imagine the aftermath of the blast: smoke, debris, bodies, men with blood streaming, limbs missing, screaming, staggering out of the doors. He'd been right earlier today. Delivering the assault team wasn't any different from delivering a bomb. If there was any comfort to be had, he could tell himself that, unlike the many devices he'd made in the past, he hadn't put the squad together, he wasn't the one sending them out; but it was small comfort, and he knew it.

The others could laugh at Cal's poor joke. Davy couldn't. If one of the peelers had been so terrified he'd shit himself, who could blame him? God help any civilians in the area. "I've a question," he said, in spite of his intention to keep his mouth shut.

Eamon looked up. "Go ahead, Davy."

"How much ammonal are you using?"

"Five hundred pounds."

"Holy Christ. With that much, there'll be a huge blast radius. You folks at the street junctions could get yourselves killed. Never mind about giving British reinforcements more time. If I was you, I'd leg it as soon as Cal gets to one of those corners."

"You would beat it, McCutcheon," McGuinness sneered. "You were always the one for running . . . even with the buggered-up leg of yours."

Davy stared into McGuinness's one pale eye until the man lowered his gaze. You wanted a truce, you bastard? You'd let bygones be bygones? The fuck you would.

"Are you sure about the size of the blast, Father?" Eamon frowned.

"Of course I'm bloody well sure. I was an armourer before you were born. I've seen what explosives can do." And seen too often. "And there's another thing. If there's any civilians on those streets, a lot of them's going to get killed or hurt."

"Collateral damage can't be helped, McCutcheon. You should know that." McGuinness glowered at Davy, who refused to look away, but the room suddenly seemed to be stifling him. Davy looked to Eamon.

"We can only hope if there are folks about, they'll have enough wit to run like hell when they see the tractor bust in through the fence or hear the first shots."

"If I was you," Davy said, knowing he was being dragged further into the thing, trying to persuade himself that he was only giving advice in the hope that civilian lives could be spared, "I'd get your armourer to set the timer for ten minutes. It'll take a few minutes to drive down the hill and through the wire."

"That's right," said Erin, glancing at Cal. "So in the time left after the tractor's inside the police compound, even if the police try to run for it, they'll get caught in the explosion."

"Right," Eamon agreed. "Will you get Sammy to see to the timer, Erin?"

"I will. He'll be here tomorrow." Davy saw her smile. "I'm glad you're here, Davy. None of us had thought of . . . what did you call it? Blast radius. We're always too far away to see any of the culvert bombs we've set when they go off."

"I've been close enough," he said quietly, thinking of a little girl behind a car window.

"We've only killed soldiers or peelers." Erin frowned. "I don't like the notion of civilians getting hurt."

And that's the way it always should have been, Davy thought. Like the old days before the Provos decided to create havoc, to try to make the province ungovernable.

McGuinness said coldly, "Quit worrying about a few civilians. If a few other folks get killed . . . tough titty." There was no emotion in the man's voice, but a trace of a smile lingered on his lips.

Davy knew he'd been right in his assessment of the man. Biblical words learned as a child danced in Davy's head, words more powerful than any he'd found in all the books he'd read in the Kesh. McGuinness "had made a covenant with death, and with hell was he in agreement." Davy turned his back and walked away from the table.

He heard Eamon say, "So, I'm sorry, Erin, but there'll be no hanging about. There'll be no need to shoot the men who survive the explosion. From what Davy says, there won't be any survivors."

The poor bastards, Davy thought, and wondered how many of the country policemen stationed in Strabane thought they were fighting some kind of holy war, and how many were like Mr. Smiley back in the Kesh, simply doing their jobs and providing for their families?

"I can see that, Eamon," Erin said, and smiled at him.

"Good." Eamon smiled back. "Cal, as soon as you get to Erin, the pair of you nip up the hill"—he pointed at the map—"to that there lane. It runs onto the right-hand side of the T, where Brendan'll have the car. Brendan, when you see them start to run, drive up to where the lane meets the right-hand street, get them in the car, and drive away to there." He pointed to the map. "Turn right on that road."

"What about you?" Erin asked. Davy saw her worried look.

Eamon laughed. "As soon as you and Cal start to run, I'll be off like a whippet up the left-hand street. When Brendan's turned right, he'll be on a road that runs to where I'll be. It leads straight to the bridge across to Lifford. There's a customs post with a swing-up barrier and a bloody great hump in the tarmac to make cars slow down for inspection."

"Have I to slow down?" McGuinness asked.

"Just a bit, just enough to get over the hump, and then smash the car through the barrier. The British Security Forces aren't allowed to pursue us into the Republic. But some bugger'll give the registration number to the Gardai, and that's why we need you, Davy."

"In the van?"

"Aye."

Davy pursed his lips and folded his arms. "Go ahead."

"Once you get to Lifford, take the road that leads to the bridge to Strabane. Just before the bridge, there's a street to the left. C'mere. Look at the map. There." Eamon pointed. "See that?"

"Aye."

"Park the van there. If you walk to the corner, you can see the Gardai post at the bridge, but none of them can see round the corner to where the van'll be. Don't worry about going to take a look. Stay with the van and get the back door open. As soon as we arrive, we'll dump our car and get in the back. You drive us to Castlefinn in Donegal, where Sean's people'll be waiting."

"Right."

"One wee thing, Davy."

"What?"

"Don't be late."

In spite of himself, Davy smiled. "Right enough," he said. "We'd enough trouble with late lorries on Sunday."

"Anybody any questions?" Eamon asked.

No one spoke.

"All right, I want us to go over the last details again on Friday night, but until then, get as much rest as possible."

"I appreciate what you're doing for us," Erin said as she rose and walked to his side and planted a kiss on his cheek. "You're a darling man, so you are, Davy McCutcheon."

Davy felt himself blush.

"Good man, m'da." Cal rose and offered his hand. Davy shook it, and in the handshake and his acceptance by Erin, Davy felt a faint sense of returning to the only family he'd known for the last thirty years, even if it was the Provos. But it was a family for whom he felt no loyalty, no filial love.

"I think," said Cal, "we could all go a wee half." He went to the dresser and produced five glasses and a bottle of Paddy. He poured and passed the glasses round. *"Sláinthe."*

Davy sipped and savoured the taste of the Irish whiskey, peaty as the aroma in the kitchen, and the heat in the spirits warmed him.

"Sláinte mHaith," McGuinness said quietly, looking from Erin to Cal and then Eamon but avoiding even glancing at Davy, before adding, "You folks here've done good. It's a grand plan, so it is, as long as the timing's spot on."

Davy felt the hairs on the back of his neck prickle. Even if he'd made a feeble joke about it moments ago, it was exactly what someone had said in the Kesh not long before the food lorry turned up late.

CHAPTER 40

Everything on the farm was running late, but the work had to go on if Erin was to leave everything ready for Sammy to take over on Saturday. On Saturday, she'd have more important things to do than muck out cow stalls. She left the barn, her wheelbarrow piled high with steaming cow clap and her Wellington boots manure to the ankles.

Eamon and his friends were in the tumulus, Cal and Tessie wouldn't be back until after they'd driven the cows to the pasture, and she wasn't sure when Sammy would show up.

Fine drizzle hid the distant hills. Erin ignored it and the stink from the barrow. She'd been out in the rain often enough and been raised among farm smells. She'd rather live with them than the reek of exhausts, the miasma of decaying rubbish that poisoned the air in big cities like Belfast and, no doubt, Boston, Massachusetts, where Eamon had told her they were going to head after they'd reached sanctuary with the Provos headquartered in Dublin.

She imagined Boston was all skyscrapers, no decent view, no open spaces. It was sure to be filled with crowds and bustle. Still, there'd be no British Security Forces. According to Eamon, who'd been in touch with a friend living out there, there was a large, sympathetic, Irish-American community, and they'd help her adapt to life in Massachusetts. The friend had even mentioned a Celtic pub there, the Róisín Dubh—the Black Rosebud. Eamon'd promised to take her there once the pair of them got settled in. He said the music and the *craic* were grand. As long as she was willing to accept the inevitable strangeness, it could all be so new and exciting—not like dunging out cow stalls.

She upended the barrow at the dunghill, listened as its contents splattered onto the heap, and trundled it back across the farmyard. She planned to spend the rest of the morning bringing the books and accounts up to date so they'd be ready for Sammy, if wee Sammy could understand them. Cal usually made a bollocks of the accounts and was quite happy to let her handle the business management.

She left the barrow in its usual spot and tutted as she noticed the damage to the side of Margaret's stall. That bitch of a cow. If she wasn't such a good milk producer, Erin would have sent her off to the slaughterhouse months ago. Sammy could fix it when he came back to work, and surely to God he must have finished his preparations by now?

"'Bout ye, Erin." Sammy appeared in the open doorway.

"'Talk of the devil and he's sure to turn up,'" she said. She'd not heard him crossing the yard. She watched as he shook the moisture from his raincoat.

"Damp day," he said. "It's likely the rain that's doing it." He nodded solemnly as if in agreement with himself.

She smiled. He didn't know he was being funny. "How are you, Sam, and how are you getting on with your work?"

"I'm rightly, so I am, and all the jobs's done. The ammonal's loaded in the tractor bucket." Sammy rubbed one shoulder. "And I finished respraying the car yesterday."

"What about plates?"

"I picked them up in Newtownstewart a couple of days ago. They're changed."

She smiled again. "You've done well, Sammy. I'm proud of you."

He glowed. "Aye, well."

"I don't know what we'd do without you. You've worked fast."

"Everything's in the big shed at my place."

She saw how he puffed out his skinny chest. She moved to him and planted a kiss on his stubbly cheek. "Good man, m'da. I always knew we could trust you," she said, even if it wasn't entirely true. He deserved credit for a job well done, and she knew that praise coming from her would please him and, more importantly, keep him willing to work. He was as easy to bring to heel as Tessie. She'd sit up and beg for a pat on the head, and so would Sammy.

"Aye, well." He hung his head, and she was sure he was blushing. "You said you wanted everything in a hurry."

"I did. Now Eamon's here with his mates, the only thing holding us up was waiting for you to finish."

"Eamon made it?"

"Aye. They're in the old grave." No harm in telling Sammy that. He'd already have guessed.

"You'll be glad to have him back."

"You don't know the half of it." She could feel herself bent over the kitchen table, the weight of Eamon on her, his hard-on in her, his breath hot on the back of her neck. "And now he's here, we're just about ready to go."

"Erin, look"—he pulled off his damp duncher and held it between both of his hands—"it's not my place, but . . ." He looked as forlorn as a man at the races who'd put his last pounds on a horse—and lost. "I wish you'd not." His hands tugged at the tweed, and he stammered slightly as he said, "You might get killed."

Good Lord, the man was scared for her. "Don't you worry your head about it, Sam. It'll be over before the Brits know what's hit them."

"Aye, so you say, but we've never done nothing like this before. It's not a night ambush or leaving a booby trap somewhere. Erin . . ." He tried to grab her arm and stared into her eyes. "You could get shot."

She shrugged. There had always been a risk from the day she'd made the Provo Declaration, but she'd never seriously entertained the possibility that it could happen to her. Other people, perhaps; Terry O'Rourke, shot in the lungs, had died the night she'd gone out on an ambush with him, and Fiach, alone in Ballydornan. Da'd come close to dying years ago, on the night when he'd been shot, but he'd gone on fighting. Eamon had been forced to surrender his freedom. But—Sammy was right. "I could get killed on Saturday, Sammy," she said quietly. "But so could the rest. So can anyone who's in the fight. I have to chance it."

"Och, don't say that." Sammy stood footering with his cap and studying the toes of his boots.

"You're sweet, Sam, but don't you worry your head about me. Everything's going to be fine." She lowered her voice. "Then it's 'over the hills and far away.'"

"What are you talking about?"

"The lot of us are leaving Northern Ireland." She glanced at the misty hills, feeling her own eyes mist, but she tossed her head and said, "No more barrows full of cow clap." She forced a smile.

"Leaving?" Sammy's brows wrinkled. "Me, too? You never said nothing about it to me." Poor wee Sammy. He never could digest sudden surprises. "I . . . I'd not mind getting out," he said, and she heard longing in his voice. He was going to be disappointed.

"Not you, Sam. We want you to stay here and look after the place until we can get one of the overseas O'Byrnes to come home and take it over."

"But . . . but . . ." One hand released the peak of his cap. His hand flew up and a finger guddled in his nostril. She wished he wouldn't do that. "If you and the rest are for getting out, will the Brits not come after me if I stay?"

"Not the way we're going to arrange things. You'll be safe as houses, safer than a bunch of peelers." She laughed.

"There's no need to make fun of me, so there's not." He sounded hurt.

"I'm not, Sam. The Brits won't be looking for you because you're not going."

"Not what?"

"Not going on the raid. We can manage without you. If you go down to Ballybofey the night before, make sure you've a few jars there with your mates and go back to the pub with them the next day. The Brits can suspect what the hell they like. You'll have an alibi. Cal'll give you a few quid to pay for a room."

Erin waited for Sammy to smile in relief. Maybe he'd been genuine in his concern for her when he'd asked her not to go, but she knew he'd been asking on his own behalf, too. He didn't want to take any risks. Whatever else Sammy McCandless believed in, dying for Ireland was not one of his aspirations. But he didn't smile, didn't rush to agree with her plan. "I thought you'd be pleased," she said.

"I need to think on that," he said slowly, frowning and scuffing one boot toe in the earth. He was like a kid who'd been promised a treat, and the promise had been broken.

"What's there to think about? We're letting you out. You'll not be taking any risks, Sam. And the boys and me will be fine, too."

"I hope you're right. I still wish . . ."

"I'm going, Sammy. I owe it to Fiach, and I want to have one more go at the bastards before I run off. Eamon can't stay here no matter what, and when he goes, I'm going with him." She softened her voice. "I'll miss you," she said, although she knew she'd not miss him the way he'd want her to. She'd yearn for the farm and for Ireland. Like them, Sammy had always been part of her life, but all she'd really feel for him would be a small sense of loss of the familiar. She didn't want him to see that, so she took his hand and squeezed.

Sammy looked as if he could burst into tears and blurted, "You don't have to go on the attack."

"Och, I do, Sam."

He shook his head forcibly. "You do not. Not . . . not if I go instead of you."

Good God. She stared into Sammy's eyes and saw the resolve. "You are sweet, Sammy, you really are."

"I would, you know," he said. "You could go down to Ballybofey and have an alibi. You could look after the farm until your family come back, maybe . . . maybe go to Eamon in a month or two."

She saw pride on his face, and he'd every right to be proud. It must have cost every ounce of his tiny courage to make the offer. What a hell of a thing for him to do. "I suppose I could, Sammy, but I'm the one who's planned this attack. I'm the one who has to see it through. You're for Ballybofey."

"Why've I to go to the Republic?"

"For your alibi, silly. You cross the border and our customs and·the Gardai'll have records. Nobody can challenge that."

Sammy managed a small smile.

"Good," she said. "Now listen . . ." Telling him the dates now would pose no risk. He had earned the right to be told. "You get yourself over the border on Friday night and don't come back until Saturday evening."

"All right," he said. "Have it your own way."

For a man who'd been so easily offended a few days ago when she'd deliberately withheld the information, he didn't seem very interested now.

"I know you, Erin O'Byrne, when you've your mind made up. Just you . . . just you take care of yourself, now, whatever you're attacking."

"Strabane," she said, "Strabane Police Barracks."

Sammy grinned and danced a few jig steps. "Jesus," he said, "Strabane? I'd never've guessed. Not in a month of Sundays. That'll really give the Brits a quare poke in the eye, so it will."

"Well, now you know, Sammy. You keep it to yourself."

"Of course I will." There was a more serious note to his voice now. "I've just had a wee notion. If I'm not going, who'll fuse the bomb?"

"You'll have to teach Cal how to set the timer."

"That's wee buns, so it is. I'll just need to take a run-race over to my place and get my stuff. I've everything I need in a knapsack hid under the coal in the coal shed."

"Are you still using fulminate?"

"Aye."

Erin chuckled. "You'd need to make sure you didn't pick some up by mistake and shovel it on the fire."

"I'd not be that daft," Sammy said seriously. He started to trot over to the door. "I'll get it right now, so I will."

"Hang about, Sam," she called, and saw his look of disappointment. "Take your hurry in your hand. There's work to do here first."

"Oh."

"C'mere here," she said, and walked along to Margaret's stall. "I want you to fix that. She's kicked the bejesus out of it."

"Right."

"And I want you to stay here tonight. You'd be a bit of company for me and Cal, and you'll have to see to the cattle in the morning because . . ." She felt moisture in her eyes. She'd tried to put the whole business out of her mind. "We're burying Fiach tomorrow."

The rain had stopped earlier in the afternoon, when Sammy came into the barn to fix the stall. He nailed the last board, stood, and surveyed his handiwork. He'd taken care of the job, and it wasn't the only thing he was going to take care of, just like he'd promised Erin.

She didn't know it, and she'd never know it, but she'd given him all he needed for him to keep her safe, and at no risk to himself. If she would have let him, he would have kissed her when she'd told him he'd not have to go on the raid. What the hell had possessed him to offer to go in her place? Was it her saying she'd miss him? The touch of her hand?

As he walked the length of the barn, he congratulated himself on his performance this morning. He'd let her think he wasn't really interested in the day or the target. When she'd told him, he'd wanted to scream, "Hallelujah." He smiled to himself. Putting on an act like that would have given the Ballymena film actor Liam Neeson a bit of competition.

Sammy wandered over to the barn door and chucked his hammer on the workbench. For a second, his eyes lit on a Black & Decker drill. That was the one the men from Derry had taken to the young drug dealer. Nobody was going to use it on Sammy McCandless. The senior Provos would have no reason to suspect him, because the plans he'd been trying to make last night had fallen into place like the tumblers in a well-oiled lock. The attack could go ahead without any interference from the Security Forces. There'd be no suspicion that someone had given them away if they weren't ambushed. And they weren't going to be, not the way Sammy had things worked out now.

He knew the day. His guess about Strabane had been confirmed, and all he had to do was phone Spud and tell him, but—and this was the brilliant part—he'd tell Spud it was going to be on Saturday week. Any plans the man might be making, because Sammy had told Spud to expect the attack soon, would have to wait. The Security Forces couldn't risk trying to remain concealed for more than a week in Strabane. The Special Branch man would be fully aware that the locals would notice something in a rural town, and the word would get back to the O'Byrnes.

Once Sammy fed his handler the wrong information, there'd be no ambush this Saturday, and Erin and the rest could attack to their hearts' content. And, Sammy relished the thought, with a bit of luck, that big shite of a policeman who'd interrogated him in the Strabane Barracks, softened him up for recruitment by Spud, would be in the barracks. Sammy hoped he'd roast in hell.

Spud would be furious that he'd not been given the correct details, but the E4A man would have all the confirmation he wanted that Sammy had been right about the target.

When the barracks were blown up this Saturday, Sammy would have his alibi that he'd been down in Ballybofey, and that should convince Spud that the O'Byrnes had lied. It wouldn't be Sammy's fault if they'd fed him a story. If Spud was mad enough, there'd be no trip to England, but why would he need to go anyway?

He'd not been making it up when he'd told the peeler that once the O'Byrnes were gone, there'd be no more information from Sunshine. The police would leave him alone. They couldn't even take their revenge by blowing the whistle to the senior Provos and letting them deal with him. If they did, word would get out that the police had fucked one of their own informers. They'd not recruit another tout in Tyrone or Counties Armagh or Londonderry either—not until apples grew on cherry trees.

It was a bugger that he hadn't been able to persuade Erin to let him go back to his cottage to get the detonators. He could have made his phone call on the way, got the whole thing over with, but it could keep until tomorrow after Fiach's funeral.

Now that he was going to put the rest right, Fiach's death was all he would have on his conscience. Tonight, when they sat round the range, he'd tell Erin not to worry. Sammy would make sure for as long as he lived in Ireland there'd be fresh flowers on Fiach's grave. She'd like that. Maybe she'd kiss him again or give him a hug.

He was smiling to himself as he saw Cal and Tessie bringing the cows in for milking. He'd have to take them out tomorrow morning and see to some of the chores while Cal and Erin were at the funeral. And while they were out, he'd use their phone. You're brilliant, Sammy McCandless, he told himself as he gave Cal a hand to herd the cattle into their stalls.

"Thanks, Sammy," Cal said when they'd finished. "When you take them out tomorrow, keep an eye on that Margaret. She's a vicious hoor of a beast."

CHAPTER 41

Fiona allowed herself a slightly vicious thought. Dimitris Papodopolous's name should be changed to *kalo pedi*. Those words had been the mother's sole contribution to the four-way discussion. The boy's father had done most of the talking, and they had brought a cousin as their translator, a gangly, olive-skinned, heavily moustachioed man. Her three visitors sat in front of her desk.

"Eno kalo pedi." Mrs. Papodopolous dabbed at her eyes with a lace-fringed handkerchief.

"Mr. Giorgiou, please tell Mrs. Papodopolous that I do know her son is a good boy, but he *is* still having difficulties."

Fiona had already decided that, since neither she nor the school advisor seemed to be able to succeed with the lad, it was time for Dimitris, who was in class, to be given specialized professional counseling. She knew the suggestion would be taken as a deep insult by his parents. They would regard as shameful the least hint that a family member might need a psychologist's help. How was she going to raise the subject tactfully?

Despite the padding of the swivel chair, her backside felt numb. She listened to rapid-fire Greek as the cousin translated and Mr. Papodopolous, brows furrowed, replied. Words flew back and forth between the two men. She waited for the conversation to end. Now it seemed Mrs. Papodopolous was finally taking her turn. It looked as though the family debate might take some time.

The dying gale tossed bursts of rain against the windows of her office, and, distracted, she looked out and saw dead leaves whirled and tossed through the air and tumbled across the grass. Bare branches of trees thrashed and seemed to rake the low, grey clouds the way McCusker sharpened his claws on her furniture.

She felt as buffeted by the events of the last two days as those branches and told herself to stop thinking about it and concentrate on the job at hand. She'd made her decision and was determined to stick to it. Jimmy's revelations about Davy had helped. Siobhan's abrupt admission about how she still yearned for her dead love had surprised Fiona. She could try to pretend to herself she'd made her decision about Davy because she'd carefully weighed all the available information, added up the pros and cons. The simple truth was that her mind had been made up from the moment she'd learned that Davy might be coming.

Everything else had been attempts to justify her decision to herself and, damnit, there was no need for justification. She was still in love with Davy McCutcheon, and that was all that mattered.

Accepting him, knowing, knowing without the slightest doubt, that she would wait for him, meant she must tell Tim, hurt Tim, and the prospect had kept her awake for hours last night.

She rubbed her eyes and leaned forward to hear what the cousin was saying.

"He say"—the cousin seemed to be searching for the right words—"he say, the family do all things you tell them to do. Dimitris washes dishes, gives dog his meals."

"Good. It's certainly an excellent start."

"*Kalo pedi.*"

Fiona smiled at Mrs. Papodopolous to show she understood. "Unfortunately . . ." Saying baldly their son was a disruptive little hellion who, in her nonprofessional opinion, needed his backside warmed would hardly do. Back in Belfast, it was precisely what would have happened. She half-consciously rubbed the palm of her hand across her knuckles, remembering the stinging whacks she'd had there from rulers wielded by the nuns of her Catholic school.

Dealing with disruptive kids was much more scientifically based here in Canada. And a good thing, too. That's why she was here today, to try to bring all she'd learned to bear on Dimitris's problem.

"Unfortunately," she said, "and I'm not being judgmental, it's not having the positive outcome on his negative behaviours I'd hoped for." She coughed and scolded herself for trotting out the educational jargon. She knew what it meant, but to expect even English-speaking parents to understand would be unreasonable. No wonder there was a puzzled look on the cousin's face.

"I mean, I don't think we've succeeded as well as I'd hoped."

Mr. Papodopolous turned to his cousin, rattled off an explosive sentence, and turned to Fiona. Was he angry or questioning?

Almost as rapidly, the cousin translated. "He say, in Greece, bad boy is punished. He now punishing Dimitris. He say, perhaps things different in Canada?"

"Yes. Yes they are." Fiona wondered if those differences might be at the root of the boy's difficulties. At his age, he'd be like a little sponge, soaking up the local way of doing things, yet at home, he'd have to fit in with the mores his parents had brought from their homeland. "Very different." It had taken her years to shed much of the cultural baggage she'd brought from Belfast and adapt to the Canadian way of doing things. "It can be very difficult for immigrants, I know."

The words bounced back and forth between the two men like the ball in a tennis match, then Mr. Giorgiou said, "He say, please, perhaps little more time to do all things you say to them last time?"

"Well . . ." Would a little more time help? Despite her intention to concentrate on the problem at hand, she couldn't help but be reminded of how she was procrastinating before telling Tim about Davy. "Perhaps it might, in fact, I'm sure it will."

The cousin translated her words.

"*Kalo pedi,*" Mrs. Papodopolous offered.

"But I honestly believe we should be considering other options, too."

She watched Mr. Papodopolous shrug and stretch his hands forward, fingers spread wide. His lips were set at twenty past eight, his head tucked down on his shoulders. She understood what he was expressing. I give up. You're the expert. Do something.

Fiona picked up a pencil from the blotter on her desk. She'd make a point of discussing her ideas about Dimitris and what recently had been termed "culture shock" with the euphemistically titled "visiting teacher."

She tapped the eraser end of the pencil on the blotter, glanced from the mother to the father, chose her words with care, and said to the cousin, "I believe we should arrange for Dimitris to see the visiting teacher." She knew she was deliberately avoiding any reference to the fact that Ethel Nelson held a Ph.D. in behavioural psychology.

How would they respond? She waited until the translation was finished.

Mother twisted the hanky between her reddened fingers and whispered, "*Kalo pedi,*" as if it were an invocation to some unknown god, a prayer to keep the evil eye away from her son.

Mr. Papodopolous puffed out his cheeks and blew out his breath. She caught a whiff of garlic. His words directed to his cousin were slow and measured.

"He ask, what is visiting teacher, please?"

Damn. She'd been hoping to avoid this part of the discussion, just as she knew she was hoping, even though she knew it was a doomed hope, to find some way to avoid hurting Tim. Fiona watched the father's face closely as she said, "A special teacher who's had extra training to help children with their . . . difficulties."

Mr. Papodopolous sat rigidly and fired a question.

"Teacher is not, I am sorry, I don't know right word, he is not . . . a head shrinker?"

Fiona couldn't suppress a laugh. The cousin looked so serious.

"I'm sorry. It's not funny, and no, she's not a psychiatrist. Not a medical doctor." But it was a half-truth, and the parents were entitled to a full explanation. "Doctor Nelson is a psychologist."

Mr. Giorgiou translated.

Mr. Papodopolous frowned, talked rapidly to his wife, who rolled her eyes and clutched her hanky, then clearly struggling to express himself, spoke through his cousin. "He say, it is difficult for him and wife to understand. They do not think Dimitris is crazy in head . . . but you are teacher. In Greece, we have much respect for teachers. He say, we believe you doing best for Dimitris. Not Greek best, Canadian best."

"Thank you," she said. "I appreciate that."

Mr. Papodopolous smiled, relaxed, and said, "OK. We do. Thank you."

"My cousin is learning English," the interpreter said with a hint of pride. "I teaching him."

"I *am* teaching him," she corrected without thinking. "That's wonderful. Keep up the good work. It's not an easy language."

She was happy to change the subject and retreat from the potential minefield she could have found herself in having suggested psychological help for the boy. She also felt a tinge of guilt, knowing full well by suggesting counseling she had shifted Dimitris and his difficulties to someone else. She'd not miss having to deal with them.

"Good," she said, rising. "Then if we are agreed, I'll make the appointment for Dimitris."

The cousin translated.

"OK," the father said, and rose, motioning for his wife and cousin to do the same. "We thank you, Miss Kavanagh."

She opened the door, and as Mrs. Papodopolous left, Fiona dropped a hand on her shoulder and said, "Dimitris *kalo pedi*," and was gratified to be rewarded with a smile.

Fiona closed the door and looked at her watch. Ten o'clock. She was free for an hour before her next class and should start writing the report for the visiting teacher, but she sat and rested her head on her hands. God, she was tired. She'd taught an extra class to fill in for the absent Becky, had precious little sleep last night, and the pressure of the just-concluded interview had sapped her.

Someone knocked on her door. "Come in."

Becky poked her head into the office.

"What are you doing here?" Fiona saw the bags under Becky's bloodshot eyes. "How's your dad?"

Becky flopped into the nearest chair. "Not good. I went home for a few hours last night, and I'm on my way to VGH, so I thought I'd just pop in and see you. I need your advice."

Fiona sat upright. Usually it was the other way around. "I'm listening," she said.

Becky folded the fingers of one hand through the others and for a moment rested her chin on the cradle. "I'm very fond of the parents," she said, "but Mum's still not willing to face up to things."

"About your dad?"

Becky nodded. "The doctors at VGH have told us they're as sure as they can be he'll never recover. He's being kept going by the ventilators and all the other gadgets."

"I am sorry."

"I think," Becky said slowly, "I think I'm going to have to take the bull by the horns and give them permission to"—she grimaced—"pull the plug. Gruesome expression, I know, but I can't think of a better one. I'm just not quite sure if I can bring myself to do it." She looked questioningly at Fiona.

Fiona waited. It was as if she had become Becky and Becky her. Usually her friend had no difficulty making decisions. "I think," Becky said, "in fact I'm pretty sure it would be the kindest thing to do for Dad, but I'm not sure how Mum would take it."

"Have you asked her?"

Becky shook her head. "There's not much point. The doctors already have. She says she'll not forbid it, but she'll not give the go-ahead either; it's not for her to decide. It's in God's hands." Becky managed a wry smile. "I very much suspect that I'm going to have to act in *loco Domini*." She leaned forward and picked up the pencil that, moments before, Fiona had been tapping on her blotter. Fiona watched as Becky clutched the little yellow stick between her fists.

"I'm not sure I can tell you what to do."

"I wouldn't dream of asking you to," Becky said, "but I would appreciate hearing what you think."

Fiona leaned forward. "I can only suggest we try to look at the facts. It sounds as if your dad isn't going to make it. I'm sorry, but it's true."

"I'm afraid so."

Fiona saw the pencil bend.

"So if you leave him on life support, it won't do much more than prolong the suffering, perhaps for days."

Becky sighed. "I don't think he's feeling anything anyway."

"No. But you and your mum certainly are."

Becky pursed her lips. "I'm all right. It's Mum who worries me."

"But she's going to have to . . ."

"It's all right. Just spit it out."

"Accept his death sooner or later."

"I know."

Fiona took a deep breath. "It seems to me you've two choices." And what had she been dealing with since Monday? Her own two options were so black-and-white on the surface: Tim or Davy? But whatever she decided would lead to a death of a kind inside her, a death of something precious to her, and one that would bring its own guilt and grief. "Becky, you can either make a decision or simply choose not to decide, if you follow me."

Becky nodded.

"I can't tell you what to do, but I have a suggestion. It's worked for me. You can drive yourself nuts haggling over options, consequences, details. Why not ask yourself how you felt in the very first minute you realized you were going to be asked to deal with this? You might have been right then."

"Turn off the life support. It's the kindest thing to do."

Fiona heard the pencil snap. She saw Becky nod to herself and throw the broken ends of the pencil on the desktop before she said, "I suspect I've known it all along, but thanks for listening, for helping me to see straight."

"I'm sorry there's not more I can do."

Becky rose. "You've done a lot. And thanks for arranging for me to have a bit of time off to sort things out. I'll get back to work as soon as I can. I promise."

"Take all the time you need. We'll manage."

"Right." Becky moved toward the door. "I'd better be running along."

Fiona rose, stood in Becky's path, and enveloped her in a great hug. "It's going to be difficult, but I think you're making the right choice."

"I hope so," Becky said, "but you were right, too. It has to be mine, nobody else's, and I should have trusted my instincts."

"I know," Fiona said. "Believe me. I know."

Becky opened the door. "Thank you, Fiona. I'll be in touch," she said as she left.

Fiona returned to her chair. Poor Becky. Fiona picked up the broken pencil and threw the pieces into a metal wastebasket. "Pulling the plug," was a gruesome expression, and yet there were occasions when everyone would have to—on a job, a love affair, and, yes, a dying parent. It took courage, but Fiona knew she had that kind of strength. She'd not hesitated when she'd had to tell one lover, the married one with the ponytail, to get lost. That had been cleaner than watching her affair with George Thompson, the Protestant civil rights worker, shrivel and die.

It was all because of him that she was now estranged from her parents. She'd come to understand how convenient their anger had been. She'd needed an excuse to divorce herself from their world of ancient, inbred hatreds. In some ways, it had been a relief to "pull the plug" on them. She'd never tried to patch up the differences between them. Then she'd met Davy and had found herself dragged once more into that world of bitterness and intolerance. It seemed the harder we tried to run away from things, the faster they pursued us. Would it really hurt now, after twenty years, to stop running, to write to her folks, even make the trip back to Belfast? The old reasons for keeping them out of her life were dead. It was strange, but with Davy on his way here, the notion of returning to Belfast felt possible. Perhaps she'd do it once Davy was safely here with her.

Somehow it felt as if he was here already. Talking to Jimmy and Siobhan, seeing the Irish pictures in Jimmy's apartment on Beach Avenue, smelling the scones cooking.

And it all meant she was going to have to end things with Tim. Talk about "pulling the plug." When he came to Whyte Avenue, she must face him and tell him the truth.

CHAPTER 42

If he told himself the truth, he was more than anxious; he was worried as hell. Inspector Alfie Ingram (aka Spud) sat in the briefing room waiting for two senior officers to arrive. Merely being in the presence of upper echelon always made him feel uncomfortable, but there was more at stake today. His career.

Alfie'd risen early, shaved with extra care, and put on his best shirt, sports jacket, and trousers before driving to Tasking and Co-ordination Group North (TCG[N]) headquarters in Londonderry. This organization had been formed after the early years of the Troubles, when army and police worked independently, the one often to the detriment of the other.

Now the combined group was responsible for collating the intelligence gathered by all branches of the British Security Forces working in a defined geographic area of Ulster and for acting in concert when mounting antiterrorist actions.

The TCG(N) was housed in a collection of nondescript police and army offices hidden behind a grey concrete wall surmounted by a high metal fence. The briefing room was in a Portakabin in the middle of the complex. The windows were curtained with thick material to hide the occupants from any prying eyes.

Alfie fidgeted on his folding wooden chair. He was proud that he was the one who would take the credit for this meeting being called, yet terrified in case he'd been misled by his informant. If he had, today's efforts and all they would lead to would be a colossal waste of everyone's time. He knew the Provos were effective in running double agents whose function was to mislead the police or army intelligence units. He didn't think Sammy was smart enough to be playing that game, but still, the wee man hadn't phoned on Wednesday as he'd promised with the final bit of the puzzle—the date. Maybe there'd be a note under the cross in Ballydornan churchyard.

He picked at the skin around the base of one fingernail and longed to light a cigarette. It was a bugger having to work with incomplete information, but that was the nature of his trade. A scrap here, a suggestion there, a good hint could lead to a planning session like this one to discuss the mobilization of forces. If it all paid off, he'd be in clover. If it didn't, he could see himself posted to desolate Rathlin Island off Ulster's north coast, hanging about in the rain, forgotten by his superiors, keeping an eye on the island's sheep, with nothing to look forward to but his pension.

The thought that his informant could have been wrong or Alfie might have misinterpreted what he'd been told niggled at him. He polished the toe cap of his brightly shined black shoe against the back of his neatly pressed pants. He was going to look a right Charlie if all this morning's planning, based solely on his word, led them on a wild-goose chase.

He ran a finger inside his collar and wished he could unknot his tie. The room was close and muggy, too small for the group of men who were present. Besides himself there were majors of the regular army and the volunteer, part-time Ulster Defence Regiment. Their units would provide ground troops to set up a cordon and block escape routes. An RUC inspector from the Headquarters Mobile Support Unit (HMSU) and a staff sergeant of the SAS represented their two forces, each trained in surveillance and, more importantly for this operation, weapons skills.

It was going to be a hell of a show, and—Alfie managed to smile—*he'd* been picked as the Special Branch (E4A) liaison officer for the combined army/RUC operation, code-named Joan. His selection was a mark of his boss's confidence in the intelligence Alfie had provided, incomplete though it might be.

Chief Inspector McMaster, Old Mac to his men, but never to his face, had been skeptical on Sunday when Alfie reported the short telephone conversation he'd had earlier with Sammy. "Your man *thinks* there's to be an attack on Strabane Barracks? Not much to go on, is it, Ingram?" Old Mac was not one to be on Christian-name terms with his subordinates.

"No, sir, it's not, but Sunshine's always been reliable. He gave us the Ballydornan arms cache, tried to warn me about the Kesh breakout. I just wish to hell he could've told me when that was going to happen."

"So do we, Ingram, so do we, by God." The chief had a mole on his left cheek and a habit of stroking it with his index finger when he was concentrating. Alfie watched as Chief McMaster poked at the thing. The poking stopped. "Right. I'll take his track record into consideration . . . and yours."

"Thank you, sir."

"I'll have a word with TCG(N) on Monday, but I suspect they'll need more to go on."

Someone laughed at the back of the Portakabin. Alfie turned to see the two majors, both with faces split in enormous grins. One must have told the other a joke. It was as good a way as any to pass the time, Alfie supposed, but he would have had trouble raising a smile at that moment, even if Frank Carson, the "It's all in the way I tell 'em" Belfast comedian, had been performing.

The chief inspector certainly hadn't been laughing when he'd spoken to Alfie on Monday evening and told him that the consensus at TCG(N) was that, if Alfie was right, there could be an opportunity to deal—for good— with certain Provos who'd been a thorn in the Security Forces' side for a long time. As he'd predicted, they needed more info. That's what had prompted Alfie to visit Sammy on Tuesday.

Old Mac had managed a small grin on Tuesday afternoon when Alfie reported the new details: his agent's certainty about the target, the extent of the preparations, the uncertainty about the actual date. It had been enough for the chief to take the file personally to TCG(N).

He'd summoned Alfie last night, right in the middle of the fish and chips he'd been looking forward to all day. They'd have to wait. No one kept Old Mac waiting. Alfie had driven straight to the chief's home in an old manse outside Newtownstewart. After his credentials were scrutinized by one of the uniformed bodyguards, he'd been ushered into a spacious lounge and told to sit.

Old Mac had paced back and forth across what Alfie recognized as an expensive Axminster, fiddled with his mole, and spoke deliberately. "You'd better be right about this one, Ingram. TCG(N)'s approved. They support your idea that the attack will come soon. So, rather than wait for your source to confirm the exact day, the SAS and HMSU will go in after dark on Thursday night. There'll be units of the UDR and the Green Army, and I'm sending you and your men. I warn you, there's going to be a lot of very pissed-off senior officers if this turns out to be tying up forces for nothing while we should still be after Kesh escapees."

So they were going ahead. It meant that Sammy's cover would be well and truly blown. Alfie hadn't forgotten his promise to the little man. The question was when to broach the subject.

"I know he's right about the target, sir."

"I hope to God you are."

"I will be." He glanced at the chief inspector's face, saw no disapproval there, and decided that now was as good a time as any to press his request. "When I'm proved right, sir, there'll be another wee thing."

"What?"

"Witness Protection for my man. We'll have to get him out."

"Why?"

"He's earned it. He's risked his life for six months now."

Alfie saw the chief's frown. "I'm not so sure. Reliable informers are bloody hard to come by. We should milk them dry."

"I know." He was going to need a stronger argument, "But he only knows one Provo cell. They're the ones who are going to make this attack, and when we hit them, he'll have no more contacts. He'll be no more use to me."

"Are you certain?"

Alfie nodded. "Absolutely, sir." He pressed his point. "We'll need him as a witness when this is over."

Old Mac raised one bushy eyebrow. "Oh, indeed. If none of the Provos survive, we'll take a lot of stick and be accused by the media of mounting a 'shoot-to-kill operation.' I suppose your man could help us deny it. A few strong words about how the Provos were bent on causing mayhem and lots of civilian deaths wouldn't hurt at all. Will he be able to do that?"

"Yes, sir." Sammy would do precisely as he was told if he wanted to be kept safe in England. Christ, Alfie thought, in the propaganda war, image was everything.

He watched the chief rub his cheek before saying, "Very well, Ingram. I'll see to it."

"Thank you, sir. I'm sure he's given me the inside gen on this one."

Alfie felt his shoulders relax. He'd kept his word. He'd done everything in his power to protect Sammy, and although it was part of his training to gain the confidence of his tout, Alfie had become more fond of the little man than he'd anticipated at the beginning.

"I bloody well hope he has. For both our sakes." Chief McMaster walked across to a tall glass-fronted cabinet and said as he opened its door, "I want you in Londonderry tomorrow morning for the planning session, Ingram."

"Right, sir." Alfie rose and was surprised when the chief asked, "Would you care to join me in a small whiskey, Alfie?"

Alfie? Good Lord. Old Mac must be pleased, and would you like a drink? Alfie had heard rumours that since his wife had died three years ago, the chief had become a lonely man. The least he could do was accept the offer, but just one. He had to be in Londonderry early tomorrow.

Too bloody early if the length of time he'd had to wait was anything to go by, but the scraping of chairs being pushed back and the movement of men standing as the senior officers came in meant the waiting was over. One nagging thought stayed with him. He had better be right.

Alfie stood and waited until the TCG(N)'s commander, a Special Branch chief inspector, and the army TCG(N) liaison officer, a moustachioed major, took their places at the head of the room. They stood behind a bare, pine trestle table; at their backs a large-scale ordnance survey map of Strabane and the surrounding countryside was fixed to the wall with drawing pins.

"Be seated," the commander said.

Alfie recognized the Special Branch man, Harry Bowman. He'd lectured to Alfie last year on a course about undercover surveillance. He was fiftyish, balding, a port-wine-stain birthmark disfiguring his left cheek, belly bulging over his belt. He remained standing. Alfie flinched as Bowman hit the map an almighty whack with a wooden pointer. His voice was husky, and Alfie had to strain to hear the words. "Pay attention." Another whack.

"The Provos' target will be the police barracks. Here." Whack. "Unfortunately, we're not sure of the exact day, but expect it will be very soon, so we'll be setting things up tonight." He dropped a hand to the seat of his pants and dragged their rear seam out of his backside before continuing. "The attackers will probably be a small group, but we're taking no chances. They could have asked for help from other Provo units. We're going to be in place with superior force." He smiled when he said, "superior force."

Alfie heard the murmur of approval. The men around him had all lost subordinates at the hands of the Provos and were eager to hit back. The RUC inspector, Charlie Dunlop, was a Catholic, one of the few in the force. His brother, Sam Dunlop, E4A like Alfie, had been shot by a Provo sniper on the steps of his own home in Grange Park, Dunmurry, on March 25, 1974, killed by a gunman in front of his wife, Mary, and one of their daughters. It was believed, but never proven, that the assassination had been ordered by one of the recent escapees, Brendan McGuinness, because Sam had been running an informer inside McGuinness's battalion. Alfie decided to forget about poor Sam and concentrate on what was being said.

"Each of your units will have a defined task. I'll deal with each one at a time." Bowman turned to the SAS staff sergeant. "Mr. Atcheson, you, I believe, will have the contingent of twenty-four troopers stationed here in Ulster, and ten more have been requested from your Twenty-Two SAS Headquarters in Hereford?"

"Correct, sir." The sergeant's voice was clipped, precise. "The men from G squadron arrive this afternoon."

Alfie gave a low whistle. The commander hadn't been fooling when he'd said there'd be superior force.

"You will be the nucleus of the observation post/reactive."

Or "ambush," in plain terms, and with such a large number of men the crossfire would be ferocious. Wee Sammy could be right in the middle.

"Mr. Atcheson, you've had a chance to study the ground. Come up here and show us where you will place your men."

The staff sergeant rose, moved to the front of the room, took the pointer, and half-turned to the map. His boots gleamed, and Alfie reckoned you could fillet a fish on the sharp creases in his khaki trousers.

"Right, the barracks are . . . here. The main road, the A5 from Omagh to Strabane and on to Londonderry comes down a hill . . . here, to the front of the station, then branches into a T-junction in front of the barracks. It's most probable the attackers will try to run a tractor with a bomb in a front bucket down this hill."

"Inspector Ingram has the details." Harry Bowman nodded to Alfie.

"Five hundred pounds of ammonal on a timer fuse. It'll be in the bucket of a red tractor, registration number HKM 561." He hadn't needed to refer to his notes.

"Thank you. If it's on a timer, we must try to stop it before it gets inside the barracks' fence. Please make a note of that."

Alfie heard a voice behind him and turned to look at the speaker. It was the regular army major. "Should we be asking for the bomb disposal squad, sir?"

Bowman again. "TCG(N)'s considered the question. They'd stick out like sore thumbs with their equipment, and we don't want to frighten our targets off. We want to send a very clear message to the Provos' high command."

Alfie had no doubts about what the message was going to be. As many dead Provvies as possible. He glanced at Inspector Dunlop. The man's grin was feral.

Harry Bowman continued. "It's probable that the device will be on a short fuse. There'd not be time for an ammunition technical officer to do his stuff. We're prepared to accept the possibility of damage to surrounding property. Civilian casualties should be kept to a minimum, however."

And how in the hell were they going to achieve that? Alfie thought, and wondered how many more people would die or be maimed. He felt a tinge of anger with his own part in this. His job, when you boiled it down, was to protect the public, and yet by passing on the information, he was probably going to be indirectly responsible for bringing catastrophe to innocent victims. If he could take any comfort, it was from the thought that had he not found out about the attack, it would have gone ahead anyway and certainly have killed some of his own, the poor bastard constables inside the barracks as well as any passing civilians.

The staff sergeant took over the briefing. "The assault group will be concealed in three locations in front of the barracks."

"You mean 'killer group,'" a voice called from the back.

"Indeed, I do, sir, but we don't call it that in public. Mustn't upset the civilians."

The staff sergeant waited until the laughter died. "We'll have Sergeant Buchan's squad in this house . . . here." He indicated the corner of the hill road.

"He was your chap at Ballydornan, wasn't he?" Bowman asked. "He did a good job there."

Killed young Fiach O'Byrne, whose funeral was today, *and* managed to avoid an enquiry. Alfie had no doubt it was the latter action that warranted Harry Bowman's approval.

"Thank you, sir. He'll have a 7.62 general-purpose machine gun. Two more squads will be in place here and here." He pointed to houses on the corners of the streets joining the T at the right and left of the barracks. If we're wrong and they come in from either end of the T or down either of these two streets, we'll be ready."

"And," Bowman interrupted, "equally well positioned to prevent escape by all routes. Carry on, sergeant."

"The houses on the far side of the T and the barracks back onto a field. On this side of the field, there's a small wood. A second machine gun will be sited in rear at the corner of the wood in case they try to come in over the field."

Alfie nodded. The staff sergeant knew his stuff. Every route to the barracks was covered, and if the rest of the SAS troopers carried their standard-issue M16s or HK 53 assault rifles, the firepower would be overwhelming.

"We'll post two cutoff groups farther out on the arms of the T, and here, off the map"—he pointed past the left side of the paper square—"we'll have an airborne quick-reaction force in two helicopters. Single men will be stationed here, here, and here as lookouts." He indicated positions on the possible approach roads. "All groups will be netted in on a secure radio frequency shared with the other deployed military forces and the constabulary." The staff sergeant coughed. "We were going to put men inside the barracks, sir, but that's RUC turf."

There was a polite ripple of laughter that died when the inspector from HMSU said, "My men will be inside supporting the local constables."

"Will that not put them at risk if the Provos get the bomb through the fence and detonate it?" Harry Bowman asked.

"Some, sir, but if the tractor comes straight down the hill, it will be aimed at the centre of the barracks. The men'll be stationed at either end of the building, and all internal blast-proof shutters will be closed. We'll leave the ones on the outside windows open until the last minute. Keeping them shut might warn off the Provvies."

Chief Inspector Bowman leaned forward to retrieve the pointer. "Thank you, both. Questions?"

There were none.

"Right. All forces to be in position tonight after dark and to remain concealed until the attack goes down or we get orders to call the whole show off."

The very thought of having the thing called off made the hairs on the nape of Alfie's neck tingle.

Bowman nodded to Alfie. "You're next, Inspector Ingram."

"Sir."

"Your detachment—you'll have how many men?"

"Seven and me, sir. We'll be working in four two-man teams on twelve-hour shifts. We've a pretty good idea who the attackers will be. I'll be with one team keeping the suspects' home base under observation. In case I'm wrong, there'll be unmarked cars on the access roads three miles from the barracks to identify the tractor, any accompanying vehicles—and I'm told there will only be one . . . black, registration LKM 136. If I'm right and it is our boyos, once we've spotted them, we'll radio ahead to the assault group and maintain distant surveillance."

"I'll not ask for the names of your suspects now, Ingram. It's not the way we usually operate. Innocent until proven guilty and all that." Harry Bowman tried to look as if he meant the last remark. The official policy was to consider all the acts of the Security Forces to be governed by the rule of law.

Alfie heard the laughter of the men round him and decided now was the time to make the request that he knew he must make. "May I ask a question, sir?"

"Certainly."

"It's likely my source will be with the attacking party. My chief inspector wants him protected. Will that be possible?" Alfie waited anxiously.

Bowman asked, "Staff Sergeant? Can we protect one man?"

"I honestly don't know, sir. How can we identify him?"

"If you're apprehending him, he'll tell you his name's Sunshine." Alfie inwardly congratulated himself for having thought of these details. "If the shooting starts, look out for a small man wearing a bright green scarf."

"Staff Sergeant, brief all of the assault group. Inspector, same for you and the HMSU team. We'll do our best, Ingram."

"Thank you, sir." It was all Alfie could hope for. He continued to worry about Sammy but paid attention as the various representatives dealt at length with details of the placement of uniformed RUC officers, regular army and UDF roadblocks.

Extra RUC constables would be brought in on unconcealed foot patrols to surround the barracks. Their function was crowd control. The minute any shooting started, they were tasked with getting civilians in the area safely out of range and undercover. The army was to provide escorts for the police squads and distant cover on all access roads and country lanes. The UDF would send a detachment to reinforce the customs post on the bridge to Lifford across the border.

None of that kind of backup would affect the roles of Alfie and his men, and if what he suspected was going to happen came to pass, there'd be no one left for the squads to arrest at the roadblocks. With the exception, as he fervently hoped, of Sammy, all the other "persons of interest" would never leave the streets around the Strabane Police Barracks.

He glanced at his watch. Good. The briefing was almost over. He'd one other thing to do before he reported back to his chief, briefed his men, and sent the first shift out to their positions. He wanted to stop by Ballydornan churchyard and cast an eye over the people who would be gathered there.

Alfie waited until everything was finished, said his good-byes, got in his car, and drove along the A5, out of Londonderry, and through Strabane. He stopped outside the barracks, picturing how it would be there—if his information was accurate. In his mind, he smelled the reek of gunpowder, saw the muzzle flashes. There was blood in the gutters, and Alfie made a silent wish none of it would have come from Sammy McCandless.

He put the car in gear and headed up the hill, the hill a tractor would come barreling down in just a few days.

He stopped some distance short of Ballydornan churchyard and took time to survey the little scene.

As was customary at paramilitary funerals, a small detachment of uniformed police officers was in attendance. The mourners would be Provo sympathizers. Some would be active members. There was no honour party of balaclava-hooded men to fire a farewell burst over the grave. That mark of respect was reserved for active Provo volunteers, and the O'Byrne family and everyone else who had been questioned had sworn blind that young Fiach O'Byrne was not, had never been, a Provo.

Anyone who believed that probably still had a soft spot for Santa Claus, Alfie reckoned, and he'd been certain for years, as he had told Sammy, that the O'Byrnes were active volunteers. The father had been a well-known IRA man in his time. But be damned if anyone had been able to prove their involvement.

Getting a good look now at the folks at the graveside would give Alfie more faces to add to his mental catalogue of potential suspects for the future. And the O'Byrnes, who would assuredly know they were suspects, would have their suspicions raised if no one from his branch showed up. He'd seen them when he'd accompanied the uniformed men to tell the O'Byrnes about the death of their brother, and the girl had seen him. It wouldn't hurt to let her see him again.

When the funeral party had departed, Alfie would check the dead-letter drop under the big cross in case Sunshine had left a message.

CHAPTER 43

He'd get a message to Spud today, Sammy thought, the phone call that would make amends and set things to rights for Erin and Cal. He sat at their kitchen table finishing his breakfast. He'd slept reasonably well last night, although at first he'd been uncomfortable when Erin put him in Fiach's old room. He'd eventually drifted off after he'd told himself for the hundredth time that the way the peelers had set it up, he'd had no choice, none at all, but to turn. Now he was going to put things straight, but—he chewed a piece of black pudding—he was going to miss Erin's cooking when she went to America.

He glanced at the telephone on the Welsh dresser. The minute the O'Byrnes were out of the house, he'd be on to Spud, and, Sammy smiled, he was going to fuck up his new friend, him and his "trusting each other" bullshite, and there wouldn't be a fuckin' thing the peeler could do about it.

Better still, no one in the townland would ever know Sammy had been an informer. They would have figured that out in no time if he'd stuck to the original plan and buggered off to England. Now he didn't have to go, he'd not have to share the shame of Mollie MacDacker or Art O'Hanlon, names remembered with hatred over the centuries.

The door to the hall opened, and Erin, in a black dress, hat, and veil, walked across the kitchen; Cal followed wearing black shoes, black suit, black tie, and black armband. Both the O'Byrnes were in the Northern Ireland uniforms of mourning.

Sammy rose. "I'm sorry I can't come, too, pay my last respects, like." He bowed his head.

"That's all right, Sammy." Erin lifted her raincoat from the coat stand. "You just get on with your work here until we get back." She sounded subdued, but Sammy couldn't see well enough through her veil to tell if she'd been crying.

"Come on, Erin," Cal said, taking his sister's arm but needing the other hand to wrench the lower half of the kitchen door open. "If you've a minute, Sam, could you take a plane to that? I've been meaning to, but . . ."

"Aye, certainly. Never you worry." Sammy was going to add that as soon as the O'Byrnes returned, he'd scoot over to his cottage and bring the detonators, but decided this wasn't the time. "Cal, say you a couple of Aves for me, will you?" Sammy knew there was little point asking Erin. She hadn't set foot in a chapel since old man O'Byrne died.

"I will." He stepped aside and let Erin out through the door.

Sammy waited until he heard the noise of the van fade, walked to the dresser, lifted the phone, and dialed. He listened to the ringing at the other end, picked his nose, and tapped one foot on the floor. "Come on, for fuck's sake." Ten double rings, and no one answered. Where the hell was Spud?

Sammy replaced the receiver. "Shite." He'd wanted to put the finishing touches to his deception as quickly as possible, but the call could wait until after he'd been to his cottage and back here. Surely to God the peeler would be in by then. And what the hell had made Spud suggest leaving a note under the cross in the Ballydornan churchyard? Today the place would be crawling with O'Byrne family friends and, like as not, a wheen of Provo volunteers. Sammy imagined excusing himself and pushing through the crowd, saying, "I just have to leave this here wee note for a policeman, so I do."

Fuck that, but the idiocy of the scene made him laugh out loud, and that was something he hadn't done for months. He'd have a few more laughs with his smuggling friends in the pub in Ballybofey, particularly on Saturday morning, when, if all went according to plan, the Strabane Barracks would be a heap of stinking rubble, the O'Byrnes safely on their way to the States, and E4A Spud shitting himself with frustration. It was about time the peeler had his own grief. Sammy had had enough, more than enough.

Still smiling, he grabbed his duncher, put on his raincoat and Welly boots, let himself out, having to shove hard at the door to close it, and whistled for Tessie. The stupid bloody cows wouldn't get themselves out to pasture. When he'd got that done, he'd pick up a plane in the barn and see to the door. Some days, he thought, Cal wouldn't bother drinking his pint if he could get someone else to do it for him. Perhaps, Sammy decided, he'd try the phone again once he'd fixed the door.

He crossed the yard, collar turned against the rain, opened the barn doors, and heard the cattle lowing and stamping in their stalls. They'd not understand why they'd had to wait. By the bawls of some of them, they were getting impatient. He walked along the aisle, opening gates and giving the beasts room to squeeze past him. Cal had said something about one called Margaret, but Sammy was damned if he could recognize her.

"Away to hell," he yelled, thumping one hard on the rump as she tried to squash him against the front of the pens. Instead of lowing and skittering away, she heaved her bulk against him. Jesus. Margaret. Sammy struggled to breathe but couldn't force his chest to expand. The cow had him pinned against the gatepost. He heard his ribs snap and felt stabs like red-hot irons in his left chest. Specks of bright light swam in front of his eyes, his knees buckled, and he slipped sideways, to tumble back into the manure on the floor of an empty stall. In the second before the darkness crushed in on him, he had time to think—Spud.

Erin held her hurt to herself as she stood beside Cal in the autumn rain. She glanced at her brother, solemn-faced, cheeks glowing in the chill, red hair darkened by the rain. It was the colour of the sadness within her. Bloodred, tinged with scarlet anger.

And if she could see Cal's emotions as a colour, they would be grey. Grey as the clouds that were stalled immobile above them. Her brother had been numbed by Fiach's death, yet more accepting than she. Perhaps grey was the colour of acceptance.

The mourners huddled sheeplike against the cold beneath the moss-grown Celtic cross or inside the drystone wall with its iron gate. The ancient, timeless gravestones sagged lopsidedly, the newer marble ones cowered in the shadows. Old Father O'Driscoll in his biretta, cope, cassock, and stole was as damp and musty as the mound of newly turned soil beside the open grave. It felt like the Irish had been attending funerals in the rain since the dawn of time.

The priest droned on,

Ave Maria, gratia plena, Dominus tecum.
Benedicta tu in mulieribus, et benedictus fructis ventri tui, Jesus.
Sancta Maria, Mater Dei, ora pro nobis peccatoribus, nunc, et in hora
*   mortis nostrae.*

Outside the wall of the Ballydornan churchyard, police officers stood with their bottle-green uniform raincoats sodden, their Sten guns reversed, heads bowed in respect. To the side of the small contingent, she could see the man with the funny triangle in his left eye, the man who'd come to the farmhouse and stayed in the Land Rover when the peelers had arrived to notify her and Cal of Fiach's shooting.

He wore a civilian coat and was bareheaded but held his head erect, eyes never still. He seemed to be interested in the Celtic cross, and for a moment she wondered why. She knew very well why he kept scanning the faces of the people. He'd be making mental notes of those he thought he should add to his list of Provo suspects. Special Branch bastard. Let him. If he was any-where near Strabane Barracks on Saturday, he'd find out for sure about some of them. Much good would it do him then. She hoped he'd catch pneumonia from getting soaked.

"*In nomine Patris, et Filii, et Spiritu Sancti.*" The priest wagged his as-pergillum and sprinkled holy water into the grave.

"Amen," murmured the priest and mourners in concert.

Erin moved to the grave's lip and looked down. The lid of Fiach's wooden coffin glistened and she saw drops of water, each one a discrete blob, shin-ing on the brass plate. His hurley and ball lay to one side.

"Rest in peace, Fiach," she whispered, lifting a handful of earth, letting the soil trickle from her fingers, and hearing it rattle off the lid. "Rest in peace here in Ireland, Fiach," she said. "We'll not forget you, darling."

She allowed herself one last look and turned aside to Cal. Tears ran down his ruddy cheeks. She'd not cry. She'd not. Not until the last shot had been fired, they were safely across the border, and she and Eamon were in Amer-ica, the land that had been the refuge of so many of her people.

She walked with Cal through the gate to their parked van. She nodded silently as family friends and Fiach's hurling teammates murmured their condolences. She didn't speak, didn't look back. She promised herself she would not look at Fiach's grave until the day she returned—when her Ire-land was whole again.

Cal said nothing as she climbed in beside him. She left him to his thoughts.

The van jolted over the grass verge and onto the road. The windscreen wipers made rhythmic squeaks as they swung across the rain-mottled glass. Cal turned on the heater, and she watched the condensation vanish from inside the windscreen, felt the warmth of the air being blown from the vents, and hoped the heater she'd put in the neolithic grave would be keeping Eamon and his friends warm, too.

Fiach had always looked up to Eamon, admired his passion, his strength. She wondered how her young brother would have taken to Davy Mc-Cutcheon.

Davy seemed an interesting man. She'd like to know more about him and hoped she'd be able to get him to open up once they'd crossed the border.

They'd've time to kill in Dublin before they went their separate ways to what used to be called the New World.

Why, she wondered, would a man like him, a man who'd given his life to the Cause, repudiate it as fiercely as she had rejected the Catholic faith? Did he still believe in an avenging God, fear his immortal soul was burdened with the people he'd killed, see himself hell-bound when he died? According to the Church, we were all sinners anyway, so what difference did it make? He was no more guilty than the old IRA volunteers who'd fought alongside Michael Collins and Harry Boland against the Black and Tans in the Irish War of Independence in the '20s. It had been a just war, forgivable as the one Davy had waged, the one she was still waging.

What thoughts had run through the minds of Collins's "apostles," his handpicked assassins, on the eve of one of their attacks on the hated G-men, the undercover policemen in the pay of the British? Had they been haunted by the fear of their own deaths? They must have been. And since Sammy had made her face the possibility yesterday, she'd been forced to consider the risk that she herself might die. She was proud to find she did not fear death. She'd regret the shortness of her life, regret never seeing Eamon again, regret not learning all the new things in store for them when they settled in America, never knowing if the Irish would win their freedom. But she had no anxiety about an afterlife. Her cause *was* just, and there was no limbo, no purgatory, no hell in store for her.

If she died on Saturday, there was solace in the thought she'd be buried in Ballydornan, beside Ma and Fiach and Da in the rich Irish earth, under a weeping Irish sky.

The van jolted over an uneven place where a pothole had been filled with new tarmac. Her knee banged on the dashboard. She told herself to stop being so morbid, that all soldiers must feel like this on the eve of battle. She stared ahead to the slopes bordering the narrow road, the bracken brown, the whin flowers chrome-yellow against the green of their thorny bushes. Take a good look, she told herself. You'll see them once again on Saturday on the way to Strabane, and after that, how many years will it be until you're free to walk these hills again? Erin crossed her arms, hands on her shoulders, and hugged herself.

The events of the last week had seemed vague, unfocused back then, but now she could not escape from the fact of Fiach's death and the reality that she would be leaving her little corner of Ireland, the land her family had farmed for generations here in the County Tyrone. She was bound for America.

Erin glanced back over her shoulder and was pleased to see there was no other car following them. She'd not have put it past the man with the odd eye to have tailed them, and with the men in the tumulus, the last thing she wanted was having a peeler sniffing round the place.

She wondered how Sammy was managing and wished he'd shown more understanding when she'd tried to explain the accounts yesterday. She was grateful for his offer to keep flowers on Fiach's grave and knew she could rely on Sammy to ensure there'd be a proper headstone on Fiach's grave, there beside his da.

She became aware of the van slowing down as Cal tucked in behind a tractor. He usually swore when he was held up like this, but today he sat tight-lipped, big hands clutching the wheel.

"Are you all right, Cal?" she asked quietly.

"I'm right enough, but I'm sad."

"About Fiach?"

"Aye. And Da, and all the rest. I wonder," he said, "is all the dying worth it?"

"It has to be."

Cal sighed.

"You're not getting cold feet are you?"

"Not at all."

"Good. We're too far along to turn back now."

"I know," he said, and stared ahead.

She saw the tractor indicate to turn right into a field and waited for it to swing across the road and for Cal to accelerate.

The van picked up speed the way all her plans had in the last few days. Erin had learned in history class that once the European powers had mobilized in 1914, no power on earth could have stopped the juggernaut that became the "war to end all wars."

The statesmen of the time found they had no more choice about changing course than—than the old trams that used to run in Belfast. She felt the same sense of inevitability. She must fight and go on fighting for her country, and for Fiach, and she must rest content with that decision, the consequences be damned.

She listened to the rain, heavier now, rattling off the van's roof, and was vaguely aware of the pungent odour of damp dog, Tessie's smell, clinging to the van's upholstery. She'd miss the collie, even miss that bitch of a cow, Margaret.

The road wound past water meadows, where cattle huddled at the hedges, heads to the rain, coats sodden, jaws working as they chewed the cud. Stupid animals trying to ignore the weather, hoping it would soon clear up, just as most of the people here in the north hoped the struggle would go away so they could get on with the rest of their lives.

Cal turned onto the farm lane. Fuchsia bushes slipped by her window. Their red and purple flowers drooped in the rain, as if they, too, were sad, and she knew that, wherever she and Eamon went, she would never again see a fuchsia bush without thinking of Fiach. She'd heard a line about a man not being dead as long as someone remembered his name. I'll always remember yours, Fiach, she thought as the van jolted into the farmyard.

The whole dairy herd was milling round. "What the hell's going on, Cal? Stop the van. Where's Sammy?"

She piled out, forced her way past the animals, heedless of the mud splattering her raincoat and the hem of her dress, and ran to the barn. In the dim light she saw a pair of moleskin-trousered legs sticking out from an empty stall. Erin strode over, fell to her knees, and bent her head over Sammy's face. His lips were slatey, but he was breathing. "Sammy. Sammy." She shook his shoulder and was rewarded with a groan.

Erin yelled, "Cal. Cal. Get in here. Sammy's hurt."

She put an arm under his shoulders and managed to have him half-sitting when Cal appeared at her shoulder. "What . . ."

"Never mind. Take his feet. We have to get him into the house."

"Right."

She was surprised how light the wee man was. In minutes, they had carried him to the farmhouse and into the kitchen. "Lay him on the table," Erin said as she unbuttoned Sammy's raincoat, jacket, and collarless shirt, scarcely noticing the darker V stretching from his collarbones to the middle of his pigeon breastbone, where days working in the sun had tanned him. The rest of his chest was white as the skin of a corpse, except for livid bruising on the left side.

She felt the grating underneath her hand there each time he hauled in a wheezing breath. She'd felt that often enough in a hurt horse. "His ribs are broken," she said.

"Should we take him up to Altnagelvin Hospital in Derry?" Cal asked.

"No," she said, thinking fast. "He's got the detonators. He's to teach you how to make a fuse. We'll have to keep him here until he wakes up. Go you and give Doctor O'Malley a call. Ask him to come out here."

She heard the telephone's "ting" and Cal speaking. She held her breath until he said, "He'll be here in an hour."

"Good. Now go and get a blanket." Erin struggled to get Sammy's clothes off, tutting at the sight of his urine-stained underpants.

Cal returned, and she snatched the blanket from his hands.

"Here." She took the blanket and covered Sammy. "Just a minute 'til I get the kettle on so I can fill a hot water bottle. Then we'll cart him along to bed."

"I'll do the kettle."

Erin waited. She remembered how Ma had stripped Da, burned his blood-stained shirt the night he'd been wounded, the night the peelers came. Dear God, would Irish women ever be able to stop binding up their menfolk? Yes, she told herself, when the Brits had gone—and any doubts she might have had earlier about the raid fled.

"Take his feet," she told Cal and helped her brother carry the blanket-wrapped Sammy along the hall. She tucked the little man under the sheets and eiderdown and, as a mother would with a sleeping child, gently used one hand to smooth his sparse hair from his forehead.

Apart from the hot water bottle, she couldn't do much now until the doctor arrived. "Come on," she said. "Let him rest."

The kettle had boiled by the time she and Cal returned to the kitchen. "Get the tea things ready, Cal. I'll make us a drop in a minute."

She sat at the table as Cal busied himself. Now what? There was no way Sammy could travel to establish his alibi. Maybe sending him to hospital would be best. But if the doctor didn't think it was necessary, she could nurse Sam here and . . . and if she could get old O'Malley to come round on Saturday, he could testify that Sammy had been too sick to leave the farmhouse.

She heard the kettle boiling and filled a rubber hot water bottle, moulded in the shape of a collie dog. It had been Fiach's.

"Erin?"

"What?'

"You said Sammy has to show me how to set the fuse. What'll we do if he's not well enough?"

Think, she told herself as she screwed the stopper into the neck of the bottle.

"I'll take this to Sammy and keep an eye to him. You drive over to his cottage. He told me he keeps the fusing stuff in a knapsack hidden in his coal house. Find them and bring them back here."

"Right. But, Erin, even if I get the gear, none of us knows how to use it."

Erin shrugged. "I'd not be too worried. Davy McCutcheon was an armourer in the Belfast Brigade for years. We'll get Davy to show you."

CHAPTER 44

Davy limped after McGuinness and Eamon. The latter two carried an Ar-maLite rifle in each arm, taken from the cache in the old grave, one weapon each destined for Eamon, McGuinness, Cal, and Erin to take with them to Strabane tomorrow. Eamon had had enough wit not to ask Davy to help. As he trudged across the dark farmyard, the light leaking from the curtained farmhouse kitchen windows gave direction.

It had been a long three days cooped up with Eamon and McGuinness in the old grave. Davy was no stranger to McGuinness's antipathy, indeed found it simpler to deal with than his unexpected offer of a truce. It had been more difficult living close to Eamon and feeling the tension between them.

By tomorrow, he'd be out of the tumulus for good and finally on his way, away from Ireland and away from all the Provo hard men.

The smell of gun oil still clung to his sweater, but he'd taken no part when Eamon and McGuinness spent the afternoon stripping, cleaning, oiling, and reassembling four of the semiautomatic rifles from the arms cache. Davy knew the ArmaLite had a muzzle velocity of 3,250 feet per second and its .223 round could penetrate a British flak jacket or the skin of an armoured vehicle. It was a deadly weapon for close-quarter use.

He stumbled on a rut, clutched for support, and grabbed for Eamon's arm. "Sorry. This bloody leg of mine."

"It's all right," Eamon said, moved ahead, then stood waiting.

Davy rubbed his thigh, the one he'd nearly blown off when, as a boy, he'd been training here in Tyrone, the one he'd smashed jumping from the farmhouse window in Ravernet. He limped to where Eamon stood.

"Look, Davy," Eamon said, as he'd tried to say several times since Wednesday, "I'm sorry about me having to rope you into this."

"So am I, Eamon." His regret was as much for a lost friendship as it was for knowing that tomorrow he was going to be part, no matter how distant from the action, of a Provo attack. "But let the hare sit."

Light streamed out through the open door.

"Come on," said Eamon, "let's get inside."

"Right." Davy walked on. He had no desire to sit through the final preparations, but the photographer who'd come to the grave on Tuesday had promised that Davy's forged documents would be delivered today, and he wanted to be sure they had arrived; otherwise, he'd have stayed alone in the old grave and let the rest of them plan to their heart's content. He walked into the kitchen and waited for Eamon to close the door.

"Evening, Davy," Erin said from where she stood at the range pouring boiling water into a teapot. "Cup of tea? No? Then make yourself at home. Sorry the place is a bit cluttered."

Davy looked around and saw a pile of anoraks, overalls, gloves, and balaclava helmets on the tabletop. Provo uniform for any attack. Once the firing was over and the attackers safe, the outer garments would be discarded along with the weapons. No residual traces of burned gunpowder would cling to the clothes or hands of the assailants.

Three bulging rucksacks stood beside the kitchen door. Erin pointed to them. "You'll be taking those in the van tomorrow, Davy. We'll all need clean clothes and toilet things once we get to Dublin. The one nearest the door has a clatter of ham sandwiches and some bottles of ginger ale."

Jesus, she sounded as if she'd been making preparations for a picnic. Some bloody picnic. If they managed to escape the devastation of that bomb blast, he wondered if they'd have any stomach for sandwiches and ginger ale. Still, when they opened the bag with the food in it, the van would be on the way to Dublin. Davy couldn't help but smile.

He looked over to Eamon and saw him staring at a khaki army-surplus knapsack covered in what looked like smudged coal dust leaning against one of the table's legs.

"Would you take a wee look at this?" said Eamon, handing Davy the knapsack. "Sorry, it's a bit grubby, but Cal had to pick it up from under a heap of coal."

Davy took the bag, undid the strap holding it shut, and opened the flap. "Holy shite." Inside, he could see an ammeter, wires, a battery, the handles of a pair of wire strippers, and a flat wooden box. He'd seen enough of those boxes in his time. Fulminate-of-mercury detonators. Fuse-making equipment. "Here." Davy thrust the bag at Eamon. "I want no part of this. That's your armourer's job."

"He can't do it, Davy," Erin said quietly. "He's in hospital. He got crushed by a cow last night. Doctor O'Malley came out, said Sammy had a punc-tured lung, might have pneumonia. He's in Altnagelvin in Derry. "

"It's nothing to do with me." Davy stepped back. "Not a bloody thing."

"But," Erin said, moving closer to Davy, "you're an armourer. You can build a fuse, show Cal how to set it."

"I can," Davy said, wondering how many fuses he'd made, how many lives his bombs had destroyed, "but I won't."

No one spoke. He saw Erin stare at Eamon.

You can stare away, girl, Davy thought. I'm not budging. He answered his own question about how many. He could identify by name or by their faces only a handful of individual people he'd killed; but it was the faceless others, the ones he'd used to think were no business of his because he only made the devices, which haunted him more.

"What do you mean, 'you won't?'" McGuinness snarled. "You'll do as you're bloody well told."

Davy's eyes narrowed. *"No."* He'd not make another bomb. He'd not. *"Do you hear me? No."* He was panting.

Christ, if they tried to force him by saying they'd not help him get to Dublin unless he made the fuse, he'd get there by himself. It didn't matter if Eamon said it would be nearly impossible to go it alone. Davy'd said he'd drive the van. He'd made that compromise. He wasn't making any more, no matter what that decision cost. He'd promised Fiona the raid on Rav-ernet in '73 would be his last, and he'd never broken a promise to her. If he did, all his telling himself he'd changed was meaningless. He'd have changed all right, but with his last shred of integrity gone, he'd not be the man Fiona could love.

His breathing slowed. "I mean it," he said more calmly. "I'll not do it." If the attack couldn't go ahead, he'd not be one bit sorry. "Gimme my pass-port and let me be." Davy waited to see what would happen.

"It's not here yet, Davy," Eamon said. "The fellow should be bringing it any minute."

"I'll wait," Davy said.

He saw Erin look at Eamon and Eamon shrug. After three years in the same cell, he must know how bloody-minded Davy could be. Cal seemed to be smiling. Was that because he'd realized if Davy wouldn't make the fuses, the attack couldn't go ahead? Davy wondered just how much the man's heart was in the thing, how much stomach Cal had for killing.

McGuinness's voice was cold. "I told you I didn't care what you did after we got to Dublin."

"That's right."

"You're for Canada, aren't you?"

Eamon must have told him. Davy stared at the man. Mind your own business, McGuinness. Keep out of this.

"And you think there's no Provos there? That we couldn't find you? You and whoever you're going to see? Jimmy Ferguson that housepainter friend of yours? Some woman?"

Davy felt a vessel in his temple start to throb. Was McGuinness threatening Fiona? Davy's fists bunched. He stepped up to McGuinness. "I'll kill you."

"I thought you'd given up killing," McGuinness sneered. "You make that fuse or . . ."

"Or what?" Davy's hand shot out and grabbed the front of McGuinness's sweater. "Or what?" He felt someone's hand on his arm.

"Back off, Davy." Eamon, still holding the knapsack in one hand, thrust himself between Davy and McGuinness, who sidled out of range and toward the door. "Sometimes Brendan gets carried away."

"He's going to get his bloody head carried away." Davy's hands tightened. How dare the bastard threaten Fiona? How dare he? Davy couldn't control his breathing. He struggled to break Eamon's grasp.

He heard a vehicle being driven into the farmyard.

Erin grabbed a blanket from the sofa and draped it over the stacked rifles. "Get you three into the hall," she snapped as a car door slammed. "Move it." Someone hammered on the back door. Erin moved toward it and shoved McGuinness out of the way. "Bedroom," she hissed, then yelled, "Hang on. I'm coming," as she waited for the three men to leave the kitchen.

Davy stood in the hall and listened. He heard the scrape of the lower half of the back door and muffled voices. A woman's and a man's. Police? Soldiers? The scraping again, footsteps tapping across the kitchen tiles. Erin pulled the hall door open. "It's all right," she said. He could see she held a buff envelope in one hand. "It was your man from Newtownstewart. He's sorry he was so late, but the job took longer than he'd expected."

His passport. Davy shot a grateful look to Eamon, who smiled back. "Thanks, Eamon." Davy stretched out his hand to Erin to take the envelope. He wondered what a passport looked like. He'd never owned one, never been out of Ireland in his life. That envelope held his ticket to a new life, and the first step to it was a small document with his photograph in it.

Davy felt himself being jostled as McGuinness shouldered his way past to grab the envelope and stride to the range. Davy charged across the kitchen, hand reaching for the package. "That's mine, you bastard," but he was forced to halt when McGuinness opened the lid of the range and held the envelope over the flames.

"Nobody can make you fix the fuse. Is that right?"

"Fuck you." Davy didn't care if he was swearing in front of a woman. "Fuck you. Give it to me." He grabbed for the envelope.

McGuinness moved it out of Davy's reach. "The fuse," he said. "Now."

Davy glanced from Cal to Erin to Eamon. All stood, arms folded, tight-lipped. There'd be no help from any of them. He felt like an apostate facing implacable inquisitors. It was as if the last nine years had never happened, as if he had never sworn not to make another bomb as long as he lived. And if he wired the timer, it would set off five hundred pounds of ammonal. The destruction would be hellish.

"Here, Davy." Eamon held out the coal-stained knapsack. Eamon's voice was hard, unforgiving.

Davy hesitated, "Eamon, I . . ."

"Take it."

Flames flickered from the open range and caressed the envelope in McGuinness's hand.

"Don't," Davy yelled.

"Then get to work. Now." McGuinness had a fleck of spittle at the corner of his mouth.

"Please, Davy," Erin asked, her voice softer, kinder. "For Ireland . . ."

Those two words, the justification for 2,510 dead since 1969, God knew how many mutilated.

"And Fiach," she whispered.

Bugger Ireland, and Davy was sorry for Fiach, but neither was cause enough.

"My arm's getting tired, McCutcheon."

Davy hauled air to the bottoms of his lungs, held his breath, thought of Fiona's eyes and what he must do to see those eyes again, exhaled, stretched out his hands, and took the khaki bag from Eamon.

"We can't make you?" McGuinness laughed, a dry, mirthless noise like dead leaves skittering across a concrete yard. "The hell we can't."

Davy walked slowly to the table, pushed the pile of clothes to one side, sat, set the bag on the table, and began to remove its contents.

Ever since Jimmy had sent her photo, he'd been striving to get to her, but hadn't let his yearning make him kill. Not Mr. Smiley, not the guards racing across their car park last Sunday even though he'd had a gun, a gun that was still under his pillow. He'd been proud of himself for holding his fire. She'd be proud when he told her. But he couldn't tell her, ever, if he didn't get to Canada.

Davy stole a glance to where McGuinness stood holding the envelope. It was too far. If he tried to rush the man, his passport and his hopes would vanish.

He'd have to make the fuse, and when he got to Vancouver, he'd have to tell Fiona and hope to God she'd understand, forgive him. He wondered if he'd be able to forgive himself.

Davy laid the makings in a rough circle in front of him. Two fulminate detonators, a battery, kitchen timer, lengths of insulated copper wire, electricians' tape, wire strippers, and an ammeter.

He lifted the first detonator, a thin copper cylinder with two wires running from its top, and held one wire to each of the ammeter's terminals. The needle flicked across the dial. The other detonator made the instrument react as violently. So they were in working order, damnit.

He attached a long piece of loose wire to one detonator and married it to a similar connector on the other. The wire was long enough so that each fulminate cylinder could be pushed through sacking surrounding two separate bags of ammonal. He used a Western Union pigtail splice for each joint and wrapped the bare copper with electricians' tape.

Nine years ago, lying behind a hedge beside a back road in the Hills of Antrim, he'd fiddled with this selfsame kind of wiring. It had detonated an iron pipe under a farmer's car, a simple iron pipe filled with the urea-nitrate-aluminium mix he'd made at home from pints of his own boiled urine.

He ran a second wire from the right-hand detonator to the anode of a nine-volt battery. The dry cell had enough voltage to power a large torch or generate the spark to blow the ammonal. He'd not used a battery on another job back in '74, just a hand-lit fuse and four sticks of TNT. The blast had killed a ticket collector who had had two little daughters in Fiona's class. Davy's hand shook as he picked up the kitchen timer. He'd need a metal screw.

"Have you any screws and a screwdriver?"

"I'll get them," Cal said.

Davy waited. He'd run a screw through the face of the timer at the twelve o'clock position and connect it to the wire from the detonator. One more strand from the timer hand to the battery's cathode would complete the circuit. The timer could be set for whatever number of minutes was required, and when the time had elapsed, the hand would strike the screw and complete the circuit.

Simple, effective, and deadly, unless—unless he left a gap in the circuit. And he could if he insulated the wire from the detonator before he attached it to the screw. He looked across to McGuinness. You think you're so fucking smart, you bastard. I'll bugger you up yet. And nobody was going to get killed by one of Davy's devices.

He smiled.

"Happy at your work, are you, McCutcheon?" McGuinness sneered.

Davy ignored him.

Cal stood at Davy's shoulder. "Here you are." Cal handed Davy a screw and screwdriver and sat beside him to watch.

Davy put the screw through the face at twelve o'clock. He attached a wire to the timer's hand and wrapped its loose end in electrician's tape. "Don't put that there wire near the battery until you've set the timer," Davy said.

"Why not?" Cal asked.

"Because the timer hand'll be resting against the screw. You'd have a complete circuit, and the whole bloody lot'll blow."

"Right." Cal peered closely at the timer. "Not until I've set the time."

Davy lifted the battery. "See that there?" He indicated the cathode. "After you put the detonators in the ammonal and set the time, strip the insulation from that wire and attach it there."

"There?"

"Right. And if I was you, I'd set the time for twelve minutes. That'll give you a couple of minutes extra to make the connection."

"Fair enough."

"Now," said Davy as he picked up the electricians' tape and ripped off a short length, "I've just to connect the first detonator to the screw, and that's the job done." He began to wrap the shiny copper filaments with the insulating tape that would prevent the current flowing to the screw. No current—no explosion.

Fuck you, McGuinness. Fuck the whole bloody lot of you. Davy knew he was taking a chance. When the attack squad fled to the van in Lifford, because the bomb hadn't gone off, Eamon might decide not to take Davy to meet Sean Conlon in Dublin.

Davy looked up at Eamon, saw his face, serious but honest, and hoped Eamon would not be so vindictive. Anyone could make a mistake. And even if he was abandoned—he glanced at McGuinness and the envelope—Davy'd have his passport. Somehow he'd get to Canada. Somehow. And he'd have no more deaths to burden him.

He hesitated and wondered about McGuinness. That bastard wouldn't hesitate to kill anyone he suspected might have betrayed the Provos. He'd have an ArmaLite in the escape car. If the bomb failed, he'd put two and two together. He'd be blazing mad, unpredictable, and dangerous. Davy thought about the .25 under his pillow. He'd stick it in his pocket tomorrow. Just in case.

"Are you not near finished yet?" McGuinness asked.

"In a minute."

"Aye. Well make sure you do it right. You've fucked up before. This one had better work."

"It'll work." Davy lifted the wire that would make damn sure it didn't.

"I know." Davy heard the venom in the man's voice. "Because, look . . ."

Davy stared across the room and saw McGuinness slip the envelope into his inside jacket pocket.

"You're not getting this until after it's blown."

Davy stopped insulating the wire. He glanced at the screw and across to McGuinness.

"No explosion, no passport, McCutcheon."

You bastard. You bastard. Davy stripped the tape free and wound the shiny copper wires around the screw. The fucking circuit would be live after all. "It's done," he said.

"Good," said McGuinness, "and when it works, I'll give you your papers . . . after you've picked us up in Lifford tomorrow."

CHAPTER 45

"Tomorrow, and tomorrow, / Creeps in this petty pace . . ." Fiona spoke the lines from *Macbeth* as she strode along Kits Beach and looked across Burrard Inlet to the evening sky above the North Shore Mountains.

The moon's rise heralded the coming of night, and after she'd slept—and she hoped she would sleep—she'd wake on a Saturday morning with the day to kill before Tim came. Tomorrow her hours would indeed be petty as she tried to make them pass before facing him.

The light faded, and she saw the half-moon hanging, a silver semicircle in its own frame of delicate blue. Between the moon and the knife-edge-sharp crest line of the brooding mountains, layers of mist were stained the soft pink of the inside of an oyster shell.

She guessed it was nearly seven o'clock, almost three in the morning in Ireland. Since Jimmy's call, she had become well practised in working out the time differences between here and there, and Davy.

If it wasn't raining, the night sky in Ireland would be velvet and pierced by starlight. Davy might still be there, and she hoped he was somewhere safe and warm and fast asleep.

He used to sleep beside her, breathing quietly unless the snores of him would have drowned the roar of a pneumatic drill. She smiled, thinking of how she'd make him roll onto his side, and he'd grunt, and snuggle against her, and stop his racket.

As the sky's colours faded, the moon's brightness slid behind a layer of thicker cloud, and her shadow faded on the rippled sand. The looming mountains melded into the darker sky, and she remembered a night when she'd taken Davy to the Hollywood Hills to watch the moon rise over Belfast Lough.

The moon's path had silvered the sea where a freighter ploughed its way to the Port of Belfast and the spray from its bow wave shimmered.

"Isn't it beautiful, Davy?"

He stood beside her, holding her hand, staring over the scene. "I never saw the sea like this before," he said. "It's as if the ship was swimming in quicksilver." And she kissed him gently, loving the poetry that he didn't know lived in him. "I wish," he said, "I could conjure up a ship like that so we could sail away from the Troubles."

She'd not sailed away; she'd flown. And soon—please, soon—Davy would fly here to her. And he would come. When, she wasn't sure, but she *knew* he would. Perhaps—and she smiled—she was fey, possessed of the gift of second sight. The gift wasn't for everyone, but those who had it could see the future, and her grandmother had had the ability. Perhaps she'd passed it on? Granny said it only worked when you thought of someone you loved, as Fiona was thinking of Davy now.

She was surprised how her certainty about her love for him had grown in five days, but recognized it wasn't really a sudden growth like the thrusting of a new daffodil shoot in January. Just as a bulb in winter lies dormant, love had been in her all along, waiting for something to force it to the surface. Bulbs needed moisture, the warmth of the sun. Had she really needed Jimmy's support, Siobhan's confession? Not at all. It was and always had been her choice to make.

As she walked along Whyte Avenue, the moon broke from the cloud, and its light filtered through the trees' leafless branches to throw whorled and tormented shadows on the sidewalk. She came to her apartment and, not ready to face its emptiness, walked on to the Korean corner store. The little shop's entrance was flanked by bunches of cut flowers—roses, carnations, lilies, irises.

On laden stands tomatoes, oranges, brussels sprouts, apples, peaches, pears, and carrots jostled each other, all in their own separate trays. The boxes of fruits and vegetables were arranged with no apparent logic. Mr. and Mrs. Kim, the owners, had used the sprouts to segregate the green apples from the oranges. The alternating patterns of orange and green made her think of the emblems of the political divide back in Ireland.

The peaches looked delicious. She picked through the fruit, squeezing each to determine how ripe it was, selected six, popped them in a paper bag, and took them inside.

Mr. Kim smiled and bowed to her from behind the counter, where chocolate bars lay in racks beneath. The shelves on walls behind him bore stacks of cigarette packets. She wondered if Davy still smoked. She hoped not, but if he did, that was part of Davy, and she'd have to put up with it.

"Evening, Miss Kavanagh," Mr. Kim said in his accented English.

"Lovely night, Mr. Kim." She handed over her purchase and a ten-dollar bill and waited until he made change from a mechanical, bell-ringing cash register.

"Thank you." She took her change and her paper bag and headed for home.

The night was dark now that the moon had gone behind thick clouds, and she wondered if it was dark in Abbotsford, where Becky was staying at her mother's. Her dad had died peacefully three hours after the doctors turned off the life support, and when Becky had phoned, she'd sounded almost cheerful; certainly she seemed to be surviving her crisis.

Becky was a strong woman, brought up with the English disdain for weakness, for shows of emotion in public. Fiona hoped she herself would be able to be brave tomorrow, to be resolute when Tim came, to tell him she was sorry, but it was over, her love for him wasn't all-encompassing, all-giving with no holding back, no reservations, no secrets. It never could be as long as Davy was there between them.

In front of the house, she fumbled for her key and heard McCusker's yowling. All that bloody animal worried about was his stomach. His calls grew more insistent as she closed the front door behind her and opened the one to her apartment. She stooped to pet him while he wove against her shins. "Davy's going to be surprised when he hears what I called you, cat," she said, closing the door behind her. "Come on. Supper."

She set the peaches on the counter and poured pellets into McCusker's bowl.

The buzzer rang.

She wasn't expecting anyone, so it was probably someone collecting for a charity or a couple of earnest young Mormons with their Bibles, spiky brush cuts, and neatly pressed, dark suits. She'd chase away whoever it was, politely of course, and then—she relished the thought—she was going to eat one of the peaches and have a long, hot bath. She went to the living room and hit the intercom button. "Who is it?"

"G'dye, darling. It's me."

Holy Mary, Mother of God. Tim.

"Come on. Open up. The bloke who was sick got better, and he wants to work tonight. I tried calling you, but nobody answered. I didn't bother to leave a message. I thought I'd just pop over."

She tried to control her shallow breathing, lost for anything to say. She must look a mess. Old jeans, sweater, hair all over the place; she patted it with one hand, wondered if her lipstick was smudged before realizing her appearance was irrelevant. What mattered was how to tell him.

"Fiona?"

"Just a tick." She unlocked the outer door.

She heard his footsteps, then Tim was standing there, grinning from ear to ear.

"Surprise," he said, and with a flourish produced a bunch of red roses from behind his back. "Useful place, that store on the corner."

What would she have done if she'd bumped into him when she was buying the peaches? They must have missed each other by minutes.

She swallowed, took the bouquet, and said, "I'd . . . I'd better get these into water." She stepped back and avoided his attempt to kiss her. "Won't be a minute. Sit down." She saw him frown and lower himself into an armchair. Should she offer him a drink? Yes, she decided. His catching her by surprise was no excuse for rudeness.

"Can I get you a beer?"

"Too right. Dry dingoes don't know the half of it, and I'm knackered."

"Coming up." She went to the kitchen and placed the cellophane-wrapped flowers in the sink.

She stood, clutching the tap, the metal cold under her hands. She put the plug in and ran the water, knowing that she was finding something to do, anything, to avoid going back to him.

"Where's my beer?" he called from the living room.

"Right," she said, opening the fridge, thinking how tired he looked. The shadows under his grey eyes were darker, the furrows on his forehead deeper, but this wasn't the time for the sympathy she automatically felt.

She found a glass and poured clumsily, making the beer foam and the head rush over the rim to drip on the kitchen floor. She grabbed the dishcloth and wiped the glass, threw the cloth on the counter, and, trying to stop her hand from shaking, carried the glass to the living room. "Beer," she said, handing it to him and stepping back one pace.

"Thanks." He took a long pull and wiped his lips with the back of his hand. "I'd not want to be all frothy when I kiss you," he said, starting to rise.

"Sit down, Tim," she said. "I've something to tell you."

"Aaw." He sounded disappointed but sat, still holding his half-empty glass.

She folded her arms and looked directly at his face, seeing puzzlement, concern. "I've had time to do a lot of thinking . . ."

"You're lucky. I've not had time to think. The hospital's been like a zoo. I'm glad to be off call now and over here with you." He frowned at her. "I thought you'd be pleased to see me. You all right?"

She shook her head. "No. I'm not all right."

She heard his concern. "What's up? Is it Becky's dad?"

She shook her head harder. "He died. Becky's with her mother."

"I'm sorry. You're upset. I understand."

"I suppose I am, but . . . that's not what I've been thinking about."

"Oh?"

"Tim. It's . . . it's about us." She stared at him.

"Us?" He lowered his beer to the coffee table. "Us? What about us?"

"I was going to tell you tomorrow night."

"Tell me now."

She tightened her arms across her breasts. "I . . . I don't think we should go on seeing each other."

"Jesus Christ." He turned sideways. She couldn't see his face, couldn't judge how he was reacting.

He turned back and looked directly at her. She saw no pleading, no anger, only raw hurt. "Say that again." His voice was controlled.

Her eyes prickled. She told herself not to cry. "I said, I don't want to see you anymore, Tim."

He stood. "I know why you'd say that." His shoulders slumped and his hands hung limply. She saw his left lower eyelid twitch. "I've seen the news about the Irish jailbreak. Your Ulsterman's escaped, hasn't he?"

She nodded.

"You can't lay his ghost, can you?"

"No," she whispered. "No, I can't." Tim knew Davy's name, and she understood why he wouldn't say it.

"He may not come to Vancouver, you know. You could be making an awful mistake."

"I know that, but . . ."

"You can't help yourself, can you?"

She felt her throat constrict. "No."

"I see."

She wondered if it was his years in practice that allowed him to speak so calmly. It would be easier if he lost his temper, even struck her, but she knew Tim Andersen would never raise a hand to anyone, and yet she deserved his ire, not his understanding and the effort he was making to spare her.

"How can you be so . . . so . . ."—she struggled for the word—"accepting?"

"I'm not. But if that's how things stand, I'll be buggered if I can see what else I can do."

For a second, her mind roared, fight your corner, you stupid man. Don't give me up without a struggle, but deep inside she knew it was her woman's pride speaking. His refusal to rear up was an affront to her ego. "I'm sorry, Tim. I really am."

He sighed. "So am I, Fiona. For a while I was beginning to believe we might have something very special, you and I. I thought I'd be good for you. We are good together. Very good."

She blinked and sniffed, determined he would not see her cry. She looked down and waited for him to speak but—God damn his medical training—he still had the knack of letting a silence hang, deadlier than any shouted words.

What had he just said? "We might have something special"—the way they laughed at the same silly things, reveled in taking *Windy* to sea. "I'd be good for you"; he had listened to her fears, never judged her, tried to help her face the reality of what she had been forced to survive in Belfast. "Good together," and she thought of last Saturday, in her kitchen, in her bedroom, and despite herself felt her nipples rise.

There was no mention of his hurt, no suggestion she hadn't played fair with him, no blame. He'd spoken as if his feelings were irrelevant. He was trying to hold on to her, but in his own, more subtle way.

"I'm not being fair, Tim."

"No," he said, "you're not. Not one bit . . ."

By the look on his face, he had just managed to stop himself adding, "you bitch." So there *was* anger inside him, and Fiona waited, ready to welcome it, knowing there must always be atonement for sins.

"But it's yourself you're being unfair to."

Dear God, she could have borne it if he'd sworn at her. She might have sworn right back and seen the affair die there and then. A yelling match would have hurt, but the pain of this was worse. How could she be angry when the man was being so patient?

He rose, and she felt his hand on her shoulder and turned to him the way she'd done so many times, expecting to be comforted by him putting his arms around her. She held her face up ready for his kiss. His lips brushed hers and she tasted beer.

Someone had told her that smell was the most evocative of the senses. The yeasty taste brought her back to Conway Street and kissing Davy after he'd been to a soccer game and then to the pub with wee Jimmy for a pint or two. In her head, she heard Davy singing "My Lagan Love": ". . . and hums in sweet, sad, undertone, the song of heart's desire."

She pulled away, out of Tim's reach, seeing for the first time the pain in his eyes, reflecting what must be his sure knowledge that he had lost her. And, God, it must be hard for him to know that he had lost her to a ghost of a man who might never materialize here in Vancouver. Tim had lost to her dreams.

"I am sorry, Tim, truly sorry, but it's for the best." The next words came hard, but they had to be said. "I'm still in love with Davy McCutcheon. I'm not being fair to you." Fiona despised herself for that last sentence, the words of self-justification of the thousands who, for their own selfish motives, jilted a lover yet needed to cling to a fragment of self-respect, but she couldn't help repeating, "It's not fair to you."

Tim said nothing.

"I think," she said, "you'd better leave."

He nodded, turned, and slowly walked to the door.

Damn him. How could he accept her rejection so easily? "I am truly sorry, Tim."

"So you said, and I believe you. I appreciate your being honest."

Did he mean it, or was he saying that for her sake, so she could try to persuade herself she had done the right thing, the honest thing? "Thank you," she said. What else could she say?

He opened the door and turned to look at her. "Fiona," he managed and she heard his voice crack, "I love you."

She wanted to run to him, to scream, "I didn't mean it, I love you, too," but she had meant everything she'd said. She didn't love him enough, and now it was too late.

"I'll miss you, Fiona Kavanagh," he said. "Look after yourself." And he closed the door.

The gentle click of the lock sounded to her as loud and as final as the slamming of a jail gate.

She sat limply, her head bowed, and tasted the salt of her tears. Oh Tim, Tim. Do you know what you've done to me? In his kindness he had unwittingly taken his revenge. She'd thought she'd hear him saying, "I love you. I'll miss you. Look after yourself" forever.

She'd been dreading the scene, steeled herself to face bitterness, anger, harsh words, recriminations. They would have been easier than his patient acceptance, his consideration for her feelings, the kind of gentlemanly respect he'd shown from the day she'd met him.

God damn the rainstorm that sent them to Bridges. God damn Bridges, where Jimmy took her photograph to send to Davy. God damn you, Fiona Kavanagh, for being such a fool.

She dashed the tears away, told herself that how she felt now was no one's fault but her own. She'd no reason to be angry with Tim, with Bridges, with Jimmy. The only one to blame was herself. Perhaps instead of feeling guilty, she should take some pride from having been truthful, for not having tried to play both ends against the middle. To keep up a pretence in case Davy didn't come would have been using Tim in the worst way. And Davy would come. He would.

She went to her shelves of records, half-pulled a disc of Irish ballads from the shelf, changed her mind, took down Puccini's *Madama Butterfly* and put it on the gramophone. The overture started, and she sat in a chair. *Butterfly*, with its dark story of love, deceit, and rejection, suited her mood far better than would Liam Clancy's songs of simple love.

McCusker came in, jumped up onto her lap, and curled into a ball. She knew the animal trusted her completely, and she fondled his head and told him she loved him. She listened attentively until the geisha, Cio-Cio-San, sang her final, despairingly hopeful aria as she watched her lover's ship sail away. "*Un bel di vendremo*"—one fine day he will return.

CHAPTER 46

It would be a few minutes before McGuinness returned from the latrine. Davy stood in his sleeping alcove, out of sight of the room at the head of the grave's main chamber. He took the .25 from under his pillow and slipped the revolver into his pants' pocket.

He fished out the remnants of Jimmy's letter to make certain her number was still legible. Not that it really mattered. He'd committed 604-555-7716 to memory. Because it was important to them, priests learned great chunks of the Bible by rote. Davy made sure he had Fiona's telephone number well remembered. He chanted it to himself like a mantra. Although he'd no idea how to get a call through to Canada, he was sure Sean Conlon would know. The first thing Davy was going to do when he was safe in Dublin was to call her.

He wrinkled his nose. The grave stank of damp and mildew, dead spiders and excrement. It was only a small chemical toilet. Davy ached to be out in the daylight, away from the O'Byrnes' farm and away to hell out of Northern Ireland.

"Are you not ready yet?" he called to McGuinness.

"In a minute."

"I'm off. Don't forget the lights." Davy went to the tunnel, dropped onto his hands and knees, and started to crawl. Christ, but spiders were persistent buggers. He brushed gossamer away from his face. How many times had someone torn that web apart in the last six days?

He heard McGuinness coming behind, so he crawled more rapidly and shoved aside the blanket that covered the entrance. The sun dappled the ground beneath the brambles.

Davy waited at the edge of the briar patch, made sure he wasn't being watched, and stood. He could see Cal and Eamon in the farmyard loading the van. Erin was walking toward them from the barn, Tessie at her heels.

He didn't wait for McGuinness but went through the back gate and limped quickly across the yard.

"Morning, Father," Eamon said as he shoved what must have been the last of the rucksacks into the back of the van. "Just about all set. Here"—he handed Davy a set of car keys—"you'll need these."

Davy took the keys, wished they were going to be driving straight across the border, knew bloody well they weren't and there was fuck all he could do about it. He went to the front of the van and climbed in. He glanced behind and saw three stuffed rucksacks and an old wooden chest. It must contain the four folded ArmaLites and a coal-dust-stained khaki rucksack. He knew too well about the rucksack—he'd made the bloody fuses hidden in it. The box would provide concealment of its contents if the van were stopped by a random patrol.

The van lurched as Erin jumped into the back. "Morning, Davy." She was wearing overalls under a hooded anorak. She was overdressed for the weather, he thought.

"Morning." He found it hard to be civil.

There was more swaying as Cal and Eamon piled in. Davy heard Eamon call, "Get a move on, Brendan. We don't want to keep the nice peelers waiting." There was laughter from the others. How in the name of Christ could they laugh?

"Move over in the bed, Cal," McGuinness said.

"'Bye, Tessie," Erin called to the dog. "Cal phoned Willy McCoubrey over by Ardstraw this morning. He'll pop over to feed you and see to the cows until Sammy gets better. Be a good girl." Davy heard the catch in her voice as she added, "I'll miss you, Tessie." He wondered what else she would miss.

The back doors were slammed. "Right, Davy," said Eamon. "Away you go."

Davy started the engine, automatically checked the petrol gauge—good, the tank was full—put the van in gear, and drove off in the bright morning sunshine, out of the yard, along the farm lane, and turned left onto the A5 to head for a big shed, along the way to Strabane. He'd dump the others and their gear at the shed, then drive back to cross the border at Clady.

He heard Cal ask Erin, "Any word on Sammy?" and her answer, "Aye. I phoned Altnagelvin. They said he's comfortable. He'll likely be out by next Thursday."

Eamon said, "Poor wee Sammy."

· · ·

Poor wee Sammy McCandless struggled awake and tried not to take any deep breaths. Every time he did, his broken ribs screamed in protest. The oxygen tubes up his nose chafed, and the intravenous line in his right arm throbbed where the needle had pierced the skin. He sat propped up on pillows, staring through the window of the ward of Derry's Altnagelvin Hospital. He could see the huge bronze statue of Princess Macha. Jesus Christ, he paid fuckin' taxes and all the Hospitals Authority could do with his money was buy an ugly lump of metal like that.

He tried to shift and ground his teeth as pain ran like green fire across his left side. Was it not time for his morphine yet? He groped for a bell push pinned to his pillow.

It seemed to take forever before a student nurse came to his bedside.

"Can I have my needle, nurse?"

She smiled and fluffed his pillow. "Not just yet, Mr. McCandless. In a wee while."

Shite. "Nurse?" He was embarrassed to ask, but he wasn't sure how long he'd been here. "What day is it?"

"Saturday," she said brightly as she turned to leave.

Saturday? Saturday? Sammy fought to remember. His mind was addled with all the medications. The last thing he remembered clearly was the awful pressure as the cow crushed him on—on Thursday. He'd been so pleased with himself because he'd thought of a way to protect Erin with one short phone call to Spud that he'd not paid proper attention to the animals in the barn. Bloody cow. Bloody cow. But for her he'd have made that call.

It was too late now. All Sammy's grand plans to safeguard Erin and, never mind her, safeguard himself were banjaxed. If the E4A man had acted on Sammy's intelligence, had persuaded his superiors to prepare an ambush, Erin and Cal and Eamon and whoever had come with them from the Kesh were going to be royally fucked—if they weren't already.

And then—then the senior Provos would know someone had touted, and they would come for Sammy. He knew it. He just knew it. His ribs grated, and he groaned, "Ah, Je-sus." He was far too sore to try to make a run for it.

Think, man, he told himself. Think. The Provos'd not know he was in here. Maybe he could get hold of Spud, have the peelers come for him here at the hospital, stand guard until he was ready to be discharged. It would work. It had to. It was Sammy's only hope of staying alive and still having a chance to get to England. Spud had promised to look after Sammy. Giving him a police minder for a day or two wasn't too much to ask.

Spud would see to it because the bugger was going to get what he wanted—a chance to stop the O'Byrnes once and for all.

And "for all" meant death. Sammy saw Erin, bullet torn, gaunt as that bloody statue outside. He turned his face into his pillow and wept, clutching at his grating ribs as he was torn by deep, shuddering sobs. He'd have killed her as surely as he'd killed Fiach, and he could confess all he wished to his priest; neither unlimited acts of contrition nor a thousand novenas would ever absolve him from what he had done.

He could always forget about phoning Spud, wait docilely for the Provos to take their revenge and put him out of his misery like a dumb animal, but fuck guilt; he'd rather live with it than face eternal darkness.

He could only try to comfort himself by clinging to the hope, as a child clings to a comfort blanket, that once he got a phone call through, and there must be a phone he could use somewhere in the hospital, Spud would protect him. He would. He would.

"Joan mobile one to Joan control, over." Alfie Ingram released the transmit button of his unmarked car's radio.

"Go ahead, mobile one," crackled from the dashboard speaker.

"The grey van has left the farmyard and is heading north on the A5, over."

"Roger that."

Good. Control was receiving the transmissions and would listen in to Alfie's conversation with another of his cars.

"Mobile one to mobile two, over."

Mobile two held a couple of Alfie's officers and was stationed at a crossroads in the village of Victoria Bridge, four miles ahead. "Mobile two, over."

"Joan mobile one in distant pursuit to peel off at the B163 junction, one half mile past you. Joan mobile two to tuck in behind us and pick up surveillance when we've gone. Mobile one will take over near Strabane. Confirm, two."

"Mobile two to mobile one, that's affirmative."

"Mobile one standing by. Out." Alfie hung the handheld microphone on its clip. He was satisfied with the arrangements. By switching the tailing cars, it was unlikely the suspects would notice anything unusual. They might if the same car kept following them. He spoke to his driver. "Drop back a bit. Mobile two's waiting up ahead at the crossroads in Victoria Bridge. We'll pull off there, take the B163, stop and observe. The 163 rejoins the A5 just outside Strabane. We'll take over from mobile two there." Alfie opened the glove compartment, took out his Ruger revolver, and laid it in his lap. He didn't expect to be close when the shooting started, but he wasn't taking any chances either.

. . .

"Everybody out," Eamon said as soon as Davy stopped the van beside Sammy's cottage.

Davy waited for them to get out. As Cal and Erin and McGuinness, carrying the four ArmaLites, walked to a large outbuilding and threw open the double doors, Eamon came to Davy's window. "You know where you've to go?"

"Of course I fucking know. Haven't you shown me the map a dozen times?"

"Aye, well. I just want to be sure. Remember, Davy, when you get to Lifford, put the van in the empty lot on the left-hand side of N14. Wait for us there."

"You told me."

"I'll say it again, Father. I'm sorry you're in this, but . . ."

"Let it go, Eamon. Just get it over with." Davy turned away from Eamon and watched as a black station wagon, the one he was to wait for, was reversed out of the building. He heard the sound of another engine. A large red tractor appeared, its front bucket held high. He could see the sacks of fertilizer. The tractor stopped, and Cal came to the van.

"Gimme the knapsack, Eamon."

Eamon handed it to Cal.

Shite, Davy thought, it wouldn't be happening if I hadn't fixed the fucking fuse. He'd had no choice but to strip off the little piece of insulation that would have rendered the detonator useless. The bloody thing was live. But it wouldn't be if that bastard McGuinness hadn't grabbed for Davy's passport. And what the fuck was he going to do if McGuinness got lifted or shot? He'd have no papers. Indeed, what was he going to do if the customs men at Clady wanted to see his driver's licence?

"Eamon?"

"What?"

"Will the customs and the Gardai not want to see my papers?"

Eamon said, "Customs don't usually ask for identification if you're driving a car with Northern plates, but I suppose with all the racing round looking for escaped Provos, they just might. Jesus, I never thought of that."

No, Davy thought, your head's been stuffed with hobby-horse shite with all your planning for this bloody attack.

Eamon moved to where McGuinness had parked the black station wagon. Davy watched as Eamon stooped, straightened, came back to the van, and handed Davy a thin plastic card. "Here."

Davy examined the thing. His own picture, auburn-haired, clean-shaven, peered at him through a pair of granny glasses. He rummaged in his breast pocket, took them out, and slipped them on. The top of the card read, DRIVER'S LICENCE BRITISH COLUMBIA. There was some kind of registration number and the name David McConnan beside the photo. He knew it was usual on forged documents to pick a name close to that of the holder of the papers. If anyone called out "Davy," there'd be no reason why he shouldn't reply.

"Tell the peelers you're here on your holidays. You've been visiting family in Newtownstewart and you're on your way to see a cousin in Ballybofey."

"Did you not get my passport?"

Eamon shook his head. "He wouldn't give it to me, and I'm not about to start a fight now. You'll get it in Lifford."

"I should bloody well hope so."

"You will. Don't worry your head." Eamon offered his hand through the open window. "All right, Davy. Time you were off."

In spite of himself, Davy shook hands. "You take care now, Eamon."

Eamon grinned. "Never you worry about that. They'll never know what hit them."

"Are you sure we shouldn't hit them now, sir?" Alfie's driver asked from inside the car, parked on a hill road overlooking Sammy's.

"Don't be bloody stupid. With only the two of us? You might want to be a hero; I don't. Now hold your wheest and let me watch." Alfie focused his field glasses. He watched as a grey van left the lane from the cottage and the shed and turned right on the A5—away from Strabane. Shite. There were no Security Forces in that direction, and he'd have to make a quick decision. He could get his own vehicle behind the van and tail it, but Sammy had said to look for a black station wagon and a tractor. Let the van go. It might not even be a Provo driving. The O'Byrnes could have persuaded some local to do them a favour by taking them to the shed.

Alfie swung the glasses back toward the buildings below. Bloody great. There they were. Three people stood beside the tractor, two with red hair. He couldn't make out their features, but he'd be damned if they weren't the O'Byrnes. "Gimme the mic," he said, and waited until the constable handed him the transceiver. The red-haired man climbed into the cab of the tractor, the others into the car. The car left first.

Alfie keyed the mic. "Joan mobile one to mobile control and mobile two, over."

"Control."

"Mobile two."

"They're on the move."

"Control. Roger that."

"Mobile two. Roger."

Alfie handed the mic back to his driver and climbed in. "Right, son. You know where to go. Get moving."

"They're on the move, Sarge." Sergeant Buchan's communications man held the headset of his radio to his ear and grinned.

"Right," said Buchan. He sidled across the floor of the upstairs bedroom and peered through a gap in the lace curtains. To his right, he could see the hill of the A5 as it came down into Strabane. Ahead, the police barracks squatted, grey and sullen behind its high wire fence. The loopholed, cast-iron shutters were open, but he knew there were constables behind each set ready to slam them shut.

He couldn't see where the two minor roads joined the T-junction but knew squads like his were in position at both corners. Beneath him, the street was empty of the cars that would normally be parked there on a Saturday morning. The police had put up NO PARKING and MEN AT WORK signs from one end of the barracks to the other. The reason, ostensibly, was a trench dug by a gang of council workmen down there, who were busily doing nothing much but leaning on their shovels. He smiled. They were part of the SAS contingent flown in from Herefordshire. He hoped for their sakes they'd made the trench deep enough to provide blast shelter.

There were several pedestrians, mostly women in headscarves and plastic hair curlers, shopping bags on their arms. Three nuns in their black-and-white habits walked slowly toward the chapel he knew was at the far end of the street. From where he stood, they looked like penguins.

He had to hand it to whoever was in charge. Buchan's officer had told him that every effort was to be made to protect civilians. Police foot patrols would be handy to hustle the shoppers to safety and the NO PARKING was a grand idea. It kept cars and their occupants off the streets, and—he glanced down at his two-man general-purpose machine-gun squad—it gave his men a clear field of fire over the kill zone.

"Right, lads," he said, "take up your positions." He knelt at the window beside the GPMG team and rested his Heckler and Koch on the sill. The house they had occupied on Thursday night, much to the disgust of the owners who were being held in a back bedroom so no word of the ambush could leak out, was on the street corner. Two more SAS troopers, M16s ready, knelt at the side window overlooking the hill. "Remember, it's a red tractor and a black station wagon, registrations . . ."

"HKM 561 and LKM 136," five voices chanted in unison.

"Good." Sergeant Buchan decided he'd not have time to go for a pee. He wondered why he always wanted one just before the action started. It was to be expected, just like the way his mouth went dry and his palms started to sweat.

"Hold your fire 'til I give the word," he said.

- "Right, Sarge."

They were a bunch of good lads, he thought. They bloody well ought to be, the way SAS troopers were selected and trained. No elite troops anywhere in the world like them. He tried to relax. Nothing to worry about. As far as Sergeant Buchan could tell, everything was ready.

"So, is everybody ready?" Eamon asked from the back of the station wagon parked behind the tractor at the top of the hill above Strabane. McGuinness was in the driver's seat. Cal had climbed down from the parked tractor and sat in the passenger's seat with his knapsack in his lap. Erin sat in the back beside Eamon and felt the warmth of his thigh pressed against hers.

"You were right, Eamon, to drive down into Strabane first and then come back up here," she said. "A couple of peelers escorted by the odd soldier and that's about it."

Eamon squeezed her hand. "It's handy about the road works. There'll be less traffic to get in our way. It was nice of the road menders to leave those metal sheets across the trench as a bridge so the peelers can drive into the barracks. Cal'll get across like a whippet."

"Can Brendan get parked where he should?" she asked.

"No problems," came from the driver's seat.

"I'm off," Cal said, opening his door. "I'll watch for your hanky, Erin." He leaned into the back and pecked her cheek. "See you in fifteen, twenty minutes." She felt him squeeze her shoulder, saw him look into her eyes. "Be careful," he said.

"And you look after yourself, too, Cal." She watched as he climbed into the tractor's cab. He had the worst job, the riskiest, and she couldn't help worrying about him. But he'd be all right. Of course he would.

She shook her head. Dear Cal. The door he'd never got round to fixing had stuck this morning before she'd closed it. It would be someone else's problem now. She'd never be seeing it again, or the churchyard at Bally-dornan they'd driven past on their way here. Erin's eyes narrowed. Fiach was the last O'Byrne they'd leave in Ireland. As long as she and Cal and Eamon—she leaned across to kiss Eamon—had just a tiny bit of luck this morning.

"If you two've finished?" McGuinness said from the front.

"Go ahead, Brendan," Eamon said. "Let's get moving."

Erin was half-roasted in the anorak, but it hid the ArmaLite. She stood at the corner of the hill road, pretended to look in a shop window, and saw to her left that Eamon was in position. Brendan had the black car parked where it should be. She pulled out her hanky.

She saw the cloud of blue smoke from the tractor's exhaust. The front bucket was lowered, and Cal, knapsack in hand, bent over the sacks. He'd be setting the fuses. Ten more minutes. She stared ahead at the bulk of the barracks. Ten more minutes, and that monstrosity, that bastion of British rule, fortified like the old motte and bailey castles that the Normans had built eight centuries before to keep the Irish subdued, would be like one of the old ruins, just a few stones standing. One day, the bloody Brits would get the message. One day.

She watched the tractor rattle down the hill toward her, bucket raised as a charging elephant held high its trunk. Cal was picking up speed, and the fence was straight ahead. He trundled past her, and she cheered him on.

She heard a series of clangs from inside the compound and saw the dark iron shutters being slammed over the windows. Someone was wide awake in there. She fumbled under her anorak.

In seconds, Cal would be across the rusty metal plates, through the fence, and out of the cab, but if the peelers who'd closed the shutters were alert, he might need covering fire before he could get to her.

The sound of heavy machine-gun fire coming from above shattered the morning, racketing on in harsh bursts of four shots. Lighter automatic weapons chattered a horrid staccato above the barking of the bigger weapon. She glanced past the tractor and saw lights winking from the loopholes in the shutters. A stray round from the barracks hit the bricks above her head and screeched off along the street behind her.

Erin stared upward, her gaze following a stream of tracer bullets as they hosed from an upstairs window and across the tractor's cab. The fire from the windows of the barracks seemed heavier. The street and the compound were laced with a stitching of lead.

"Cal," she screamed, hauling out her weapon, unfolding it in one deft movement. She slid behind the street corner, slammed the ArmaLite against her shoulder, and started firing up at the window above. Bullets from the barracks ricocheted from the bricks.

She felt a presence beside her. What the hell was Eamon doing there? He was meant to be providing covering fire, and why wasn't McGuinness firing?

The tractor had slewed sideways and stopped outside the wire. A row of circular holes, silver-rimmed against the red paint, ran diagonally across the cab door. She could see Cal, slumped in the cab. He was moving.

"Cal's all right," she yelled. "I'm going for him."

"Stay where you are." Eamon ran bent and doubled over across the few yards between the corner and the tractor.

Erin wanted to watch but knew her job was to try to suppress the incoming fire. She ripped off four aimed shots at the nearest barracks window, seeing gashes appear in the rusty shutter. She spun and pumped four more shots at the window above, where she could see the snout of a machine gun and hear its incessant chatter.

She heard a scream ahead and spun to see Eamon, carrying Cal in his arms, fall on the street, spilling Cal's limp body into the gutter. Bloodstains bloomed on his chest. "*Eamon. Eamon.*"

The machine gun clattered on. More shots were coming from God knew where. Erin clapped a hand over one ear and begged the racket to stop. She barely noticed a black station wagon speed past her up the hill road. McGuinness was running. The bastard hadn't tried to help.

She sobbed, fumbled for her white hanky, tied it to the muzzle of her rifle, and stepped out into the street, waving her pathetic flag of surrender. She tried to find some shelter in the lee of the tractor. "*Stop it. Stop it,*" she screamed up at the machine gunners. "*For the love of God, stop it.*"

She felt the thump of a bullet strike her thigh. There was no pain, but its force hurled her to the ground. She crawled ahead, dragging the leg behind her. "I'm coming, Cal. Hang on, Eamon." The firing seemed to have slackened. She forced herself to her knees, made another yard, then collapsed facedown on Eamon's unmoving chest.

Her thigh throbbed and burned now, but suddenly there was quiet. The firing had stopped. From where she lay, she could see two uniformed policemen herding a group of civilians and two nuns along the T and away from the barracks. A third nun lay crumpled on the street, limbs awry, black habit and white wimple bloodstained. She looked like a shot magpie.

Erin struggled to get her back against the wheel of the tractor and stared up at the bucket above her head. The fuse had only minutes to run.

She tried to crawl away but was too weak. Blood had soaked her trouser leg, and a pool slowly spread on the tarmac. She looked into Eamon's milky eyes and at Cal's hands as they clutched empty air. And for Eamon and Cal, and for Ireland, because it wasn't for herself, she began to whisper, "Hail Mary, full of grace . . ."

Davy left the van in Lifford where he'd been told to and tucked into a corner of the vacant lot behind a wall, out of sight of the Gardai post on his side of the bridge. He'd ignored Eamon's instructions to stay with the van and crouched behind the wall to watch the bridge, wishing the black car would get a move on.

He heard birds bickering behind him and glanced over to where a huge chestnut spread its boughs over a field at the back of the lot. It grew on the banks of a stream he'd crossed on the outskirts of Lifford. The tree's branches were alive with a flock of jackdaws. Their cawing intensified as the birds exploded into the air. Davy could hear nothing but their strident shrieking. Something had frightened them.

He had to wait until their racket faded as they flew away before he could hear the distant clatter of automatic weapon fire. He'd heard enough in his time. The deeper note was a GPMG, and he'd never mistake the bark of a Heckler and Koch. It had always been his weapon of choice. Oh, Christ. They were all carrying ArmaLites. They must have run into trouble. Bad trouble, by the way the distant guns yammered and spat.

He craned round the corner, but all he could see was the bridge and the houses of Strabane. He strained to hear and was able to pick out the sharper cracks of an ArmaLite. At least one of the attack party was returning fire.

It took little imagination for him to picture the battle that must be raging round the barracks. His first thought was that McGuinness still held on to the passport, and if he'd been shot or taken, all Davy'd gone through would have been a waste of time.

He'd tried to tell them it was bloody madness to press ahead with this attack when they were so close to getting away. Damn them all. Damn that Erin, beautiful, spirited, in love with Eamon—and so bloody bound and determined to go ahead. Damn Eamon, even if he had been Davy's friend, a friend Davy knew he could have tried to forgive for roping him in, but whom he might never see again.

Davy looked at the bridge. Across the river, he could see Ulster Defence Regiment troops spilling from the customs shed, rifles held at the high port. They formed a cordon lining the approaches to the bridge.

Three men of the Gardai detachment on the Lifford side stood behind a red-and-white-striped barrier gazing toward the sound of gunfire that yam-mered to a crescendo, fell, then, after a few single shots, died.

The sudden silence was broken by the sounds of a black station wagon he could see approaching the bridge. Some of the attack party had got away. Perhaps some of them were in the car, wounded. Davy caught his breath as he waited for it to speed up and smash through the barrier, but it slowed as it neared the customs shed on the Northern side.

He saw soldiers of the Ulster Defence Regiment surround the station wagon. One stood in the middle of the road, hand held aloft, and the rest knelt, rifles pointed at the vehicle's windscreen. Shite, whoever was in it couldn't hope to shoot their way out. It was over. The car's occupants were fucked—and he'd never get his passport now.

The soldier in the middle of the road bent and seemed to be speaking in through the driver's window. Davy waited to see how many would get out, hands raised in surrender, but the soldier stood, stepped out of the way, and must have given an order to the covering troops, who lowered their weapons.

What the hell was going on?

The red-and-white-striped barrier swung up, and the wagon was driven slowly across the bridge, only to stop at the Gardai post as if it simply held a carload of tourists on an excursion to the Republic.

How they could be able to talk their way through was a mystery to Davy, but whatever was happening, his job was to get back to the van. He slipped from the corner and limped to where he had left the vehicle. The faint grat-ing noises of gravel under his shoes were covered by the sounds of tires crunching toward him.

He spun to see the black wagon lurch into the lot. McGuinness was driv-ing. Someone with blond hair sat in the passenger seat. There was no one else inside. Davy wondered if anyone could possibly have survived back in Strabane.

He watched the wagon skid to a stop, the driver's door open, and Mc-Guinness struggle out, dragging a little girl by one of her pigtails. The child was in tears. McGuinness hauled her over to Davy.

"Get that fucking van started. There's only me coming. The rest's shot. It was an ambush." His voice trembled. "And if they'd known to look out for the tractor, they'd've had the number of this car. I'd never've got through the border, so I grabbed this wee one for a hostage. They had to let me through."

"Are you being followed?"

"No fuckin' way. The Brits can't cross the border, and I told the Gardai to stay put for fifteen minutes, or this one"—he jabbed the gun muzzle under the child's chin—"gets hers."

The girl howled, and McGuinness snarled, "Shut the fuck up."

"Let her go," Davy said quietly. "Let her go."

"I will not." McGuinness tightened his grip on her arm. "She's old enough to get the number of the van and tell the Gardai. We need the van to get to Sean's people in Castlefinn. You'd feel fucking stupid if we got picked up between here and there." He kept glancing over his shoulder as if expecting pursuers to appear at any second.

Davy tried to keep his voice level. "Christ, Brendan, it's only ten miles. If we go right now, leave her here, it'll take her a fair while to walk back to the Gardai post. By the time they . . ."

"I'm taking no chances." McGuinness screamed and pushed the child from him.

Davy caught his breath as she landed on her knees in the gravel. He started to move to her to pick her up but was halted by McGuinness's yell of, "Stay where you are."

As Davy turned, he heard the "snick" as McGuinness released the rifle's safety catch and saw him tuck its butt into his shoulder. Mother of God, he was going to shoot her. "Brendan, for fuck's sake, there's no need for that." Davy positioned himself between the child and McGuinness. He could see death staring at him from the ArmaLite's muzzle. "Put the fucking gun down."

"Get out of my way. " McGuinness moved sideways to clear his line of fire.

The wee girl screamed, "Pleeeease." Just like the one in a burning car in 1974.

Davy snatched the .25 from his pocket and shot McGuinness. Once. Through his forehead.

Davy heard the ArmaLite clatter to the gravel, ignored McGuinness where he lay, and pulled the little girl to her feet. "It's all right," he said, knowing it wasn't. "It's all right." He hugged her, then held her at arm's length. He looked into her tear-stained face, saw her grazed knees, then put a hand under her chin and said, "Now run you away on to the nice Garda man at the bridge. He'll get you back to your mammy."

"Yes, Mister," she sobbed, and started to run.

Davy bent over McGuinness, fished a Canadian passport out of the man's inside pocket, flipped it open, confirmed that it was his own photo inside, and stuffed it in his jacket pocket.

He grabbed a handful of mud from the lot's verge and smeared it over the van's rear number plate, climbed in, and drove to the corner of the lot. A quick glance reassured him that the Gardai had obeyed McGuinness's instructions and were still standing on the bridge.

Moving deliberately, he eased the van onto the street and drove slowly to the corner, glancing twice in the rearview mirror to make sure he wasn't being followed. Once out of sight of the bridge, he accelerated along the road to Castlefinn, hoping to God Sean's people would be there, that they'd get him to Dublin by tonight, and that Sean would help him telephone Vancouver.

He stopped the van as he crossed the bridge over the stream at the outskirts of Lifford. Davy hefted the .25, the one Erin had smuggled into the Kesh, the one Davy had refused to use on Mr. Smiley in the corridor of H-7 or on the guards in the car park on the day of the jailbreak, the one that had snuffed McGuinness out like a guttering candle. It was McGuinness or the wee girl, Davy tried to reassure himself.

He stepped out, stood on the parapet, and hurled the revolver as far downstream as he could manage.

Davy didn't hear the splash. The morning was riven by the roar of five hundred pounds of exploding ammonal. He turned and saw a smoke cloud rising above Strabane, staining the sky and uniting in its stinking, all-embracing pall the steeples of the Catholic chapel and the Presbyterian church.

Davy climbed into the driver's seat, released the brake, and started on his solitary journey to Castlefinn, to Dublin, to Vancouver, and to Fiona.

EPILOGUE

In the twenty-five years of internecine strife (1969–94) in Northern Ireland, 3,268 people were killed and more than thirty thousand wounded. In late August of '94, Sinn Féin, the political wing of the Provisional Irish Republican Army, announced a ceasefire and called for talks with the British government. At the time of writing for initial publication in 2005, those talks still struggled on but were derailed by a December 2004, $43 million robbery of the Northern Bank in Belfast, which was blamed on a still-active Provisional IRA, and by the Republicans' refusal to decommission their secret arsenals.

Some weapons will never be found. A .25 revolver lies rusting on the gravel bed of a stream on the outskirts of Lifford, County Donegal. Six ArmaLites and two Lee-Enfield .303s are gradually corroding in County Tyrone in a neolithic passage grave, where spiders spin their webs over four camp beds and a chemical toilet.

Sammy McCandless managed to contact Inspector Alfie Ingram, who sent constables to sit by Sammy's bedside until he was discharged. The Provos were known to have walked into the Royal Victoria Hospital in Belfast and assassinate informers who were patients. Sammy read in *The Belfast Telegraph* about the outcome of the Strabane attack and the deaths of Eamon, Cal, and Erin. The story was accompanied by graphic photographs. When he threw up, the pain in his broken ribs was intense.

He was taken to England and housed alone in disused army married quarters at Catterick Camp on the dismal Yorkshire moors. Six days after he arrived, Sammy whispered "Erin" once, before he hanged himself with the belt of his nice, new, provided-by-the-British-taxpayer trousers. His discarded old clothes were found strewn over the army-issue furniture. Three days' worth of unwashed plates cluttered the sink. His name is reviled in County Tyrone, and along with Mollie MacDacker and Art O'Hanlon, he will never be forgotten.

Erin and Cal O'Byrne and Eamon Maguire, more "martyrs for old Ireland," have been mostly forgotten by the people of Tyrone. Erin got her wish, and her remains were buried under an Irish sky beside Fiach, Cal, and Da in Ballydornan churchyard, close to the old Celtic cross. Eamon Maguire lies in the Maguire family plot. A black-framed photograph of each adorns their gravestones with the lines, only changing where the name of the victim is inserted:

> *I Gcuimne, Óglach*
> *Erin Ó'Broin, Óglaight na hÉireann*
> *A fuair bás ar saoirse na hÉireann.*

Here lies Erin O'Byrne, volunteer of the Irish Army. She died in the cause of Irish freedom.

Turloch O'Byrne, Erin's brother, came back from Australia and still farms the family place. Tessie and Margaret are long dead.

The Gardai, as required by law, turned Brendan McGuinness's body over to the Lifford coroner. The cause of death was obvious, and it was a weekend after all, so the coroner decided to forgo the formality of a postmortem and signed the death certificate. As no one claimed the remains, they were sent to the medical school at University College, Galway. A student in the dissecting room remarked on McGuinness's glass eye and also asked the anatomy teacher if the heart of this particular cadaver wasn't abnormally shrunken.

Inspector Alfie Ingram's contribution to the success of the ambush at Strabane was recognized. He was promoted to chief inspector and continued his undercover work. On June 2, 1994, he was one of twenty-eight people accompanying RUC Detective Inspector Ian Phoenix on RAF Chinook helicopter HC2 ZD576. It flew into the Hill of Stone in the Mull of Kintyre, Scotland, at approximately 6:00 P.M. All twenty-nine people on board died.

CANADA

Fiona Kavanagh and Davy McCutcheon live on Whyte Avenue. McCusker is long gone, as is his successor, a ginger tabby also named McCusker. Davy answers to the name Davy McConnan and, when he remembers, wears a pair of plain-glass granny glasses. Davy and Fiona are old now, and their lovemaking, though tender, is infrequent. Davy is less prone to flatulence but still insists on making tea, even though he grumbles about the water and says Canadian tea is not a patch on the Northern Irish brands.

Fiona's nightmare has never returned, but Davy sometimes wakes up trembling and sweating. Like most veterans of a war, he never speaks of his memories, but Fiona understands and comforts him.

Fiona retired in 1999 as principal of Charles Dickens Elementary School. Davy, after a rapid start in Expo '86 construction, managed to secure a loan from the Royal Bank of Canada and branched out in partnership with Jimmy Ferguson. They sold their construction company in 1997.

Davy and Fiona had an anxious few weeks in 1987, when Davy applied to renew his Canadian passport, but the new one arrived without any questions having been asked. The document withstood the scrutiny of the social worker when they adopted two Vietnamese girls in 1988.

Erin and Siobhan McConnan attend Simon Fraser University. Their da, usually accompanied by his friend Jimmy Ferguson, comes every Saturday in the season to watch them play varsity soccer. The two men can often be heard arguing about the relative merits of women's soccer and the Celtic matches they remember watching back in Belfast. After the games, they take their pints in Sean and Erin Heather's pub, the Irish Heather, in Gastown.

After the death of her father, Becky Johnston left teaching to move to Abbotsford and care for her mother. When her mother died in 1989, Becky surprised her friends in Vancouver by selling up and moving back to Henley-on-Thames. Every year, she and Fiona exchange Christmas cards. Fiona has noticed how spidery Becky's handwriting has become in the last few years.

Doctor Tim Andersen devoted himself to his patients and his research for two years. In June 1985, he entered *Windshadow* in the annual Round Bowen yacht race. His crew for the day failed to show up at Burrard Civic Marina. He sailed single-handedly to Bowen Island's Union Steamship Company Marina. At the prerace skippers' meeting, he was approached by a stranger of Danish extraction, Pernille Olafsen, who was willing to crew. He grudgingly agreed to take her aboard. During the race, when Squamish winds blew up to forty knots, it became apparent that she was a first-class foredeck hand, a fine helmsman, and fearless in a stiff blow.

Three years ago, Tim and Pernille, in their fifty-foot Swan-Cooper, *Windshadow II*, left Burrard Inlet on the first leg of their round-the-world cruise. Tim, then seventy-two, brushed aside any suggestion that he was too old and reminded people that Sir Francis Chichester had been in his seventies when he'd circumnavigated the globe single-handedly in *Gipsy Moth IV*. They were last heard of six months ago in Portsmouth, when Tim phoned Becky in Henley and arranged to meet her for dinner.

Dimitris Papodopolous graduated in 2001 from the Faculty of Engineering at the University of British Columbia. He lives with the Turkish daughter of his Greek father's business partner. Dimitris cannot tolerate Greek cooking, but both have appetites for sushi. They have two young children.

Jean-Claude Duplessis and Siobhan Duplessis (née Ferguson) live in Montreal. He is a senior producer at Radio Canada. Their children are grown, and Siobhan takes great pleasure from her grandchildren. She works as a volunteer for the Society for the Preservation of Grosse Isle, where, after the famine of 1845, Irish immigrants were quarantined and where thousands died of cholera and typhus fever. Every year on April 22, the date of Mike's funeral in 1974, she goes alone to the Saint Lawrence and drops in a single red rose, just as she had dropped a bouquet of red roses on his coffin.

She kneels and, as she did back then, crosses herself and says a quiet Ave.

Hail Mary, full of grace, the Lord is with thee.
Blessèd art thou among women and blessèd is the fruit of thy womb,
    Jesus.
Holy Mary, Mother of God, pray for us sinners, now and in the hour of
    our death.

PATRICK TAYLOR
Bowen Island, British Columbia, 2005

AUTHOR'S NOTE

Now and in the Hour of Our Death is the sequel to *Pray for Us Sinners*. The titles are taken from the Roman Catholic prayer Ave Maria, or Hail Mary.

The reader will be reacquainted with Davy McCutcheon, ex–Provisional IRA bomb maker, now British prisoner, and Fiona Kavanagh, who has left Davy and lives and works as a school vice principal in Vancouver, British Columbia. How their estranged love for each other is resolved and how this resolution affects the lives of people around them are the forces that drive the story.

The scenes are set against two backdrops: the sectarian carnage that was Northern Ireland in the mid '80s, and the multicultural tranquility that was, and still is, the peace of Vancouver.

The events that occurred before and during the breakout by a number of Provisional IRA inmates from the Maze Prison in Ulster on September 25, 1983, are described as accurately as research allows. Names of historical figures are used fictitiously, and I have imagined their dialogue. Margaret Thatcher was the British prime minister at the time. Bobby Storey was the prisoner in charge of the escape, and Bic McFarlane the Officer Commanding the Provisional IRA inmates of the Maze Prison, always referred to by the Provisionals as the Kesh.

My characters and what happens to them are fictional, as is the raid on the police barracks in Strabane. No such raid actually occurred, but I have borrowed from the description of the intelligence-gathering operation by the Security Forces and their dealing with a similar attack by members of the Provisional IRA on the police barracks at Loughgall in 1987.

Scenes set in Ireland are flavoured by my having lived there for thirty-two years.

The city of Vancouver and an episode in the waters surrounding Bowen Island are drawn from personal experience. I have lived in Canada for forty years, Vancouver for four, Bowen Island, British Columbia, for thirteen, and Salt Spring Island for nearly four.

I hope my late friend Al Byers forgave me for borrowing the name of his vessel, *Windshadow*.

Although this work may be thought of as a thriller, it is really a story about love. It concerns the love of men for women, of women for men, and of a woman for her family. The principal actors must also deal with their feelings for Ireland, their country of birth and nurture, and Canada, their new and welcoming adopted country. The universal love of the human race for freedom, both physical and political, lives in many of the characters.

Which of these loves transcends the rest I leave for the reader to decide.

PATRICK TAYLOR
Salt Spring Island, British Columbia, 2013

ABOUT THE AUTHOR

Patrick Taylor, M.D., was born and raised in Bangor, County Down, in Northern Ireland. He is the *New York Times* bestselling author of the Irish Country series that began with *An Irish Country Doctor*. Dr. Taylor is a distinguished medical researcher, offshore sailor, model-boat builder, and father of two grown children. He now lives on Saltspring Island, British Columbia.

www.patricktaylor.ca